D0392021

CHAUCER
AND THE
DOCTOR OF PHYSIC

Also by Philippa Morgan

Chaucer and the House of Fame

Chaucer and the Legend of Good Women

CHAUCER
AND THE
DOCTOR OF PHYSIC

PHILIPPA MORGAN

CARROLL & GRAF PUBLISHERS
New York

Carroll & Graf Publishers
An imprint of Avalon Publishing Group, Inc.
245 W. 17th Street
11th Floor
New York, NY 10011-5300
www.carrollandgraf.com

AVALON
publishing group incorporated

First published in the UK by Constable,
an imprint of Constable & Robinson Ltd 2006

First Carroll & Graf edition 2006

ISBN-13: 978-0-78671-824-5
ISBN-10: 0-7867-1824-2

Printed and bound in the EU

PROLOGUE

After the heat of the day, the cool of evening was refreshing. People were strolling in the streets or chatting on corners. Breezes stirred round the minarets before slipping through the carved wooden *mashrabiyyah* which are placed in private windows as both barrier and ornament, and which allow women to peer out at the world beyond their quarters even as they remain indistinct to men in the street. But the shutters – they were warped and not ornate – to the house in the street near the long white walls of the Ibn Tulun mosque remained firmly closed. True, there was no woman in the house who might have wanted to gaze at the world outside, for the dwelling was occupied only by Ragab and his male assistant, who happened to be a cousin of his late wife. True also that there wasn't much to see from the chamber where Ragab conducted his principal work, nothing more than a view into an enclosed yard occupied by a white mulberry tree that was older than the house itself. Beyond the yard was a fence and a narrow alleyway, and beyond that the wall of a cemetery.

The interior of the room where Ragab worked was close and smoky from the oil-lamps and the fumes which spiralled out of the glowing pans of charcoal. These were situated under alembics containing liquids that varied in colour from a translucent lime to an inky black. Ragab was an old man with a seamed face. He had been toiling here since early morning, weighing and measuring, breaking off from time to time to

1

consult bound volumes or sheets of manuscript full of numbers and symbols even though he knew their sequences by heart. Now he was sitting on a stool and squinting, with rapture almost, at the tendrils of smoke which crept along a network of glass tubes and funnels arranged along a bench in front of him. He was oblivious to the occasional noises from a chamber immediately above him on the upper storey, where Ja'far, cousin to his wife, was going about his business. Ragab's hearing was not so good these days but even so, if he had attended more carefully, he might have noticed that young Ja'far seemed to be pacing about his room, up and down, side to side. And if he'd noticed the pacing steps, he might have wondered why Ja'far was so restless.

Ragab trusted Ja'far, trusted him absolutely, but nevertheless this was an experiment he preferred to conduct by himself, though he'd hinted in general terms to the young man what he was striving to achieve. Ja'far's brown eyes had widened as if in disbelief, then narrowed slightly. He commented on the priceless nature of what Ragab was attempting. If Ragab succeeded, the world would be theirs, he said. They could move from the dilapidated old house by the cemetery. They could afford a palace and gardens by the river, and servants to wait on them day and night. They'd never have to lift a finger again. Ja'far saw the expression on his cousin's face, and swiftly turned his remarks into a joke about his own idleness. Ragab rebuked him sharply for his frivolity – not in making a joke but for thinking of fine dwellings and gardens in the first place – then, seeing the hurt in the other's brown eyes, he smiled and forgave him. But he was disappointed that Ja'far should have understood 'priceless' in such a literal sense. He thought that perhaps it was typical of the younger generation. Then he considered that he was being unfair, for the old always want less than the young. But it had never occurred to Ragab to move from the house near the cemetery nor did he relish the idea of having a gaggle of servants to command or more rooms than he would know what to do with. Ragab worked for the joy of discovery, and the glory that would come with it. He did not think of profit and luxuries.

Every now and then Ragab stretched out a thin, knotty arm to adjust a seal in one of the tubes or to move a charcoal pan closer to or farther away from its position under a flask. The seals connecting the pipes and tubes were made of a gum-stiffened fabric held in place by thread and, since the seals were not completely airtight, stray puffs of smoke escaped to deliver their pungent, oily scent into the already stuffy chamber. But most of the smoke and fumes were channelled along the network of tubes until they fetched up in a large distilling jar. The smoke rose to the top of the stoppered jar then, as if realizing that no final escape was permitted, began to turn into droplets that slid greasily down the sides towards the base of the jar. A yellowy deposit had been gathering there for the best part of two hours. Even so, only a small amount of mixture had been created by the process. That so little had been created, and laboriously too, was somehow reassuring.

When Ragab judged that he had distilled enough for his purposes, and before the liquids in the various flasks were quite exhausted, he moved the charcoal pots away from the bases of the blackened alembics. He watched as the final wisps swirled along the pipes and entered the distilling jar. When he was sure that there was no more to come, he carefully removed the seals which linked the jar to the rest of the equipment and carried it towards the shuttered window. He placed the jar on the ground and unlatched the warped, ill-fitting shutters. As he did so he became conscious of the sounds made by Ja'far in the chamber overhead, a deep regular beat. It puzzled him for a moment before he understood that it was the young man pacing backwards and forwards. Was his cousin even now troubled by his rebuke? The old man reminded himself to speak words of reassurance to Ja'far.

Ragab gazed out at the world beyond his house. Evening was well advanced. The sky stretched over the white mulberry tree and the fence at the end of his yard and up towards the first stars and a crescent moon. Ragab leaned out and breathed deeply to drive the fumes of the chamber from his old lungs. He picked up the distilling jar and held it aloft so that it might catch the last gleams of daylight. The yellowy liquid lay thick and uninviting at the bottom of the jar.

As Ragab went to replace the jar on the floor before closing the shutters, a surreptitious movement from the alley on the other side of the fence snagged his eye. But, like his hearing, his sight was not so good – his eyes dimmed by age and by many years of close work – and he scarcely paid the movement any attention. Instead he closed the shutters and returned to the bench, cradling the distilling jar in his ams. If he should drop it now! But he did not drop it, of course. Once the jar was safely deposited on the bench he took a vial made of thick glass from a stand of similar items. He removed the stopper from the vial and a cork bung from the base of the distilling jar and, tilting the jar with one hand, he held the vial under the lip of the bung-hole.

A viscous thread oozed out of the tilted jar and spooled into the vial. It looked like dirty gold. The small quantity in the jar filled the vial almost to the top. Ragab righted the jar. He held the open vial under his nose. His sense of smell remained sharp, honed by years of sniffing at mixtures and compounds. If he'd been expecting a sweet or tantalizing scent, he was to be disappointed. The contents of the vial smelled bitter, like a sacrifice. All at once, his surroundings – the fume-filled chamber, the oil-lamps burning with steady persistence, the intricate arrangement of flasks and piping on the bench, the piles of books and curling parchment – seemed to take on a menacing edge. Ragab couldn't understand how what was familiar could at once grow so strange.

4

Although it was close in the chamber, he shivered.

Outside in the yard, the man called Ali also shivered, in fear and expectation. He'd been waiting in the alleyway between the fence and the cemetery. There were few passers-by at this late time of day since the alley led only to waste ground which was haunted by dogs. Ali was crouching below the fence when Ragab opened the shutter. Alerted by the noise, he ducked out of sight. Through a gap in the fence he glimpsed the old man lean out of the window, before holding up a flask to the fading light and scrutinizing its contents. Ali wondered if he was going to swig from the flask since there appeared to be some liquid at the bottom, but instead the old man withdrew and closed the shutters once more with an air of finality like someone about to retire to bed. Ali waited for a few moments then clambered over the fence, tearing the cloth of his sleeve on a nail as he did so. He dropped to a crouch and made ungainly progress towards the shelter of the mulberry in the centre of the paved yard. Several of its aged branches were supported by crutch-like props of younger wood. The mulberry may have been old yet it continued to produce fruit, as the deep purple stains on the pavement testified. Then, despite the fading light, Ali noticed that some of the stains were fresh. He felt his sleeve where the nail had torn as he climbed the fence. He'd gashed his right arm. It was bleeding. He tore a strip of cloth from his robe and wrapped it tight about the wound. It was a little wound, it was almost nothing.

Once in the shelter of the ancient tree, Ali was able to breathe more easily. He did not think it would be so difficult to gain access to the house. With a practised eye, he'd already taken note of the old shutters over the window to Ragab's ground-floor room. The shutters were cracked and warped. However they were secured on the inside, it should be simple enough to smash through them with a blow or two. Then it occurred to Ali that he would need some implement with

5

which to make his entry. Ja'far had been very precise in his instructions that this had to look like a robbery committed by an outsider and carried out without his – that is, Ja'far's – knowledge. Ali glanced towards the upper storey of the house, to the window of Ja'far's chamber. There was a light burning inside. He thought he detected a shadow behind the blind of oiled cloth over the window. The shadow disappeared only to reappear a few moments later, as if the person inside was walking rapidly backwards and forwards. There was no doubt about the identity of that shadow. Ali sensed Ja'far's fear and restlessness. Curiously, it calmed him.

He wondered whether his friend upstairs would have the courage to lift a corner of the blind to peer into the yard. After all, he was working according to Ja'far's plan. But Ali doubted he'd choose to look out the window. Old Ragab's cousin pre-ferred to remain in ignorance, leaving the hard work to others. And thinking of hard work . . . Ali might have neglected to bring anything with him to force an entry but luckily an instrument lay to hand. He required hold of one of the crutches holding up a mulberry branch. It took more effort than he'd expected to work it loose, so heavily did the mulberry branch bear down on its support, but he finally freed the forked prop and grasped it in both hands like a club. He waited. His wounded arm throbbed. He heard the evening call to prayer. Overhead the sky darkened and more stars emerged. The crescent moon grew sharp as a scimitar. Surely he must have gone to bed by this stage, an old person like Ragab? He, Ali, wouldn't have minded being warm in bed now with Munya at his side. But a man had to work in order to live and buy things to satisfy his wife. Ali waited until it was almost completely dark. He hoped that Ja'far was ready to do his part. Eventually, unable to contain his impatience any longer, he moved out of the shade of the mulberry tree and crept towards the shuttered window, clutching the staff of wood.

But, inside the house, Ragab had not retired to bed although he had extinguished most of the lamps in his chamber. Instead he was wide awake and sitting on the stool by the bench. He was concerned for the security of the stoppered vial which he held in the palm of his right hand. The dirty-gold liquid lay sleeping in the glass tube. Who could be certain what properties and virtues it really possessed? All he knew was that he had consulted the best (because most ancient) authorities, that he had summoned up a lifetime of trial and error, that he had weighed and measured and assessed quantities and mixtures for many months, all so as to produce this . . . dirty-gold elixir. The *ab-e-hyat*. It was too late in the day now to conduct any trials. That would have to wait until the next day, or later. Maybe Ragab was afraid of actually putting the substance to the test.

Now that he held the object in his palm, he was gripped by a sudden fear. It was physical, this fear, like a band tightening round his chest and causing his breath to come short. Perhaps, he thought, possessors of large wealth always lived in this state of apprehension, terrified that someone was about to deprive them of what was theirs and never knowing an instant's peace of mind. For certain, it must be so for those who lived in the palaces by the river. But there were certain practical things he could do to make sure that the vial and its contents were safe, if anybody was minded to rob him – but then who would trouble to rob an old and impoverished physician? Nevertheless, Ragab rose and, clutching the vial, looked around the chamber for a place of concealment.

As he gazed about, Ragab strove to put himself in the place of an intruder, searching for something of value. In truth, there was nothing of much worth either in this chamber or anywhere in the whole house. The sole object to attract the eye, apart from the tangle of flasks and tubes on the bench, was a small chest sheathed in filigree silver. Oh, his herbs and crystals and powders were valuable enough but only to the practitioner who would know how to combine them in the right proportions – in the same way that his books and papers would be comprehensible only to that man who could not merely read but interpret them.

What were the usual hiding places? Under the floor? (But the floor to this room was covered with tiles that were cracked and uneven.) Inside the filigree chest? (But that would be the first place an intruder would look.) At once Ragab remembered a story he'd heard about a cunning young wife who'd hidden love letters which she didn't want her husband to see. She hadn't put the letters in a chest or under the floor but had hidden them in plain sight among a pile of household accounts. Best therefore to hide the vial containing the yellow liquid in plain view. To put it back where it had come from. On a shelf to one side of the room was an array of tubes and vials, slotted into a wooden frame. If he placed the vial there it would lost among many similar items.

He was unaware of it, of course, but two men were watching or listening outside the chamber. One of them, Ali, stood poised in the dark by the shutters, forked staff in hand, ready to force an entrance. The other, Ragab's young cousin Ja'far, was standing in the lobby beyond the door to the chamber and wondering when the old fool was going to go to bed. He could see the interior of the room through a crack in the panelling of the door. There was just enough light to see by. He had been standing there for some time, having spent much of the evening pacing up and down his room. He knew that Ali would be waiting in the yard outside the house and prayed that his friend would have the sense not to break in as long as there was any light still showing in the downstairs chamber.

Now Ja'far observed Ragab dithering before a bank of vials on a shelf. His cousin was clutching one of them. Something about the care with which he was handling the vial, and the way in which the lamplight picked up the gleam of gold inside, told him that this must be the sacred mixture . . . the potion . . . the *ab-e-hyat*. Far from hiding it away, he was placing it in the open. The young man saw that the older one had a cunning he wouldn't normally have credited him with. Ja'far continued to squint through the crack in the door. He watched as Ragab delicately inserted the vial into a space on the shelf. He did his best to note its position before Ragab turned away. The man's frame seemed to shrink as if he'd relieved himself of a great burden.

Ja'far was touched by a moment of pity. But he steeled himself. The old physician did not understand the value of what he had created. He was as likely to give it away as to sell it. And if he sold it, he would probably accept the first offer he received. Ja'far's mind was dazzled by visions of that palace on the river, with its fountains and servants. Ragab might be a clever man but he was unworldly, like all men who were happiest with their books, and he had no idea of true market value. Looked at in one way, Ja'far was doing his elderly relative a favour. What Ja'far planned was that the vial should appear to be stolen in the course of a robbery committed by an intruder. Done properly in this fashion, he, Ja'far, would be left free of blame. He had already arranged a buyer for the vial, a merchant who was prepared to pay the highest price and who had already given him a down payment as a token of good faith. After it was all over and the dust had settled he would of course ensure that his cousin was not left out of pocket. Once he and the old man were installed in that riverside palace . . .

At that instant there was a cracking noise and the shutters to the chamber burst open and Ali scrambled over the sill, clutching a queer-shaped stick. Ja'far was horrified. Didn't the idiot know that Ragab was still in the room? Why hadn't he waited until all the lamps had been put out? Now it was Ja'far's turn to dither. What should he do?

But things turned from bad to worse. As the shutters burst open, Ragab spun round to face the intruder. The old man was either slow or fearless for he did no more than move a couple of steps backwards. Ali seemed almost as surprised as Ragab. The robber – who had grown tired of waiting outside and assumed that the extinguishing of most of the lights showed the old man to have quit the room – stood helplessly by the window. He waved the forked stick about. Ragab took a further pace back. His heel caught on the ridge of a floor-tile. He lost his balance. His withered arms flew up and flailed at the smoky air. All might have been well, since the distance to the floor wasn't so great and Ragab was a wiry old bird who would have sustained no more than a few bruises. But the back of his head struck the edge of the filigreed chest with a crack. Ragab's body arched and then he slumped, expelling his breath as if he was settling down for the night, using the chest as a makeshift bolster.

Breathing deeply, Ja'far took a lamp from a table outside and entered the room. Ali was staring at the body, from which blood was beginning to pool in the region of the head. It was obvious that nothing could be done for Ragab. Ali looked up at Ja'far. He did not know that Ja'far had witnessed the last few moments.

'I didn't touch him!' said Ali.

Ja'far was about to agree with his friend but then thought better of it.

'There's blood on your sleeve.'

Ali gazed in bewilderment at his bloody sleeve and said, 'A nail. I cut myself on a nail on the fence. I didn't touch your cousin, I tell you.'

'Even so . . .' said Ja'far, quickly working out how this might be turned to his advantage. 'What's that you're holding?'

'This? I took it from the tree outside.'

Ja'far looked at Ali as if he was mad. 'Throw it out the window.'

Ali flung the staff out of the window. Holding the lamp and doing his utmost to avoid looking at the body on the floor,

Ja'far went towards the shelf where he had observed Ragab deposit the gold vial. Straightaway he saw it, nestling among the other philtres. He plucked it from the shelf and gave it to Ali.

'Go through the window now. Leave the same way you came. Barak is waiting in the house with red shutters down by the harbour. Give this to him. Do not on any account drop it or mislay it.'

'Barak will pay me?' said Ali. His wits hadn't quite deserted him.

'He will pay *me* before he sets sail tomorrow and then I will pay you,' said Ja'far. But Ali was reluctant to move and a look of cunning crept over his fat face. Ja'far at once grew irritated with his friend – some friend, since he was responsible for the death of the old man lying on the tiled floor! He hid his irritation even as he saw that more words would be necessary. 'Very well, I will pay you later tonight. Come back but only after you have delivered that . . . item . . . to Barak. He will give you a gold ring as proof of exchange. Be off with you now.'

'What about . . .?' said Ali, gesturing at Ragab.

'I will take care of him. After all, he is my cousin. Go now.'

And Ali slipped through the window and darted across the yard and over the fence, this time without doing himself an injury, and raced down the alleyway flanking the cemetery and sped off in the direction of the harbour where Barak was indeed waiting in the house with red shutters. It was a miracle he did not drop the precious vial but handed it over to Barak, intact, and in return the merchant presented him with a ring of gold.

In the meantime Ja'far pondered what to do with the body of Ragab. The pity that he'd felt earlier for the good old man expanded until it filled his heart. Then the pity was driven out by anger, anger at the turn events had taken, anger at the way in which Ali had bungled things. What to do? He must act quickly for Ali would soon be back to claim his share, which Ja'far would pay him out of the advance he'd received from Barak. But why should Ali get anything, considering how he'd botched this simple plan?

Ali knew nothing of Ja'far's thoughts. He was retracing his steps to the house by the cemetery, moving at a slower pace now. To be honest, he was exhausted by the night's work. The injury to his arm (which was still throbbing and leaking blood), the hanging about in the yard, the break-in, the unfortunate death of Ragab, the dash to the house with red shutters. All he wanted was to get from Ja'far what was owed him and then to retreat to his warm bed and his warm Munya. He arrived at the alley and the fence at the back of the yard. The scimitar moon picked out the tips of the mulberry branches. Ali clambered over the fence once more and approached the window. The shutters hung free. He hoped that Ja'far had disposed of the body of Ragab by now. Certainly he didn't intend to wait around and help.

But he heard voices from the interior of Ragab's chamber and caution made him pause. Just as well he did, for he saw that Ja'far was talking to a man he recognized. It was the kadi or magistrate in his black robes. Nor were Ja'far and the kadi alone. The magistrate was accompanied by two of his men, each wielding their canelike rods of office. Ali straightaway grasped that he had been betrayed. Ja'far had no intention of paying him what he was owed. In fact, he probably intended to . . .

At that moment one of the kadi's men glanced out of the window, his eye drawn by movement in the yard. He saw Ali. He shouted something to the others, and they crowded to the window. Ali panicked and stumbled back over the fence. This time he tore not his arm but his leg on the protruding nail, although he wasn't aware of it. Confused, he turned not left in the direction which would have taken him towards the city but right, towards the wasteland of dunes. When he reached the open he fell down. Fear of pursuers pushed him to his feet and he staggered over the uneven surface, sliding down slopes of rubbish-strewn sand. Eventually when his breath ran out and he could go no further, he sat down heavily in a depression in the ground. He stilled his panting, he listened for sounds of pursuit. But he could hear nothing apart from the baying of the dogs that haunted this edge of the city.

Ali was tired. The ground was warm. He pulled his robe about him, noticing as he did so that blood was welling from a bad gash on his calf. He made ineffectual efforts to staunch the flow by binding his leggings tighter. Now his leg throbbed worse than his arm. He wondered what to do next. Best to remain here a while, to wait until the kadi's men had given up the search, to sleep a little perhaps. He lay down and gazed up at the stars and the scimitar shape of the moon.

1

As the evening grew gloomier, the two men and the woman scrambled down the slope. The men, tall and bearded, were wearing thick leggings and leather jerkins. Their progress was made more awkward by the axes which they carried. The woman, who slithered behind them, was gripping a long club which she used like a stave to steady her progress or keep her balance. The three did not speak but concentrated their attention on avoiding the outcrops of rock and the slides of scree littering the hillside. The rain, which had been falling steadily all day, was coming down harder and made their descent treacherous in places. When they reached the gully at the bottom, they paused to catch their breath. Still no one spoke. Ahead of them the ground rose again to a bare ridge which stood out against the sky. Down here they were out of the worst of the wind and away from the booming sounds of the sea.

One of the men was evidently the leader for the other two appeared to be wating for him to move first. He had a Z-shaped scar on his cheek which showed through the thinner growth of beard there. He nodded and began a diagonal ascent of the opposite slope. There was no track but he seemed to be looking for a specific route for, at several points, he stopped and sought out a marker – a pile of stones or a stunted tree just visible in the gathering gloom – before altering his course slightly. The other man and the woman followed his lead. As they climbed, the ground turned steeper, split by fissures that were enclosed by outcrops of rock.

Eventually the leader reached the spot he was seeking. He halted by a stone promontory which nestled in a fold of ground. From its base sprouted a tangle of thorny shrubs. The man waited for the others to join him. He heard their panting before he saw them. Even though it was only mid-evening in spring, it was almost completely dark now because of the black clouds massed overhead. When all three had gathered by the stone, they once again waited to catch their breath. Then they stooped as one and – using their hands and the woman her stavelike club – began to tug at the bushes. The thorns must have pricked through the thick mittens which the men wore, but if this caused them any discomfort they did not show it. Some of the bundles of branch and thorn had been piled here for concealment rather than growing naturally. When they'd cleared a small space at the base of the stone, the woman dipped forward and using her club as a kind of probe slipped into the darkness.

They always did it this way. The woman was the first to go into the hole in the ground. After a couple of dozen yards the space widened and there was less difficulty in crawling forward. But the tunnel immediately beneath the outcrop of rock was tight, so tight that on a previous excursion one of the men had got stuck in the hole. It had taken a deal of tugging and cursing, and jokes about having to wait until he starved himself into thinness, before they'd been able to pull him out by his feet. Now it was the woman who took the lead because, if something happened to her companions, at least she would reach the far side and do what had to be done. Above ground the men listened until the faint scrabbling sounds below had died away before they stripped off their jerkins and, clad only in leggings and undergarments, proceeded into the hole, pushing their jerkins in front of them. Before they did this they discarded their axes beside the tunnel entrance. The second man did his best to cover the entrance with branches before he slithered inside.

Ahead of them the woman wormed her way further into the earth, scrabbling with the hand which wasn't grasping the club and pushing with her feet. She would not abandon her club for any reason, even if it made her advance through the passage more difficult. Although the men mocked her for this, they were secretly impressed by her determination. They were also a little fearful of her. If the woman had been inclined to feel fear, which she wasn't, she might have been overwhelmed by the way in which the tunnel of rock and soil closed tight about her, by the trickles of earth which pattered on her limbs and by the dangling tendrils of root that brushed her face. Above all, there was a darkness so absolute that it seemed as solid as rock. Whatever the weather, it was always dank and cold within the tunnel.

If the woman had possessed an imagination, she might have sensed the immense weight of rock and earth above her. If she'd stilled her gasping breath, she might have heard occasional scratchings and scufflings which would have told her that she was not the only occupant of this burrow. But she did not stop to listen. Indeed, she did not think at all and became merely a creature of the dark. The woman had no imagination, or at least not an imagination of a quick and fearful kind. So she inched and wriggled her way forward like the sightless mole.

The tunnel initially ran downwards before abruptly shifting to a slight upward slant. This was the most difficult stretch to negotiate since the crawler had to scrape under a knifelike blade of rock which ran across the ceiling. Knowing what was coming, the woman drew in her breath and pushed the club ahead of her. Arching her back, she eased herself forward across a boggy stretch. Now the tunnel broadened out further and the going became less difficult. The air remained heavy and foul but there was the odd waft of something fresher. Sometimes scrabbling in loose earth, sometimes grasping at firm flanks of stone, the woman felt for handholds on the sides and floor of the tunnel.

After perhaps a half-hour of this, during the last part of which a faint glimmer of light grew stronger, she neared the end of the shaft. The draughts of air turned colder still and the tunnel echoed with distant booming sounds. Then the passage levelled out and the roof and walls drew away so as to make a small gallery or cave, though not quite large enough for standing. Immediately ahead lay the mouth of the cave. The woman propped herself up on her elbows and gazed, almost unseeing, at the leaden line of the horizon and the shifting sky, almost as dark as the sea. She got into a crouching position, giving some relief to her aching limbs, and edged closer to the lip of the cave. The cliff face reared above her and fell steeply away beneath. Rain mingled with spray stung her face. Icy water from a land-spring trickled through the roof and ran down spikes of rock. It gathered in a hollow on the floor which was fringed by a clutch of ferns. The cavern was far above the surface of the sea but the very rock seemed to tremble as the larger waves struck the base of the cliff. There was a booming and bellowing from within the cliff face itself. This entire area was honeycombed with caves and fissures. Sometimes the sound died away as the wind abated, and the crashing was replaced by whispers which were worse to listen to because more eerie.

Behind her the two men made their more gradual advance. When they came to the knifelike projection at the upward bend of the tunnel, they chose to go on their backs and wriggle through in that fashion, even though it meant they had to twist their bodies round. Eventually they too arrived at the cave mouth. The woman was sitting with her back to them, her head slumped forward, not so much asleep as oblivious to everything despite the crashing of wind and waves. The first

18

man, the one with the Z-shaped scar, clapped her on the shoulder and she came to with a start, whirling round with the wooden club in her hand and her teeth bared.

'Thought it was old Nick, did you?'

The woman's snarl turned to a grimace. The man's scar stood out pale against his beard. He laughed at her response although, if the same trick had been played on him, he would have lashed out. And if he'd been alone here he might well have believed it was old Nick since he – unlike the woman – was imaginative enough to feel fear. It was well known that the network of caves in the cliff was the haunt of demons and devils. Any shepherd or wandering tinker who put his ear to the slopes on the far side of the cliffs could hear them groaning and whispering together. None of the locals would fall asleep on the hillside, not even in high summer, in case demons emerged from the cracks in the ground and carried them below.

'God's bones, it's cold in here,' said the man, trying to keep clear of the icy drips from the roof as he shrugged himself back into his jerkin. The woman ignored him and returned her gaze to the darkening sea until the second man shouldered his way into the cave. He held out his hand to the woman. She retrieved a canvas pouch from the depths of her clothes and gave it to the man. He removed his mittens. Working more by touch than sight, he drew out from the pouch a flint and steel and a piece of charred cloth. He placed the items on the ground. He reached sideways, running his fingertips over the wall of the cave.

He located a kind of recess, natural not man-made, and thrust into the hole with his arm. His hand closed around a square, metallic object. He brought it out and put it next to the flint and steel and the fragment of cloth. He fumbled at the catch on the lantern. He removed the stub of a candle from the interior and he replaced it with a fresh stick of tallow. Then, holding flint and steel above the charred cloth, he scraped one against the other until a little shower of sparks descended on the material. The cloth glowed red and a tiny flame struggled into life. The man crouched lower as though to shelter what he'd created against the blast of the elements. He touched the burning cloth to the wick of the candle. The smell of tallow tickled his nostrils as he waited to see the flame take hold before latching the shutter on the lantern. A soft glow filled the inner part of the cave.

The woman and the other man, who were nearer to the mouth of the cave, shifted towards to the lantern as if it was capable of sending out warmth as well as light. Now that their faces were illuminated properly for the first time, an observer would have seen that the two men were indeed brothers, with similar broad brows overhanging deep-set eyes. The woman was, if anything, more weather-beaten than they, with a complexion as brown as a nut in autumn. Their clothing, dull greens and russets smeared with mud, absorbed the glow of the lantern.

The woman turned back in the direction of the cave-mouth. She squinted into the near-darkness, broken only by ridges of white out to sea and spaces in the clouds which were like tears in a curtain. Was there anything out there? If so, it was ill weather to be abroad. Any fishing vessel or wallowing cargo ship should be hurrying for shelter.

The man who had seen to the lantern lifted it in both hands and, as delicately as if he was bearing some wounded bird, placed it at the lip of the cave. There was a square indentation in the rock here, which was very convenient. It might have been intended by Providence herself as the spot to place a warning light. A warning light or a welcoming one. Then the trio sat or squatted at the sides of the cave, but carefully so as not to obscure a single thread of the candle's bright beams.

The vessel was wide and pot-bellied. It was not designed for war or speed, and certainly not with an eye to grace. There was no nonsense about the boat. It had a single bridge and mast. It did not ride the heavy seas so much as clatter over them like a plate skimmed across a table by a drunken diner in a tavern. Nevertheless the *San Giovanni* had endured rougher weather in its time and the master was an experienced shipman, familiar with this stretch of the English coast. Some time ago, as the wind picked up from the east and the sky darkened, he had given orders for the sails to be furled.

The voyage out from Genoa, and lasting the best part of three weeks, had been uneventful so far. They had travelled in convoy part of the way, putting in at Cadiz and Bordeaux, where they had offloaded some spice cargo and taken on board fresh supplies of water. In fact, the voyage had been smooth as a dream. In the master's experience this was a bad thing. If fate had it in mind to store up trouble until the last stages of a voyage, then that trouble was likely to take a particularly malevolent form. The master of the *San Giovanni* sent up a swift prayer to the saint of his native city, in whose honour his vessel was also named.

Water was sloshing about the deck and the sailors had to cling to the ropes and bulwarks to keep their footing, while the salt wind and rain lashed at faces and hands. The *San Giovanni* was on a lee shore and on the starboard side the darker mass of the land was just visible. Standing near the bows the master scanned the coast anxiously every few moments, searching for the pinprick of light which would tell him that he was nearing landfall. Another sailor standing a few paces off struggled to keep his balance on the pitching deck. At last the master saw his light . . . a single speck in the gathering dark. Cuffing the man lightly about the head – his frequent means of getting attention – the master told him to give orders to the men at the rudder-post.

By the time the *San Giovanni* had begun to veer towards the shore, the trio had abandoned their post, leaving the light to burn, steady and unflickering, in the gloom of the cave entrance. It had been the man with the scar who first glimpsed the ship, a darker fragment against the inky sea. He observed the way in which its fitful progress seemed to be checked by more than the buffeting waves as the crew struggled to bring it closer to safety. Realizing what they were about, he grunted and shifted from his crouching stance by the cave-mouth. The others did not need telling what to do next.

The three wormed their way back through the tunnel, the woman once again in the lead. When they emerged from below the ground by the pillar of rock, the men retrieved their axes. They moved along the valley as rapidly as the gloom permitted until they reached a track that cut through the hillside like a knife-wound. They turned down the track, skidding on loose stones and tumbling more than once when they misjudged their footing. The wind was less audible here in the gully but the sound of the sea, which had been muffled by the blanket of the hillside, burst on them with renewed force. There was a thunderous noise as the waves struck the rocky strand followed by a sigh when the water drew back, then a moment's pause, then another thunderous blow. But to all of this the two men and the woman were oblivious. They knew the sounds of the sea. If anything was filling their heads it was the image of the ship, rolling and pitching its way towards what the master believed to be the entrance to the river mouth.

Some miles to the west of the point where the *San Giovanni* was wallowing out at sea a woman was lighting a candle on land that was more or less dry. Her name was Mags. She lived by herself in a tumbledown house in a fold of land among the hills which served as a natural shelter for the estuary and protected the harbour and town inside. But this particular spot was a gloomy one even on a sunny day. It was dotted with trees bent double against the wind. The house was no more than a single chamber, with a view through an embrasure directly out to sea. The wind whistled between flaws in the walls and rain dripped through the roof but the structure held to its place as tenaciously as one of the trees. The names of those who had constructed the house or who had originally lived there were long forgotten. Its occupant before the arrival of Mags – a solitary man who scraped a livelihood gathering samphire from the cliff faces – had been stricken during an outbreak of the plague in the middle of the century. Whether it was because of some sense of ill luck attaching itself to the place or because of its inherent gloominess or simply because it was off the beaten track, no one had moved into the simple dwelling after the samphire-gatherer's death. Mags did not care about these things. She did not mind the gloom or the isolation, never having known anything else. Besides, she had a cat called Gib to keep her company.

And she was not left entirely alone. People from the town and the countryside round about did quite frequently beat a path to her door (which hung from a single rusty hinge). They came to get her advice, to hear about their futures, to know the faces of their enemies. Mags was believed to have special powers. A fisherman might want to know if his wife had another man. In order to discover the truth, Mags would break an egg into a bowl, separating the yolk from the white. The egg had to be brought by the visitor; that was important. Mags would tilt her head and swallow the yolk straight from the shell. Then turning her back on the fisherman she would add some preparation of her own devising to the egg-white, stir them together, and instruct the man to gaze into the opaque mixture. If the wife had taken a lover, then that rival's face might appear – appear in miniature, dim and shadowed – on the pale liquid in the bowl. But not always. Mags was careful to say that the fisherman might see nothing more than the shadow of his own visage. Sometimes the fisherman would go away with a scowling expression, his suspicions confirmed. At other times such a visitor might leave, reassured or still baffled.

Nor were her visitors confined to the plainer folk from the surrounding country. Prosperous merchants and tradesmen from the big town had been known to pick their way down the squelchy path and knock on the door which hung from a single hinge. These merchants and tradesmen wanted to discover whether it was worth investing in a new warehouse on the harbourside, whether to take a part-share in a shipment of wine from Bordeaux. Mags was no fool. She knew these gentlemen were seeking reassurance rather than predictions about the future. If she detected uncertainty in a man's tone, then she suggested he ought to keep his money tight and dry in his purse. If she saw a hidden eagerness in his face, then she nodded and said, yes, it might be worth his while making a small outlay – only as much as he wouldn't mind losing, mind. And, of course, whatever her advice, something from that purse found its way into her palm.

It was perhaps surprising that, although she was whispered about and although people were wary of her, Mags had never been accused of harm or wrong-doing. If any word of her reputation as a witch reached her ears, she laughed it off, claiming she possessed no special powers. So she kept herself out of the hands of the law. Besides, she had an air of authority. She was old but did not look it. She was not bent and wizened and be-whiskered, but tall and hook-nosed and with flowing grey hair. She looked more like the wife of a nobleman than a devil's consort.

There was one other task which the woman called Mags performed and which, above all, helped to keep her safe from persecution. It was a task for which she was paid an annual sum by another woman, one who had been widowed when her husband was lost at sea off this very shore. This man was a sailor whose vessel ran aground on the rocks to the east during a storm very like the one raging at this instant. His boat and life had been forfeit, perhaps for want of a light. The widow determined that, in memory of her husband, a candle should be lit whenever the weather threatened peril to those at sea. Its purpose was to mark the entry to the estuary and the harbour. It is surprising how far a single light will carry on a dark night. Seeing it, a night-bound vessel could begin to change course and, by the grace of God and those saints who protect seafarers, make harbour.

Mags was able to sniff a storm at a distance, she knew the turns of the wind, she could read the deceptive surface of the sea. And, when she knew a storm was brewing, she struck a light and touched it to the wick of a large tallow candle in a shuttered lantern. This she placed in the embrasure in the sea-facing wall of the house. From here it might be seen across many miles of water. She did not keep watch after that but instead, her task done, lay down to sleep through the wind and rain. She did not know how many vessels her light had guided to the safety of the estuary, although the widow-woman who paid for the candle sometimes referred to this or that vessel which had come through perilous conditions. Of course, ships might still be driven on to the rocks, since a solitary light cannot save the whole world.

There were rumours too of false lights, deliberately placed to entice boats to disaster on the cliffs further east. Mags believed these rumours. She was versed enough in human wickedness. But she could do nothing about the false lights. All she could do was to tend her own flame, to ensure that it burned bright and clear during foul weather as she was doing now.

Out at sea on this foul evening, the master of the *San Giovanni* grasped their danger, their real danger, when he saw the uninterrupted fringe of white which marked the breakers. What he was searching for, with growing desperation, was the clear stretch which would indicate the mouth of the river and the calmer waters beyond. But through all the spume and spray he could discern nothing more than the deadly line of breakers. Together, the wind and waves were moving the *San Giovanni* steadily and inexorably towards the rocks. He glanced at the light which still glimmered near the top of the cliff. Where before he had seen it as a beacon guiding him and his ship to safety he now realized it was more like the marsh-light which tricks the unwary traveller and leads him to disaster.

He did not give the alarm, at least not straightaway. The sailor who'd been standing nearby earlier had returned. He was a slight, anxious-looking man. He was the master's nephew. It was his first time at sea. The source of the danger would not be apparent to him. Even so, he must have sensed trouble.

'Something wrong, uncle?' said the sailor, shouting to be heard above the boom of the waves and the roar of the wind.

'Never say so,' said the master. 'Never say so.'

As if he had just recalled something, the master left his position near the bows and, struggling to keep his balance on the pitching deck, reached his personal crib in the aftercastle. He was a tall man with a mane of hair which he kept tucked beneath his sea-cap. He had to duck his head as he entered the little chamber, clinging to the doorposts for support. Inside it was black as the pit but the master was acquainted with every square foot of his crib, the only truly private place on the *San Giovanni*. He kicked the door to behind him. The sounds of the weather were strangely magnified inside the crib. The shutter which covered the small port rattled furiously. A sudden surge of water running beneath the ship threw him with a crash on to the bed which occupied almost half the cabin. He cursed but did not rise from the bed. Instead he fumbled beneath it with one hand and dragged out a small wooden chest. Then he swung round until he was in a sitting position and brought the chest on to his raised knees. He slipped a cord from about his neck. Hanging from the cord was a cross, as well as a small sheathed knife such as most sailors carry about their necks – and a key.

He might have struck a light but he did not have time. Instead he reached back and unlatched the shutter over the port. It flew back with a clatter as if the salty air and spray could not wait to enter the crib and drive out all the fustiness. Little enough illumination was admitted from outside but it was sufficient for the master to have a glimpse of what he was doing. Using the key on the cord, he unlocked the chest and lifted the lid. He had large hands with fingers that were surprisingly elongated and supple. He felt among the various items which lay at the bottom of the chest. Only one thing was of concern. It was a pouch of soft leather secured with a drawstring, such as might have been used to store money. He cradled it in his palm. Whatever was inside was small and lightweight. The master of the *San Giovanni* did not open the pouch but transferred it straight to an inside pocket of his doublet. The pouch lay over his heart.

He remembered the circumstances in which he had acquired it. The confidential meeting in the tavern near the waterfront of the city of Genoa. A dark corner of smoky candles and smeared goblets, a corner where men retreated when they wanted to discuss terms or argue quietly before reaching a deal. There was a back door by this corner, useful if a man wanted to make an unobtrusive exit. He recalled the merchant from the East, a man called Barak, a man whose eyes glittered with more fire than the smoky candles of the tavern and whose skin was almost the colour of the leather pouch that he cradled in his palms. The pouch was handed over unwillingly, it seemed, even though the gentleman was being well paid for it. The master was used to the practised reluctance of the vendor, the way in which goods would be parted with as though they were the most valuable items on earth. But there was something different about this transaction, as if the merchant genuinely believed he was delivering an item of supreme value. Perhaps it was so.

The master recalled how he had taken possession of the purse, tugged at the drawstring and, with his delicate fingers, lifted out what it contained. He held it up to the candlelight and heard the merchant's indrawn breath. The gasp was another piece of salesmanship maybe, intended to emphasize the value of the object which the ship's master then replaced in the leather pouch. From his own purse he poured out a stream of coins and counted them out, separating them like counters in a game. He recalled the glint of the gold as the coins lay for an instant among the flasks and candles on the table before being scooped up by the man from the East. The deal was done. The merchant called Barak drained his goblet, then without another word he stood up and quit the tavern by the back door. The ship's master secreted the pouch in his doublet. Next morning, when he boarded his vessel, he would put it under lock and key inside the chest stowed under his cot. For tonight he intended to keep the pouch secure about his person.

But before the *San Giovanni* weighed anchor the next morning, the master heard some disturbing news. It seemed that a trader from the East had been discovered floating in the waters of the harbour. He went by the name of Barak and was a frequent visitor to the port of Genoa, one who dealt in spices and other goods. The death was not outwardly suspicious. It must have been an accident, and certainly no murder or the result of an attempted robbery. It could not have been otherwise, for there were no marks of violence on the body and, more significantly, a purse full of gold coins had been discovered on the corpse. The presence of the gold was a tribute to the honesty of the folk who'd fished him out of the harbour and then handed the corpse over to the authorities. The money would revert to the city after a certain sum had been deducted to pay for his funeral. The circumstances of the death were not much of a mystery. The merchant, perhaps the worse for wear after a night in one of the waterfront taverns, had taken the wrong turning – or been looking at the view by night and lost his footing – and had tumbled into the dark waters of the harbour. The master of the *San Giovanni* was troubled by the information. It made him wonder about the nature of the item which was concealed within the leather pouch. Perhaps it brought ill fortune to those who handled it. Some superstition prevented him from even looking at it again once it was safe inside the chest in his crib.

And now oblivious to the blast of the storm raging outside, the master reflected for a moment (ought he to take anything else from the chest?) before deciding that there was nothing apart from the leather pouch which demanded saving, should the worst happen. For all that, he relocked the chest, pushed it back under the bed and looped the cord with the key about his neck once more. He fastened the latch of the port-shutter and stood up, with some difficulty because of the motion of the vessel.

The ship's master left his crib and emerged once more into the open. He clapped his hand to his sea-cap as the wind threatened to unfasten it from his head. The *San Giovanni* was stern on to the weather, and each wave as it passed carried the vessel forward with a motion that was somewhere between a leap and swirling lift. There was no power on earth that could change their course now. The mast quivered in its supports and the furled sails snapped and cracked like whips, as if they were dying to be torn free. By this stage the terrified crew had seen their danger and several were clustered about the forecastle, shielding their eyes against the rain and spray and looking at the deadly line of breakers which drew closer with every instant. Some were kneeling or crouching, in prayer or fear.

'Oh, what is to be done?' said his nephew, cupping his hands and speaking direct into his uncle's ear.

'Nothing but to pray to Our Lady and all the saints. To Giovanni especially.'

'Will the saint save us, uncle?' said the man, as if he was a child.

'God ordains, while we arrange,' mouthed the master.

And, privately, the master promised that he would light a five-ducat candle to the saint if they should survive. No, ten ducats' worth of candles. At the same time, he felt the outline of the pouch which nestled in his doublet. He wondered if its contents might have the power to save the *San Giovanni*. Or were they responsible for the fate which was now rushing towards them?

When they emerged from the gully and arrived at the shore, the threesome whose false light had caused the *San Giovanni* to veer off course picked their own way over jagged outcrops of rock and across the slippery weeds and shingle. They halted some distance from the breaking waves and took shelter as best they could behind a natural ledge of rock, their faces turned towards the sea. The same wind and rain which buffeted the *San Giovanni* buffeted them, but they were glad at each ferocious blast and tearing gust. They had scarcely spoken in all this time. The scarred leader glanced back in the direction of the light which glimmered to one side and far overhead in the cliff face. Then he gazed at the ship which was being drawn towards the beam, as if the threads of light were strong enough to drag all that massy weight across the ocean. Now the two men flourished the axes which they had carried all this distance. There was some ragged light coming through gaps in the clouds. The men held up their axes as if to admire the workmanship of each blade and the curved hooks which protruded from the opposite side to the blade. For her part, the woman hefted her club and smiled to herself.

These weapons were not merely for display. They would serve a bloody purpose if any member of the ship's crew staggered ashore, battered and near-drowned, once his vessel had come to ruin on the rocks. A swift cut from the edge of the blade, a swipe with the curved hook, a swingeing blow from the club, would settle that sailor's fortunes for ever.

Any survivors must be destroyed. It was what the law demanded. For it was all a question of law – and the men and the woman were familiar with the law of the sea, or with this particular branch of it, even though they'd never handled a legal parchment and none of them could read or write. If the threesome had known which King of England to thank for the law they might have lighted an honest candle to his memory. But they didn't know, or care. All they knew was that the law of England stated that a ship could not truly be considered a wreck if a single man or beast escaped from the vessel. Escaped alive. So it was their duty to ensure that the false hopes of any man, or beast, emerging from a stricken ship were soon dashed.

It was both their business and pleasure to see that there were no survivors. Most often the violence of the sea cheated the wreckers of the chance to kill. Sailors and other travellers on a boat that was driving on to a lee shore would frequently leap overboard, preferring to trust to the water than to take their chances with a vessel that was about to be smashed to smithereens. Others would jump or topple from the side as the boat grounded, only to be crushed by falling spars or dashed on the rocks. The very few that outlived the wreck of their craft would clamber down ropes or jump from the bulwarks. They would stumble across the slippery foreshore and – if they had any space remaining in their poor brains – give thanks to God and all his saints for their preservation. They might look up and, wiping sweat and seawater from their eyes, see figures in their way. They might even, if they had a shred of reason left in their heads, observe that the figures were wielding weapons and that in consequence they were further from salvation than ever. But there was usually no fight or spirit left in these survivors. The boiling waves and the terror of the wreck had seen to that. They would move blindly forward, like cattle to the slaughter, not believing the evidence of their battered senses. For how could any human being intend harm to one who had suffered the blows of the sea? And then the survivors would be felled like cattle by the men with axes and the woman with the club, their bodies to be discarded where they'd fallen or thrown back into the tossing waves once any valuables had been torn from their corpses. It didn't matter if these corpses were recovered later. It was easy to blame their injuries, their shattered limbs and broken heads and trunks, on the violence of the sea.

The prizes from the dead were small pickings, of course, and the property of the wreckers. The real meat was to be found in the ship's cargo, whether it was wine or salt, silks or spices. Some of it would inevitably be lost in the smash of the ship but much could be salvaged. Out of this the wreckers took their share, although they were not the only ones to benefit. So it had always been.

So it would be now. The three wreckers crouched behind the rock ledge, hands clutching their weapons and eyes straining out across the sea at the boat which was being drawn steadily and hopelessly towards them.

But it did not happen as the wreckers expected. Whether it was on account of extraordinary good fortune provided by their patron saint Giovanni or the stocky solidity of the vessel, or whether it was because of the prayers which the master and men had been offering up with all their hearts or because of the good seamanship and steady nerves which meant that no one leapt overboard before the boat grounded, not a soul was lost. No man perished while the *San Giovanni* was borne across a patch of deeper water and then lifted up by a final black wave and deposited on a shelving stretch of rock and shingle.

The crash was ear-splitting. Men were thrown flat on the deck or against the bulwarks, breath knocked from their bodies. White water foamed about the sides of the boat and hissed as it withdrew but the force of that final throw had been sufficient to push the boat out of the way of immediate harm. If the *San Giovanni* had been a more elegant vessel, if she'd been designed for any other purpose than to carry goods in a no-nonsense fashion from one port to another, then the timber of her frame might have shattered under the hammer blows of the pounding. But even when some of the planking sprung and the boat shook relentlessly, she held herself together. After a few moments the wind dropped and a strange lull followed. The waves continued to batter at the rocks but the *San Giovanni* lay just out of reach of the very worst of them.

The wreckers could not believe their eyes. It was a disaster. In all their experience of wreck and ruin, they had never seen anything to match it. They watched as the ship was carried up and deposited to their left on a shelf of rock and shingle, as if to put her out of harm's way. The great crash and grinding she made was audible above the roar of the wind, and they instinctively turned away from the sight. They waited for the sailors to flee the carcass in fear of imminent destruction. But the boat held its position and the wind eased. On deck figures were visible, strangely immobile. Eventually they came to life and several of them slipped over the side, dangling down by their hands or using ropes. There were half a dozen of them.

One of the men and the woman hefted their weapons. They were about to emerge from the shelter of the rocky ledge and confront the sailors. Or rather to wait for them to make their way further up the shore. But the first man, the one with the Z-shaped scar, put out a restraining hand.

'What's wrong, brother?' said the second. His blood was up and he was eager to get to grips with the band on the shore.

'They are too many of them,' said the first.

The woman looked at him. But it was so, there were too many. The half-dozen had been joined on the rocks by another handful of men. They stood, little figures set beside the rocks and the boat and with the sea raving away behind them. The threesome would not usually have baulked at cold-blooded murder. But there was a difference between cutting down the odd straggler and slaughtering a whole crew, which, it would appear, they must do before the vessel was accounted a wreck. Yet they might have accomplished even this. They had surprise on their side, and they wielded fearsome weapons.

But something held the leader back. Perhaps he was struck, despite himself, by the near-miraculous preservation of the *San Giovanni*. He had noted the way the wind dropped abruptly and was aware that the tide was on the turn. Perhaps he quailed at the idea of cutting down one man after another, with the likelihood that some would fight back or escape along the foreshore. Perhaps he was frightened at the secret cargo which the vessel was reputed to carry. He had heard rumours, no more, of some priceless freight, something rarer than gold or silver. Perhaps the *San Giovanni* was protected by magical influence. If it was so, then to attempt to overpower the survivors would be not merely useless but dangerous. It would not be the sailors who would be struck down but the man and his brother and the woman who was his doxy.

So there was no wreck for them to loot but a boat which, though damaged, seemed to have been lifted clear of harm. There were no scattered goods to scavenge from the shore. No stragglers to be felled with an axe-blow, but a numerous band of sailors who would most likely fight for lives which had been so providentially spared. There was no future in it.

The leader of the wreckers was a ruthless man. He was also a canny one. He and his little band would not have survived so long had it been otherwise. He knew when the moment had come to retreat. He indicated as much to his brother and the woman. There was a brief argument among the three of them, interspersed with curses, all conducted in hisses and whispers against the crashing of the sea. But the man with the scar prevailed, as he usually did. The others could see that there would be no prospect of gain this night. So they slunk back the way they had come, across the shore and up the gully.

The crew of the *San Giovanni* had no idea how close they'd come to another assault, not from the sea but from the shore. They were dazed and bruised and shivering. They kept an instinctive distance from the beached boat towering over them like a Leviathan, as if they feared it might even now fall to pieces and crush them. But the master strode about, counting heads and occasionally cuffing them and speaking cheerfully. He had lost his sea-cap and his hair flared out like a mane.

Eventually, as the storm calmed, he permitted some of the men to clamber back aboard the *San Giovanni*, to get warmer clothing as well as some provisions. They found a sheltered place in the lee of some rocks (the very place where the wreckers had been crouching earlier), and they lit a fire and chewed on salt meat and salt fish, and shivered again, and lay down to sleep fitfully on any patch of shingle they could find. Tomorrow at first light they'd be better able to assess the damage which, in keeping with their miraculous escape, appeared to be slight. Those Genoese boat-builders knew their business! Praise be to the stout timbers of their country! It might even be possible to patch up the *San Giovanni* and float her off on the next day's tide, since they could not be far from the river mouth and harbour. The master had suspicions about the light which had led them to this place. He could still see it, glinting delusively, a pinprick further down the coast, but in the dark it was impossible to tell whether it marked a dwelling place or served a more sinister purpose. He put the suspicions to one side for the time being.

'We are saved, uncle,' said his nephew.

'Then you should thank Giovanni and all the saints,' said the master, clasping his hand to his breast and feeling the outline of the pouch which lay there. And wondering whether there was truly some magic power in its contents.

A few miles to the west, in the small stone house nestling in the fold of hills above the estuary, Mags slept undisturbed. Her candle burnt clear and bright, a warning and welcome to benighted sailors.

'Tell us a story,' they said, 'tell us a story.'

'Very well,' he said, 'let me think.'

Geoffrey Chaucer looked down and stroked his beard, neatly trimmed now after months of travel. He gazed towards the window as if inspiration might lie among the stormy clouds outside. He tapped his foot, as though to jog his thoughts into motion. But all the time he had a story in mind. It had occurred to him as he was riding on the outskirts of Florence some weeks before. He and his companions had been passing a rackety small-holding. An old woman was standing in a crooked doorway, gazing at the riders without expression. The yard was full of hens and a single cock with a bright red comb. Unlike his owner, the cock paid the riders no attention. However impoverished the surroundings, the bird was king of this dusty arena.

'This is a story about animals in a farmyard,' said Geoffrey. 'It takes place in the days when the animals could talk.'

'When was that?' said Elizabeth.

'A long time ago, according to a book called the *Physiologus*,' said Geoffrey. Elizabeth nodded as if she knew what he was talking about. Her father hurried on with the story.

'The farmyard belonged to a woman who lived a very simple life,' he said. 'Among the farmyard animals were a cock and seven hens. The cock had one hen out of the seven which was a particular favourite of his. You might almost say that they were husband and wife. The pair were called Chauntecleer and

Pertelote. Chauntecleer the cock was a showy bird, fond of parading about the yard and certain that whatever he thought must be right. One night he was sleeping on the perch next to Pertelote, his wife and favourite hen, when she was awoken by the sound of groaning. She turned to gaze at her husband.'

Geoffrey paused. He closed his eyes and imitated the noise of Chauntecleer groaning in his sleep. He looked at his daughter and son. Thomas chuckled with pleasure at the noise but Elizabeth looked as she usually did, rather solemn and serious for her age.

'When Pertelote the hen heard him making these odd sounds she grew alarmed and said, "O my dear, what's the matter with you that you're groaning like this?" "Madam," he replied, "don't take this in the wrong way. But I dreamed just now that I was in bad trouble and it's given me a real scare."

'"Well?" said Pertelote.

'She sounded impatient and merely waited for Chauntecleer to continue, which he did once he'd calmed down a bit.

'"I dreamed that I was wandering up and down in our yard when I saw a beast like a hound which wanted to seize hold of me and kill me. His coat was a yellowy-red colour, his tail and his ears were tipped with black. His snout was small and his eyes were glaring – even now I'm almost dead with fear at the look he gave me. That's what made me groan in my sleep."'

Geoffrey saw that Elizabeth was about to name the hound-like animal and signalled with his eyes that she was to keep it secret from Thomas. The boy was four. Elizabeth was seven. Both children were quick. They loved hearing stories. Telling stories was what he did sometimes when he was with them. But he'd been absent since before Christmas of the previous year, returning only a couple of days ago on the brink of summer. He hoped to be at home for a while longer. Not that this chamber where he was sitting with Elizabeth and Thomas could be counted as home or even a part of it. Not his proper home, for this was the grand palace of the Savoy on the banks of the Thames. Now the wind rattled at the windows of the grand palace. The day had started fair before suddenly turning chill and Philippa, Chaucer's wife, had ordered a fire to be lit for the evening. Geoffrey was sitting in a chair by the fire but a draught was blowing in from somewhere. His children were sitting nearby among the rushes strewn on the floor. They'd been playing outside and Geoffrey had called them in out of the wind and rain with the promise of a story. Suddenly conscious that Elizabeth and Thomas were waiting for him to continue with the cock-and-hen story, he took up the thread once more.

'Pertelote the hen was not impressed by her husband's story. "What!" she exclaimed. "Shame on you! By God, you've lost my heart and my love now you've told me you're frightened of dreams. How can I possibly love a coward? Whatever women say, every one of us wants a husband who is tough and clever and generous – and a man who isn't afraid of any threat or weapon. How dare you say such things to your loved one. Who could be scared of dreams? Dreams don't mean anything, they're the result of over-eating or some kind of upset in your system."

'And, she continued, when they flew down from their perches and into the farmyard, she would find him the right herbs and remedies to clear his system, starting with a purgative. What he really needed, she said, was a diet of worms.'

'Worms?' said Thomas.

'Birds eat them,' said Elizabeth.

Thomas looked at his sister. 'I'm not stupid,' he said.

'But Chauntecleer was,' said Geoffrey.

'Why?' said Elizabeth.

At that moment the door opened. Philippa Chaucer stood in the entrance. Slightly behind her stood a squat nurse holding a small child by the hand. It was the Chaucers' third child, little Lewis. Elizabeth and Thomas glanced round for an instant. It was only their mother and their little brother. They turned back to their father.

'Why was Chauntecleer stupid?' repeated Elizabeth.

'Because he didn't listen to his wife when she advised him about his diet,' said Geoffrey.

'Husbands should listen to their wives,' said Elizabeth.

'That's my opinion too,' said Geoffrey. 'Husbands should listen to their wives if they want a quiet life.'

He sensed Philippa shifting by the door, but couldn't tell whether she was amused or impatient.

'But Chauntecleer was not prepared to listen to his wife,' Chaucer continued. 'The cock went back to some stories which he'd read once and which showed that dreams could predict the future and that it was right and sensible to take notice of them. Chauntecleer told the stories, which he'd got from the Latin. They showed that if you didn't pay attention to dreams then disaster would overtake you. "So, my dear," said Chauntecleer triumphantly when he'd finished, "you ought to know that we should take dreams seriously. There's nothing wrong with being frightened of them. But, madam, let's change the subject and talk of something more pleasant. Whenever I gaze on the beauty of your face, whenever I see that lovely scarlet-red colour around your eyes, it makes all my fear just die away. Feeling you beside me on the perch gives me joy and pleasure – I'm ready to defy my dreams and my visions."

'You can see that Chauntecleer was feeling more confident now. By the time he flew down from the beam, accompanied by his wives, he had forgotten all about the dream. He looked like a fierce lion as he roamed about the place on his toes, hardly laying his foot on the ground and clucking so much when he found some corn that all his seven wives ran after him.'

Once more Geoffrey paused for effect. He glanced towards his wife. She'd come further into the room now. Yes, it was definitely amusement on her face. Behind her stood the short nurse hand in hand with Lewis. Even she seemed to be listening. He would continue with the story until . . .

'They say pride goes before a fall, don't they? Listen to what happened later that morning. A . . . fox, yes a fox – '

'A fox!' said Thomas.

'I knew it was a fox,' said Elizabeth.

'Yes, it was a fox with black markings which had lived in a grove of trees for three months. He had been waiting for his opportunity to pounce on Chauntecleer and now the time had come.'

'What was he called?' said Thomas.

'Foxes don't have names,' said Elizabeth.

'This one did. He was called . . . Russell. Well, Pertelote was around, playing very happily in the sand with all her sisters near her in the sun while Chauntecleer, now a very cheerful fellow, sang his heart out. It so happened that as he was idly following the flight of a butterfly above a cabbage patch he became aware of the fox . . . of Russell . . . lying low there. Straightaway he stopped singing, to cry out in terror.

'But the fox was quick. He spoke immediately: "Why, my good sir, where are you going? You're not frightened of me, surely? I'm your friend, your true friend and admirer. I mean you no harm, I haven't come to pry into your secrets. All I want is to hear you sing. I have to say, your voice is as fine as an angel's in heaven."'

Chaucer imitated the fox's refined voice. He made it sound like the voice of a courtier whom he knew slightly and disliked a great deal.

'Chauntecleer was caught by this flattery,' he said.

'Fattery,' said Thomas, puzzled.

'*Flattery*,' said his sister.

'But fattery is a good word too,' said Geoffrey, 'because that's what it was. Thick slippery words spread like grease. Chauntecleer

41

was so taken in by this *fattery* that he missed the double meaning in Russell fox's next words.

'"My lord your father (God bless his soul!) – and your mother in her kindness – have both visited my house and given me the greatest pleasure," said the fox. "But while we're talking about singing I have to say that, apart from your good self, I've never heard anyone sing so well as your father did in the early morning. Every note came straight from the heart. To make his voice even stronger he would close both his eyes when he sang. And he would stand on the tips of his toes and stretch forward his long, slender neck. I tell you what!" said the fox as though the idea had just come to him. "Let us see if you can imitate your father!"

'Chauntecleer was so overwhelmed by these smooth words of *fattery* that he began to flap his wings with delight. He stood high up on tiptoe, stretched out his neck and shut both his eyes. He started to crow as loud as he could.

'Russell the fox leapt up at once and grabbed Chauntecleer by the bare throat. No one was nearby to pursue the pair and the fox made off, with Chauntecleer lying across his back, in the direction of the wood . . . '

Geoffrey paused. He'd reached the high point of the story. Both Elizabeth and Thomas were agog to know the fate of the gullible Chauntecleer. Even Philippa seemed eager to know what happened next. This was a good place to stop.

'You must go to bed now, children. Your mother is here with Lewis.'

'Just a little more, mother, please,' said Thomas, recognizing where the true authority lay in the family. 'Only a little.'

'Tomorrow,' said Philippa. 'Tomorrow, I expect. Now you should say goodnight to your brother.'

The nurse brought Lewis right into the room, still holding him by the hand. He was two and a half, and smiled to see his father. Philippa kissed him first and whispered something in his ear. Then she kissed Thomas and Elizabeth and said, 'Silly boy, your clothes are damp.'

'They were playing outside,' said Geoffrey. 'I called them in.'

Philippa's look suggested that Elizabeth and Thomas should have been told to change. Now she watched as the nurse ushered all three out of the private chamber.

She sighed and sat down in the chair on the other side of the fire. The wind rattled at the window. They might have been in the middle of winter rather than May.

'Fattery,' she said.

'It's a good term,' said Geoffrey. 'Perhaps the boy will turn out to be a wordsmith.'

'Like his father, no doubt. What happens to the cock in your story . . . whatsitsname?'

'Chauntecleer. Oh, I'm not sure yet.'

'Liar, Geoffrey.'

'All right, I am sure but you'll have to wait till tomorrow like everybody else.'

'I'm not certain there's going to be a tomorrow.'

'Eh?'

Chaucer glanced at Philippa. She was watching from the far side of the fireplace. He couldn't read her expression. Or perhaps it was that he didn't want to read it.

'I've just heard that Sir Thomas wants to see you tomorrow morning.'

'Elyot?'

'The very same. Gaunt's secretary.'

'I hadn't heard that.'

'You forget my privileged position in this place,' said Philippa. She put a half-ironic emphasis on 'privileged'. 'I hear things before other people.'

'What does Sir Thomas want, I wonder?'

'To send you off on the road again, I expect. Another mission.'

'Another "mission". More rotten food and worse lodgings. I

hope not. I shouldn't think so. He probably just wants to clear up some business from my last trip.'

'I've heard differently.'

'How is your sister?' Geoffrey said, wondering if this was Philippa's informant. 'How is Katherine?'

'It is not easy for her,' said Philippa, closing off this attempt to turn the conversation with a shrug. There was not much more to say in any case, since Chaucer knew or could guess why it was 'not easy' for Katherine Swyneford in the palace of the Savoy.

'At least *you* must be comfortable here,' he said, 'comfortable if not easy.'

But Philippa gave no answer and continued staring into the fire.

'I must go to the Aldgate house,' he said. 'I haven't been there since I got back.'

'You want to see your mistress?' she said and, observing her husband start, went on, 'Calm yourself, Geoffrey. I mean that you wish to visit your library.'

'The house at Aldgate is also our home.'

'And we shall be back at home . . . as soon as Katherine has no more need of me here.'

Which could be some time, thought Geoffrey Chaucer as he made his way down the passages of the Savoy Palace and into the blustery air outside. Philippa's sister Katherine had an eminent position in the Gaunt household of the Savoy. Doubly eminent. Officially Katherine was there as *magistra* to John of Gaunt's children by his first wife, and unofficially she was there as Gaunt's mistress. Because of her sister's status, Philippa and family had choice lodgings on the south side of the palace overlooking the river. Her own duties were as one of the demoiselles in attendance on Constanza, the austerely beautiful Spaniard who was Gaunt's second wife. The existence of Constanza was the reason for Katherine Swyneford's uneasy role in the household. Chaucer had no idea how the situation would be resolved, but he doubted that it would be soon since it seemed to suit John of Gaunt to have his two women under one roof. A bit like Chauntecleer. Meantime he crossed the Fleet river and strode along Thames Street, relishing being back in his home town and hoping that his interview with Sir Thomas Elyot the next day was not to be the prelude to some further adventure.

Recalling his wife's comment about going to see his mistress, he smiled slightly. She was right enough there. He was dedicated to his library and his books. As for real mistresses . . . he wondered if his wife thought about what occurred when he was on his foreign expeditions. He wondered what she was thinking now.

In fact, Philippa was thinking about her husband at this moment. After he'd quit their chamber she remained sitting by the fire. Then she stood up and stretched. She wandered over to the window. The wind shook the branches of the fruit trees on the terraces and ruffled the waters of the river beyond. There were a few ferries plying to and fro. Grey clouds scudded across the sky. She put her hand to one of the cold panes of glass, which quivered slightly in the wind. She could see the pale reflection of her image, the round cheeks, the homely looks. She wasn't in the habit of gazing at herself in mirrors. Her sister Katherine's apartment in the Savoy had enough mirrors for the pair of them.

Philippa Chaucer had no illusions about herself. When she'd married Geoffrey Chaucer, it had been half by arrangement, half by her own choice. Under the patronage of Edward the Third's late queen – another Philippa, and also from Hainault – she had made her selection from the wide circle of suitable bachelors associated with the English court.

Chaucer wasn't exactly a catch in the sense that her fine sister Katherine would have understood the word. He was the son of a vintner, born little more than half a mile from where she presently stood staring at the tousled skies above the river. His family was prosperous, better off than hers. But that didn't count for much against lineage. Philippa occupied a place at court through birth and blood, even if neither were of the highest. Geoffrey had acquired his through luck and merit.

He stood only a couple of inches taller than her. She doubted he'd ever been lithe or lean. And now, whatever he said about the poor food and the privations which he experienced on the road, he was growing slightly stouter by the year. True, he'd campaigned and fought in his youth. He had even been captured in France and ransomed – for sixteen pounds, the sum having been paid by the Keeper of the King's Wardrobe. (He was fond of saying he'd be worth more now.) Yet her husband had never been an authentic knight or warrior. For him, warfare was not a calling, not even a profession. Rather it was a regrettable necessity, something to be avoided if at all possible. Philippa considered that, at least in this, her husband was more in keeping with the spirit of the times. The great days of the warrior-heroes were dying. The King was in his seventies. The King's oldest son, also Edward and known for his black armour and his prowess in the field, was a sick and swollen figure, unlikely ever to fight again and one who might not even outlive his father since the doctors seemed able to do little or nothing for him.

Perhaps, Philippa thought, the future belonged to men like Geoffrey, the sons of wool-traders and wine-shippers, men more at home with an account book and a pen than with sword and shield. Books – now there was an item which her husband certainly was at home with. Not account books but books of fancy. Geoffrey had plenty of them, two dozen at least, which he kept at the Aldgate house. And it wasn't just the reading or amassing of books but also the writing of them. He called himself a 'maker' and scribbled verses to prove it, love verses even. Philippa didn't have much time for such stuff and Geoffrey, sensing this, rarely troubled her with his effusions. For which she was thankful. There was something inherently comic about the idea of her husband as a love poet anyway, since he seemed far beyond romance, so middle-aged by nature. Why, he might have hopped out of the womb already middle-aged!

The idea of the account book brought to mind those columns where profit and loss are balanced against each other. So, having considered his debit side, Philippa considered her husband's credit column.

He was a good enough husband (when he was present).

He was an attentive father to Elizabeth and Thomas and little Lewis (when he was not gadding about) if a bit careless of their welfare. She wouldn't have allowed her son and daughter to sit on the floor in damp clothes.

He had a dry sense of humour. That had been the thing that attracted her at first. He had the habit of making a comment with a straight face, using his slightly hooded eyes to good effect.

He was courageous in his way. Philippa was no fool and understood that when her husband went abroad on his 'missions' he must sometimes run into danger, even though he spoke very little about his activities.

She could think of nothing further in his favour, at least without having to try too hard, although she supposed that four entries on the 'credit' side wasn't a bad tally. She recalled the words of Pertelote in the story he'd recounted to her children. She'd been listening outside the door before she entered, with the nurse and Lewis in her wake. She'd heard Geoffrey's words about what women want. *A husband who is tough and clever and generous – and a man who isn't afraid of any threat or weapon.* Well, it was true enough, wasn't it? She turned away from the window. The dark clouds scudding about the sky had turned the chamber dark. More light came from the flames in the hearth than through the window. She was about to call out to one of her attendants to light some candles but instead she went back to her seat close to the fire.

3

Geoffrey Chaucer knew better than to protest or make a fuss. It would be useless to say that his bones ached and that he was weary of travelling. Useless to say that he'd enjoyed only a couple of days at home and that, if he had to spend much more time away from his family, he would begin to forget not merely what his wife and children looked like, but their very names. Useless to say that, anyway, this did not sound like a task requiring his special skills – whatever those skills happened to be, precisely. Then he decided to make this final point, after all: this was not a task for which he was fitted. It was the only argument which might have some effect on Sir Thomas Elyot, secretary to John of Gaunt.

It didn't work.

Sir Thomas looked at Geoffrey Chaucer from under his bushy eyebrows. Geoffrey squinted back. It was an early morning in the early summer. They were sitting in an outer office in John of Gaunt's quarters. The sun was coming right through the casement window behind Sir Thomas, causing Geoffrey to shift his head in an attempt to block the light. It put Geoffrey at a small disadvantage, which was probably deliberate. For his part, the knight wore his perpetually indignant look, enhanced by those bristling brows. He was sitting on the far side of a table on which papers and scrolls and writing implements were immaculately arrayed, everything aligned or set at right angles. Geoffrey wondered why he chose not to keep his eyebrows as trim as he kept his table-top.

'What do you mean, Master Chaucer, you do not have the skills? You are acknowledged as an expert diplomat and negotiator. Our master has said so, often.'

'Our master' also called me a desk-man once, thought Geoffrey Chaucer, someone who shouldn't stray far from his books and verses. But he would not quibble over the words of John of Gaunt. Sir Thomas Elyot was one of Gaunt's most trusted assistants, someone who liked to believe that he had the private ear of the man he invariably called 'our master'.

'I did not say that I lacked the skills, Sir Thomas. I said that this particular . . . errand . . . does not sound like the kind of business where I could usefully intervene.'

'Oh, I know that you are accustomed to talk with dukes and counts and wealthy bankers – '

'It's not that.'

' – and now we are asking you to go on an "errand", as you call it, to a little town by the sea where you will have to converse with plain citizens and burgesses,' said Sir Thomas, unwilling to relinquish the chance to make Chaucer out to be too big for his boots.

'Sometimes these things are better settled at a local level,' said Geoffrey. 'Can't you send someone from, I don't know, someone from Plymouth?'

'Plymouth?' said Sir Thomas, as if it was a town on the moon.

'When an official person comes all the way from London, everyone leaps to the conclusion that there must be a lot at stake. They get worried.'

'Which is exactly why we need someone with your gifts, Master Geoffrey,' said Sir Thomas. 'If anyone has the ability to put people at their ease, it's you with your silver tongue. Our master says so, often. He also comments on your tact and your reticence, which everyone knows are more valuable possessions for a diplomat than his letters of credit.'

John of Gaunt had particular reason to be glad of the tact and reticence of Chaucer and his wife Philippa. But Chaucer knew Gaunt well enough to recognize that any compliments paid to him by the Duke of Lancaster were heartfelt, and not mere flattery . . . or fattery, as his son Thomas would put it. At the same time Geoffrey realized that further comment was useless. Whatever he said about his suitability or unsuitability for the task would only be twisted to exert more pressure on him. He sighed slightly and shrugged with what he hoped was a good grace.

'Very well, Sir Thomas. Explain to me exactly what I have to do. If you would be so good.'

Sir Thomas did not show any pleasure at the concession but instead reached behind him and tugged at the window curtain. He said, 'I fear the sun is in your eyes, Master Geoffrey. Is that better?'

'Thank you.'

'Your mission to Florence was successful, I understand.'

'There were some small difficulties but it was successful, yes.'

The difficulties had included several murders but Chaucer did not want to enlarge on that. He had achieved his primary aim in Florence, which was to negotiate a loan from the Lipari banking house to the English throne in order that the English King might continue with his lifelong task of showing France the benefits of war.

'And your knowledge of the Italian tongue, Master Geoffrey, how is that?'

'Enough to get by, Sir Thomas.'

'Good, good. And, if I'm not mistaken, you stopped off in Genoa on the way to Florence.'

Chaucer nodded. Of course, Sir Thomas knew perfectly well that Chaucer had 'stopped off' in Genoa for several weeks on the way to Florence since the two of them had discussed the matter together before he'd even set out the previous year.

Bound on double business as the King's envoy, Geoffrey had also been charged with negotiating the establishment of a trading centre for the Genoese on the south coast of England (its exact whereabouts was not yet settled but the plan had been approved in principle).

'Your business in Genoa was successfully concluded as well?'

'There is a treaty.'

'And the Genoese are now our friends.'

'I hope so.'

'We must ensure that it *remains* so,' said Sir Thomas, picking up a pen and laying it down again in the same place. 'Did I mention to you that the ship, the one that was wrecked, is from Genoa?'

'You said only that a ship had been driven ashore near Dartmouth without loss of life. You didn't say where it had come from.'

'It was carrying a cargo of alum. It was driven ashore during a storm. By a miracle no one was harmed and the damage to the *San Giovanni* is not so great, I understand, although it will take several weeks of repairs to put it right. Is that how the word is pronounced – *Jo-vah-nee*? I have only seen it written down.'

'Giovanni – the Baptist to us – is one of the patrons and protectors of the Genoese, especially those who go to sea,' said Geoffrey.

'Well, he doesn't seem to have done them much good on this occasion,' said Gaunt's secretary.

'If no one's life was lost I would say they'd been well cared for by Saint Giovanni.'

'The cargo was lost though. The alum was lost,' said Sir Thomas, fixing Geoffrey with his hard, bristly-browed stare. When the other didn't respond the secretary started to say, 'Alum is used for – '

'Used for fixing dyes in cloth, yes, I know,' said Chaucer, uncertain where this was leading and wondering what was so significant about the loss of a cargo of alum. It was valuable enough but hardly the same as a consignment of gold or silver. 'I suppose the cargo getting washed overboard is preferable to the crew sharing the same fate.'

'The cargo was lost, I say, but it wasn't washed overboard. It didn't leak out because the ship was stove-in, either. In fact, the damage to the *San Giovanni* was quite minor. No, the cargo was stolen by the good citizens of Dartmouth *after* the ship had been safely towed into port.'

'The area has a reputation for pirates and rogues,' said Geoffrey.

'Not every rogue can tear up a treaty between states.'

'The Genoese are threatening to abrogate the trading arrangement because of the loss of a single cargo of alum?'

'It is possible,' said Sir Thomas. 'It seems that the master of the *Giovanni* is cousin to someone important in the office of the Doge. We are aware of this because of two merchants from Genoa living here in London – Jacobo de Provano and, er, Johannes – Johannes . . .'

'Johannes de Mari,' said Geoffrey. 'I know them. I've travelled in their company.'

'Which is exactly why you are the very man for this business, Geoffrey. You've got all these connections. What was I saying?'

'I suppose you were about to say that Jacobo and Johannes have got to hear about the shipwreck in Dartmouth and the disappearance of the alum and that, knowing of the link between the master of the *Giovanni* and the Doge's office, they have hinted that this is a matter which can't be left to fester.'

Sir Thomas leaned back in his chair. He looked less indignant than usual. Another man might have smiled.

'I couldn't have put it better myself, Geoffrey. You must be able to read my mind. Your Genoese friends are also friends to England and to this court, but they have let our master know that there could be trouble if this affair is not quickly settled. Someone of sufficient . . . weight . . . must travel to Dartmouth without delay. Once there he must establish what has happened and restore the stolen cargo of alum to its owners and punish the culprits, and generally see that justice is done . . .'

'Its owners being . . .?'

'That is a nice point of law,' said Sir Thomas with relish, 'since it vanished before it could be delivered. As long as the cargo was in transit it belonged to the sender, the Genoese exporters, with the ship's master as its custodian. It only becomes the property of the importer once the necessary bills have been exchanged on arrival.'

'What if the cargo of alum has already been broken up and despatched to the four corners of Devon?'

'Then you are authorized to offer compensation to the master of the ship as a last resort. We do not want him thinking that the English are a bunch of lawless scavengers and reporting this opinion back to the Doge of Genoa. It would be highly damaging to relations between us.'

'There is some authority in Dartmouth? The justice of the peace or the mayor, for example?'

'There is a difficulty in that regard.'

Sir Thomas Elyot paused, leaned forward and once again picked up a pen. It was a sign of his agitation that when he replaced the pen on the table, it was not quite in alignment with the other items. Chaucer waited for an explanation of the 'difficulty'.

'You mentioned the mayor of Dartmouth. He is an individual by the name of William Bailey.'

Again, Sir Thomas paused. It was as if he expected Chaucer to demonstrate his skill at mind-reading again. But this time Geoffrey couldn't oblige.

'You see, Geoffrey, it is the mayor himself who has been accused by the master of the *Giovanni* of stealing the cargo. The mayor William Bailey and his associates. While, for his part, Bailey has threatened to clap the master into jail for slander and false report.'

Chaucer was beginning to see that all the talk about the need for tact and diplomacy in this situation was well founded.

'Is the master of the ship right? Has the mayor stolen the cargo?'

'Our information is that it is not impossible. You said yourself that Dartmouth has a reputation for its shipmen. It is a wild land down there in the west. Not that there's any danger of course. Just a few heads to be knocked together.'

'Who's passing this information back, about the mayor and so on?'

'We have a reliable man in place. A gentleman of influence called Richard Storey. He is a physician and well known to us because he has given an opinion more than once on the afflictions of our Prince Edward. He has a fine house overlooking the town and the river, I understand. That is where you will be lodging while you are investigating this business, Geoffrey.'

'This has all been planned, hasn't it?'

'I don't follow you.'

'Planned that I should be despatched to Dartmouth to investigate this theft.'

'Why yes.'

'What if I had not returned from Florence just now but had been held up by contrary winds or – or pirates? What would you have done then, Sir Thomas?'

'Your progress has been tracked, Geoffrey. We had reports when your ship reached Calais and then again from Sheerness. We knew the day you were coming back and almost to the hour when you would land at the London wharves. But it was John of Gaunt himself who said that you must be allowed a day or two with your family before you were called on to serve your country once more. You shall leave tomorrow.'

Very considerate of Gaunt, thought Geoffrey. There was something unnerving, however, in the way in which his return had been spied on and the exact length of his family reunion laid down. That he might refuse to go to Dartmouth had never been contemplated. Yet what Sir Thomas said next took him aback even more.

'You know Alan Audley and Edward Caton?'

'Alan and Ned? Why yes, though I haven't seen them for some time.'

'Not since you travelled with them to Aquitaine, I believe.'

'You know all this, Sir Thomas. I think you are much better acquainted with my wanderings than my wife is – or than I am for that matter.'

'What I do not know, Geoffrey, is your opinion of Audley and Caton.'

'Not much at first but I grew to like them. They made reliable travelling companions once the road had knocked a bit of sense and patience into them.'

'Good, good. Because they are to accompany you once again, this time out to the West Country. Hearing that you were going, they have requested it. In fact Ned Caton has a particular reason for wishing to travel westwards with you.'

That Geoffrey would require company or some sort of escort was no surprise. The roads were near their best at this time of year, most easily passable, yet the conditions that suited the highway rider also suited the highway robber. No one travelled alone, not unless they were desperate or too poor to be worth bothering with. What puzzled Chaucer was why Alan and Ned should want to go with him. Not just for the pleasure of his company, surely, even though the idea gratified him. Sir Thomas explained.

'Edward Caton is betrothed to the daughter of Richard Storey. He wishes to discuss arrangements for the wedding with the family. Alan Audley goes with him and you, Geoffrey, will make the third of the trio. The senior third naturally.'

'Naturally.'

Geoffrey Chaucer might have made more of the fact that he was required to leave his wife and children only a couple of days after getting home (and those days apparently at the express command of John of Gaunt). But, if he was honest with himself, he objected more to the *idea* of travelling again than to quitting home once more. Home in the London residence of John of Gaunt – otherwise the Earl of Richmond and Derby, of Leicester and Lincoln, and also the Duke of Lancaster – wasn't exactly home. Chaucer flitted between two places, the gatehouse at Aldgate, which he owned, and the palace of the Savoy, which he didn't, feeling that he truly belonged in neither. Though, if he'd been pressed, he'd have to say that the spot where he kept his books and writing materials was the one which he regarded as home (and those items were in Aldgate).

In fact, Geoffrey sometimes considered that his presence in the Savoy Palace was an afterthought. Whenever he returned from travelling, he felt as if he were arriving at an inn – a very grand and lavish inn, true, but a place where he did not properly belong and where he was looked at with indifference or, at best, curiosity. This attitude extended to his children, Thomas and Elizabeth and little Lewis, who had changed during his most recent absence in subtle ways that he couldn't quite put his finger on. Maybe they were just growing up. His wife Philippa seemed preoccupied and it would have taken several days, if not weeks, to restore the not unharmonious relations that usually existed between them. When he'd told her after his meeting with Sir Thomas Elyot that he would be leaving the next morning, she said that was to be expected. Philippa had shrugged and sighed in a matter-of-fact way. The shrug meant unconcern and the sigh meant regret. Perhaps the sigh meant regret. Geoffrey had wondered whether she couldn't have shrugged less and sighed more. She – they, his family – would manage without him, Philippa said.

So, one way and another, Elyot's 'request' that he should depart for Dartmouth wasn't altogether unwelcome. There were worse prospects than riding through the English countryside in early summer. After the difficulties of his Genoese and Florentine business, it did not sound as though a tussle over a ship's cargo would pose many problems. Nor would this be a protracted expedition across seas and plains and mountain ranges. Say, a week to ten days' travel in each direction and a few days on the spot to sort out the little local difficulties.

Chaucer had to admit to himself that he was looking forward to the company of Audley and Caton. When he'd journeyed with them three years earlier to Aquitaine they had been more of a liability than an asset, tending towards drink and lechery. He recalled an incident at an inn in Chatham, involving the wife and daughter of the innkeeper. He remembered the fondness which Ned Caton had shown for a young woman in a troupe of travelling players. Audley and Caton were inclined to be snobbish, too, at first looking down on Geoffrey as the mere son of a vintner whereas they had been born into court circles. But, as he'd said to Gaunt's secretary, the road had knocked a bit of sense and patience into their heads, and in the end he'd grown quite attached to them while they, for their part, had been badgering him to tell stories to while away the tedium of travel.

And, talking of stories, he remembered that he'd promised to finish the tale of Chauntecleer and Pertelote and Russell the fox that evening. But young Thomas was running a slight fever, the result (Philippa hinted) of his having been allowed to play outside in wet weather the previous day. Now he was sleeping and when Elizabeth asked her father to finish the tale he said that it wouldn't be fair in the absence of Thomas. He'd conclude it when he returned from a little trip which he had to make.

Despite Thomas's sickness and Philippa's coolness, or perhaps on account of these things, his departure from the Savoy Palace was a cheerful rather than a tearful affair. On the morning following Chaucer's meeting with Sir Thomas Elyot, he said farewell to his wife and children – Thomas more or less recovered, with the resilience of the very small – and was reunited with Ned Caton and Alan Audley. They were young men still, but something in them had filled out and grown more settled in the interim. Caton's compact shape had grown rather stockier, and Chaucer suspected that in time it might come to rival his own. Audley's features, chiefly a prominent nose and heavy jaw, seemed more at home on his face. Their hair – Caton's pale, untidy thatch and Audley's coal-black curls – were subdued by contrast with the last time Chaucer had seen them. If the day had been overcast or Geoffrey's mood more sombre, he might have reflected on the passing of the years and the difference which even a handful of them can make. But the sun was out, the sky was cloudless, the walls of London glinted at their backs and, apart from a scattering of walkers and horse-drawn carts, the road in front was clear. Getting back in the saddle was enough to remind Geoffrey just how much of the previous few months he'd spent on horseback. Somehow, though, this seemed preferable to all the comforts of life inside the Savoy. The aches and sores would come later. When they did, he'd be ready to greet them like old friends. Rather like Ned and Alan in fact.

The first thing that Alan Audley said to him once the preliminary greetings had been exchanged was, 'You have a story for us, Geoffrey?' Then he laughed as though to show he wasn't being serious.

4

Geoffrey Chaucer had been right to look forward to a relatively pleasant journey through the English country in summer. Apart from an unseasonable storm on their first evening, by which time they were already snug inside a Chiswick inn, the days turned out fair. They rode along roads and tracks that were largely dry and free of mire. The places they stayed might not have been in the first rank for comfort but they were adequate. Their horses were well cared for. No rapacious innkeeper attempted to cheat them nor did any lubricious innkeeper's wife set her hat at Geoffrey's more youthful companions. They encountered no trouble on the road from their fellow travellers. On the contrary, they were greeted with cheery smiles and waves. They were not waylaid by thieves or intercepted by highwaymen. They took no false turnings until near the end. The aches and sores of the saddle did come, but as Chaucer had foreseen they were half welcome. It was an unusual journey, a quiet one, during which Chaucer reflected that it was odd that he knew some foreign realms better than he did parts of his own country.

Alan Audley and Ned Caton seemed intent on proving themselves to Geoffrey as statesmen or justices in the making. The early request for a story wasn't followed up. Rather their conversation was measured and they wanted to discuss serious matters. They were well aware of Geoffrey's connections with the house of Savoy although, if they knew of his sister-in-law's true role there, they were too circumspect to mention it. But there were safer subjects which could be aired, to do with royal deaths and the question of succession. What was the likelihood that Prince Edward would survive the year? Prince Edward's younger son, Richard, what manner of man was he? (Edward's older son had died and Richard was accordingly destined for the crown.) How did John of Gaunt regard his nephew? What part was to be played by his new Duchess, the lady from the land of Castile? When Geoffrey turned aside some of the more detailed questions or professed ignorance, they assumed that he was being cautious. He didn't have the heart, or the modesty, to disillusion them. Really, fellows, I don't know much more than you know. Go to my wife now if you really want to find out what's happening. To be honest, after many miles of such queries he would have welcomed a flash of the old misbehaviour and ribaldry from Alan and Ned.

Ned Caton frequently talked about his forthcoming wedding to Alice Storey, and Chaucer was too tactful to remind him of his earlier passion for another Alice, the daughter of travelling players (though he did wonder whether it was no more than coincidence that Ned had been drawn to a woman of the same name). Ned talked in respectful, even reverential terms, as of a knight about his lady. Again, Chaucer recalled the more robust attitude the young men had formerly taken towards women. It was different when you fell in love, of course, or different enough to make it seem like another thing altogether. Edward Caton – he preferred to be called Edward to his face these days – and Alice Storey had met when she was visiting London with her father, the physician. The fame of Richard Storey was widespread, and he had on more than one occasion been summoned to town to give advice on the intractable condition afflicting Edward. Like the other physicians, Storey had been able to do little or nothing and was honest enough to say so, but word that he had attended the

Prince of Wales enhanced his standing even more and he had been consulted by many of London's rich and famous.

Edward Caton had paid a single visit to the house of his bride-to-be and was full of praise not only for her and her father but also for the attractions of the surroundings, the tree-clad slopes, the hidden combes, the glittering estuary of the river Dart. Even the air, the delicate air of Devon, was superior to the close stenches of the London streets. And marriage was in the very air, for it transpired that Richard Storey had quite recently remarried after the death of his first wife. She was young in comparison to her physician husband, young and shapely, according to Ned, but she did not of course compare to his Alice.

'And you, Alan,' said Geoffrey, after he'd heard once too often of the great beauty and accomplishments of Alice Storey, 'are you any nearer marriage?'

'My mother gives heavy hints that if I do not choose for myself soon, then she will have to choose for me.'

'At least I do not have to consult my mother or father,' said Ned. 'That is the orphan's blessing.'

'I sometimes think parents may choose better than one could choose for oneself,' said Geoffrey. 'They are not blinded by lust or love, you see, and can look at the matter more objectively.'

'So it was your parents chose for you, Geoffrey, was it?' said Alan.

'It was a higher authority at any rate,' he said, making light of the distant part played by the Queen in arranging a match between him and Philippa. 'But I also had some say in the matter. Does anyone really choose in marriage, though? More time and care go into picking a hat or hose to put on in the mornings.'

The two laughed but were sufficiently conventional to express their disagreement with such a heretical opinion.

And so the trip from London to Dartmouth passed amiably enough, under clear skies and along clear roads.

Finally, two days out of Exeter where they had hired fresh horses, they came to the last stages of their journey. It was late afternoon. Chaucer and the others were growing tired – and hungry. They'd stopped briefly in the morning to consume bread and cheese and ale, purchased at their last overnight stop. The bread was stale, the cheese was hard and the ale was sour. He'd be glad to arrive to a warm welcome and some refreshment.

Just as Ned had described it, the landscape was one of rolling hills and steep hidden valleys. The track wound now across open stretches of higher land and then suddenly plunged into deep hollows where overhanging trees almost cut out the sunlight and where there was the smell of damp and mould. They had occasional glimpses of huts and ramshackle dwellings among the trees or on the fringes of woods. These were the homes of charcoal-burners or sheep-herds, and signs that they were entering a less deserted area. At one point they came upon a man hunched by the side of the track, head down on crossed arms. Dozing or simple-minded, he seemed surprised as they rode past and started up in confusion, pausing only to give them a squinty gaze before blundering off into the trees.

Shortly afterwards they reached a sharp fork in the track. Ned Caton dismounted and looked both ways. He removed his hat and scratched his head. He examined the ground as if that might give an indication of which route to take. He peered ahead but both tracks soon veered into sun-dappled shadow. Then he said, with unconvincing confidence, 'It's this way. Look at the marks on the ground.'

It was true that the fallen leaves were trampled and mashed into a black mould as if there'd been some traffic here while the right-hand fork looked fairly untrodden. So Ned remounted and led them down the left-hand fork. The path began promisingly enough and the three of them relaxed in the belief that they were heading in the right direction. But after a mile or so it narrowed as it followed a downhill slant. The tree branches clustered thicker and nearer to the ground and the riders frequently had to duck their heads. The sunlight grew dim. On either side was dense foliage. Chaucer, who was in the rear, found himself glancing over his shoulder more often than necessary. He couldn't escape the thought that this would be a good place for an ambush and the hand which wasn't holding the reins hovered near the dagger which he wore on his belt.

None of them spoke. No birds sang. The only sound was the jingling of the bridles and the scuffling plod of the horses' hoofs. Geoffrey would have suggested they turn back but preferred to leave the decision to Ned since, if this territory was anyone's, it was his. He felt the pangs of hunger in proportion as their destination grew more elusive. The path eventually ran into a large open area with a tangle of bushes and brambles fronting a crumbling, fissured rock face that stretched up like a cliff. The trio had no choice but to halt. They gazed around as though they might actually have arrived somewhere. But they were nowhere. Far overhead at the top of the cliff was a thin strip of blue sky.

'I thought you knew the way, Edward,' said Alan Audley, 'the way to your true love's house.'

'The path of love is neither smooth nor straight,' said Ned, striving to put a brave face on his mistake. 'It must be the other turning.'

They were glad to retrace their passage and arrive at the original fork where they took the right-hand turning, the one that had seemed the less-travelled. The diversion had perhaps taken a couple of hours, but what were two hours over many days of travel? What was a single wrong turning among so many forks and turnings on the road?

This second path soon began to rise gently and the trees started to thin out among a sea of bushes and ferns. They passed a dead oak which had been struck by lightning. It stood by itself, as if shunned by its living brothers.

'This is the right track,' said Ned, relief in his voice. 'I recognize that tree from the last time I rode past. Like a pair of hands, I thought then, and one of them pointing the way.'

Indeed the bare branches of the tree were splayed out a little like elongated fingers. A thick stubby branch was angled out like a thumb, curving downward at the end, a projecting sliver of wood even providing a fingernail. A fanciful sort of imagination might have likened it to someone casually giving directions, thumb jerked over a shoulder. A lover's imagination might well see such things, Chaucer thought, since lovers are always on the alert for signs and tokens that they are on the correct path. But, were he a lover, he would have preferred a different sign – a turtle dove flying overhead, perhaps, or a young tree in blossom. There was something grim about the oak tree. If it was a hand then it was one stripped of its flesh, with the white of the bone showing through.

Then they climbed higher and their spirits lifted. A while later they emerged into the open and Ned Caton indicated that they were getting closer to their destination. He sounded more certain of himself this time.

'We are nearly there but you do not see the place until the last moment for Semper House is tucked below the brow of a hill and all surrounded by trees.'

'Semper?' said Chaucer.

'It means always in Latin,' said Ned, eager to show knowledge and to atone for his error in the woods. 'It is the father's name for a house that he has determined never to leave. He is a learned physician. I have never met one who is so familiar with the humours.'

And a determined physician as well as a learned one, thought Chaucer, the sort of man who wants to announce to the world that he is fixed in one spot for ever. He himself hadn't yet found the place that he never wanted to leave, certainly not his old father's dwelling on the London wharves nor his family house in Aldgate nor his wife's comfortable accommodation in the Savoy Palace.

Ahead of the three riders the track began to run at a downhill slant through an area of short-cropped turf. There were intermittent glimpses of the river and the tang of the sea was borne in on a strong breeze coming over the lip of the hill. Also ahead and to one side of the track was a small stone hut, a place where a sheep-herd might get out of the rain. The thatched roof was holed and there were gaps in the walls but it would do to keep out the worst of the wind or rain or the summer's heat. Sycamore trees clustered by the side of the hut as if for company and in their immediate vicinity the grass grew longer and more ragged.

The hut lay about a hundred paces to their right. It looked derelict and the riders were surprised when the figure of a woman rose from the grass when they drew parallel. She was waving her arms. She was shouting but her words were carried off by the breeze and the sound of their horses thudding across the downland. Geoffrey checked his progress and the others instinctively slowed. The woman stood, almost waist-deep in the long grass. Her posture, her flailing arms, indicated that she was in distress and now they could hear that she was yelling for help.

Ned Caton was the first to pull his horse off the track and canter towards the hut. Geoffrey and Alan followed. The woman, seeing them coming, lowered her arms and fell silent. The grass immediately in front of the entrance to the hut was trampled flat and a man's body lay face-down on the ground. The woman stood over him, wringing her hands and glancing now down at the body and now towards the riders who had drawn up their horses at a few yards' distance. She was quite young and ferocious-looking. Her smock revealed the outline of generous breasts and her arms and face were chestnut-brown from the sun. The man was injured or dead. He lay quite still, blood covering one of his sides and soaking through his leggings. His right arm was flung out, the hand grasping at the earth. Blood had also pooled on the ground. The man's face was turned away from them so that all that was visible was a mass of bushy black hair. Nearby lay an axe in the grass together with some chunks of wood, also bloodstained.

It was easy to see what had happened although, as if to confirm the nature of the accident, the woman mimed the act of chopping wood and then clapped her hand violently against her lower thigh in the place where the man's leg looked at its most bloody. He'd been cutting up wood when he'd lost his footing or mistimed his stroke or the axe had flung free from his grasp, and somehow the edge of the blade had sliced into his leg. The blade was sharp. Chaucer could see its honed edge glinting in the grass. Now the man moaned softly and a tremor ran down the length of his body and his right hand clenched convulsively at the earth. Still alive then.

Geoffrey Chaucer saw that he was wrong in his supposition that no one lived in the hut. There were charred twigs and branches by the opening and a scorched area on the ground, together with a scattering of bones and a water-bucket and a skillet next to it. There was a woody, smoky smell in the air, and the scent of roasted flesh too. Something shifted in the interior of the hut and a pair of eyes glinted in the dark entrance. Chaucer started, but it was only a dog, keeping out of the way of a human disaster. In fact the dog was so uninterested in the proceedings that it growled and went back to tearing at a piece of meat grasped between its front paws.

Ned Caton dismounted. The woman came towards him and clutched him by the upper arms. She was mute, as if words were no longer needed, but her face was stiff with shock and fear. Alan Audley also got off his horse while Geoffrey remained in the saddle. Their horses immediately began cropping the grass. It was not clear what the newcomers could do apart from staunch the wound although, as far as Geoffrey could see, the blood was no longer flowing. He wondered why the woman hadn't attempted something of the sort herself. No doubt she was too shaken to act. Ned wrenched himself free of the woman's grasp. He pointed in the direction in which they were riding and said something about Richard Storey. Of course, there was a physician living close at hand in Semper House, if the injured man could somehow be moved there.

Geoffrey had seen plenty of injuries on the battlefield, and a pile of dead men too. Physicians had told him it was usually possible to tell at a glance whether there was any prospect of survival, although he'd witnessed men succumb to an apparent scratch while others sometimes recovered from the direst of wounds. The man on the ground might live or die. It would depend on how swiftly he could be attended to.

But instinct told him there was something wrong with the scene. Something badly wrong, apart from the grievous wound on the man and the distress of the woman. Their journey had been peaceful so far, it had been free of trouble. That was about to end.

Ned and Alan hovered by the man's body. Perhaps there was a reluctance in them to touch him, to attempt to pick him up or turn him over. Perhaps they were waiting for Geoffrey Chaucer, as leader of the party, to issue some instruction. Or they were simply waiting for him to get down and help, since the body was large and cumbersome. Meanwhile the woman stood by, her gaze shifting in a distracted way from the prone body – was it her man lying there? – to the two upright ones. Then she glanced up at Chaucer and held out her hands in appeal. It was as if she was inviting him to descend from his horse as well and join the others on foot.

But Chaucer stayed where he was.

He remembered what a canny old soldier had told him on his first campaign in France when he was scarcely out of his teens. Never go up against a man on a horse if you're on foot. A man on foot is always at a disadvantage against a mounted man, it doesn't matter how heavily armed that foot-man is or how lightly armed the rider. If you're lucky enough to find yourself on a horse, stay on it. And ride away, if you're able to.

Chaucer remembered the squinty-eyed man they'd startled in the woods earlier, the one who'd blundered off into the trees. A vagabond who'd sat down to rest in the woods on a hot afternoon – or a lookout who'd nodded off by the side of the track? Which, he wondered, vagabond or lookout?

He wondered too why the man with the wounded leg had been cutting up wood on a fine day in early summer, when all that was necessary for a cooking fire were a few handfuls of twigs and some broken branches, easy enough to forage from the sycamores clustering by the hut. Why did they need a fire? Hadn't they just eaten? The air still smelled of smoke and cooked meat. Was the man already preparing for next winter by chopping up logs? Very provident of him, if so.

He wondered why the woman – who from her complexion looked as though she spent her life outside and must be used to cuts and blows – had been so shocked by an accident which was not out of the ordinary, so shocked that she had been unable to tear a strip off her own smock and bind it around her man's upper thigh to stem the rush of blood from further down.

He wondered why the blood had seemingly ceased to flow from a wound that was surely fresh.

He wondered why there was blood everywhere, blood generously spilled on the ground and along the man's stained leggings, blood dabbed on the billets of wood which lay scattered about the place, but not on the axe itself. Not on its haft or its blade. The blade glinted, clean and sharp, in the long grass, scarcely a pace from man's outflung right arm.

He wondered what was the source of the blood and his eyes instinctively flicked towards the dog in the doorway. But the dog was concerned only about its meal, tearing at a bloody chunk of flesh, in between watchful glances before and behind. There was blood on the dog's muzzle too, he'd be bound. Blood from the same source as that which had stained the man on the ground?

All this speculation took only a handful of seconds, these impressions which Chaucer had been absorbing unawares ever since they'd pulled up at the scene of the accident and which now came together in an instant of revelation.

'Don't!' said Chaucer. 'Don't touch him!'

It seemed that the woman had the same idea for she once again flung her arms about Caton, as if to prevent him doing the very thing she had wanted him to do moments before, to give help.

'This is a trap,' said Audley, almost in a whisper.

'Get back on your horses!' yelled Geoffrey.

The woman looked up at him over Ned's shoulder. They were embracing like lovers. Suddenly there was danger in the air, pungent as the woodsmoke and roasted flesh. Now the woman's nut-brown face registered a kind of surprise. The reason why she was grasping Caton hard was to prevent him reaching for his weapon. Not that he would have done so anyway. He was too slow and confused. From his vantage point on horseback, only Geoffrey could see more clearly the real nature of this 'accident', the man starting to stir on the ground, his right hand unclenching, the woman hindering rather than helping her rescuers. Alan Audley responded more quickly than Ned. He was groping for the dagger at his belt. At the same time the man on the ground rose to his feet, one hand reaching out for the haft of the axe. The blood with which he'd smeared himself made him look as if he'd already come off worse in a fight, but of course he had the advantage of surprise. He was a very big fellow, brawny and bearded, almost a giant, and he was ungainly on his feet. One of his cheeks, the one that had been resting on the grass, was badly scarred with a white zigzag shape showing through the beard. He lurched towards Ned, but the woman shook her head urgently and nodded in the direction of the more dangerous Audley. The man took a couple of steps then staggered, off balance. Perhaps the signal of their approach had been given too early and he'd been lying there too long, in imitation of someone badly wounded, and his leg had given way.

Chaucer urged his horse forward and the man, still off balance, reared back and then stumbled over the scattered logs behind him. He let go of the axe in his fall and this time it flew out of his immediate reach. Ned Caton at last awoke to his predicament and tore himself out of the woman's embrace. Audley swung to and fro, dagger in hand, now facing the woman, now the man who lay sprawled on his back. Chaucer's horse was thoroughly frightened by this stage and he struggled to bring it back under control. Alan and Ned's mounts had shied away but they'd not gone far. All might still have been well.

'Get the horses!' said Geoffrey, yanking at the reins of his own mount.

Alan and Ned started to back away from the hut. Both men had their daggers drawn. They might have got away, the three of them. They almost did. But now another figure emerged from the stone hut. Whether he'd held himself in reserve or was merely late on the scene, Chaucer neither knew nor cared. This one burst out of the doorway, kicking the squealing dog to one side and yelling at the top of his voice. His words were not audible. They weren't meant to be. It was a war cry. Like the fellow who'd 'injured' himself with the axe, this one was bearded and burly. They might have been brothers, these near-giants. He too was toting an axe, which he now whirled about his head. At the same instant the first man regained his balance and his own discarded axe, while the woman scrabbled in the grass and produced from somewhere a crude-looking club. Ned and Alan seemed transformed to stone, unable to decide whether to stay and fight (daggers against axes!) or to take to their heels. And, even if they ran, the others had the advantage of size and surprise.

Like Ned and Alan, Geoffrey carried only a knife, in his case as much for cutting up food as for protection. They weren't knights-at-arms parading about the English countryside, equipped with swords and lances. Nor were their horses accustomed to fight or battle. Chaucer might have saved himself. He could have cantered off and left his companions to it. *If you're lucky enough to find yourself on a horse, stay on it. And ride away, if you're able to.* But he mastered the instinct to flee, and urged his horse back towards the fray, well aware that none of them might survive the next few minutes. If it had been just a single one of his companions who was on foot Geoffrey might have hoisted him up on to his own horse and ridden away. But with two of them down on the ground . . .

The men with the axes and the woman with her club formed a half-circle and were advancing slowly towards Alan and Ned who, by now, had left it too late to run and had bunched themselves together, throwing frantic glances over their shoulders at Chaucer who was perhaps twenty yards to their rear. Even the dog, booted to one side by the man as he charged out of the hut, was circling around the edge of the group, its bloody teeth bared. The first axeman grinned, his teeth showing through his shaggy beard. The second of the axemen then did something more unnerving than grinning or uttering his warcry or brandishing his weapon above his head. He opened his mouth and let out a great barking guffaw of laughter. It was as if their opposition was too puny to warrant anything more than derision.

A few minutes' survival would have been a grace. A few seconds was more like it. The three assailants paused but only so that the two men might adjust their hold on the axes. Chaucer was familiar with the manoeuvre. Unwilling to get within reach of the quivering daggers, they were going to use the 'beard', the hooked end opposite to the blade, to engage with Ned and Alan and their weapons. A man with a dagger extends his reach by a matter of inches but a man with an axe gives himself a couple of feet. The barb can be employed to slash at an outstretched hand or to dash away the opponent's weapon. And, once the opponent is disarmed or disabled, the blade will come into play . . .

The two giantlike figures still paused, as if reluctant to take the final steps which would bring them within striking distance. Geoffrey Chaucer tensed himself to dig his spurs into his mount. The best he could do was to drive into the middle of the group and attempt to scatter them so that Alan and Ned might yet get away, even if in the process he or his horse was likely to suffer an axe-stroke. But now the woman was gesturing with her club-hand and the attention of all three was diverted. They were gazing off to their right.

Geoffrey looked behind him. Where the immediate horizon had been empty, a ridge of grass bisected by the line of the descending track, it was now occupied by half a dozen riders who were surmounting the lip of the hill. With the sun behind them, they grew in size by the instant to fill the sky. They were yelling, their cries carried on the wind.

'Now!' shouted Chaucer. 'Run!'

Taking advantage of the temporary distraction, Ned and Alan at last had the presence of mind to stumble away from the area of the hut. The woman, showing more fire than the men, ran forward and flung the club at them, but her aim was poor and the implement itself seemed to falter in the air before crashing harmlessly to earth. Without hesitation, she produced a knife in replacement. One of the men brandished his weapon, but indecisively this time, and his mouth gaped without a sound emerging from it. And Chaucer knew then that this was no do-or-die mission, for their attackers would instinctively preserve themselves even though they might still have closed with Ned and Alan to do some damage. The riders, silent now, drew ever closer and Chaucer sensed that the advantage had shifted.

The three assailants, the brawny men and the nut-brown woman, hesitated for an instant before taking to their heels. The dog slunk back inside the hut. The human beings put the ramshackle building and the clump of sycamores between themselves and the oncoming party. By the time the riders had drawn up near Chaucer, they'd almost arrived at the dark line of trees which fringed the far side of the plateau.

Several of the riders took off in pursuit. Meanwhile the leader of the horsemen looked first at Geoffrey Chaucer then down at Ned Caton and Alan Audley. He was a tall man, with a hooked nose and a neat beard. There was the glint of excitement in his eyes. He was enjoying himself, much as the attackers had been enjoying themselves.

'I thought it must be you,' he said to no one in particular. 'You are safe now. You may put your weapons away.'

'Master Storey,' said Ned, sheathing his dagger. His voice was hoarse as though he'd been shouting. 'I . . . we . . . thank God.'

'Thank Griffin rather than God,' said the hook-nosed man, nodding towards another of the riders. 'He was keeping watch for you.'

The rider called Griffin looked familiar. Chaucer recognized the squinty-eyed fellow whom they'd encountered earlier dozing by the side of the track, the fellow he'd assumed was the lookout for their ambushers. Well, he did have a villainous, vagabondish air to him. Geoffrey raised his hand in acknowledgement, not just of Griffin but of Master Richard Storey, and indeed of the whole party which had arrived just in time to save them from death. He bowed his head. He was aware of his breath coming short, aware of his hands tightly gripping the reins of his horse.

'And you, sir, must be Geoffrey Chaucer of London,' said Richard Storey, physician of Dartmouth and medical counsellor to Edward, Prince of Wales.

'I'll add my thanks,' said Geoffrey, speaking with effort, 'to you and to Griffin who gave warning of our arrival, and thanks to God for preserving us.'

'You must not think that you have entered a region of thieves just because of this misfortune,' said Storey, indicating the scene around the hut, the staged accident with its scattered logs and spilled blood.

'Thieves? I think not.'

'What did they want then?'

'Our lives only,' said Chaucer. 'This thing was carefully prepared.'

Richard Storey looked as though he was about to say more but at that moment the group of horsemen who'd ridden after the three fugitives returned.

'They've got away, sir,' said one. 'No use to follow them into the woods.'

'No use,' echoed Storey, then to the others, 'There are a hundred paths and caves and gullies down there. Our friends will have scattered and could be anywhere.'

Alan Audley had picked up the club which had been thrown by the woman. He was examining the object but without really seeing it. As if to stop his hands from shaking he was gripping tight to the shaft, which had been crudely trimmed to make a hand-hold. Meantime Ned Caton was staring fixedly at the ground. Chaucer recognized the marks of fear which often come after an assault. He felt them in himself.

'Get your horses,' he said to them. 'You should never have dismounted in the first place.'

As the two young men went to retrieve the mounts which were grazing a hundred yards off, Geoffrey quickly outlined for Storey the way in which they'd been decoyed from the track and tricked into the belief that they were helping at an accident. As he spoke, the expression on Storey's face grew graver and he stroked his trim beard.

'As you say, Master Chaucer, it seems that these were no chance thieves. They knew you were on your way and meant to prevent your arrival. Alice will be more than pleased to see you. She'd never have forgiven me if harm had come to my prospective son-in-law.'

These last remarks were directed at Edward Caton, who had now ridden across to join the party together with Alan. Chaucer was glad to see that his companions had recovered something of their composure. Ned even smiled to hear the name of Alice. For his part, Alan had retained the club which had been flung at them and was lodging it awkwardly in the straps securing his saddle-pack. Chaucer wondered that he thought to bring it with him, but supposed it was better in his hands than left on the ground for their attackers to retrieve. Perhaps the fact that it had been wielded by a woman made it a more curious weapon.

Introductions were swiftly made between Audley and Storey, and then the group cantered off. Geoffrey glanced back at the hut and beyond to the line of trees where their assailants had made themselves scarce. He wondered if their departure was being observed. The dog was certainly watching them though it had returned to its interrupted meal in the entrance in the hut. For sure, the man playing injured had smeared himself with blood from the sheep or whatever animal it was whose remains had been tossed to the dog.

A minute or so brought them to the edge of the hill where they filed in pairs down the track. Below lay wooded slopes leading towards the river. The sun shone bright in their faces and clouds sauntered across the sky. It was hard to believe that they'd just escaped death or injury. Geoffrey found himself riding next to the squinty-eyed retainer called Griffin, the one who'd been keeping lookout in the wood. There was something that bothered him. After thanking the man for his promptness in raising the alarm, he said, 'But why didn't you warn *us* of the ambush instead of running off? We would have ridden straight by or taken a different road – or at the least been prepared for an attack.'

'I had my orders, sir, which was to look out for your coming and tell the house so that food and drink were ready,' said Griffin. He pulled his hat down over his brows to shield himself from the sun. He didn't look at Chaucer.

'You knew they were there, our attackers?'

'I did not know they were laying in wait for you. I saw them when I was running over this hill behind us. Saw them and thought they were up to no good though I did not wish to approach them. So I said as much to Master Storey and he gave command that we should saddle up.'

'You don't know who they were, a pair of big men and a woman burnt dark by the sun?'

'No idea, sir. Rogues and villains is all I know.'

Seeing he'd get no further, Geoffrey put the subject to one side. There'd be time later to speculate on reasons for the attack and how it was likely to affect their mission.

As Ned Caton had described, Semper House remained hidden until they were almost on it. The approach from this side was overtopped by trees while on the farther side the land stepped down in a series of open terraces, offering fine views of the Dart as well as glimpses of the town itself and the hills on the opposite bank of the river. Storey reined in and beckoned Chaucer and the other two to draw up beside him. He swept his hand across the scene.

'Welcome to Semper,' he said.

'Edward talked of nothing else on our journey,' said Alan Audley. The remark was light but there was an edge to it.

Geoffrey said, 'But even so this place beggars his description.'

78

'It would take a poet to do it justice,' said Ned, giving a sly glance at Geoffrey.

'Oh, I'll warrant this young man is not thinking of the house when he requires a poet,' said Richard Storey. 'Nor is he thinking of its inhabitants – bar one.'

Geoffrey was glad to see the unaffected good humour between Caton and the physician. He was glad to be here himself, although he didn't have a woman waiting for him but instead an errand to undertake in Dartmouth, an errand that looked as though it might be more dangerous than he'd foreseen.

Even if Chaucer hadn't known that Richard Storey was an eminent and wealthy man, it would have been obvious from the size and style of his dwelling. Semper House was a fine, two-storeyed building, framed with heavy timbers. It looked to be relatively new. On both sides of the manor house were the offices, a cluster of penthouses and sheds containing the stables and store-rooms and doubtless some of the servants' quarters. A high fence of palings enclosed the estate and the area immediately round about it was clear of trees and shrubs. Semper was not in the style of the older country houses, places built to be easily defended, but nevertheless it would have been difficult to approach it unseen. Judging by the size of the company which Storey had brought with him to the rescue, there was no shortage of manpower in the house and there would always have been someone on the watch.

Leading the way, the four riders entered a gate in the fence by which stood a small lodge. A very wrinkled old man, presumably the lodge-keeper, stood in the door. A woman in a pale white dress was also waiting in the shadow of the doorway and she called out as they passed and then ran forward. She was young and attractive. A dog accompanied her, a little hound, greyish silver in colour and thin. Chaucer assumed that the woman must be Alice Storey but, if so, rather than greeting Ned Caton she grasped at the bridle of Storey's horse.

79

The physician halted, leaned down and took her hand. She clapped her other hand on top of his as if she was going to pull him from the saddle.

'It's all right, my dear,' he said. 'We are safe and sound.'

'There was talk of an ambush, Richard. Griffin told me.'

'We saw the villains off,' he said, easing herself from his grasp.

Storey paced forward and the woman walked beside his horse. She'd scarcely glanced at the three newcomers. Chaucer realized that this must be the new wife, the one whom Caton had referred to as young and shapely. He was right about that, although there was something frail about her, an impression enhanced by the paleness of her robe. What was her name now? But perhaps Ned hadn't supplied this particular piece of information. Despite himself, he felt a momentary pang which he could not avoid calling envy. It had been a long time since Philippa greeted his return with such gladness and relief, even after months of absence. Perhaps, indeed, she had never greeted him so.

While the rest of the party, Storey's retainers, dispersed to the outhouses, they dismounted in front of the main entrance to Semper and left their horses in the charge of a stable-boy. Storey gave instructions that the guests' luggage should be brought round. Then they were ushered through the door by the owner, his wife grasping his other arm as if afraid that he might take it into his head to leave again. Inside was a spacious hall and dining area. A staircase led off at one side to a gallery which ran round half the chamber. The floor was laid with fresh green rushes, among which crouched several dogs gnawing at bones or fast asleep. A small table by the door was occupied by chess pieces, neatly arranged on a board. A buffet was loaded with plates, and servants were bringing in fresh dishes and tankards and flagons. Geoffrey's hunger pangs, which had disappeared while they'd been under threat, returned at the sight and smell of food. There was an air of order and comfort to Semper House.

'Our guests, my dear,' said Storey when they were standing in the hall. 'Edward you already know, of course. This is Geoffrey Chaucer who is come from London to inquire into the recent shipwreck. And this is Edward's friend, Alan Audley. My wife Sara.'

Now that her husband was safe indoors, Sara bestowed smiles on the new arrivals. She was young indeed, and had a high-strung look. From a silken cord about her neck hung a valuable pectoral, a cross which was studded with pearls. Her little dog circled round her. It had something of her thin restlessness and occasionally whimpered as if it was in pain.

'Forgive me, sirs, but when I heard that an ambush had been laid for you I feared the worst. I have been pacing about the place for the last half-hour, my heart in my throat.'

'It nearly was the worst,' said Geoffrey. 'But don't let's dwell on it.'

Ned Caton, who'd been casting his gaze about without paying much attention to the introductions, suddenly broke into a smile as another young woman entered the hall from an inner room. Chaucer didn't have to be told that this was Alice Storey, Ned's intended. It was obvious who she was from the way they embraced under the eyes of her father, with a kind of eager decorum. She had something of the physician's neat features, but with a feminine softness to them. She must have been only a little younger than Sara, and Chaucer noticed that the two women did not look at each other but concentrated instead on their respective men.

'Where's Edgar?' said Richard Storey.

'I am here, father,' said a gangling youth peering over the gallery at the top of the stairs. There were enough similarities to his father to make his identity also obvious, even without his words.

'Come down and greet our guests.'

Reluctantly it seemed, the youth descended the stairs. One of the sleeping dogs rose up on stiff legs and walked over to Edgar who paused, as though to show he was in no hurry to obey his father's command. He stroked the dog's black muzzle and bent down to whisper something to it before coming across to join the party near the entrance. Servants continued passing to and fro, putting food and drink on the buffet.

'Where were you, Edgar? I sent out to find you but we couldn't wait.'

The young man shrugged and said, 'Down by the river.'

'You have missed some excitement. You should have been with us.'

'Another hunting expedition?' said Edgar. His tone indicated that he was indifferent to missing some excitement.

'You could call it a hunting expedition,' said his father, 'though the quarry got away.'

'But it was Edward who was the quarry – and these gentlemen,' said Sara.

'Oh no!' said Alice. She clutched hold of Ned's arm. 'What happened? Why didn't I hear about this? Why didn't you tell me?'

This last question was directed at Sara. It was apparent that Alice Storey did not know of the attempted ambush. Sara seemed confused. She glanced at her husband as if for some explanation then said, 'I am sorry, Alice. I could think of nothing else but went pacing about the place, my heart in my throat.'

'You should have told me, Sara. I have as much right to know as you do.'

'I expect you did not want anybody else to be alarmed, my dear,' said her husband and Sara smiled, as if this was indeed the explanation she'd been looking for.

'Well, let us all give thanks to God that you are safe – especially Edward,' said Edgar Storey in the direction of Caton, who nodded in acknowledgement.

Chaucer couldn't tell whether the young man was being sincere or not. Surely a brother could not wish any harm to befall his sister's intended, even if he was unconcerned about the fate of two strangers? Amost simultaneous with this thought was the next one: of course, a loving or a jealous brother might wish exactly that. He caught Alan Audley's eye. They were the outsiders here. Geoffrey sensed some undercurrents in this household, where only moments before he'd seen comfort and order.

Perhaps Ned detected it too for he said to Alice, 'Then I shall tell you the story now and reassure you that we were never in any real danger, thanks to your father's quickness. It won't take long. Shall we taste the air . . .? I have been telling my friends about the quality of the Devon air, how delicate it is.'

'Don't go far,' said Richard Storey. 'The table will be ready soon. Our travellers must be hungry.'

Chaucer nodded, trying not to display too much eagerness. Even Alan looked pleased at the chance of food. The young couple went outside. No doubt, as well as Ned's readiness to tell their adventure, they wanted a few moments away from the eyes of the family. Chaucer would have felt the same, in their position.

At that moment, the squinty-eyed Griffin entered carrying their cap-cases and bags which he handed to Geoffrey and Alan. Richard Storey indicated that he should show them to their quarters. They climbed the stairs and Griffin led them along the gallery. The windows were larger on this floor, where the house was less vulnerable, and they were glazed, a sign of Storey's prosperity. They turned down a passage off which were several doors. If all these were entrances to separate chambers then that was the clearest index so far of Storey's wealth and status, since even the most well-to-do families generally contented themselves with a couple of apartments above the communal hall. Now Griffin showed them into a spacious chamber on the far side of the house. He left them without saying a word. Still he did not meet Chaucer's eye but kept his hat low on his brows as though he was still out in the sun.

There were several beds in the chamber with testers to ensure some privacy. Also a couple of chairs and a large coffer. By instinct, the two men went to the window to see a fine prospect leading the eye down the terraces and out across the glinting river. There was a landing stage down there which must serve the house. Geoffrey opened the window and craned forward, scenting that delicate Devon air. A few small boats scudded about on the water while other, larger ones remained sedately at anchor. With an effort, he could just make out small figures among the winches and hoists on the quayside across the water. He was reminded of his boyhood view from the house on the London wharf, the sense of invisible lines and threads leading across whole seas and oceans. Dartmouth was a busy harbour with links to Bordeaux and Cadiz and other great ports.

'Look at the love-birds, Alice and our Ned,' said Alan. 'Edward, I should say.'

On one of the grassy terraces Ned Caton and Alice Storey were wandering arm in arm. Their heads were close together. The sound of her laughter reached the two at the window.

'Jealous, Alan?'

'I have known love too,' said Alan.

'I didn't mean to imply that you hadn't.'

Geoffrey drew his head in and put his hand on the young man's shoulder. Audley turned from the view to look at him.

'What is my part here, Geoffrey? You have come to Dartmouth as the emissary of John of Gaunt and Sir Thomas Elyot, while Ned is here because this is where his true love lives. But I'm not certain of my part.'

'I'd have said companionship if you'd asked me three hours ago. But I have a feeling this errand is not going to be as straightforward as it was presented to me in London. You'll be needed, Alan, someone I can depend upon. I saw that just now on the hill.'

'I did nothing.'

'You saw something was wrong sooner than Ned. And you held your ground while I didn't even get off my horse.'

Audley seemed mollified, slightly. Then his brow furrowed. 'I'd give a deal to have those two at my mercy now. Yes, and the woman too. I'd show them what an axe or a club can do.'

He mimed chopping and swiping motions before realizing that he must look slightly absurd. Geoffrey once again clasped him by the shoulder before glancing out of the window. This time his attention was caught not by Ned and Alice, still entwined, but by a figure standing closer, almost under the eaves of the house. It was Edgar Storey. He was stroking the head of a black hound, perhaps the same one that had greeted him in the hall. And he was staring fixedly at his sister and his sister's intended.

Edgar Storey was not the only person to be looking intently at what was taking place in the grounds of Semper House. On a flank of the hillside overlooking Semper, and in a spot fringed by trees, lay the two men and the woman who had so recently attempted to waylay Chaucer and his companions. The one who had played dead shaded his eyes against the declining sun and gazed at the house and outbuildings. He was still streaked with the sheep's blood that had been intended to suggest a severe wound. What this man's given name was had long been forgotten. Instead he was known as Zed, after the shape of the scar which formed white furrows across his bearded cheek. Zed could not read of course, though even he might have spelled out the shape of the letter which had given him his nickname. The man who had given him the scar was dead (killed while he was asleep). So too was the individual who had examined the scar of the wound and christened him Zed – dead not for providing the nickname but because he had also called him a 'whoreson' as well as an 'unnecessary letter'. Zed might not have fully understood the insult but he had grasped the other's mocking tone.

The habit of nicknames had spread to the second man, brother to Zed. His given name was William or Bill but, on account of his build and choleric temper, he was called Bull. The woman was Molly, doxy to Bull. Molly was faithful to Bull, faithful out of choice (though he would have killed her and the other man, if she hadn't been). And Zed, who might in other circumstances have tried his luck with the large-breasted Molly, had sufficient respect for – and perhaps fear of – his brother's impetuous temper to keep his hands off her.

The dog that been crouching in the hut, tearing at the bloodied remains of the meal they'd enjoyed before mounting the ambush, was by their side. It was nameless, spoken to only to be cursed.

This threesome and the dog lived half-wild in the woods on this side of the estuary, where the remit of the Dartmouth justice did not run, or at least did not run so effectively. These land-pirates made a good living out of plundering wrecked ships and other acts of theft and ruin, and sometimes murder. But they had lately been frustrated. The attempt to lure the *San Giovanni* on to the rocks had failed, and now they had been deprived of the chance of attacking three travellers on horseback. The ambush had been well laid, with Zed playing the part of a man injured by his own axe and Molly the grieving goodwife. But the travellers had been slow and cautious – or at least the older one had been. And by the time the band had mustered their forces for an attack, rescue had arrived in the shape of the good doctor and his household. Zed and Bull and Molly were not being paid to get themselves arrested or injured, let alone cut down like dogs. As they had on the shore during the wrecking of the *Giovanni*, they could see when they were outnumbered. So they took to their heels and lost themselves among the trees.

But they had not given up hopes of salvaging something from the wreck of their plans. In particular, Molly was angry over the loss of her club. She still possessed her knife, a wicked little thing, sharp as her gaze. But she mourned the loss of the club. She had chosen and whittled the birchwood until it sat in her hand as naturally and easily as her thumb. When the riders had quit the upland, Molly had been the first back to retrieve the club which she had been foolish enough to throw at one of the travellers. The nameless dog cowered up to her, wagging its ragged tail, but Molly paid it no attention. Instead she cast about in the grass for her weapon and eventually was forced to the conclusion that it had been taken from her — stolen! — by one of the riders or by a member of the doctor's posse. Which meant that the club must now be in the possession of someone within Semper House. But the land-pirates had not taken the risk of getting so close to Semper in the hope of recovering a club made of birch, however dear to its owner. Rather they were looking for other pickings, other leavings.

There were two more members of the Storey household whom Geoffrey Chaucer had yet to meet, a man and a woman, and both were present at the meal. The woman was placed at table on Chaucer's right hand, as an indication of his importance as a visitor and of her rank within the house. This was Bridget Salt, the mother of Storey's first wife Agnes, and so the grandmother of Edgar and Alice. With her own husbands – no fewer than three of them – now dead, she had been given an apartment in Semper House in the latter years of Richard and Agnes's marriage. She had overseen the upbringing of the children, at least of Edgar, and even played a part in running the house since, as Geoffrey was to learn, her daughter Agnes Storey had been a somewhat sickly woman.

No trace of sickness or feebleness attached to Bridget Salt, who had a broad, beaming countenance, a girth to match and an unstoppable tongue. Or rather her tongue was only stopped when she was filling her mouth with the ample food and drink laid out on Storey's table. If anyone might have been expected to look askance on the physician's remarriage it might have been her, not because she was in a position to disapprove of new wives (or husbands) but because it might have threatened her position in the household. However, she went out of her way to praise Sara Storey and to express her pleasure in her son-in-law's decision to remarry. She explained that Sara Storey was a delicate young woman, whom the good physician had taken under his wing. Sara was recently orphaned, the death of her father (who had been a shopkeeper in the town) being followed almost immediately by her mother's demise. Her father had been deeply in debt and Sara was left unprotected. Storey had rescued her from a life, if not of destitution, then of privation and struggling. There'd been gossip – said Bridget Salt in a tone that suggested that this garrulous woman disapproved of gossiping – about the unequal nature of the match between the older man and the younger woman, more to do with their difference in rank than the gap of years. Yet, said Bridget, such unequal matches were more common than people supposed. Nor was the gain entirely Sara's.

'For, you know, Master Chaucer, a man should have a woman. A man without a woman is like a boat without a sail. He can get where he wants to go, perhaps, but it takes a deal more effort.'

Geoffrey supposed that such nautical comparisons were natural if you lived near a river-port. He said, 'And what about the other way round? A woman without a man . . .?'

'Oh, we can manage with you or without you. No offence, Master Chaucer.'

'None taken, Mistress Salt.'

'I know what I'm talking about. I have been three times at the church door. Did I mention that I had had three husbands?'

'You did, I think.'

Bridget Salt put down the knife with which she had been spearing her food. She held up three fingers and with the index finger of her other hand she enumerated each husband with a twinkle in her eye. She might have been recalling so many good meals. 'There was Antonio.'

'Antonio?'

'Yes, Master Chaucer. He was an Italian as you've probably guessed. He came from Pisa. He came, he saw me and he conquered. With his tongue he conquered me. The Italian language is fitted for romance, no? By the end I had a smattering of it, I

90

can tell you. More than a smattering. Where was I? Ah yes, Antonio. He was older than me but no wiser. He died falling from a roof, trying to make repairs. I told him not to go up there but he did not listen to me. Then there was Eric. We were of an age and he was the father of Agnes. Like Agnes, he did not enjoy good health. He would not take the remedies which I recommended and he perished of a fever. And last of all was Edward, who was younger than me and the master of a ship.'

Geoffrey waited to be told how this one had died. Bridget Salt paused, with one finger outstretched. 'Oh, you are curious, I can tell. Edward Salt, he was drowned.'

'Though you tried to teach him how to swim . . .' Geoffrey could not resist adding.

'Do not be ignorant, Master Chaucer. Do you know any sailor who can swim?'

Geoffrey shook his head.

'They say that it merely draws out the business of drowning if you know how to swim,' said the widow.

'I have heard something of the sort.'

'Do not believe I am heartless in the matter of my late husbands, however lightly I talk about them. I pay my respects to their resting places and say a prayer for their immortal souls. I visit the graves of Antonio and Eric. And in memory of Edward Salt I go and gaze at the sea in spring and autumn when the tides are highest, for he was drowned off this coast. This is a dangerous shore. You are here to investigate a shipwreck, are you not? The Italian vessel that came to grief?'

'The *San Giovanni*. It is not the harm to the ship but the fate of the cargo I have been commissioned to look into. But I have heard nothing yet beyond the barest bones,' said Geoffrey. Then, to avoid more discussion of his mission, he changed the subject. 'Tell me, mistress, with three husbands behind you, surely you would have been able to take another one without breaking your stride?'

'Are you married, Master Chaucer? You have the married look.'

'Is that a hen-pecked look?'

'Now you mock me and all wives. No, you have that . . . settled look about you.'

'There is your answer then. I am married, with a wife and children in London. But you have not answered my question yet about further husbands.'

'It's a wise woman who knows when she's had enough,' said Bridget, leaning confidentially towards Chaucer. 'Let me tell you something for I can see at a glance that you'll appreciate what I mean. Ever since Richard sensibly invited me to live here when poor Agnes was so tired and sickly, I have enjoyed many of the benefits of a wife but without suffering the penalties of one. I have a voice in Semper House, more than a voice. It is my domain you might say, especially since Richard is distracted with his new wife.'

And especially, thought Geoffrey, with such a young and unconfident woman as Sara Storey. She would be putty not so much in the hands of her husband, who – from all that he'd observed so far – attended to her with a kind of tender patience, but in the hands of an older and more experienced matron like Bridget Salt. Nevertheless there was a touch of resentment or impatience in Mistress Salt's references to Sara. Perhaps the older woman was not as content with the situation as she claimed to be.

'So you have what you want, madam?'

'It is what all women want, you know, Master Chaucer. To be mistress in their own realm. Let the men go and play with their toys, whether they are boats or charts of astrology, as long as we are left undisturbed in our own domain. I am sure your wife would say the same in private with her gossips.'

'She would. She probably does.'

Bridget beamed at Chaucer, pleased at having proved her

point, and picked up her knife once again to jab it into a bowl of shrimps. Geoffrey leaned back and looked along the length of the table. With one exception, the company had fallen into talking in pairs. There were Edward Caton and Alice Storey, who had several months of absence to make up for and who chatted in whispers and laughter, pausing only occasionally to feed themselves or to pay attention when some remark was directed at them. The doctor's son, Edgar, was seated next to Alan Audley, and Chaucer was glad to see that these un-attached men – man and youth, more correctly – had struck up some sort of acquaintance. They seemed to be talking about the merits of various hunting dogs. The black hound which was evidently Edgar's favourite was lying at his feet.

Then there were Richard and Sara Storey, with the doctor of physic sitting on Chaucer's left and his wife on the far side. Though he and Geoffrey had already exchanged a few words, he'd indicated that he wanted a more private conversation later on. He spent much of the meal reassuring his wife that he had indeed been in no danger during the attempted attack on their guests. Sara's attention was distracted from time to time by the little silver-grey hound which fidgeted and whimpered about her feet and which she fed on fragments of meat or bread dipped in milk. The dog was called Millicent or Milly for short. Storey acted the host in an easy, unforced style, distributing jokes or compliments among his family and inquiring just often enough whether the food and drink were to his guests' liking. If there were any tensions or antagonisms here – and Chaucer was pretty certain that there were – then they were submerged for the course of the meal.

The last diner at the table was a stringy, stoop-shouldered, bespectacled figure called Alfred Portman. From his appear-ance Chaucer would have taken him for a clerk, and he would have been half right. Alfred was a cousin to Richard Storey, but his position in the household wasn't so much on account of any family connection but because he assisted Storey in his work, preparing medicaments, making talismans for his master's patients, drawing up astrological charts, and so on. When the physician had introduced Chaucer to Portman before the meal, he had generously acknowledged the other's skill and industry.

Alfred put out a hand that was dry and patched with grey-brown stains as if he spent his time rootling around herbs and dyes. In a voice as soft as the rustle of a leaf he said to Geoffrey, 'My cousin is too kind, sir. His is the name which the world knows while I am no one.' Chaucer had to lean forward to catch the words. There was something disconcerting about such humility, seemingly uttered without any desire for contradiction. Alfred Portman turned away to take what was doubtless his usual place at the table. Geoffrey didn't hear him say another word during the repast. Nor did he appear to take any interest in the conversations around him but bent over his food, spectacles glinting and attention fixed on his trencher as if he was casting someone's water or examining a root that he had just dug up.

The servant called Griffin entered the hall and came over to whisper something in Storey's ear. The physician nodded, waved a hand in dismissal and turned to Geoffrey.

'Word spreads quickly. I sometimes think the birds must carry messages across the river.'

'What is it?'

'We have a visitor, sooner than expected. You will have to pardon us, Sara.'

Storey got up, indicating that Geoffrey should accompany him. The two men walked out of the hall and into the air. It was yet early in the evening and the sky was high and clear. As they paced along the landward side of Semper House, Storey explained, 'I had hoped that you would have a good night's rest before you began to inquire into the matter of the *San Giovanni* but it seems that other people have different ideas. William

Bailey is our visitor. He is the mayor of Dartmouth. As you know, Master Chaucer, he has been accused of stealing the cargo from the ship by the master, a Genoese gentleman called Pietro Cavallo. In turn, our man Bailey has threatened to shut Cavallo up in jail if he continues to make such accusations. From what I've just heard, the mayor is on his way over here to get in the first word with the important emissary from London.'

Chaucer and Storey rounded the house and emerged on the highest of the grass terraces overlooking the river. A sizeable rowing boat was already halfway across the channel, the oarsmen pulling hard against the tug of the evening tide. There were two rowers and a canopy of red cloth in the stern beneath which another figure could be discerned. It was the only boat on the river moving towards the eastern shore and its evident destination was the landing stage below Semper House. In the stillness of the air, the regular splash of the oars reached the men on the terrace. The departure of the boat out of the harbour must have been noted from this side and its occupant recognized or guessed at – perhaps the mayor of Dartmouth was always ferried about in the red-canopied craft. Geoffrey appreciated anew the situation of this large house, with its clear views to both east and west. Storey liked to know in advance if he was receiving callers.

'What manner of man is he, this William Bailey?' he said.

'A stout, sanguine fellow though he is too fat for his own good health,' said the physician. 'He gives the impression he'd knock heads together as soon as shake hands with their possessors. It's a useful skill in a mayor – or in our mayor at any rate for a port is a rough place, you know, Master Chaucer. Sailors will fight each other and when they're tired of that they'll fight with landsmen.'

'You should call me Geoffrey. And I know about ports. My father was a vintner and I grew up on the London wharves.

Between ourselves, Richard, is there any truth to the charge that the mayor had a hand in stealing the *Giovanni*'s cargo?'

'It is possible,' said Storey cautiously. 'But that is what you are here to find out and I do not want to prejudice your investigations. When a man is sick, I want to hear about it from his own mouth and to consult the astrological tables. I prefer to make my own observations, not rely on others'.'

'Very well.'

Chaucer registered the mild rebuke and saw that he wasn't going to get any further with this line of questioning. Nor did he speculate aloud on the reasons for Bailey's evening visit. Was the man's readiness to call and, presumably, to make his case in person so soon after Chaucer's arrival a sign of innocence – or of guilt? Chaucer had one more question for Storey.

'The master of the *San Giovanni*, this Pietro Cavallo, have you met him?'

'We have exchanged a few words only.'

'You have Italian?'

'I have enough of it.'

Geoffrey did not ask the other for his opinion of the Genoese ship-master. Even if the physician had been willing to give one, it wouldn't have been based on much evidence. From the river came the soft collision of wood on wood as the rowboat fetched up against the landing stage. One of the rowers scrambled out and made fast and then stood by to help as a figure levered himself from beneath the canopy. Geoffrey shaded his eyes and saw a portly individual scramble ashore together with the second oarsman. Then the landers were lost to view as an intervening lip of land came between him and the men down below. Beside him, Richard Storey chuckled.

'I will tell you one thing, Geoffrey, and that is that Master Bailey must be eager to see you. He would not make the journey across the Dart otherwise. More especially he wouldn't choose to make the climb to Semper House. He's complained about it often. He'll have to stop for breath. It'll take him a good few minutes. While we are waiting tell me how things are at court. What is the latest news on the King's health, the Prince's health? Reports are not encouraging.'

Geoffrey might have replied with a similar reticence to Richard Storey's when he was asked about the mayor, since the well-being or otherwise of the King and his oldest son was a confidential matter if not actually a state secret. But he was speaking to the physician who had already attended Edward the younger and he saw no reason to deliver anything other than the truth – that the King was ailing although not as fast as the Prince of Wales. Rapidly he told Storey what he knew, which wasn't a great deal. The physician nodded and tutted appropriately but none of what he heard seemed to come as a surprise. From time to time as they were speaking, they had glimpses of the boat-party ascending the path which wound, snakelike, along the terraces and in between clumps of trees and bushes.

Eventually the trio – a fat man wheezing and puffing, escorted by the two oarsmen – appeared immediately below Chaucer and Storey. The fat man stopped and put his hands on his hips. When he recovered his breath he looked up and said, 'Christ's bones, physician, you might have despatched one of your horses to pick me up at the bottom.'

'I have more respect for my horses, William Bailey.'

'And less respect for the mayor of the town. Well, it is always good to know where we stand,' said Bailey. 'I shall come up to your level now.'

The fat man indicated that the two oarsmen should remain down below. They were his opposites, minnows to his whale. With an effort, the fat man drove himself up the final slope. He stood panting at the top, sweat gathering in the creases of his brow, looking at Geoffrey and the physician as if he expected to be complimented on his achievement. Everything about him was round, even the features on his face, a button of a nose, a bud of a mouth. It was a face constructed for good humour but there was a watchfulness about the eyes, just as there had been a frosty edge to the banter between him and Storey. It was easy to believe that he could knock heads together. Chaucer looked at him with more than ordinary curiosity, and not just because in comparison to this individual he felt undersized.

'To what do we owe the honour of this visit?' said Storey without much ceremony.

'I have come to pay my dues to your guest from London, Master Storey. You, sir, must be Geoffrey Chaucer.'

'I would have recognized you for a Bailey,' said Geoffrey, 'even if you had not been announced as such. I know your . . . brother, is it?'

'Old Harry! You know my brother Harry? Of course you must do, sir. I've always thought that London is no more than a small town writ large, a place where everyone is familiar with everyone else, especially old Harry.'

'This gentleman's brother is the keeper of an inn in Southwark,' Geoffrey explained to Storey, who was looking bemused and slightly displeased at the turn in the conversation. 'An inn that I have visited from time to time.'

'The Tabard in Southwark,' said William Bailey. 'A fine spot. He tells me that an innkeeper's life is the best of all. Drink and talk, talk and drink till the crack of doom. How is the old bugger? Still watering his ale and serving wine from Cadiz while pretending it's vintage Bordeaux?'

'Oh, his customers will keep him to the straight and narrow,' said Geoffrey Chaucer, 'especially the holy people on the way to Canterbury. He is honest as the day is long.'

'Then you must be referring to St Lucie's day,' said William Bailey, 'for it is the shortest in the year.'

'Come now, Master Bailey,' said Storey, 'we must not stay out here where all may watch our doings and speculate on what nonsense we are talking. Let's go inside and have some refreshment in private. You'll be in need of it after your climb up here. You men, go and search out Griffin. He will see to you.'

Nodding at the two little rowers, he led the way back towards the house. Geoffrey noted the slightly milder tone in the physician's words. No doubt he was surprised at the connection between Chaucer and the Dartmouth mayor, even if it was at one remove. Geoffrey was, as he'd described it, an occasional visitor to the Tabard Inn on the south side of the Thames. This was the place where many of the travellers and pilgrims on the way to the shrine of Thomas the Martyr at Canterbury gathered before they set off from the capital. Hence his remark about the 'holy people'. Geoffrey had passed the time of day with Harry Bailey and he remembered that the tavernkeeper had more than once referred to having come from a family in the West Country, as if that wasn't already apparent in his voice. In truth, Geoffrey had no idea whether old Harry was an honest fellow, though he was certainly a shrewd one. Nor had he seen the innkeeper lately. But he was inexplicably pleased to have traced out this link between the mayor of Dartmouth and the proprietor of a London tavern. The exchange brought back the last time he'd been at the Tabard, during a spring evening of the previous year, watching the pilgrims assembling for the two- or three-day journey to Canterbury. The memory brought back a pang for his native place. When this business was finished he would gad about no longer but spend time at home, even if it was no more than a 'town writ large' according to William Bailey.

But this business wasn't finished of course. Indeed the investigation into a ship's stolen cargo was hardly begun.

Instead of returning to the dining hall of Semper House, they entered a side door in the building and shut themselves up inside what was evidently the physician's private office, Storey stopping a servant on the way with orders for some drink to be brought. The office was a panelled room with a window set quite high in the external wall so that none could easily peer in from outside and through which the evening sun streamed in dusty beams. Even so, several candles were burning and added their sweet aroma of beeswax to the scent of herbs and an undercurrent of something darker and earthier, almost dungy. There were several comfortable chairs in the chamber. The surface of a large trestle table was covered with a neat array of bottles and vials, mortars and pestles, and boxes containing small metal plates or talismans. There was a shelf of books – more volumes, Chaucer rapidly calculated, than were contained in his Aldgate house, even if the doctor's library was mostly made up of leech-books – together with charts on the wall showing human figures circled by the appropriate sign of the zodiac, such as Aries for the head or Taurus for the neck.

The physician's assistant, Alfred Portman, was sitting on a stool drawn up to the table. He was in the same posture as Geoffrey had seen him at supper, bespectacled head down over a bowl, his fingers plucking at its stringy, unidentifiable contents. Chaucer had rarely encountered anyone who took such a doglike interest in his immediate surroundings and little in anything else beyond. He must have quit the meal immediately after Storey and Chaucer, obviously eager to get back to his work. He barely glanced up as his master entered. It was only when Storey said, 'That is all, Alfred, you can go now,' that he appeared to take in the presence of the other two men. He unbent himself and shuffled towards the door, saying in his leaf-dry tones, 'Of course, cousin, of course.'

William Bailey clapped him on the shoulder and said, 'How goes it, Alf?' and was rewarded with the tremor of a smile. Chaucer was surprised that the mayor of Dartmouth should know the physician's assistant but then Bailey was plainly someone who made an effort to be at ease with all kinds and conditions of men. As Portman was leaving the room a woman entered with a salver on which was a flask and some goblets. The three men seated themselves, with the mayor in the middle, and were served with wine. Richard Storey waited until the servant had left before looking expectantly towards Bailey. In turn, the mayor looked to Geoffrey. Some of the bluff, hearty manner had dropped away from him. Geoffrey decided to begin with a simple statement of the reason for his presence.

'I have been deputed by the secretary to the Duke of Lancaster to inquire into the diappearance of a cargo of alum from the Genoese ship, the *San Giovanni*. Sir Thomas Elyot, Gaunt's secretary, is particularly concerned that the loss of this valuable freight should not impair relations between England and Genoa which are at a delicate juncture at this present. I am authorized to establish what has happened, if possible to restore the missing cargo to its owners, and generally see justice done.'

'Then we are of one mind, Master Chaucer,' said Bailey, 'since I desire those very things as well. It is hardly for the good name of my town if we earn a reputation as a nest of pirates though I can tell you that it would please the town of Fowey. Oh, Fowey would be very pleased.'

Chaucer didn't have to ask why. Fowey was the other

principal harbour in the West Country and there was a sharp rivalry between the Cornish and the Devon ports. He refrained from saying that Dartmouth already possessed something of a reputation as a nest of pirates.

'Very well, William Bailey,' said Richard Storey, 'then perhaps you should give Master Chaucer here your side of the story.'

'My side, physician!' said Bailey. He'd been in the act of raising the wine goblet but the other's remark made him pause. 'There are no sides here, only the truth.'

'Even truth has another side – a backside known as lies,' said Geoffrey, noticing that while William Bailey had been quite happy to make jokes about his Southwark brother's honesty (or the lack of it) the mayor was much less relaxed when it came to the good name of his town or of himself. 'Simply tell us the tale of what happened as far as you know it.'

Slightly mollified, Bailey started to speak. By the mayor's account, the Genoese ship – 'one of those heavy vessels which they call tarets, Master Chaucer' – had been driven onshore during a spell of bad weather more than three weeks previously. The boat had foundered on some rocks in a cove near the estuary. There'd been talk of false lights and wreckers. But in Bailey's opinion, the misfortune was due to the weather, poor English weather. And to even poorer Italian seamanship, for the *Giovanni*'s master, Pietro Cavallo, wasn't fit to be in charge of a cockboat. Pietro which was Peter and Cavallo which meant horse, didn't it? Well, Peter the Horse had only got the job of master because he was connected to some high-up in the office of the Dog in Genoa.

'*Doge*,' corrected Storey. 'The *o* is long and the *g* is soft.'

'I know what I'm saying, physician,' said Bailey.

'Then please continue to say it.'

The damage to the *Giovanni* was minor but sufficient to require a period in dock while everything was made good. With some temporary patching over the hull the *Giovanni* had been refloated with the tide and then rowed and towed into a mooring next to the principal repair yard in Dartmouth. But the seawater had already got into the hold and threatened to reach the crystals of alum, which was stored in sacks and which – as Master Chaucer surely knew – it was most necessary to keep dry. So the master of the vessel, this Peter the Horse, decided that the alum must be unloaded and stored on land while the repairs to the boat were completed. The precious sacks could be returned to the hold later when it was dried out.

'A moment, Master Bailey,' said Chaucer. 'Why was it necessary to return the cargo to the hold at all since it had already reached its destination? Couldn't it simply have been handed over to the Dartmouth merchant who'd purchased it?'

'I see that you are not so well informed after all, Master Chaucer,' said the mayor, shooting a glance at Richard Storey, as if this ignorance was all the physician's fault. 'The *San Giovanni* was never bound for Dartmouth in the first place but for Fowey. If the sailors were to be cast ashore anywhere it should have been further west. It would have saved us a deal of bother.'

Geoffrey said nothing but wondered why he'd never been told this in London, even if its significance wasn't immediately clear.

'The alum, and the other goods they carried, were destined for Fowey,' repeated William Bailey. 'There is a merchant in that town called Latchett who is a busy trader with Genoa. There is even a distinguished doctor of physic there by the name of Lamord, Raymond Lamord. Isn't that so, Master Storey?'

Chaucer noticed that Storey's mouth tightened, as if he was displeased at this mention of a rival.

'But back to the business in hand,' said Bailey, who'd also observed Storey's response and who seemed pleased to have disconcerted his host. 'We are not concerned with doctors of physic here, however distinguished. Our merchant Latchett is unhappy that his goods have gone astray even if he has not yet paid for them. But the town of Fowey is another matter. Our misfortune is their good luck. You see now why I said that only Fowey would be glad at this.'

Whether it was the effort of speaking at length or, more likely, irritation at the other port's pleasure, William Bailey's breath was coming short and fast.

'To the quick of the matter, William Bailey,' said Storey. 'I am sure that our guest from London is not interested in the rivalry between Dartmouth and Fowey.'

Now it was the mayor's turn to look as though he might take offence at the remark. He shrugged instead and took a restorative gulp from his goblet, which Storey then refilled. Bailey continued with his account. It seemed that the sacks of alum had been taken off the *Giovanni* and stored in a warehouse near the repair yard. This warehouse was a sturdy building, well secured against thieves with bolts and bars and shutters. Knowing the value of his cargo, the master of the *Giovanni* had detailed members of his crew to guard the alum. One sailor was to keep watch on the warehouse during the hours of daylight from the bridge of the *Giovanni*, which was moored opposite the building, and be replaced by another for the night. It was really a version of their sea-going task, where they would have to watch out for currents, rocks and pirates. Except now they were on dry land and keeping an eye on the security of the warehouse. Nevertheless, the theft of the alum – if that's what it was, a theft – had occurred late in the evening as darkness was descending.

The sailor on watch at first claimed that he'd been attacked and overcome by a gang of villains who'd beaten him senseless before making off with the alum sacks. He even had the cuts and bruises in apparent proof of it. He'd been discovered, muddied and stinking and face down close to the warehouse door, by the crewman who came to replace him on night duty. This story of a violent assault, this disgraceful slur on the good name of Dartmouth town, held good until it came to light that the sailor, growing tired of watching a building, had in fact abandoned his post in quest of the carnal delights which the port of Dartmouth offered – 'For you know, Master Chaucer, my town may contain the odd house of pleasure for the diversion of foreign sailors,' added the mayor.

It appeared that this lusty seaman, who like his ship went by the name of Giovanni, had disobeyed his master, skipped off the bridge of the *Giovanni* and gone off in quest of flesh early in the evening. He had gone looking in Sheep Street, one of the lanes that led off from the waterfront. He had drunk deep at one or two establishments. Had staggered back towards the harbour but at some point fallen and injured himself (hence the cuts and bruises), got up only to fall down again, this time into a midden (hence the mud and stink), before arriving back at the warehouse where he fell for a final time by the door, too pissed to go any further. In which prone position he'd been found by one of his fellows, who alerted the master Pietro Cavallo, who became suspicious. He roused the mayor who discovered that the valuable cargo had vanished from the warehouse. Meanwhile Cavallo was bringing Giovanni back to consciousness by throwing him into the harbour, after which sousing the sailor luckily came up for air. Not wishing to reveal that he'd abandoned his post, he also came up with the tale of a violent gang which had somehow got into the depot and stolen the sacks of alum. Hearing this, the next thing the furious ship-master had done was to accuse William Bailey of having a hand in the theft.

'Why, Master Bailey?' said Chaucer. 'Why should you be called out to examine a warehouse which proves to be empty? Why *you*, the mayor of Dartmouth?'

'Because the warehouse belongs to me, Master Chaucer.'

'I see,' said Geoffrey, thinking that there was a lot he hadn't been told.

'I rented it to this Horse fellow,' said Bailey, 'this Cavallo fellow. He rented it for the few days it would take him to get his ship repaired. He summoned me because the door was still locked when the theft was discovered.'

'Then how did anyone know that a theft had occurred? Was there damage done to the doors or the bars and shutters of the place?'

'No. But a sack of alum was found close to the drunken sailor. Peter the Horse recognized it for part of his cargo. That's when he demanded that I open up the building. Then this gentleman from Genoa straightaway jumps to the conclusion that I must have done it myself since it is my warehouse. But the gentleman shows that he is a fool even to think it.'

'How so?'

'If I was going to rob my own warehouse I'd at least make it look like a robbery, wouldn't I? To divert suspicion from myself in this suspicious world.'

'I see. I wonder you did not mention that the depot was your property at the beginning. How did the true version of what happened to this Giovanni come to be known? Indeed, if the man was as drunk as you say, how did he know how many times he'd fallen over and where he'd fallen and so on?'

'That is easily answered. This Gee-vanny went to Sheep Street like I said and was frustrated in his desire to find a girl. Instead he bought a piece of cloth to take back to some sweetheart in Genoa. He paid up but left his purse behind him – he was pissed, like I said, he was forgetful – and the owner of the place, who's a woman of good heart, went after him to return it. Mistress Barton witnessed how he tumbled down not once or twice but thrice, then thought better of it when she saw him tumble down for the last time by the warehouse and crept away without having the chance to give back the man's purse. Though by then Gee-vanny had bigger things to worry about.'

'The purse has been returned to this unfortunate Genoese by now?' said Richard Storey.

'I expect so,' said Bailey, suddenly finding something of deep interest in the contents of his wine goblet. 'You know Mistress Barton. She keeps a house full of needlewomen.'

'That is one word for her house,' said Storey.

Geoffrey caught Richard's eye. It was growing darker in the physician's chamber and it was not easy to read the other's expression. Nevertheless he knew that the physician must be thinking what he was thinking. The story about the sailor buying a piece of cloth was rubbish. And the idea that the madam of a house full of needlewomen (by which one might understand a brothel) would run after one of her girls' clients in order to return a dropped purse was about as plausible as the idea of the madam becoming Queen of England. Much more likely was that Mistress Barton had noted where Giovanni stowed his purse while he was paying her and set off after him when he quit the brothel, meaning to take advantage of his drunken state to relieve him of the rest of his cash. This she had done, probably when he was face down by the warehouse door. As for the idea that she might have given the purse back to its rightful owner . . . well, that was about as likely as her voluntarily surrendering her crown, were she actually Queen of England.

'And why did Mistress Barton come forward to describe all this,' said Geoffrey, 'about how she'd witnessed the drunken state of the sailor and started off after him to return his purse? Why not simply keep quiet about it? After all, not everyone will believe her tale of the purse in this suspicious world.'

'Gentlemen,' said William Bailey, casting his gaze either side of him, 'I could be less than open with you. I could say that Mistress Barton acted out of loyalty to her native town and because she was unhappy with the slurs which these foreigners were casting on us. But the truth is that Mistress Barton is a long-time . . . friend of mine . . . and so when she heard that William Bailey was being accused of breaking into his own property at the head of a gang, she determined to speak up and tell God's honest truth. Which is that Gee-vanny abandoned his post and neglected his duty, so eager was he to come to grips with one of the fair ladies of the Shorn Lamb.'

'The shorn lamb?' said Geoffrey.

'That is the name of the needlewomen's establishment in Sheep Street – as I believe.'

'Come now, mayor,' said Richard Storey, 'it is reputed that you have shares in the Shorn Lamb. Even your good wife Constance must know about it.'

'I have many business interests, which I am not obliged to divulge to you, Master Storey, let alone my wife.'

'Can we get back to the matter in hand?' said Geoffrey Chaucer, amused at the way the brothel had been named for the street and not much bothered by the mayor's investment in it and whether the man's wife was aware of it or otherwise. 'You say that the door to the warehouse was locked?'

'It was.'

'The master of the ship had access to the warehouse?'

'No.'

'Is that the usual practice? Shouldn't a ship's master have an extra key?'

'Why should he?'

'I don't know. In case he needs to inspect his cargo?'

The mayor patted his heavy frame, spilling some of his wine and causing something to clank. 'I keep all my keys myself, Geoffrey. Here about my waist. Even my men are not permitted to carry them but must come to me each time.'

'There was nothing else stored in your warehouse?'

'There were some barrels of wine.'

'Which were not taken?'

'Only the sacks of alum.'

'Well, the fact remains that the cargo was stolen, whether the thieves broke in or walked in to get their hands on it.'

'Indeed, Master Chaucer. It's my belief that it was taken by – '

Bailey was interrupted by a shriek from the front of the house, a woman's shriek. It was an eerie noise in the darkening chamber. Chaucer was startled. Storey sat up straighter in his chair but did not otherwise react. After a moment William Bailey picked up the thread again.

'I think this precious alum was stolen by the master of the vessel himself.'

'Why would he take his own cargo?' said Chaucer. 'How would he gain access to the warehouse if you had the only keys?'

'The first is easily answered, Geoffrey. He means to sell it on to some unscrupulous merchant and pocket the cash, and blame the theft on the good citizens of Dartmouth, and on me in particular. That way he comes out with a profit and clear of blame.'

'And the second? The matter of the keys?' said Richard Storey, putting Chaucer's question.

'I wasn't born yesterday, physician, nor the day before that either. I guard my keys carefully but a man must take his rest and . . . other things.'

'So you're saying that someone took a copy of the warehouse key?'

'Someone? It was Peter the Horse had it done.'

'You have no proof though.'

'Why was he so quick to accuse me otherwise? It's my belief that he probably put his man Gee-vanny to watch over the depot, knowing the sailor's weak head. Maybe he was waiting for him to desert his post. Or maybe Gee-vany was in on the plan the whole time.'

'I thought you said the master nearly drowned him in the harbour when he found out what had happened.'

'All for show, Master Chaucer, all for show.'

'I will have to talk to the master of the vessel, to Pietro Cavallo.'

'He's foreign, he doesn't have much English.'

'I expect I'll make myself understood.'

'He knows that if he repeats any more accusations against me,' said Bailey, 'then I'll take him to law. I'll haul him before

Justice Mortimer. The Italian may not understand much but he understands that. I'll see him behind bars if he slanders the mayor of Dartmouth again. What is going on in your house, Master Storey?'

Ever since the woman's cry, there had been increasing sounds of disturbance in Semper House, feet running down passages, shouts, doors rapidly opening and shutting. The physician, who'd been growing more and more distracted, jumped up and left the chamber. Chaucer and Bailey followed him.

The source of the disturbance was in the entrance hall where they'd taken supper. The table was cleared but the room was fuller than before. By now it almost dark outside and, from the light of the few candles in the hall, it was hard to see at first what had happened. A group of figures, servants and family, were standing in a circle round something or somebody lying on the floor. On the edge of the group stood Alan Audley and Storey's son, Edgar, holding tight to his hound by the collar. Ned Caton was grasping equally tightly the hand of Alice Storey. The circle opened to admit Richard Storey, and as it did Chaucer glimpsed a figure kneeling amid the rushes on the floor. It was Sara Storey. She had her hands to her face and she was sobbing quietly. Over her stood Bridget Salt and, for an instant, Chaucer assumed that the old woman was the cause of the younger one's distress. But not so. As the circle widened he perceived that Sara was kneeling by a little silver-grey corpse. It was her dog Milly.

'What has happened, my dear?'

Storey crouched down next his wife. She seemed oblivious to his presence until he touched her on the shoulder. She shuddered and then, seeing who it was, threw her arms round his neck so that he nearly overbalanced. One of the servants brought a candle closer and the scene was bathed in a deceptively soft glow. Meantime Chaucer, who was standing close to Edgar, heard the son say to Alan, 'It wasn't Hector, I tell you. She'll say it was but it wasn't.'

He bent down and stroked his own hound protectively and Geoffrey understood that this must be Hector. Geoffrey went over to Ned and asked him if he knew what had occurred. It was Alice Storey who answered, hardly troubling to keep her voice down.

'My new mother's dog is dead. She came in here to find Hector standing over the little thing, sniffing and snuffling. It looks as though my brother's hound attacked Millicent. The bitch is as new to the house as Sara is. You know that dogs don't like newcomers who trespass on their territory, Master Chaucer.'

Geoffrey understood that the remark had a wider application than to a mere pet dog. It must have been Sara's cry on discovering Millicent's body that they'd heard earlier. He glanced behind him. William Bailey was watching with interest rather than concern. But then why should the mayor of Dartmouth be bothered over the death of a dog? He looked back towards the scene, the husband and wife both on their knees by the body which was rigid in death, its legs stretched out stiff as sticks. The candlelight showed up white flecks on Millicent's muzzle.

'I can't see any marks of violence,' said Geoffrey.

'Probably died of fright,' said Ned Caton. 'It was a twitchy little beast just like . . .'

He left the remark unfinished. He didn't have to complete it since he obviously meant 'like its owner'. Again Geoffrey observed how rapidly Ned had absorbed the hostility of Storey's children to their father's new bride.

At that instant Alfred Portman crept to the centre of the group. He ignored his master and Sara but, like them, got down on hands and knees. He touched the dead dog's fur, he brought his spectacles close to its tiny head, he smelt its muzzle for all the world as though he was himself a hound. Then he levered himself to his feet. He gazed round at the assembled company. To no one in particular he said in his dry tones, 'This dog has been poisoned.'

7

Geoffrey Chaucer clambered into the rowing boat, waving aside the hand which Alan Audley held out in mock helpfulness. He settled himself beside Audley in the stern, feeling the boat rock under his weight. The morning sun dazzled along the water. The physician's man Griffin, sitting on a thwart in the prow, gave the order to cast off and the second of the two oarsmen unhitched the mooring rope and scrambled into the vessel as it began to swing away from the landing stage. Richard Storey had put his personal ferry at Chaucer's disposal so that he might be transported over the river to Dartmouth, there to pursue his inquiries into the theft of the alum. He hadn't offered to accompany his visitors to the town but was sending Griffin across together with two of his retinue as rowers. The mayor William Bailey had promised he would be waiting in the port to show Geoffrey to the house where the Genoese master of the *San Giovanni*, whom he persisted in referring to as Peter the Horse, was lodging. 'It's the least I can do for any friend of my brother Harry, though don't expect me to say hello to that Horse fellow – that Dog of Genoa,' he had said the previous evening before embarking for his return to the other side of the river.

Geoffrey was not unhappy to be working alone, or with only Alan for company. Ned Caton had stayed behind with Alice Storey while the physician was busy with his own concerns in Semper House, not the least of which was consoling his wife for the death of her little dog Millicent. Sara Storey seemed stricken by grief and was keeping to her chamber on this fine summer's morning. The accusation of poison made by Alfred Portman had not been well received by the head of the house or his wife. Sara had looked up and, for an instant, the grief in her face was replaced by anger. Storey had raised himself from where he was kneeling by his wife and, using his greater height and authority, had said quietly to Portman, 'Do not be absurd, man. Who would poison a poor harmless creature like this?'

'If you say so, cousin,' said his assistant. 'You must be right of course.'

'My wife's dog has died a natural death,' said Richard Storey to the company at large. 'The dog was a sickly little thing. Ignore what you have just heard.'

Portman bowed his head in submission but Chaucer would have bet a great deal that he was still convinced of his diagnosis of poisoning. And indeed, even to an untutored eye, there was something odd about Milly's corpse – the rigidity of the body as if it had been dead not minutes but hours, the white flecks around its muzzle. In the flickering light Geoffrey noted the expressions of the bystanders, both servants and family. There were bemusement and uncertainty, and even a taint of pleasure on one or two faces, perhaps glad to see Sara's misery. Truly she was not a popular member of Semper House. Only Bridget Salt went out of her way to condole with Sara, putting an arm round her and helping to raise her up from the floor. Edgar Storey now looked reassured that his own hound Hector could not possibly be suspected of having done Milly to death. The household went back to their own interrupted affairs, mostly preparing for bed. Two were detailed to deal with the little corpse, Storey enjoining them to handle it with delicacy. Chaucer wondered what would happen to the body. In London, a dead dog would usually be thrown on the midden or into the river but he suspected Milly might be given a proper burial in the grounds. After the scene in the hall, the mayor quickly took his departure though not before making arrangements for Chaucer's visit to Dartmouth the next day.

And now they had reached the middle of the river. The tide was on the turn and the oarsmen grunted with effort. Their boat was the only vessel on this stretch of water but ahead of Geoffrey and Alan lay the port, bustling with life and bathed in the morning sun. Geoffrey glanced over his shoulder. The full extent of Semper House and its grounds could best be appreciated at such a distance, the terraces still partly in shadow, the timber-framed buildings dominating the skyline. Beside him, Alan Audley shivered as the breeze blew along the corridor of the river. He pulled his hat lower.

'You do not feel the cold, Geoffrey?'

'I'm better covered than you.'

'Remind me of what we are about.'

'We shall visit the Genoese master of the *San Giovanni* and hear his side of the story.'

On the way down to the jetty at the foot of the Semper grounds, Geoffrey had given Alan a brief account of the tale told by the mayor the previous evening. As things stood, it appeared that the theft of the alum sacks could be laid at the door of two individuals. One was the master of the boat and the other was the mayor of Dartmouth himself. Each was accusing the other. To Chaucer, however, the reasons for the theft did not hold water, or not enough water. Why would the mayor compromise his own position and reputation by thieving from his own warehouse? And if he had done it, he wouldn't have done it so foolishly, surely, as not to make it look like a robbery rather than an inside job, a point Bailey had made himself? Bailey was no fool. Equally, would Pietro Cavallo be stupid enough to damage his standing at home by filching the freight he'd brought all the way from Genoa? It was possible, of course. There was no saying whether greed or a sudden requirement for cash mightn't drive a man to act foolishly. There was a third possibility – one which Alan Audley had quickly seen, although the same thought had already occurred to Geoffrey Chaucer – which was that there might be other copies of the warehouse keys in circulation. And a fourth possibility too: that there might be some other means of gaining access to the warehouse and removing its contents.

Now, on the rowing boat crossing the Dart, Audley said, 'How many men would have been required to take away the alum?'

'I don't know. It depends how long they had. It is like a number problem in a school. Take this quantity of sacks and so many men and so much time, and try to get everything to add up.'

Audley seemed about to say something more but Chaucer shook his head, indicating the two grunting men plying the oars amidships and the figure of Griffin sitting in the bows and twisting round to look at Dartmouth town. He didn't altogether trust the squint-eyed servant and certainly did not want their musings listened to. Although he had journeyed down here to investigate a missing cargo, he wondered whether there were not equal or worse problems brewing at Semper House. It might be true that Sara's dog had been poisoned, and that there was someone intent on stirring up trouble in the household. Nothing to do with him, of course, but trouble was no respecter of persons. Then there was always Ned's connection to Alice Storey to complicate matters.

They drew nearer to the harbour, the oarsmen manoeuvring the little rowboat round the cogs and merchant ships which were anchored offshore. Although Chaucer knew of the reputation of Dartmouth – a port not only large enough to support a flourishing trade with foreign cities but also important enough to be the gathering place for campaigns departing for the Holy Land – he had not appreciated the scale of the place.

Perhaps because of the way the boats towered like walls over Storey's dinghy while their crewmen paced the deck or peered incuriously over the side, Geoffrey was reminded of his early days as a child in the Vintry Ward. Then he had stood on the wharf gazing at masts which seemed to stretch up to the sky, wondering at the sheer bulk of the vessels which transported his father's wine from France, asking himself how constructions so awkward and lumbering could ever float on water, let alone plough a furrow across the seas.

The rowboat fetched up at a flight of steps leading to a stone jetty which was intended for smaller craft. As he got off, Chaucer looked a query at Griffin.

'I have my orders, master. We will return here in a couple of hours.'

Leaving the three men in the boat, Geoffrey and Alan scrambled up the steps. At the end of the jetty, the large figure of William Bailey was waiting for them as he had promised. Chaucer found himself oddly pleased to see the mayor's fat, round face. Again, he was accompanied by the pair of minnow-like men who'd ferried him in the other direction the previous evening. They didn't acknowledge Chaucer or Audley, scarcely looked at them. This town was as full of watermen as London but unlike the Thames variety, who were rowdy and foul-mouthed, the Dartmouth breed seemed to be tight-lipped. Chaucer might have wondered that his and Alan's business was important enough to summon the mayor to the quayside but he sensed that where the good name of Dartmouth or himself was concerned, Bailey would go to considerable lengths to meet his visitor. At least he assumed that was the reason.

Grasping Chaucer warmly by the hand and nodding at Audley, Bailey asked whether they had slept well, lulled by the soft air of Devon. Then, without waiting for an answer, he indicated that they were to follow him and his men. Bailey steered a course among the knots of people on the waterfront, as well as navigating his way past the barrels of wine and the bales of wool and baskets of fresh fish which were distributed the length of the quay. He moved along with the gravity of a clog or merchant ship himself, making a bit of a splash and enjoying it too while the others bobbed in his wake. Gulls swooped down and stalked along the quay, even more assured of their right to be there than the mayor.

There was the usual mixture of purposefulness and idleness which you get in any port, with harbour-workers and sailors going about their business observed by large numbers who had no business at all. The sunlight glittered on the scales of the piled fish. It made most people cheerful. William Bailey was greeted with waves and shouts on every quarter, and he slowed down from time to time to administer a pat on a shoulder or to exchange a hand-clasp. He was evidently a popular face, a familiar face, and Geoffrey suddenly understood that an additional reason for his meeting them at the waterside was to show just how strong was his standing with the townsfolk (and, by implication, how much more important he was than any passing visitors).

An idea occurred to Chaucer, something he should have thought of earlier. He quickened his pace to draw level with the popular mayor.

'This is a fine town,' said William Bailey, speaking first and gesturing to his right. 'Admire our new church of Saint Saviour.'

The streets beyond the harbour slanted uphill. A church tower was prominent, its crenellations standing out clear against the blue sky.

'Master Bailey – '

'William, if you please.'

'William, then. I should like to look first at your warehouse, the one from which the alum cargo was taken.'

'Is it necessary? I have told you what happened. The place is empty.'

'Nevertheless I should like to see it for myself.'

The friendliness was momentarily banished. William Bailey neglected to wave at a woman who was selling fish at a stall and ignored a shouted greeting from the other side. He appeared to consider the request. He glanced at his escort who were on his other side, before saying, 'You do not want to visit the master of the *San Gee-vanny* first? He is lodging in Fore Street.'

'In due course. I'd rather see the scene of the crime beforehand.'

As the mayor became more reluctant, Geoffrey grew more insistent. Bailey saw that he was not going to dissuade the other man.

'Very well, Master – Geoffrey.'

'We could see it now.'

'Now?'

'No time like the present. You said that the place was on the waterfront.'

'Very well.'

It occurred to Geoffrey that the mayor's reluctance might mean he had something to hide. But what if the warehouse was empty? Perhaps he was put out at being asked a simple request.

By this time they were reaching the end of the waterfront. Here, closer to the mouth of the estuary, were muddy slipways up which various vessels had been hauled although they were only partially out of reach of the tide when it was at its highest, as it was now. Some of the boats were in such a decrepit condition that they looked as though they would never float again while others were being repaired or repainted. Workmen and sailors were hammering at deck-boards which had sprung or stitching torn shrouds with bodkin-like needles and bundles of pack-thread. Others were standing in the sludge of the slipways and caulking the seams. Above them wheeled the squawking gulls.

William Bailey stopped opposite a wide, pot-bellied boat whose stern-post rudder was lapped by water but whose bows were on land which was more or less dry. The vessel was secured to posts on the shore by a web of ropes and its deck could be reached by precarious-looking planks. It had a single bridge and one mast. The boat was the reverse of graceful. It was designed to carry goods over a distance without comfort or ceremony. A new section of timbering was visible among the older boards of the hull, standing out like the bandage on a wounded limb. There was no one in sight. The boat looked oddly exposed and forlorn.

'There it is,' said Bailey, indicating the vessel. 'That's the *San Gee-vanny.*'

'It looks ready for the sea again,' said Geoffrey.

'It is ready but old Peter the master won't leave without his cargo. You can see where he drove it on to the rocks, the silly bugger.'

By this time all five men were assembled on the bank over-looking the Genoese craft. Bailey's two companions, yesterday's oarsmen, laughed at their employer's joke.

'You speak as if he did it deliberately,' said Alan Audley.

'I speak things as I find them, young man. There is the place you want to see.'

He pointed towards one end of a line of sheds and storage houses facing the slipways. They walked over to it. The building was the last in the row and easily visible from the bridge of the boat. At the end of the row of buildings the ground rose sharply. The ground in front was marked with wheel ruts and scattered with rusty iron nails and fragments of timber and oyster shells. A mangy dog which was rootling on the ground slunk away at their approach. Bailey's warehouse looked newer and more substantial than the other edifices on this stretch. In the centre of the two-storey wooden building was a pair of doors wide enough to accommodate a small cart.

Overhead there was a smaller door surmounted by a beam and a hook and pulley so that goods might be hauled directly to the first floor.

Geoffrey looked at the churned-up area in front of the doors.

'This was where the Italian sailor Giovanni was found?'

'This was where the Italian sailor Gee-vanny fell down pissed,' said Bailey. The mayor banged his fist on the wooden planking by the door. 'Well-made stuff, solid stuff. Our Dartmouth carpenters are second to none. Not even a crack for a rat to get through.'

'Not a rat or a pi-rat,' said Geoffrey.

'What? Oh yes, very good, Geoffrey. Not even a pirate. Isn't that right, Francis?'

One of the minnow-like men who'd been hovering in attendance nodded and said, 'Sir,' although it wasn't clear whether he was agreeing with his employer or merely acknowledging his words. William Bailey drew a key from a bunch about his waist and, with a flourish, inserted it into a great padlock which secured a hasp on the double doors. Both the key and the padlock had the sheen of newness. Chaucer was minded to make some remark about horses and stable doors but he kept quiet. Without removing it, Bailey hefted the padlock in one of his plump hands as if its weight proved its worth, then pushed at the doors with his other hand. They swung open with scarcely a creak.

'There you are, Geoffrey. See for yourself – though, like I said, there's nothing to see.'

'You said there was also some wine in storage?'

'No longer. It was removed by the merchant who'd shipped it. After the alum had gone.'

'A Dartmouth merchant?'

'A man called Weston.'

'Did Master Weston remove his wine because the building was no longer secure?'

'No. Master Weston removed his wine because he was selling it on. And the building *is* secure. The first thing I did was change the locks. See.'

He held up the new key, he pointed to the new padlock.

'Why was the wine not taken?'

'I don't know, Master Chaucer. You'll have to ask the thieves that.'

'So you leased only part of the building to the master of the *Giovanni*. You haven't thought to rent it again?'

'Not yet,' said Bailey firmly, as if it was none of Chaucer's business what he did or didn't do with his own property.

And indeed now they were here Chaucer wondered why he'd insisted on visiting the warehouse. As far as he was able to see from here, the interior was bare. He had some further questions to ask Bailey, though, and they were ones that required a certain delicacy. He put his hand to one of the mayor's well-padded elbows and drew him to one side, out of Alan's hearing and that of his two men.

'Forgive me, William, but last night at the physician's house, you seemed very sure that this Cavallo had acquired your keys and made a copy. I asked you about proof and for answer you said that he had accused *you*, as if that was sufficient.'

Bailey looked a little uncomfortable.

'Very well, man to man, I don't mind telling you, Geoffrey. Seeing as you know my brother Harry . . . I have said that I am on friendly terms with a lady called Mistress Barton, Juliana Barton . . . '

'In the house called the Shorn Lamb. A house of needle-women.'

'Just so. I am accustomed to visit her from time to time for . . . conversations.'

'I understand.'

'Would that my wife Constance understood.'

'You know wives,' said Geoffrey.

'Oh, I know wives. Well, Peter the Horse is also a visitor to the place, as are some of his men like Gee-vanny.'

'To a house of needlewomen?'

'Man to man, Geoffrey . . .?'

'Man to man.'

'It may be that other things go on in the Shorn Lamb. *May* be, I say no more. I believe it was on one such visit, when I was perhaps off my guard, that my keys were borrowed and copied.'

'By Juliana Barton?'

'No! She is as honest as the day is long, as you said about my brother. Remember that she was trying to return a purse to that sailor. But I cannot vouch for all the ladies in the house.'

Chaucer forbore to remind Bailey of his response to his brother Harry being described as 'honest as the day is long'. However, the situation was becoming clearer. The mayor was a regular visitor to the brothel. Someone, whether the mistress of the place or another woman, perhaps urged by Cavallo, had filched his keys and taken copies. If the mayor hadn't thieved his own warehouse then he'd been guilty of carelessness over his keys. It wasn't surprising that he had not revealed this on the previous evening, particularly given the hostility between him and Storey.

'Has the ship's master repeated his accusations against you?'

'He knows better than to do that. I have the power to clap him in jail. But no, he has just changed his tune. I've been informed that he no longer holds me responsible.'

'Why has he changed his tune?'

Bailey shrugged his solid shoulders. 'How should I know? I would say that he's seen sense except that he's a foreigner, and sense and foreigners don't go together. Have you heard enough now?'

He spoke in a tone that was at once abashed and defiant.

'Thank you. But I should still like to examine this place.'

Geoffrey beckoned to Alan that they should go inside.

Bailey, together with his men, remained firmly outside. The mayor said, 'Take your time, sir. I shall repair to the Mermaid Tavern along the waterfront with Francis and John. You'll find us there.'

'What are we expecting to find, Geoffrey?' said Alan once they were inside the warehouse. 'This looks like a waste of time. Why has the fat mayor abandoned us?'

Because he knows there's nothing here, thought Geoffrey. *Or because he knows that we shall find nothing.* Aloud he said, 'I don't know. Use your eyes now, Alan.'

Geoffrey waited a few moments to allow his own eyes to get used to the change of light. The morning was bright and there was enough sun coming through the open doors to reveal an earthen floor which was bare apart from some coils of rope and piles of empty sacking. Above them was the second floor of the depot, the beams and joists supported on rough-hewn pillars driven into the earth. There was a ladder at the far end leading to a small trapdoor in the ceiling. These pillars, and the planking overhead, looked comparatively new. Of course, it would make sense to increase the capacity of the warehouse by installing an extra floor. The interior was cool and there was a mixture of smells. Among them Chaucer caught the vinous scents of his childhood, of oak and alcohol mixed together. Again he recalled his early time in Vintry Ward.

They came to the foot of the ladder, a somewhat rickety one.

'You first,' said Geoffrey.

'After you, Master Chaucer, I insist,' said Alan, sweeping him a mock bow.

'If I go first, I may fall and hurt you – or break a rung of the ladder. If you fall I shall be here to catch you.'

Audley sighed and gripped the ladder. Halfway up he stopped and turned to Chaucer.

'If you break the ladder we won't be able to get back down again.'

'Get on with it, man.'

Alan arrived at the top and pushed at the trapdoor, which fell back with a clatter. He clambered through to the upper floor. Geoffrey followed suit, manoeuvring himself through the hole. He wouldn't have said as much to Alan but one reason for wanting his companion to go first was to avoid the indignity of being seen squeezing through the trapdoor – or not squeezing through it. In the event, it was big enough for his frame. It crossed his mind that William Bailey would probably be too large to get through. He supposed that the mayor, if he wished to inspect his property, would have to be hauled up from the outside like a sack of his wares. But, as a man of many interests, perhaps he didn't inspect his properties that closely.

There was no window on this storey but, for all the solid construction of the building, there were enough cracks and knot-holes in the planking to admit threads of light as well as a small amount of illumination coming up through the open trapdoor. By now Geoffrey was growing used to the gloom. At either end of the building was a gable wall while on each side the roof of the warehouse sloped down until it was almost at floor level. There was a scrabbling sound along one of the walls, suggesting that Bailey's comment about rats wasn't altogether accurate. There was no space wide enough, though, for a pirate or any other kind of thief to creep in.

There was nothing much to see up here either. At the far end, fronting the river, was the set of doors through which goods hauled up by rope and pulley would be swung inside. Nearby there was a windlass secured to the floor and more coils of rope. Alan was already standing near the upper doors.

'Come and look at this,' he said, his words echoing in the bare space.

Geoffrey walked over. The floorboards creaked underfoot. The sound of his steps together with the smell of the sea air, which penetrated even here, made him feel as if he was on the deck of a ship. He was able to see the outline of a pair of stout little doors – more like a pair of shutters since a man would have had to stoop to pass through them – secured by an inner wooden bar crossing their mid-section and resting on iron brackets on either side.

'It's not pinned,' said Alan, 'though there are holes bored to take the pegs.'

He was feeling above the bar to one side of the shutters.

'And here is a peg. It is hanging down on the end of a piece of string. See.'

Alan held out the wooden peg triumphantly, as if he had secured a vital piece of evidence. This system of securing doors, or more usually shuttered windows, was about the simplest that could be conceived. Even a child would be able to fix the bar once it was in position by inserting thick wooden pegs into holes bored into the uprights on either side of the opening above the bar. In this way no one from outside could force a knife or other implement through the small gap between the two doors and work the wooden bar free of its metal brackets by easing it upwards. Or at least they would not have been able to do so if the pegs had been in place. Geoffrey thought that the pegs were probably not much used. Since the doors to the upper storey of the warehouse were frequently opened and closed, the storemen would simply put the beam or bar back at the end of the day, without troubling to replace the wooden pegs. In any case, their distance from the ground would make the chamber less vulnerable. Meanwhile Alan was lifting the bar. He required two hands, more for the balance than the weight of the thing. The bar came clear of the brackets which held it.

'It's not so heavy,' he said.

'But strong enough to keep these fast,' said Geoffrey, putting his hand to a catch on one of the doors. They swung towards him. Sunlight streaked into the interior and both men blinked.

A view of the river was revealed and, closer to, the pot-bellied Genoese boat squatting on the slipway. Geoffrey stuck his head out. The drop to the ground was fifteen feet or more, he estimated. Down below the mangy dog had returned to forage among the rusty nails and discarded oyster shells. Geoffrey glanced up. The projecting beam with its hook and pulley looked much more substantial when seen from close to.

'You are thinking that someone might have got in through here, Alan?'

'It would not be so hard to remove the beam from the outside.'

'You could only get up here with a ladder. A man might manage to open these doors, true, but it would be precarious perched so high above the ground. And this is a public place. It's not just a matter of getting in but of getting all those heavy sacks out. You'd be seen.'

No one was looking at them now but they could see more than a couple of dozen individuals at work on the neighbouring boats, hammering, caulking, painting. Others, men and women, were strolling in either direction, singly or in twos and threes.

'By night, Geoffrey, they would do it by night. What man robs while the sun is out?'

'This theft occurred in the evening by all accounts, a few weeks ago. It would have been light then – or not dark enough. There'd still be too much risk of being seen.'

They closed the doors and replaced the wooden beam. But Alan Audley was reluctant to abandon his theory that someone might have broken into the warehouse on this level. Well, his younger eye might spot something that Geoffrey had over-looked or never even noticed. Alan spun round on his heel. He gazed towards the gable wall at the other end of the warehouse.

'There's another entrance over there.'

'I don't see it.'

'I noticed it when I first climbed up.'

Audley strode across the floor, his steps resonating on the bare boards.

Chaucer followed, glad to let him have his head. As Audley said, there was a second pair of doors on this side similar to the first. It was darker at this end but still possible to see that the entrance was secured by a bar resting on brackets, this time with the holding pegs in place.

'Why do they need two ways on to this floor – three if you count the trapdoor?' said Alan.

'There's a path or a street on the other side of this wall,' said Geoffrey. 'Goods arriving by water must go to the front of the building while anything which is being shipped out from the town will probably be delivered at this end.'

'Then it can't be used as frequently . . .'

'. . . otherwise they wouldn't have replaced these pegs.'

This time Chaucer removed one of the wooden pegs from its post. It was a snug fit but slid out easily because it had been greased. Like the others it was fastened to the wall by a length of cord.

'Take out the other peg, Alan.'

Audley did so and together they lifted the bar and placed it on the floor. Chaucer released the catch and opened the pair of doors. As he'd surmised, there was a wide and muddy path running underneath, more of a ditch since there was a bank on the far side topped by rank weeds. The ditch was in the shadow of the gable wall. What was surprising was that instead of a long drop, the ground was only a few feet below them. You could have jumped out from here without coming to much harm. The land behind the waterfront was irregular and rose on a diagonal behind Bailey's warehouse, which was the last building in the row. On this landward side, therefore, the ground floor was more or less below the level of the earth. Chaucer wondered that Bailey had ordered the construction of a storehouse in a place that must have demanded the removal of many cartloads of soil, but he supposed that it had to be set back this far because of the danger of flooding from the river. Perhaps the canny mayor was able to buy the land cheaply because no one else had thought to build on this spot.

The view from this aspect was not as pleasing as the view across the River Dart. To their right were the backs of other sheds and warehouses, also accessible from the muddy track. Beyond that lay the town and on a neighbouring slope the castellated tower of Saint Saviour's. The bells of the church were ringing. To their left the track or ditch petered out in long grass and clumps of trees. There was no one in sight. That the track was occasionally used for delivering or collecting goods was evident from the faded wheelmarks on the ground and the scuffed state of the mud and weeds in the area. There was a scatter of rubbish here, discarded pieces of timbers and rotten sacking. The approach did not appear to be as convenient as the frontward entrance. Nor was there any arrangement of windlass and pulley on this side, presumably because any items could be handed straight through the opening, especially if delivered from the back of a cart.

'This is secured as fast as the other opening,' said Geoffrey. 'You couldn't get in here if the beam and pegs were in place.'

Alan Audley was leaning out of the entrance and scrutinizing the surround to the doors. He had one foot on a wooden ledge protruding from the base of the doors. He drew his head back in.

'I'm not so sure, Geoffrey,' he said, gathering himself and leaping to the ground outside. He landed awkwardly but quickly scrambled to his feet and looked up at a surprised Chaucer, ignoring the mud on his hands and leggings.

'Could you fasten the doors again, with the beam and pegs and all? I want to try something.'

Alan's mood of impatience had gone. In its place was a schoolboy's eagerness. Geoffrey shrugged, and did as Alan requested, shutting the little doors and replacing the beam and the greased pegs. From outside came sounds of clattering and thumping. Chaucer waited. He hoped that William Bailey and his men were well occupied in the Mermaid Tavern and would not be returning to check on their activities.

Alan banged on the outside of the gable wall at about the level of Geoffrey's head.

'Look, Master Chaucer,' he said, his voice muffled.

'What am I supposed to be looking at?'

The renewed dimness of the interior made it hard to discern anything. There was more thumping and scraping from the outside. Still he could see nothing, but then he heard a soft thunk right in front of his face as one of the pegs securing the cross-beam fell out and swung against the wall, prevented from falling further by the cord. It was like the removal of a bung out of a barrel. He peered out through the new hole, about an inch across. He could see the rank grass which straggled on top of the bank opposite. He realized what Alan was about.

'Wait there,' he said, putting his mouth to the hole. 'I'm coming round.'

He replaced the peg in the aperture and retraced his steps across the floor to the trapdoor. Quickly he went down the rickety ladder and across the earthen floor at ground level and out through the main doors. The sunlight struck him full in the face. He looked round, at the single mast of the *San Giovanni* protruding above the slipway, at a couple of men now standing on the bridge of the Genoese boat, at the scavenging dog which regarded him without curiosity, at the view along the river-front. His heart was beating hard, not merely from the exertion but from the expectation of finding . . . what?

He looked over his shoulder to his right where the land rose beyond the buildings. Then he walked in the other direction along the front of Bailey's warehouse. It was not flush to the building next to it but the space between the two was so narrow that even the dog would have had difficulty slipping through. Chaucer walked further. After two more storage houses he came to an alley which led inland. This too was scarcely wide enough to accommodate him but he squeezed down it, treading on things that squelched and slid underfoot and were best not examined. He was glad that he wasn't wearing his best boots. Soon he emerged into the lane that ran behind the row. He looked along the line of the path, which became more ditchlike as it went upwards. Alan Audley was standing precariously on a plank balanced between the top of the bank and the wooden ledge at the base of the back entrance to the warehouse. He must have retrieved the plank from the timber debris which lay about. Audley was gazing in the opposite direction as if he expected Chaucer to come from round that corner. Geoffrey whistled softly and Alan's head jerked back and he almost fell from his perch in surprise.

Geoffrey climbed the track until he reached the gable end of Bailey's building. Meanwhile Alan remained on the plank, keeping his balance with one hand to the wall. There was a mixture of triumph and apprehension on his face. His eyes kept on flicking behind Chaucer as if someone might come into view at any second. But it was deserted here. There was no sound other than the crying of gulls from over the river and the church bells ringing out across the town.

Chaucer gazed up at the young man swaying on the plank several feet above his head. Audley took his hand away from the wall and held up something that looked alarmingly like a human finger. He lost his balance and fell forward, landing almost on top of Geoffrey. Both men tumbled down, Chaucer on his back, Alan on top of him. Neither of them was hurt but they got up muddy, winded and, in Chaucer's case, feeling ridiculous.

'I hope this is worth it, Alan.'

'It is, it is.'

Audley went scrabbling about on the ground again, finally found what he was searching for and held it up under the other's gaze. It was not a finger but a small cylinder made of some kind of resinous substance, slightly malleable to the fingers.

'Don't you see how it was done, Geoffrey?' Alan began a breathless explanation. 'Someone bored through the walls above here from the outside and then pushed the pegs through. They covered up the hole with this. I'll wager anything that there's another one in the second peg-hole. That way a thief could remove the plugs, push the pegs through from the outside, lift the beam with a knife or any thin implement, get inside the warehouse and take the goods. The wood around this plug has been newly bored with an auger, I'd say. And the pegs on the other side were well greased so they'd slide out straightaway.'

'It would be difficult,' said Geoffrey.

'Oh, it's difficult all right but it can be done. It would take several men but it can be done from this side. You said yourself it was too busy on the waterfront, someone would see. But it's quiet as the grave round here. There'd be no trace of a break-in either. It might have been prepared days ahead. Perhaps Master Bailey's warehouse has often been pilfered.'

'You're right, Alan. But there's one small objection to such a clever scheme.'

'Objection? What objection?'

Chaucer was sorry to see the sudden deflation on the other's face.

'You've done well to get so far, Alan,' he said, then quickly added, for fear of sounding like a schoolmaster, 'You have seen what I did not see. As you say, it looks as though this has been set up as a means of getting into the warehouse without making a robbery immediately apparent. But if the pegs securing the beam can be removed so ingeniously, then remember that someone has to replace them afterwards and put the cross-beam back – from the inside.'

'I hadn't thought of that.'

'You would have done so with more leisure. It is not an insuperable objection either. We should go in search of Master Bailey now, he'll be wondering what's taken us so long. Better remove that plank first.'

Alan jumped up and dislodged the plank from where it was resting between the bank and the side of the warehouse. It fell among the other discarded pieces of timber lying along the ditch.

With Audley at his heels, Chaucer retraced his footsteps down the path and along the narrow gap leading to the waterfront. He was genuinely struck by Alan's discovery – or rather by the other's sharp wits – and he reminded himself to make a point of complimenting him again, without patronage. Even so, there were two or three things about the warehouse robbery which baffled him. If it was correct that the thieves had gained access through the back entrance, and had done so by boring holes in the gable wall in order to push through the restraining pegs from the outside, they had gone to a deal of trouble.

Why? Why go to such lengths to conceal how you'd entered the warehouse when the theft would be obvious enough the moment the alum was discovered to be missing? What had the thieves gained by making such a surreptitious, ingenious entry?

Had they gained time? No, because the theft had been revealed soon after it had occurred. But they had not known it would be discovered, had they? It was only because the sailor had been found face down in front of the warehouse together with a sack of the alum – dropped? discarded? – that anyone had thought to check inside. So, once the cargo was gone, had anyone set off in pursuit of the robbers? No to that as well, because the ship's master thought he knew who was responsible – the mayor. While William Bailey also thought he knew the identity of the guilty party – the ship's master. Or so each had claimed, even if they'd subsequently changed their opinions. (But then, if you were going to be accused of theft, your best defence would be to accuse someone else, wouldn't it?) However, if someone other than Bailey or the Genoese was responsible, they had inadvertently created for themselves the circumstances for a clean getaway, in that no one went looking for them.

With these thoughts running through his head, Geoffrey emerged into the open by the river. He scarcely noticed his surroundings. Another consideration came to him, another odd aspect to this affair. He must ask the mayor when . . .

'Geoffrey!'

'Huh? What is it, Alan?'

'William Bailey's back, with our doctor of physic.'

It was surprising, to see Richard Storey together with William Bailey. The large mayor was again walking, rolling rather, along the path which led to his warehouse. Keeping him company was the doctor of physic, while his two-man escort hung respectfully in the rear. Nearing Chaucer and Audley, Bailey raised his arm in greeting while the physician contented himself with a small smile. Closer to, the mayor said, 'Here is a coincidence. I was leaving the tavern to come in search of you when I encountered Master Storey.'

'I did not think you were coming to Dartmouth this morning, Richard,' said Geoffrey. He wondered that their host had not come across at the same time as he and Alan made the journey. The rowers would have to make two trips across the river when a single one would have done.

Perhaps divining his thoughts, Storey said, 'I could not come earlier. My wife needed consoling after the death of her dog. She is a delicate woman.'

He looked at the others as if to say, *You know women*, but there was something rueful rather than dismissive in the look. Chaucer, however, was more conscious of the mayor's gaze. Bailey's eyes were darting over his and Alan's hands and clothing, spattered with mud from the ditchlike track at the rear of the building. Those eyes were watchful but he said nothing about the mud.

'All done?' said Bailey. 'I was starting to wonder what had

happened to you when you didn't turn up at the tavern. I thought you might have had some mishap.'

'No harm done,' said Geoffrey, without elaborating. 'You were right, William, there is absolutely nothing of interest to see inside there.'

Chaucer jerked his thumb in the direction of the warehouse. Taking his cue, Bailey indicated to his men that they should go to the building and make it secure. The two, Francis and John, sloped off across the waterfront and disappeared through the open doors.

'Nothing?' said Storey, as if he couldn't quite believe it.

'Nothing,' repeated Chaucer.

He was speaking the literal truth. There was nothing of interest inside the building – the *outside* was a different matter. Was it his imagination or did the mayor look more comfortable at his reassuring words?

'There is one thing though, William . . .'

'Yes?'

'The cargo, the stolen sacks of alum. Which floor were they stored on?'

'The upper floor, I believe.'

'But they were only going to be there for a short time, weren't they, while the ship was being repaired. Wouldn't it have been less trouble to store them on the ground floor for a few days?'

'I do not know, Geoffrey Chaucer. I am too busy to concern myself with the disposition of some cargo sacks.'

'Even in your own property?'

'Christ's bones, man, I am the mayor of this town, not a carrier or a carter.'

'Of course, of course,' said Chaucer. He was about to go on and ask who had been in charge of depositing the cargo when there was a great shout from the slipway where the *San Giovanni* lay. Up one of the gang-planks strode a tall, bearded figure, one of the two men he'd noticed earlier on the ship's bridge.

'That is Peter the Horse,' said Bailey. 'You will not have to go to his lodgings after all now.'

As the man drew nearer, Chaucer recognized that there was some justice in the mayor's literal translation of his name. The master of the *Giovanni* was large-limbed and had a long, equine nose. Moreover, his hair was bunched behind his head in a manelike fashion. Again the Genoese called out something in his own language. It might have been a greeting, it might have been an insult, it was impossible to tell. Pietro Cavallo was so large that he almost obscured another man walking at his heels. This one was small and wearing a sorry face.

'That is Gee-vanny with him,' added Bailey.

Gee-vanny? Ah yes, the sailor who'd been detailed to guard the warehouse but who preferred to visit a needlewoman – or a whore. If Cavallo had been angry with his man, he'd evidently forgiven him for he paused for an instant to allow the other to draw level and put a great arm round the diminutive sailor's shoulders. The hug might have been threatening or consoling. If the latter, then it didn't seem to have worked since the small man continued to wear his woebegone expression.

The pair of Genoese came face to face with the English foursome. Cavallo did a little bow and said, '*Buongiorno, Signor Podesta. Buongiorno, Signor Storey.*'

If there was mockery intended in greeting William Bailey by his mayor's title, Chaucer couldn't detect it. Indeed, Pietro Cavallo not only seemed pleased with life in general – something which on this fine morning wasn't so difficult – but gratified to see Bailey in particular, the man who had threatened him with jail for slander. For his part, the mayor did not appear quite so glad. Cavallo cast his large brown eyes over Chaucer and Audley. Richard Storey, whose grasp of Italian was more than the 'enough' he'd mentioned to Chaucer, swiftly introduced the two *gentiluomi di Londra* who had come to *investigare* the theft of the alum.

Even this news did not seem to disconcert Cavallo. His smile might have faded slightly but he shrugged his great shoulders and said, 'Is liddle problem, but we are all friends, eh, Giovanni?'

He turned to the sailor who stood a pace or two behind him. Giovanni nodded without apparent understanding. Richard Storey looked at him for the first time and with a physician's eye. Giovanni was not in the best of health to judge by his trembling limbs and his complexion, which showed a coppery green under the burnish of the sun.

'That man is sick,' said Storey. '*Morbisciato.*'

'*Si, si, e vero,*' said Giovanni, speaking for the first time.

'Is nothing,' said Cavallo, sweeping an arm in the direction of the water and making a splashing sound. ''E go in water, 'e get liddle – *come s'e dice? – febbricita. Eh, mio figlio.*'

Geoffrey recalled that Giovanni had been flung into the river by his master after the theft from the warehouse. Maybe he'd caught a chill which, going untreated, had led to his present feverish state.

'He needs attention, Signor Cavallo,' said the physician decisively. 'Bring him over to Semper House this evening and I will cast his horoscope and make other investigations. I know too that Master Chaucer here wishes to speak to you about the theft of the alum. It will be a good opportunity for you to talk, away from any curious eyes in Dartmouth.'

Having said all this in English, he repeated it in Italian, speaking so fast that Chaucer had some difficulty in following the sense. Cavallo nodded and once again put a large arm about Giovanni's shrunken shoulders. Then, bowing for a second time to the Englishmen, he turned round and steered his man back in the direction of the *San Giovanni*. They negotiated the gang-plank, although the frail Giovanni looked as though he might topple off it at any moment, and went out of sight towards the stern of the boat.

'Do you wish me to come over to Semper House this evening, Master Storey?' said William Bailey.

'Why no, you have already had your say, haven't you?'

'Geoffrey – Master Chaucer here – might have some more questions he wishes to put to me.'

Chaucer was surprised at the eagerness in the mayor's tone, particularly because he hadn't shown himself that willing to offer assistance up till now.

'It is possible that I will have more questions for the mayor when I've spoken to Signor Cavallo,' he said, looking towards the physician.

'You are always welcome at Semper House, William Bailey. Visit us when you please.'

This was about as gracious as Storey was going to get in his dealings with the mayor. Knowing he would get nothing further, Bailey took his leave of the others and made his way towards the warehouse. When he was out of earshot, the physician said, 'Tell me, Geoffrey, did you really find nothing inside?'

Audley, who'd not spoken a word so far but had been listening intently, shifted on his feet as if he was about say something about the secret access which they'd discovered at the rear of the building. But Chaucer glanced at him, and he kept silent. Geoffrey shook his head.

'It is as the mayor stated. The cupboard is bare.'

Richard Storey looked dubious. It was evident that he was reluctant to accept the mayor's explanation. 'I wonder what they're up to in there,' he said.

'A man is entitled to enter his own property,' said Geoffrey. Nevertheless he too wondered exactly what William Bailey was doing when, presumably, his only task was to secure the doors.

At that moment, in fact, the Dartmouth mayor was standing on the ground floor of his building. As Chaucer had surmised, he was too large to squeeze through the trapdoor to the first floor. Nor did he need to, since he had servants to do that for him. Instead he stood warming himself in the strip of sunlight entering through the open doors, waiting for his men to climb back down the ladder. The first to return was Francis.

'Well?'

'Everything is safe and sound.'

'No signs of disturbance?'

'No, master.'

'Francis, who was it gave command that the alum should be stored up there?' said Bailey, indicating the first floor.

Francis gave the matter some thought before saying, 'There was already Master Weston's wine stored down here.'

'There still would have been enough space.'

'It was the master of the ship who told us to put it upstairs,' said Francis after another moment. 'He said it'd be drier up there. Leastways that's what he said as best as I understood his foreign words. He waved his arms about a lot.'

'That's how they speak to each other, foreigners do,' said Bailey. 'They wave their arms and speak loud.'

The mayor might have gone on to describe other foreign habits but he was interrupted by the raised voice of a woman from outside. She sounded as though she too was speaking as loudly as possible but Bailey knew from experience that this was a relatively restrained display.

'Christ's bones,' he muttered under his breath, making his way as fast as his portly frame would allow back into the open air. The three men, Geoffrey Chaucer, Alan Audley and Richard Storey, were standing in a defensive semicircle. Facing them, but with her back to William Bailey, was a woman who was formidable not on account of her size, which was small, but because of her fiery manner. She was dressed in a red gown of the softest and most expensive wool, as William Bailey knew, since he had both paid for it (once) and felt it (often). She was wearing an elaborate headdress in a matching shade, which added perhaps an extra fifth to her height. She might have been one of Bailey's foreigners, she was waving her arms about so much. Certainly she was very voluble, and as the Dartmouth mayor approached he picked out fragments of sense.

' . . . disgrace to the good name of Dartmouth . . . our honourable mayor . . . don't trust these foreigners . . . take an Englishman's word over theirs any day . . . bugger off back to London . . . '

William Bailey gripped the woman tight by the shoulders. She started and made to lash out but something about the grip must have been familiar to her for she suddenly smiled and, without turning her head, said, 'Is that you, Will?'

'It is, Julie. What are you telling these good gentlemen?'

'I am giving them a piece of my mind.'

'Now is not the time and here is not the place, Julie,' said Bailey gently.

'It is for their good – and as healthful as any of your medicine, Richard Storey,' said the woman, singling out the doctor of physic rather than answering Bailey, who continued to clasp her by the shoulders. Then to him, 'I am telling your visitors to return to London. They are not welcome here if they have come down to accuse you of thieving.'

'Hush, hush, no one has accused me of anything,' said the mayor.

'*They* may not have done but what about the Italian shipmaster, the one you call the Horse?'

'Signor Cavallo has changed his tune, Julie.'

Slowly William Bailey coaxed the woman away from the hearing of the others. Once at a little distance, he whispered in her ear while kneading her shoulders gently. By degrees he succeeded in calming her down. They spent some time talking low, with occasional glances in the direction of the others.

Meanwhile, for the benefit of Geoffrey and Alan, the doctor of physic was identifying the woman as Juliana Barton, mistress of the Shorn Lamb in Sheep Street and mistress to the mayor, although Chaucer had already guessed who she was. It wasn't difficult. They'd endured only a few moments of the woman's tirade once she observed them standing outside Bailey's warehouse and come striding across, her dress like a travelling flame. Without introduction or preamble, she launched an attack on the physician for bringing down Londoners to inquire into Dartmouth affairs. Not just their presence in the town, but the reason for it, seemed to be known. Juliana Barton was stout in her defence of the mayor's honesty. Geoffrey was half amused, half impressed by her protective attitude towards Bailey, and now he said as much to the physician. Storey again did his *you know women* expression, although there was less indulgence in it than when he'd been talking about his wife.

Eventually Bailey soothed Mistress Barton. She returned to the group and made a cursory bob with her head before saying, 'My William here tells me that I must apologize if I have mis-said anything. And so I do, if I have, which I haven't . . . '

'Juliana,' said Bailey more firmly now, 'I am sure you have matters to attend to. These are busy men and I have things to do also. Be on your way to Sheep Street.'

'You will join me later, Will?'

'If I can. Off with you now.'

'Mistress Barton,' said Richard Storey, 'you found a sailor's purse recently, I understand. Has it been returned to its owner?'

The remark seemed designed to needle Mistress Barton. Storey had not taken the woman's harangue in good part. The woman bristled and Geoffrey feared she was about to start again.

'I am an honest woman, Master Storey.'

'As honest as the rest of your profession.'

'How is your wife, the young Sara?' countered the woman. 'I

hear that she has been deprived of a favourite companion and has taken to her bed.'

There was more mischief than malice in her tone but the mayor grew anxious again. Presumably he'd just told Juliana what had been happening over at Semper House, the death of the little dog and so on. 'That's enough, Julie,' he said, ushering her away. Nevertheless, the woman got in a parting shot over her shoulder, 'Strange it was the dog that died, Master Storey.'

'A foolish person,' said the the physician, watching the couple retreat. 'And Bailey is a foolish man to have anything to do with her or with her establishment.'

'She doesn't like you?' said Alan Audley. The remark hardly needed saying but he had been startled by the ferocity of Mistress Barton's attack.

'She does not greatly like me, Alan, any more than I care for her. I've more than once said that her house is a nest – '

' – of disease?'

'No, of disorder. And one which is protected by the mayor. It is strange, gentlemen, that Mayor Bailey is married to a meek and mild woman who fully lives up to her name of Constance, but that he keeps company with that termagant.'

Storey spoke with detachment but Chaucer could see that he had been ruffled by the encounter. It was apparent that the physician was not the most popular man in town, at least with the mayor and his associates. He had a rather high-handed manner, either because of his natural temperament and his London connections or because he was the king of his estate over the water and used to being obeyed.

Their business in Dartmouth being concluded at least for a time, Chaucer and Audley returned with their host across the river to Semper House. Here news of a domestic crisis lay in store. Alice Storey was waiting with Ned Caton by the landing stage for the return of her father's ferry. As soon as Storey stepped ashore she took her father to one side and poured a torrent of words into his ear. Geoffrey and Alan soon heard what had happened from Ned.

It appeared that Sara Storey, still grieving for her little dog, had accused her stepson Edgar of having been the cause of Milly's death, either through urging his own hound Hector to attack the creature or possibly through administering some poison himself. All this despite the fact that the dead animal bore no signs of a physical assault and the denial of the doctor that it had been poisoned.

'I was there when she attacked him with her wild words,' said Ned. 'Alice and I were both there and so was their grandmother Mistress Salt. Alice didn't know what she was saying, she was hysterical, but Edgar took her seriously. She used the word "murder" to his face. He was hurt. He is a sensitive individual.'

'That's true,' said Alan. 'And he is very fond of Hector.'

'So fond that when Sara said that she would see to it that the vicious brute of a hound – her words – was dealt with, Edgar grew very angry in his turn. He declared that he'd rather go and live wild in the woods with his dog than spend another moment under his stepmother's roof. His grandmother tried to stop him but he brushed her aside and stormed out of the house, taking his precious Hector with him.'

The affair of the missing cargo of alum was temporarily forgotten in this fresh excitement. Geoffrey had been correct in his intuition that there were intractable problems within Semper House. Mostly, he guessed, they had to do with the doctor's remarriage to a woman not so much older than his own children. Alice Storey was too sensible to feel jealousy, or at least to give way to it, and besides she had her own prospects of marriage. But Edgar was a different matter. He was young and moody, and resented the female who had usurped his mother's place even though she had died some years ago. He could no longer count on getting a fair hearing from his father and when his own hound, or he himself, was accused of 'murder' it had been enough to drive him over the edge.

For his part, Ned Caton obviously felt impatient with the woman who, should he marry Alice, would be transformed into his own mother-in-law. Even Alan Audley, who really had no share in these proceedings, sympathized instinctively with Edgar. In particular he thought that the accusation of murder, when applied to a dog (whether as perpetrator or victim), was absurd. Common sense said it was absurd. Chaucer was inclined to agree with him, but he also knew that common sense was a commodity in short supply.

Not for Richard Storey though. He had a robust attitude to his son's disappearance.

'Edgar will come back to us soon,' he said to Geoffrey when evening had come and there was still no sign of Edgar or his dog Hector.

'You're very sure of it.'

'He is not suited for life in the wild.'

'The wild?' said Chaucer, looking up at the slopes which stretched away on either side of Semper House.

'Yes. These woods and pastures are not for those who enjoy domestic comforts. There are wild people out there. My son will creep back soon enough, his tail between his legs. His dog too.'

He's probably right, thought Geoffrey, remembering the attack on him and his companions the previous day by the ruined hut. It wasn't so much the woods that were wild, but the denizens of the woods. Chaucer and the doctor of physic were once more walking in the grounds of the house. They were waiting for the arrival of Pietro Cavallo with his ailing crewman, the diminutive Giovanni. Chaucer was to talk with the Genoese ship-master – something which he was not much looking forward to – about the theft of the alum, while Storey was going to exercise his physician's skills on the sick sailor.

Unlike on the previous evening, which had been fair and fine, the weather had shifted, and not for the better. Storm clouds scudded across the estuary from the west and rain was in the air. A growing breeze shook the new leaves of summer. Ripples raced across the water of the Dart, a few whitecaps just visible. Nevertheless, a couple of boats were setting off from the Dartmouth shore at this instant to make their choppy way towards the landing stage at the lower edge of the grounds. One of them was the mayor's boat, the craft with the red awning over the stern. The other was presumably bearing Pietro Cavallo. Even from here, it appeared that the little boats were keeping a politic distance from each other. Although the mayor and the ship-master had apparently stopped accusing each other of theft, nobody was any nearer to discovering what had happened to the cargo. Chaucer had the uneasy sense that both men were coming to plead their case, and that he was to be the adjudicator between them. He'd already been here for more than a day yet a situation which was supposed to be easily resolved – according to Gaunt's secretary, Sir Thomas Elyot – looked very far from any settlement.

As if this wasn't enough, there was all the disturbance within Semper House itself. Sara Storey had kept to her chamber for most of the day, her husband having spent much of his time soothing her. Judging by his expression it had not been an easy task. Meanwhile Ned and Alice, together with Alan, could be observed talking frequently together, an alliance of the young against the rest of the world.

'You have been attached to the court for a long time, Geoffrey?' said Storey, evidently wishing to turn discussions away from his family troubles.

'Do I look so old?'

Geoffrey spoke with slight reproach but he wasn't really offended. He was used to having a few years added to his stock of three-and-thirty. It was not merely that his beard was greying or that he was growing stouter. Rather, it was a question of his attitude to life, he knew. Nevertheless Richard Storey put out a placating hand and said, 'Maybe it's just that you sound older than your years, Geoffrey.'

'I have not been attached to the court for that long,' he said. 'And, if it is an attachment, it's not altogether voluntary. I'm like the hunting bird who can't go far because of its jesses. I must return to the Savoy Palace because my wife and children are there.'

'I was wondering whether you remembered John of Gaddesden who was physician to the old King, but of course you would not be old enough.'

'I've heard him spoken of,' said Geoffrey.

'He treated the King's brother for smallpox. He wrapped him in scarlet cloth, and covered his bed and the chamber walls with scarlet hangings.'

'Did it work?'

'It did not work. Come this way. I've something to show you. We have time before those Dartmouth fellows arrive over on our side.'

Under the scudding sky he led Chaucer towards an enclosed quarter of the garden. A box hedge grew high enough to prevent anyone peering inside. There was a wicket gate at a gap in the hedge. Storey unlatched the gate, which was not locked, and ushered Geoffrey through. Beyond was a herb garden. Some of the beds were half-moons, some straight-sided but all were laid out as neatly as the figures on the chess board on the table in the hall of the house. The air was heavy with rain, as yet unfallen, and the scents of herbs, concentrated by their enclosure behind high hedges. A handful of the plants Geoffrey recognized, such as feverfew and St John's wort, but others were unknown to him. It was not surprising that the doctor of physic should grow the materials with which to concoct his remedies. Nor was it surprising somehow that they were not

147

the only visitors in the garden, for Alfred Portman was already there, on his hands and knees and with face and nose thrust close to a withered-looking plant. He seemed to be scrabbling in the topsoil. He scarcely glanced up as the others entered, and Storey did not acknowledge him. Perhaps this was because there was another person in the garden, Sara Storey. The physician was evidently taken aback to see his wife here. She was standing at a distance from Portman, who gave no sign of being aware of her presence either. She was white-faced and hollow-eyed. Chaucer had never seen a woman grieve so for the death of a mere animal. Nevertheless, it was the wife who spoke first.

'I am following your advice, husband, when you said I should seek a remedy for sorrow. I have asked cousin Alfred to make me a preparation of valerian and marjoram.'

'You should have asked me, my dear.'

'You have better things to do, Richard.'

'But nothing better than to care for you.'

'Even so, I have already spoken to Alfred here.'

She spoke tremulously but clearly, laying her fingers on the pectoral cross she wore on a silken cord about her neck, as if to prove the sincerity of her words. She made to move past Storey and Chaucer but the doctor put a restraining hand on her arm. He smiled, bent down and kissed her on the cheek. Sara smiled in return, before making her way from the garden. Storey looked after her – somehow wistfully, as it seemed to Geoffrey – as she unlatched the garden gate. Then he turned his attention back to Chaucer.

The paths between the herb-beds converged in a circle at the centre of the garden. Here, in a place of honour, was the sculpted head of a man set on a kind of pedestal. The head was old and grave, with blank staring eyes and a ring of sparse hair like the wreath on a Caesar. One of the ears was broken off and the head had been stained by time and weather. Chaucer had seen similar heads and busts during his time in Genoa and Florence.

'I had this brought from the East,' said Storey. 'I was assured by the merchant who sold it to me that it is the head of Aesculapius and if not him then Hippocrates, and if not *him* then it is the head of Dioscorides.'

'All the fathers of physic,' said Geoffrey.

'It is good to talk to an educated man, to a man of letters,' said Storey, reaching out and putting a hand on the bald pate in front of him as if to protect it from the first drops of rain which were beginning to fall. 'Who knows, the merchant might have been correct about Aesculapius. But whether he was right or not it pleases me to have this gentleman here watching over our plants and seeing that they grow aright. Watching over visitors to the garden too. Isn't that so, Alfred? Aesculapius watches you while you toil.'

Storey raised his voice to address Portman. The cousin looked up from his sniffing and scrutinizing of the soil, and smiled faintly. He did not reply.

'You will be pleased to do as my wife requests and make up a preparation of valerian root and marjoram?'

'Of course, cousin,' said Portman. 'It shall be done.'

'These herbs are a great physic,' said Storey, 'but they do not take us much further down our road. They are balms only, remedies known to our grandmothers, and to their grand-mothers too. Old wives' remedies.' Then the doctor leaned in close to Chaucer as if to impart a confidence and said, 'And, by God, we still have far to go before we can move beyond the old wives and penetrate body and soul, before we can reach our destination.'

'I don't understand. What is our destination?'

Storey's usually controlled features were alight with some inner fire. He appeared about to say something then thought better of it. He pulled back.

'Oh, to live a little longer and to live a little happier.'

'Surely our length of life is in God's hands?'

'Yes, of course it is in God's hands,' said Storey. 'Our happiness too, is that his?'

'We are all bound on Fortune's wheel,' said Geoffrey. 'Up one day, down the next.'

'You make us sound like buckets in a well.'

'Then at least we shall be guaranteed some refreshment from time to time.'

'We must see to our visitors,' said the doctor, seeming to grow impatient with the conversation and leading the way out of the herb garden. Chaucer followed, latching the gate behind him. Portman remained, doglike, close to the ground. Geoffrey was not taken aback by the other's words about God and human life. Doctors were famous for their impiety. Was it not said that where any three physicians were gathered together, then two of them would prove to be little better than atheists?

By now, the boats had docked and two little groups were making their separate way up the terraced slopes. The rain which had been coming down in single drops now began to descend in earnest. Geoffrey and Richard retreated under the eaves of the house to await the arrival of the mayor of Dartmouth and the master of the *San Giovanni*. But the party was larger than expected for, in addition to Cavallo and his men, and William Bailey (with Francis and John), came Juliana Barton. The little figure, dressed in red but covered with a dark mantle, climbed up the slopes with a will, outpacing the mayor. Richard Storey pulled a face.

'What's she doing here?' he muttered.

Mistress Barton, almost as red in the face as her dress, was full of smiles.

She had come, she said when she'd recovered her breath, to make amends for her rudeness that morning. She had brought a token of her respect for the doctor's wife: a decorative brooch and pin. Richard Storey did not seem much mollified but by now they had been joined by the others and any objections were muffled by the need to make a show of welcome to William Bailey and the Genoese ship-master, as well as to get out of the rain.

9

Chaucer's encounter with Cavallo wasn't very enlightening. He spoke to the ship's master alone, and for the most part was able to make himself understood and to follow the man's Genoese speech, except when Cavallo got carried away with his words. Storey had put one of the chambers of Semper House at their disposal and ordered refreshment for them, while he ushered the sick crewman off to his own office to be dosed with something or other. Giovanni looked worse than he had that morning. He could scarcely walk and had to be supported by Cavallo and another crewman called Marco. Giovanni was shaking like a leaf, his condition doubtless made worse by the wet and wind while they crossed the Dart. He had been too weak to take the oars, and Cavallo had been compelled to row beside Marco.

During all this, William Bailey hung about in the background, indicating that should Chaucer wish to speak to him again he would be prepared to answer any questions. Geoffrey couldn't help wondering whether the mayor's co-operative attitude was related to the scene by the warehouse that morning and the behaviour of Juliana Barton. Bailey wanted to prove himself a respectable, responsible citizen for all that he consorted with the madam of a brothel.

On one point Chaucer noted that Bailey was correct. Whereas immediately after the theft Pietro Cavallo had rounded on the mayor and accused him of thieving from his own premises, now the Italian went out of his way to clear

William Bailey of blame. In fact, his story was remarkably similar to the one already given by Bailey. He'd been alerted by the discovery of the prone body of Giovanni – the *povero* who was even now being treated by the good *dottore* – together with a sack of the alum cargo. This led him to believe that some mischief was afoot and he had ducked his man in the cold waters of the harbour solely, he assured Chaucer, to bring the silly fool back to his senses. Then he had roused the mayor and demanded that the warehouse be opened to check on his goods. Only to find them gone. *Con suo grande stupore*, as he said, for he considered the warehouse to be thief-proof. His first reaction had been to blame Bailey because the man had the keys to the place while he, Cavallo, most assuredly did not. But, thinking on the event, he'd concluded after all that Bailey had had nothing to do with the disappearance of the alum.

'So who did steal the cargo?' said Chaucer in Italian.

Cavallo shrugged his heavy shoulders. Who knew? he said. There were thieves in every port just as there were rats in every ship's hold. No doubt if the alum was not found and returned, his losses would be made good by London, for he understood – as Signor Geoffrey must certainly understand – that it was in the best interests of both Genoa and England that trade should continue between the two states in a spirit of goodwill.

Chaucer nodded. This was very close to what he'd been told by Sir Thomas Elyot. It was better that a comparatively small compensation should be paid than that a treaty should be imperilled. Cavallo evidently grasped the diplomatic niceties. Even so, Geoffrey was taken aback by the relaxed attitude of the ship master. Not only had he endangered his vessel but he had lost her cargo. Yet here he was sitting in the good doctor's house and drinking the good doctor's wine, apparently without a care in the world.

Geoffrey rose from his seat and went to gaze out of the window, which gave a view across the river. The rain was falling hard and the wind was whipping at the trees. The far shore was obscured by the downpour. As far as he could see, he'd reached a similarly misty and obscure end to his investigations. The simplest course would be to return to London and request that Cavallo be indemnified for the loss of the goods. Then, when he'd received the necessary assurances and when the *San Giovanni* was seaworthy again, the master and his boat could quit Dartmouth and be on his way to Fowey. It was unsatisfactory, but if Chaucer's principal mission had been to soothe ruffled feelings then that seemed to have been achieved without his intervention. As he was gazing from the window, his attention was suddenly caught by a shadowy figure sheltering among the trees on a lower terrace. He wondered why anyone would be out in such weather. He thought too that he glimpsed a black dog cowering by the figure, and it occurred to him that it might be the errant Edgar. Perhaps Storey was right to think that his son wasn't really cut out for life in the wild and would soon be slinking back, tail between his legs, unable to withstand a single night of summer rain.

This was more than a mere passing storm, though. As the clouds pressed down heavier and the wind blew more fiercely, it soon became apparent that there would be no possibility of the two groups – the mayor's and the ship-master's – crossing back over the river that night. And there was an additional reason to stay in Semper House. Richard Storey informed Pietro Cavallo that his man Giovanni was in an even worse state than he'd at first thought. He had done his best to relieve the man's fever but it would be preferable if Giovanni was not exposed to the elements again that day. He should rest and be cared for by Storey and his assistant Portman. All this was conveyed in an urgent conversation between the doctor of physic and the ship-master. Chaucer heard fragments of it while they were assembling in the hall for supper, an unusually large gathering since it had been decided to lodge these various guests in Semper overnight. But the house was spacious, with a surplus of chambers, and there were the outbuildings also to accommodate those such as the mayor's oarsmen John and Francis, who did not warrant any better lodging.

As on the previous evening Chaucer found himself examining the motley collection of guests and residents assembled under Storey's roof. The immediate family were there with the exception of Edgar. Sara Storey had emerged in public, still looking grieved. Chaucer wondered whether she'd yet taken the valerian and marjoram preparation that Portman was supposed to have prepared for her. Even the doctor of physic seemed to think his wife had mourned sufficiently for the death of her dog and his earlier forbearance in the garden was replaced by a more brusque approach. When he put his arm about her as she came downstairs and was impatiently rebuffed, he whispered something sharp in her ear. Only the presence of Bridget Salt, mother to Storey's first wife, seemed to be tolerated by the young woman. Chaucer observed that ruddy matron's face thrust close to Sara's. Instead of a display of impatience, a single tear rolled down Sara's cheek and she grasped the older woman's hand in gratitude. But when Juliana Barton went to greet her and present her with the gift of a brooch, it seemed to Geoffrey that she flinched even as she brought herself to smile and accept the offering. Meanwhile the younger people – Ned Caton and Alice Storey, together with Alan Audley – kept their own company and counsel, paying no attention to Sara, probably because they blamed her for driving Edgar out of the house. Alfred Portman was there but might as well have been on the moon for all that he contributed to the evening's cheer.

If there'd been any remaining animosity between William Bailey and Pietro Cavallo over the theft of the alum, it was well washed away by the wine which flowed across the table. The Dartmouth mayor had no Italian – Chaucer had identified him as the kind of Englishman who positively prides himself on ignorance of any foreign tongue – while the Genoese master had little more than a few fragments of English, but they managed to make themselves understood in the universal language of liquor. In the background were Francis and John, the mayor's servants, together with the sailor who had ferried Cavallo over the river.

The evening was a convivial one, or would have been convivial except for a particular occurrence. With one or two exceptions like Sara Storey, everyone might have gone to bed happy or at least drunk, which frequently amounts to the same thing. But then Griffin appeared for an urgent consultation with his master, and the doctor of physic disappeared in the direction of his office. When Storey came back a few minutes later, he was grim-visaged. He looked round uncertainly until his eye caught Chaucer's.

'It is as I said, Geoffrey. That fellow Giovanni was in a more sorry plight than I thought.'

'He *was*, you say.'

'Yes, he is out of it now.'

'He cannot be dead?'

'Dead during these last few minutes. Griffin came to tell me.'

The two stood awkwardly for a moment. Even though Chaucer had only glimpsed Giovanni on a couple of occasions and the man meant nothing to him, the news of the death was shocking and surprising. It occurred to Geoffrey that the Genoese sailor had died far from home and family, if he had one.

'But you were treating him, weren't you?'

'I would have cast his horoscope tomorrow when I discovered his nativity – if the man knew when he was born, that is,' said Storey, a touch defensively. 'Then I would have treated him for fever which, as you know, is caused by an excess of yellow bile. He would have been bled or given cold baths. But for tonight I gave him no more than a feverfew. Something to drive away his fever.'

Which seems to have worked a little too well, reflected Geoffrey. As if divining his thoughts, Richard Storey said, 'Oh, do not blame the remedy, Geoffrey. It was a mild concoction, more to procure sleep than anything else. If you're searching for anyone to blame, then you should blame that fool.'

'Which fool? You mean Pietro Cavallo, the master?'

Chaucer glanced across to where Cavallo and the mayor were laughing together at some shared joke. On the other side of Bailey sat Juliana Barton, her red dress seming to take new fire from the liquor she'd imbibed. The two men presented quite a sight: the mayor, round and squat, sitting next to the Genoese giant, with his great shoulders and mane of hair.

'If the master hadn't ducked him in the harbour, the man would never have caught a chill. If he'd had him attended to earlier, the chill would never have developed into a fever. Even then, if informed a day earlier, I might have saved him – although I suppose *you* would say it was all in the hands of God or fortune.'

It seemed somehow indelicate to refer to this earlier conversation only minutes after a man had died and Chaucer did not reply. Storey continued, 'Well, as I said before, we have far to go before we can fathom the secrets of the human spirit and soul.'

'May he rest in peace,' said Geoffrey.

'Amen to that. Now I must go and tell Cavallo.'

The doctor strode across to that part of the table where Cavallo was sitting in company with the mayor. Without ceremony he broke into their conversation, or rather their laughter, and spoke rapidly in Italian. He did not trouble to keep his voice down. The rest of the table, alerted by Storey's manner or the angry edge in his tone, stopped their chatter. It quickly became clear, without anyone's explicitly translating the doctor's words, what had happened. Geoffrey, by now recovered from his initial shock, observed Cavallo's response to the news of his crewman's sudden death. He knew that Italians were given to displays of feeling, but even so he was surprised by the way in which Cavallo's face crumpled as it changed from good humour to grief. He carefully placed his goblet on the table and bunched his fists. An audible groan issued from his mouth. Storey looked half gratified, half abashed at the effect he'd created.

Cavallo rose from the table. He was about the same height as Storey but much more massy than the lean doctor. The Genoese raised a hand that was almost the size of a hoof. For an instant it looked as though the two might come to blows but the doctor stood his ground until the ship's master thought better of it and lowered his arm again. He said something to Storey, who nodded and led the master from the hall, no doubt to view the body.

For the second time in as many days a death had occurred in Semper House. The little dog Millicent and now the diminutive Giovanni had gone from this place, never to return. As on the previous evening, the news cast a pall over the household even though scarcely a member of it had glimpsed the foreign sailor. The chatter round the supper table was replaced by whispered comments.

Geoffrey made his way to the doctor's office, under some impulse to see the corpse. By now, with the skies overcast, it was growing dark. A few candles shed a subdued light in Storey's sanctum. The body of the unfortunate Giovanni had been laid out on the trestle table, cleared of its bottles and vials and boxes. The Genoese seaman, slight to begin with, was further shrunk in death. Around him stood Cavallo and Storey and Griffin and, inevitably, Alfred Portman. Chaucer wouldn't have been surprised to see the doctor's assistant sniffing at the corpse but instead that stringy man was arranging a sheet over Giovanni, wrapping it around the body as securely as a mother seeing a child to bed. Portman left the face exposed.

Storey was saying something in Italian to the ship's master, who stood with his great head hanging down. Judging by the postures of both men, their anger had gone as suddenly as it had come. Griffin stood in a corner of the crowded room. Chaucer sensed someone come up behind him. It was William Bailey. His ebullience too had vanished.

'This is bad,' he said. The town mayor crossed himself before putting a consoling hand on Cavallo's shoulder. He was one of those people capable of an instinctive sympathy. Now he said, 'You were here when it happened, Alf?'

Portman looked up in surprise and glanced at Storey who, in turn, turned his head towards Griffin.

'I was here when he died, sir,' said the squint-eyed servant. 'The foreign person sighed and shook and shuddered, then went quiet and still. There was nothing to do. I told my master straightaway.'

Richard Storey nodded in agreement. For all the feeble light in the room, Chaucer could see uncertainty, even confusion on the doctor's face. It was as if the impact of this death was taking its time to sink in. Pietro Cavallo turned away from the body on the table. He pushed his way out of the room without saying a word. When he'd gone, Storey spoke half to himself, half to the others.

'I did not know that he was that gentleman's nephew. He told me just now.'

'His nephew?' said Bailey.

If there'd been any doubt whom he was referring to, Storey put out his hand and laid it on the forehead of Giovanni. It was a protective gesture, rather like the one he'd made when touching the head of Aesculapius in the herb garden but, of course, by now there was nothing left to protect.

10

Outside Semper House, while darkness thickened and the rain came down faster, Edgar Storey shivered and drew his cloak more tightly about him. He was crouching at the base of an oak near the river-bank. His dog Hector huddled nearby, looking at his master occasionally as if to question whether the sacrifice of dryness and shelter was really worthwhile.

Uncomfortable as he was, Edgar did not regret the fight with his young stepmother. In fact, as he brooded on it his anger flared all over again. Sara was an ignorant woman. As if he would harm a dog! Even a wretched yapping little creature like his stepmother's! The dog was a sickly thing, always coughing and whimpering and crawling round its mistress. The dog was sickly and the woman was a fool. From this point his thoughts and his anger grew broader.

Sara was not fit to be his father's companion or mistress of Semper House. Edgar resented the way Sara clung to his father, as ivy wraps itself about a tree and sucks the life out of its supporter. He wondered why his father couldn't have married someone older, if he had to marry at all. He had small memories of the mother who'd died some years previously and who, in his mind, remained a fading figure, prone to illness. The only woman whom he admired (and loved) was his sister Alice, although he had some respect for his grandmother Bridget even if he sometimes found her talk and attitudes a little . . . well . . . a little on the salty side and unbecoming in a beldame. But he was grateful to her for taking his part in the quarrel with Sara. It was more than he would have received had his father been present. Edgar also had an odd liking for Alfred Portman, perhaps on account of the assistant's quietness and taste for solitude. It may be, too, that he saw Portman as being under the thumb of his father.

The principal emotion which Edgar felt towards his father was fear. Richard Storey was an imposing man, clever and sometimes stern and cold. Edgar sensed that he was a disappointment to the good doctor and that, in truth, Alice was much closer to the ideal son. Alice was strong and independent-minded and quick-witted. Edgar had shown an inclination towards books and the secret lore which they contained, something that he hoped would win his father's approval, but he had been rebuffed when he tried to talk about them. When books failed, he did not go in the opposite direction and develop a taste for manly pursuits. He had no wish to joust or to go and fight in France or the Holy Land. Oh yes, Edgar Storey enjoyed hunting but that was more because it was an activity done in the company of the dogs which he loved.

Edgar shifted his position at the base of the tree as what had been a steady drip of water from the leaves above turned into a trickle. He looked out across the river. The far bank was shrouded in dark rain. He could hear the river slopping at the landing stage nearby and the occasional thunk of the boats moored there. He liked this spot, whatever the weather. He often came down here to get away from Semper.

He suddenly recalled an occasion, many years ago, when he had been walking with his father along the shore near this place. It was a bright day in spring. Intimidated by his father's presence and struggling to keep up with him, he slipped and tumbled down a slide of mud and dead leaves into the fast-flowing current. Edgar could not swim, of course, but he was fortunate in that the shock of the cold water prevented him from flailing about straightaway, something which might have sunk him. Instead he was spun along on a series of eddies quite close to the shore. His father might not have noticed if it hadn't been for the sharp, involuntary yelp which Edgar gave as he fell. The doctor of physic ran along the bank, hardly keeping pace with his son, not crying out or calling the boy's name but grim and tight-lipped.

After what seemed like ages, but was only a matter of seconds, Edgar did begin to struggle and flounder. His clothing turned heavy as armour. Icy water poured into his mouth and nostrils. His eyes were tight shut against the spray. At once he felt a great blow to his chest, which knocked the little remaining wind out of him. Instinctively he reached out and grasped at a slithery limb. A tree-branch, broken off somewhere upstream, had wedged itself almost at right angles to the bank. The branch bobbed and swayed but it kept the boy from being swept away. The branch was Edgar's salvation.

He looked towards the bank. His father had drawn level with him. Richard Storey came to the very edge and crouched down on his hams. Whereas before Edgar's senses had been drenched in cold and confusion, he now saw and felt and smelt everything. The roaring of the waters, the slimy branch under his small hands, the brackish odours of the river. For an instant he saw Richard Storey's face – the beard neatly trimmed, the sharp hook of the nose – not as his father's face but as someone else's. He observed the eyes, grey ones, as they seemed to observe *him* with interest rather than concern. Then his father reached out and, telling the boy to cling hold as fast as ever he could, he struggled to free the branch from where it was wedged before drawing it slowly inshore. He succeeded in bringing Edgar within arm's length and at last to safety.

Afterwards, though he couldn't have put his feeling into words, Edgar felt perturbed by his father's reaction, since the son was (as Chaucer and the others correctly saw him) a

163

sensitive and moody individual, even as a child. The doctor of physic had not clouted him about the head for his carelessness in falling into the river, he had not rebuked him in so many words. He had merely instructed him to run back to the house and get changed into dry clothing. It was a spring day, bright and cold.

What he recalled afterwards was that look in his father's eyes of . . . detachment . . . as he clung to the branch in the river. He'd seen a similar expression when his father pored over the little creatures which he had trapped, killed and cut up, as if to plumb or penetrate their secrets. The legs of the frog, the wings of a bird, how did they operate? What was the hidden, animating principle which drove their limbs and organs? Could it be discovered by taking them apart and examining the individual items of which they, or their legs and wings, were composed? In Storey's office on his trestle table were often to be seen little jumbles resembling uncooked food, red threads and tendrils, jelly-like blobs and fragments of bone, hide or feather. In attendance, even then, would be Alfred Portman, bent over his own collection of seeds and herbs. That was the division of labour, the doctor taking care of the higher forms of life, albeit birds and toads and the smaller vermin, while his assistant studied things which grew up from the ground.

Edgar's knowledge about his father's activities came not from the good doctor but from his sister. It was Alice who was favoured by her father. It was Alice who was allowed to peer inside the leech-books which contained advice and remedies, just as she was permitted to be present while he sliced up the thrush's wing or the fox's paw. (This was how Edgar was aware that his father sought for the secrets of motion and propulsion.) To Alice he explained how sickness in the human body is caused by ageing or by sin or an imbalance of the humours. We all grow older and we are all born in a state of sin, but at least we may do something about an imbalance of the humours. There are remedies like cupping, purging, leeching, bathing, and so on. Edgar listened while Alice explained in turn some of what had been explained to her. The boy stored up as many gobbets of information as he could remember – that the ankles are linked to Aquarius, the sign of the water-bearer; that vomiting is healthy since it restores the equilibrium of the body; that those born under Gemini are inclined to be phlegmatic. He stored up these items in the hope that he might be able to impress his father one day. And he'd tried more than once to display his little knowledge, only to be rewarded by a baffled and angry look from the doctor, as if as to say 'Why are you concerning yourself with my business, boy?' After a time Edgar Storey realized that his father was not prepared to share any of his secret lore with him. For company and understanding, apart from his sister, the boy turned to his dogs.

As he now turned to Hector, huddling under the dripping oak tree by the river-bank, and stretched out a hand to stroke the hound's damp flank. The dog groaned. Perhaps Edgar did too. He didn't relish the prospect of spending a night in the open but some shreds of pride prevented him from creeping back up the hill to Semper. Anyway he knew that the house would be crowded this night since, from the concealing trees, he'd observed the arrival of that fat town mayor and a woman in a red dress as well as some other visitors he hadn't recognized. One of them was pretty sick, he'd been supported by his fellows as they walked to the house. The visitors' boats, pitching up and down in the water, were still moored to the landing stage. It was unlikely at this late hour and in this foul weather that any of them would be returning to Dartmouth town. Most probably Edgar's own quarters in the house – a poky chamber under the eaves, and little better than the common servants' accommodation – would be given over to one of the guests, so little did he count for in his own home.

But he could not live long in the wild. The hunger he felt was stronger than the darts of anger. Pride did not stop you from shivering with cold and damp. He would have to return sooner or later. He would be compelled to apologize to his young stepmother if he wanted to regain admission to his own home. He'd have to swallow his pride and anger. Edgar wondered if anyone was thinking of him now. Only Alice, and she was probably far too wrapped up with Edward Caton to spare him more than a moment. Ever since Caton's arrival in Semper House, the brother had done his best to ignore the man who was going to take his sister away from him. The two of them were decided on marriage, weren't they? His sister would go off to live in London, which was where Caton came from, wasn't it? London, a city far away. And when Alice departed with Caton, Edgar would have no protector or friend in Semper.

Caton. Edward Caton. Edgar saw him in his mind's eye. A well-born man, no doubt, though he had something of the peasant about him, with his unruly fair hair and his thick-set frame. He preferred Alan Audley, who had at least deigned to talk with him and who was knowledgeable about dogs. He even preferred the portly older man who'd come with them and whose name he couldn't quite recall, Geoffrey something-or-other.

There was nothing much to hate or even to dislike about Edward Caton (except for the fact that he was set on marrying Alice), but Edgar would not be sorry if he met with an accident. If that happened then Edgar could console his sister. Edgar pleased himself with various visions. Caton might tumble into the fast-flowing Dart and be swept away, as Edgar so nearly had been when young. He might succumb to the pestilence, although it would be better if that occurred in London and, of course, without Alice being nearby. Best of all would have been if the ambush which had occurred on the afternoon of their arrival had succeeded, and the visit of all three London guests had been . . . forestalled. That was a loss which Edgar could have borne quite comfortably.

In his misery and irritation, Edgar thought too of how convenient it would be if Sara Storey was somehow no more, if that young usurping female in Semper was to meet with her own kind of accident . . .

His musings were interrupted by Hector growling. The dog, more resigned than his master to the discomfort of outdoors, was looking into the darkness. His ears were cocked. Edgar soothed him. He listened but could hear nothing beyond the rush of the river and the sweep of the wind.

Not so far off crouched two men and a woman, as well as the nameless dog. Like Hector, Edgar's animal, their human senses were fitted for the dark and, even though they could not see anyone, they were already aware that someone was there. Hector's growling, faint on the wind, confirmed it and caused their own hound to prick up his ears and give an answering murmur until one of the men clapped him about the muzzle. The three had made their way into the Semper grounds by following the river-bank. The boundary was marked by palings but they were easy enough to surmount.

One of the men, the one known as Bull, reached for the axe which he had laid on the ground. The woman restrained him. Not yet, her gesture said, not yet.

11

Within Semper House the occupants were preparing for bed. Not all were permitted to sleep in the main building. Even in such a fine dwelling there were insufficient chambers for the extra guests. The Genoese sailor, for example, the one who'd accompanied his master Cavallo across the water, had been told by Griffin that he should bed himself down in the stable, this information being conveyed in dumb-show. The sailor might have been offended at being put with the horses but he was already so sozzled with drink and grief for Giovanni that he would have slept on a pitching deck on the high seas. At any rate he was better off than the unfortunate Giovanni, even if that gentleman was accommodated where it was dry and warm. But then he was sleeping under a shroud in the doctor's office.

Pietro Cavallo was allocated the room under the eaves which belonged to the son of the house, as Edgar Storey had foreseen in his angry ruminations. This was a low-ceilinged chamber and there was no part of it in which Cavallo could stand fully upright. The ship's master, who'd drunk deep in the early part of the night, had been abruptly sobered by the death of his nephew. His first reaction, which was anger against the doctor of physic, had been replaced by a colder, more pensive state of mind. When he returned to Genoa he would have to account for Giovanni's death to the young man's mother, his sister by marriage. This did not weigh too heavily on his conscience,

169

since to go voyaging was a dangerous enterprise and men died at sea (and on land) all the time. He would blame it on the incompetence of the English physician. Altogether Richard Storey owed him a great deal . . .

Meanwhile, as mayor of Dartmouth, William Bailey had been given a proper chamber in deference to his rank. He was preparing for bed and wondering whether he could be bothered to undress even in the most rudimentary way when there was a tapping at his door. He recognized that tap. Juliana Barton rustled into the room, in her red finery. She pressed herself against him and he almost fell backwards. In truth he wasn't so steady on his pins at this instant.

'I thought you were bedding down in the women's quarters,' he said.

'I will not bed down with the servants,' she said. 'I, Juliana Barton, who have my own establishment in the town.'

She reached a hand down beneath the belly of her friend.

'Now, my Julie?' said William Bailey. 'Here? The bed is narrow.'

It was not so much that he objected to what she was trying to do. But he had drunk a lot and was by no means sure that he was up to it.

'What better time, Will? We are all alone and your wife is on the other side of the river.'

'A man has died here tonight.'

'I don't know about you, Will, but I find death always gives me an appetite, if you know what I mean,' she said, then added quickly lest she should seem unfeeling, 'As long as you aren't too familiar with the deceased. Which we are not since he was Italian.'

'But the sailor visited your house, Julie.'

'Many men visit my house,' she said, unarguably.

'Even so it is not respectable, here and now.'

'Oh, I forget that this is such a respectable place. To look at them you would think that butter wouldn't melt in their whatsits. Especially that Sara Storey.'

'You gave her a token this evening, my dear.'

'A mark of my *respect*, Will. Do you not think that she would make a good needlewoman in my house?'

'The physician's wife? You're joking of course.'

'Believe me, it is those quiet demure girls who go best. You should know that, Will.'

'Banish that thought, Julie. Promise me you will never say anything to Mistress Storey even in jest. I can protect you as far as is in my authority but – but . . .'

'But what?'

Bailey slumped down on the small bed, which sagged beneath his weight. He'd lost the train of his thought. All he wanted to do was lie back and close his eyes. He struggled to complete his sentence.

'The doctor of physic is a powerful man. Leave his wife well alone.'

'No harm in teasing,' said Julie, leaning over him, filling his face with her breath, sweet and sour with alcohol. 'I have teased Mistress Storey in the past when she was a simple unmarried chit without prospects. William? William, are you listening to me?'

But the mayor lay unresponsive on the bed, his pudgy legs dangling over the side, snoring his head off. After a time she gave up the attempt to wake him. She considered shoving him off the bed and on to the floor – it mattered little to a drunk man where he slept – and taking his place on the narrow bed. She gave a couple of tentative pushes to Bailey's body. Christ's bones, he was as impossible to shift as stone! She looked, not unfondly, at his doubled chins and rounded belly. Strange she did not object to all of that when it was on top of her, she thought. But her heart was not really in the effort to dislodge her lover. Let him sleep soundly and snore in comfort, as befitted the mayor of the town. She would go back and take her shared bed in the servants' quarters. That was her place in this *respectable* house.

In truth she had come to Semper less to make peace and more to make mischief, in the same spirit in which she'd addressed Richard Storey that morning or given the token of a brooch to that stuck-up woman Sara. Juliana did not like the good doctor and was unwilling to pass up the chance to discomfit him by turning up on his doorstep. Also she was pleased to be with her William. He couldn't deny her that, particularly when she announced that she wanted to atone for her rudeness of that morning by accompanying him to Semper. The mayor was so busy with town affairs, and his warehouse business, and his wife Constance (whom Juliana considered a shrew), that he was able to give little time to his Julie. They had to snatch what moments they could together. Trust Will to get so drunk that he was incapable of staying awake let alone getting it up. It might have been a good session, despite the narrow bed and the dead man lying downstairs. Death did give an edge to things sometimes.

She exited the room quietly. The passage outside was illuminated by a single candle in a sconce. At the far end Juliana saw the very person she'd been talking of. It was Sara Storey. She was still in her evening-gear, a white gown. The doctor's wife was oblivious of her presence. Instead she was standing outside another door. She put her face to the door and Juliana understood that she was trying to see whether the occupant was still up, whether there was any candlelight showing through the panels. Evidently the occupant was awake for Sara raised her hand as if to knock but then seemed unable to carry the action through. Well now, thought Mistress Barton, whose chamber is that? Who is it that the young wife is calling on in the small hours of the morning? She hung back in the shadows, thinking she might catch a glimpse or hear a whisper if Sara

172

summoned up the nerve to knock and if her knock was answered.

In the room behind Juliana, William Bailey opened a single eye. He wasn't quite as drunk or incapable as he'd pretended. For an instant he thought of rising and calling after Julie. But he could not be bothered to shift from his position, and in a while he must have fallen asleep.

Juliana Barton was not the only woman in Semper House who was thinking of Sara Storey. As Mistress Bridget Salt sat musing in her own comfortable and spacious apartment, she reflected on the fashion in which the young woman had come to dominate life in the household. It was not because Sara was a decided and vigorous individual (as Bridget thought of herself) but the reverse. Sara possessed a kind of negative power which grew out of feebleness of temper. It sometimes seemed to Bridget Salt that it was her fate to be surrounded by individuals who were less robust than she was. She excepted the doctor and her grand-daughter Alice from this charge, but her husbands had proved themselves less strong than her by going and dying against her best advice. She was glad that, in Edward Caton, Alice had chosen a proper man, that is one who shared a name with her most recent husband, one who was well formed (albeit on the stocky side) and who seemed the sort to appreciate her grand-daughter's spirit. Mind you, if it had been her decision, she might have plumped for the rather better-looking Alan Audley. She thought of their third visitor from London, Geoffrey Chaucer. Was he the kind of man to let his wife have her way? His remark at supper the previous evening about having a hen-pecked look was self-mocking, but there might be a grain of truth in it. For sure, Master Chaucer was intelligent enough to see that the wiser course was to let the woman have her head.

For many years now, after she'd moved into Semper when her daughter Agnes grew sick, Bridget had been accustomed to having her own way. She relished the dominant part which she'd boasted of to Geoffrey Chaucer. But ever since the doctor's remarriage – which she had not welcomed quite as much as she proclaimed – she had found herself consulted second and not first in domestic matters. This was because Richard Storey was so engrossed in his work and projects that he preferred to delegate household affairs to a woman, a situation that was in any case perfectly normal in households up and down the land. Bridget had been that woman but now – in deference to the master of the house and not on account of any command in the new wife – it was Sara to whom the servants turned.

To Sara's face, Bridget showed concern and kindness because she knew that the only way for her to retain any shreds of influence in Semper was to pretend affection, given the manner in which her son-in-law danced attendance on Sara's every whim. But she had been enraged by Sara's attack on Edgar. Her grandson should have had the spirit to defend himself or ignore Sara altogether, but Bridget could understand how exasperated he had grown with the young wife's accusations of poisoning and murder. Of a dog, for God's sake! Edgar did not have a great deal of stomach, true, and Bridget enjoyed shocking him sometimes with her ribald comments about men and other matters. But in this instance Edgar wasn't altogether to blame. It was the young wife's rash words which had driven her grandson from the house, and Bridget would not quickly forgive her. In fact, life in Semper would be better in certain respects if Sara was elsewhere . . .

She was alerted from her reverie by a soft scraping. At first she imagined it was a mouse behind the wainscot but then realized it was someone at the door. Her next thought was that it might be Edgar, sneaking back into the house, but when she opened the door a crack she saw Sara Storey standing there, her hand uncertainly poised to scratch again. There were marks of strain in the young woman's expression. Like Bridget, Sara was not dressed for bed. Mistress Salt adapted her best face and looked a query.

'I hope I am not disturbing you. I saw your light was still burning. Can I come in?'

Every sentence seemed to cost Sara an effort. Bridget stood aside to let her enter. She glanced into the passage as she closed the door but, by the uncertain light, she did not notice Juliana Barton in the shadows at the far end.

'What is the matter, Sara?'

The young woman, pale as a ghost in her white garb, stood alternately wringing her hands and grasping at the cross which hung about her neck but saying nothing.

'Where is your husband?' said Bridget, putting kindness into her tone and thinking that if the girl couldn't say what was wrong she might at least respond to a straightforward question.

'I don't know,' Sara said haplessly. 'I fell asleep and he was gone when I awoke just now. I expect he is in his office. He often works there through the night.'

More fool him, thought Bridget, to leave his bed when it is equipped with a fresh young wife, although she was aware of Richard Storey's habits of reading and working late. Well, that was sometimes best for man and wife, each to their own realm.

'What is the matter then?' the widow repeated.

'Someone is trying to kill me,' she said.

In the doctor's office the dead sailor from Genoa lay under his sheet on the trestle table. Giovanni's face was covered now but his nose stuck up like the prow of a little ship. He was by no means alone in death. The doctor's assistant and cousin, Alfred Portman, was sitting on a stool at a smaller table positioned beneath the high window, as if he was a paid watcher over the corpse. But Portman had his back to the body and his mind was elsewhere. Rain beat at the panes and the wind gusted outside. The assistant seemed oblivious to all this although at one point he heard a different sound, not the pattering of rain or the gusting wind, and he lifted his head. He glanced over his shoulder at the shrouded shape. Satisfied that it was merely the house settling down for the night, Portman went back to his task. He was in his usual posture, but crouching forward over a book rather than a pile of herbs or seeds. Portman was a great reader, with a knowlege of several tongues. He could understand even the Genoese ship-master's guttural dialect. A single candle burned on his right-hand side. The script in the book was small and Portman had to bring his spectacled face almost within grazing distance of the page to make out the words. Unhurriedly he brushed his finger along the lines until he found the point he was looking for. When he reached it, he read the passage over several times, mouthing the words silently and nodding slightly to himself.

He shut the volume and returned it to its place among the other leech-books on the shelf. Then he picked up the candle and ran the light along other shelves which contained a selection of jars and pots and vials. Here were plant roots and feathery tendrils suspended in thick amber liquid, or fragments of animal skin with fur or bristle still attached, items such as desiccated toads' legs and bats' wings. Portman found the earthenware pot he was searching for on a lower shelf. From it he removed a small leathern bag. The bag, like the pot, was plain, easy to disregard. You would have to know what you were looking for. Portman did know. Taking up a small mortar, he brought both items to the table. He set down the candle and wiped clean the inside of the mortar with a scrap of cloth. Portman's long fingers loosened the drawstrings to the bag and he tilted it over the bowl until a trickle of grains had filled the bottom. The grains were the pale colour of wood-ash. When this was done he made the bag fast again and returned it to the plain pot on the shelf. Back at the table once more, he bent over the mortar as if he intended to snuff up its contents. He took care not to touch the grains in the bottom. His entire attitude and the pains he'd taken in pouring them out, just so much and no more, suggested that he was dealing with a substance as valuable as gold dust.

Portman sighed slightly and rose from the stool. He went over to the body and folded the sheet away from the dead man's face. In the few hours since Giovanni's death, his features had sunk and his complexion, which had been an unhealthy green when he'd been brought in, had darkened. It would be necessary to remove the body from the office tomorrow and to do it early. Portman did not know whether the ship's master would wish to take him back across the water or see him buried in the grounds of Semper. Whatever happened to the man's remains was really no concern of his.

He nodded as he gazed at the other's face and said something. Accustomed to his own company, Portman perhaps talked more to himself than he did to anyone else. Now he spoke so softly that, even had there been a second living person in the room, his words would not have been audible. He retrieved the bowl from the smaller table and took up a smaller item which glinted in the candlelight. It was a small square of polished metal such as a woman might use to check her face-painting before she emerges from her chamber. Now he positioned the three objects – bowl, candle and metal square – on the trestle table close to the dead man's head. All of Alfred Portman's movements were precise, as if everything in life and death was to be measured out in small quantities. He put the square of metal close to Giovanni's nostrils and slack mouth. An observer might have thought that he was ascertaining whether the man was truly dead. The metal mirror did not go cloudy, of course, nor was Portman expecting that. For the second time some external noise apart from the rain and wind made him pause about his business. But it was nothing. Just the creaking of a house as it settled down for a short, stormy summer's night.

Juliana Barton was listening outside Bridget Salt's room. Something about the nervous, surreptitious way in which Sara had knocked on the door had whetted her interest. But she was able to pick up no more than a few stray words, even if two of those words were 'kill me'. At once she heard light footsteps coming towards the door, and she retreated a few paces into the gloom of the passage.

But she didn't move far or fast enough. Sara Storey emerged and stared straight at Juliana. She seemed confused but gathered herself with an effort and said, 'What are you doing here, Mistress Barton?'

'I couldn't sleep,' said that lady, accurately enough.

'I must return the brooch to you,' said Sara. She fumbled uncertainly in her placket and produced the brooch. She held it out to Juliana. The brooch had a long pin, and Sara seemed to be flourishing it like a tiny knife.

'It was a gift, my dear.'

'I do not want your gifts.'

'But it is inscribed with a saying.'

'I saw it. *Amor vincit omnia*, it says.'

'Love conquers all,' said Juliana.

'I know what it means,' said Sara, continuing to hold out the brooch. 'Take it. You meant to insult me just as you have insulted me in the past. You imply that I married my husband not for love but for money and position.'

Now Juliana Barton had not really intended anything by the gift, or at least no such ironic message. But she saw how over-wrought Sara Storey was, and inclined to misread every gesture. She put out a placating hand but Sara misunderstood this too and dropped the brooch into her palm. Automatically, Juliana closed her hand about the brooch.

'What are you doing in our house with William Bailey?' said Sara, not content with one tiny victory. 'Does his wife know that he is here?'

Juliana was taken aback and, before she could come up with a reply, Sara said, 'Husbands should not deceive their wives.'

Something about the young woman's priggish manner began to irritate Mistress Barton and she said, 'I suppose you're proposing to tell Mistress Bailey, are you? The good Constance would be glad to hear.'

Sara stood indecisively, hands fluttering over her chest. Then she turned about and walked off in the direction of her quarters. Juliana Barton stared after her. The pin of the brooch had pricked her closed hand and added to her discomfort and irritation. She did not think that Sara would go telling tales but, if she did, it might prove awkward for her and William . . .

'His nephew? My God, Geoffrey, I didn't know,' said Alan Audley.

'None of us knew. Why should we? Though he did call him *mio figlio* on the quayside this morning.'

'My son?'

'It was his affectionate way of referring to Giovanni – affectionate and perhaps a touch mocking.'

'But wait a minute, Geoffrey, he didn't exactly show much care or concern for this nephew of his, did he? The ship's master, who's supposed to be his uncle, ducked him in the harbour where he might have drowned. And then when Giovanni caught a chill which turned into a fever, Cavallo didn't seem too bothered about it.'

'Probably because he thought it was nothing worse wrong than a slight fever. The master of a ship must be used to seeing his men sick and ailing. He's most likely buried a fair few over the side in his time. I don't suppose he really meant to drown the man in Dartmouth harbour either, but merely to shake him up. He was angry because the cargo was gone. He's a man who acts on impulse. And you're right, from the way Cavallo was talking this morning he did not appear too concerned about Giovanni.'

'In fact it was the doctor of physic who demanded that Giovanni be brought across here for treatment,' said Alan. 'Master Richard Storey showed more tenderness for the crewman than his own uncle.'

'That may be the very reason why Cavallo is angry,' said Geoffrey. 'He feels guilty. He started the sequence of events which have led to this unfortunate death.'

'An accident though?'

'An accident,' echoed Geoffrey. Then he remembered something he'd intended to say to Alan. 'You did well this morning in the warehouse. I wouldn't have seen what your eyes saw, nor would I have come so quickly to your conclusions. There is some trickery there.'

'But what?'

'I don't know yet.'

'We shall find out,' said Alan, then he yawned as if to disguise his pleasure at Chaucer's compliment.

It was later the same evening of Giovanni's death. Geoffrey Chaucer and Alan Audley were in the apartment which had been set aside for their use in Semper House. Both men were lying in the security of their beds, which were canopied. Ned Caton was not present. He was keeping company with Alice Storey, no doubt, as he had on the previous evening. A bed had been set aside for him and he'd been slumbering in it that morning, but Chaucer had no idea at what time of the previous night he'd crept into their shared chamber.

'There is more, Geoffrey. I have found out something of interest although I don't know where it leaves us.'

Obviously this process of investigation had its attractions for Alan.

'Tell me.'

'I have been talking with Alice Storey. She is a woman of spirit and intelligence – beautiful too. Edward Caton is a lucky man. Alice was telling me about her father's recent wife. You know that her parents have lately died and that they left her quite unprovided for.'

'Her father was a shopkeeper in Dartmouth, wasn't he, and died in debt?'

'Yes. She has no family or resources. There were not many paths open to her. Apparently she'd always given herself airs. Too good for the locals and so on. The whole family in fact. That is why there was little sorrow at her parents' death or for the way she was left.'

'Well, if she wasn't to marry then she might have taken the veil,' said Geoffrey. 'Shut herself up behind the walls of a convent.'

'There is a kind of piety in her perhaps. She is shy and easily startled and such women are not always equipped for the hurly-burly of the world.'

'Be careful, Alan. You're sounding wise, older than your years. Someone said that to me recently. It was like an accusation.'

'But there was a third course of life,' said Audley, undeterred. 'Sara is also attractive . . . and refined. It seems that she was approached by Mistress Barton to make up the numbers of her women.'

'Those who live by the prick of their needles in Sheep Street?'

'Just so.'

'I can't believe this was a serious suggestion – that Sara should become one of the shorn lambs?'

'I don't know. It may have been no more than a casual comment intended to wound. On the other hand, there's no denying that women like Mistress Barton are always on the lookout for new flesh, especially if it is young and fair and well bred. Or so I've been told.'

Geoffrey was surprised, almost shocked. The idea of Sara Storey in a house of ill-fame was incongruous. Yet, as Alan said, it was true that many madams would pride themselves on having a girl who was a cut or two above the run of her stable. It was good for trade, no less, no more.

'That would explain the bad feeling between Barton and Richard Storey,' he said. It also explained the madam's snide comments about the doctor's new wife and the latter's flinching response in the dining hall.

'How does Alice Storey know of this? Did Sara tell her?'

'They had a heart-to-heart talk one day. Sara was expressing her gratitude to Alice's father. The story of Mistress Barton's approach came out then. Perhaps Sara considered she could confide in Alice because there is little difference in their ages. Alice hardly troubles to conceal her feelings for Sara. Nevertheless she can feel for the woman's plight even if she does not like her.'

'So Richard Storey turned up like a knight in shining armour to rescue the girl from the clutches of Juliana Barton.'

'That is a poetic way of seeing things, Geoffrey.'

Satisfied with the information he'd given, Alan Audley now tugged at the curtain which hung from the canopy over his bed as a signal that he at least intended to sleep rather than talk further.

In the doctor's office, Alfred Portman had finished his business. He pulled up the sheet once more over the dead man's face. He emptied the contents of the little mortar or bowl into a jar, and tucked it out of sight behind some larger items on a shelf. He was about to snuff the candle when the door opened. It was Richard Storey. The doctor of physic did not seem surprised to see his assistant but in a better light Storey might have detected some trace of unease or guilt on the other's expression.

'Still at work, Alfred?'

'As you see, cousin. Your wife asked me to make up a pre-paration for her.'

'I thought you had already done that.'

'I have, but I was looking for ways to refine it.'

'Very commendable of you, Alfred.'

'I have finished now.'

'Leave the light burning. I have things to do.'

Portman inclined his head slightly and slipped through the door which Storey held open for him. When the man had gone, the physician moved towards the trestle table bearing the corpse. He reached out his hand as if he too would examine Giovanni but at the last moment he paused. Instead he lowered his head and mouthed some words. Geoffrey Chaucer, who'd come to the conclusion that the doctor was probably an atheist, would have been surprised to know that he was uttering a prayer.

There was one further conversation in Semper House during the early part of that night. It was between the doctor's man, Griffin, and the mayor's man, Francis. Griffin had just returned from the stable, where he had taken some pleasure in showing the Genoese sailor Marco his bed amid the straw and dung and dirt. But the shipman was so pissed that he would have dropped down in a sty and, if Griffin had been intending the foreigner to know his proper place, the mild insult was lost.

One of Griffin's tasks was to make the house tight and safe when darkness fell. He carried a bunch of keys and a lantern as if they were badges of office. He encountered Francis near the kitchen. The soft glow of a fire, banked up for the night, emanated from the partly open door of the kitchen together with old food smells and the sounds of clattering pans. One of the women was still at work, clearing up. It was probably Bessy, a slatternly girl in Griffin's view who made a habit of showing a good deal of tit. Judging by the way the mayor's man was using his sleeve to wipe grease and crumbs from his mouth, he'd been scavenging among the supper remains and sniffing round Bessy too, most like. Francis was a slight, ratlike figure but Griffin knew for a fact that the fellow stuffed his face whenever he got the chance. Taking after his fat employer, no doubt, and it was a wonder that he hadn't swelled to Bailey's size.

'You should be abed, Francis,' he said. 'Your fellow John is tucked up by now. And your master too.'

Francis didn't answer, which irritated Griffin. And, thinking of the mayor, he remembered he had a bone to pick with Francis.

'What's that Barton woman doing here?'

'What's it to you?' said Francis, unpicking a shred of meat from between his teeth. He examined it before flicking it to the floor.

'My master doesn't like her.'

'But mine does.'

'We all know about Bailey and Barton. I hope they are not planning anything naughty under this roof.'

'They are grown man and woman. It is no business of yours what they get up to, Griffin.'

'I've quartered *Mistress* Barton with the servants and that is better than she deserves.'

Griffin shook his keys for emphasis and so Francis said, 'Locked her in, have you?'

'I should have done. The woman is rampant,' said Griffin.

'Trouble is she just hasn't ramped in your direction, eh, Griffin,' said Francis, turning his head very slightly and spitting some further fragments of food on to the floor.

'Be careful, Francis. I could tell one or two things about you to William Bailey.'

The remark did not seem to unsettle Francis. He said, 'You point the finger at me and I'll weave the noose will hang us both. Where is my reward?'

'The matter is not yet concluded,' said Griffin.

'Oh, the matter is not yet concluded,' Francis echoed, putting on a fluting tone. 'You talk very fine, Griffin. It must be the clever and learned company you keep in this house. We had a bargain, you and me. I did my part. Where's my payment?'

The argument might have gone further but suddenly a face appeared round the kitchen door, alerted by the raised voices. It was Bessy. By the light of the lantern, Griffin saw a half-smile on her face. The smile was directed at Francis. 'Oh, 'tis you,' she said to him. 'Not abed yet, Frankie?' She emerged more fully and smeared her damp, smudged hands down her front, taking care that the exposed upper part of her breasts caught the light. For sure, Francis had been sniffing around and warming himself by more than the kitchen fire.

'Get back to your work, Bessy,' said Griffin.

The woman opened her mouth to say something, saw the expression on his face and disappeared again.

'We will talk of this in private,' said Griffin. 'Later.'

'Oh, we'll talk, all right,' said Francis, removing a final fragment of food from his uneven teeth.

'Do not threaten me,' said Griffin. 'I have friends outside. *We* have friends outside, I should say, since you're up to your neck in this. They are only waiting. One word from me and they would send you into a place darker than the night.'

'I am not frightened of you – or them,' said Francis. But his tone indicated otherwise.

12

It was dark inside the chamber where Geoffrey Chaucer and Alan Audley were lodged, and darker still beyond the chamber windows. Rain beat at the glass and the wind sent cold draughts down the chimney. Geoffrey tried to read by the flickering light of a candle placed in a recess in the headboard. He was cradling a volume of Dante's *Inferno*, given him as a gift on his recent journey to Florence. It was a precious volume, and one that had played an odd part in solving a murder mystery. But the fine, ornamental script blurred before his eyes. His head was awkwardly angled on the pillow propped up against the headboard, yet he could not be bothered to make himself more comfortable. He abandoned the attempt on Dante. In any case, his mind was not on the travails of hell.

Geoffrey adjusted the curtain round his bed, placed Dante in the recess behind his head, extinguished the candle and lay down to sleep. But the moment he did this he became alert and wakeful. In his mind he went over the events which had occurred since their arrival at Semper, and beforehand if he included the attack on the upland above the estuary. Was that connected to his business in Dartmouth? A violent assault to stop him and his companions ever reaching Semper House? If so, he could only be thankful for the intervention of Richard Storey. If the doctor of physic hadn't arrived in time then he, Geoffrey, and Alan and Ned would surely be dead at the hands of the axemen.

They'd survived the attack but the incident seemed like a harbinger of worse things to come.

Chaucer recalled the way in which the supper hours had twice been interrupted by the news of a death, first of Millicent, Sara Storey's little dog, and then of Giovanni, nephew to Pietro Cavallo. He thought of the strange scene outside Bailey's warehouse that morning, the instinctive hostility between Richard Storey and Juliana Barton, the righteous anger of the madam when she was defending the good name of the mayor. That hostility was not so strange now that he'd heard Alan's account. Was the gift of the brooch which Chaucer had observed Mistress Barton making in the dining hall a peace offering?

It was all very odd. Just as odd perhaps was the way in which the former antagonism between Cavallo and Bailey seemed to have been dissolved by a few glasses of wine. Neither man was now accusing the other of thieving the alum. What had happened to make them change their tune? Cavallo no longer appeared very troubled by the disappearance of his cargo, but perhaps that was natural given that he expected the English treasury to make good his losses. He was probably more concerned now with the death of his nephew than with any theft from the warehouse. Chaucer thought of Alan Audley's discovery of how access might have been gained to Bailey's depot. Was that proof that the crime had been committed by an outsider? Yet, as he'd said to Alan, someone would surely have been required to secure the bar and pegs again from the inside.

Geoffrey got no further in these speculations, which were anyway going round in futile circles. He must have fallen asleep because the next thing he knew was a confused awakening from a dream in which he was being pursued by a screaming man whirling an axe about his head. The axe . . . hadn't Alan taken one of the axes as some kind of memento? No, it wasn't an axe but the club, the vicious woman's club. He must ask him what he'd done with it. He sat up in bed, sweaty, heart banging.

He looked around. For some reason he expected to see the glimmer of daylight through a gap in the curtains which surrounded his bed. But it was pitch dark. He wiped at his soaking forehead and plucked his nightgown from where it had stuck to his back and under his arms. Outside, the wind still gusted but sounding slightly abated. A dog was barking in the distance. He lay back down again and fell asleep within moments.

When next he awoke it was indeed nearer to day. A watery light poked between the bed-curtains. Needing to relieve himself in the jordan which was in the corner of the room, Geoffrey swung himself out of bed and padded on bare feet across the boards. He noted that Ned Caton had returned to his friends at some time during the night. The young man hadn't bothered to draw his own curtains or even change into night-gear but lay sprawled across his bed, face down and dead to the world. For sure, he had been up half the night with Alice Storey and needed his rest now. Alan Audley too was sound asleep, judging by the gentle snoring which emanated from his bed.

Geoffrey made his way towards the window near which the chamber-pot was placed, perhaps so as to give any gentleman relieving himself the pleasure of a view. Outside was no summer's morning. The rain had ceased but clouds hung so low in the sky that they seemed to be brushing against the house. Without a thought in his head, Geoffrey gazed out. What he saw caused him to forget the need to make water. Below him stretched the descending terraces of the Semper grounds, intermittently glimpsed. Beyond was the invisible river. Immediately below and to his right was the enclosed area which contained the herb garden behind the box hedge. He could see the wicket gate. It was shut. Because of the angle from which he was gazing down, Geoffrey could see only a segment of the garden, the part of it further away from him, with the varied greens of the herbal beds and the pale tracks of the paths which threaded between them. In the centre was the diminutive head and shoulders of Aesculapius. Through some trick of the light and the mist, the head seemed to be floating in the air. But it was not any of this which took Geoffrey's attention.

There was a figure moving in the garden. It was dressed in white. Geoffrey caught his breath. He rubbed the sleep from his eyes and wiped at the window glass. The panes of glass were thick and irregular, causing little distortions in the view. The figure, slight and bare-headed, was pacing to and fro in the central area near the bust, now coming into view, now obscured by the dark wall of box. It was a woman. Chaucer was fairly certain that it was Sara Storey. For a moment he wondered whether she was still grieving over the death of her dog for there was something distracted in her movements, something that suggested she was not altogether conscious of her surroundings. Then a swathe of cloud or mist descended and the view beyond the window turned greyish-white. Geoffrey remembered what he was about. He relieved himself in the jordan. No reason, he told himself, why the mistress of Semper House should not be walking in the grounds early in the morning. Yet it was very early in the morning, and hardly for a person's health that she should be drawing in the damp vapours of the dawn, going out without a hat and dressed to all appearances in her night-gear. Did her husband know she was outside? Sara was a delicate creature. The doctor of physic surely wouldn't approve.

Geoffrey looked out again. The mist or cloud lifted, or rather a corner of it did, as if someone was turning the page in a book. Once more the herb garden was revealed, the neat green beds, the gravel paths, the floating stone head. But Sara – if it had been Sara – was no longer in sight. Obscurely glad that he could no longer see her, Geoffrey made to turn away from the window. Then stopped. Another figure, a different one, had suddenly materialized in the garden, a figure moving down one of the paths, moving quickly and purposefully. So quickly that all he could be certain of was that this one was dressed in darker clothes. Geoffrey leant closer to the window, resting a hand on the cold, clammy stone of the surround. His breath fogged the glass and he wiped at it. Once again, there was nothing to be seen except the bare paths and verdant beds. If anything was happening down there it was happening out of sight, behind the stockade of the box hedge. Fearing that something was wrong, Geoffrey fumbled with the window catch. It opened with a creak. A damp, unwholesome blast of air buffeted his face. He leaned out. He listened. But there was no sound at all, no birds singing, no dogs barking, no human sounds. Then, for the second and last time, the mist swept across like a curtain and the whole scene was reduced to its hazy outlines.

Geoffrey stayed by the open window but with no idea what he was expecting. He jumped at a voice behind his back.

'For God's sake, close the window. It's cold.'

It was Alan, his voice muffled by sleep. He had the bed nearest the window and was peering through the canopy, blinking in Chaucer's direction.

'What is it, Geoffrey? What are you doing?'

'Nothing. Go back to sleep.'

'God's sake, close the window,' said Alan again, falling back on his bed. Geoffrey fastened the window and returned to his own bed. He left a gap in the curtains but pulled the covers about himself. He too was cold and not entirely from the draught of morning air. It took him some time to compose himself. What had he seen exactly? A woman dressed in white who might have been Sara Storey. Another figure whose identity was unknown. Man or woman, he could not even be sure which, the glimpse had been so quick. All that he was sure of was that whereas the woman had been moving in a dithering, distracted fashion, the second person had been acting with a purpose. Why? What were two people doing in the herb garden at some God-forsaken hour of a summer's morning?

Maybe he'd imagined it, he told himself. The light outside was poor, the view of the garden obscured by mist. His sight was not so good these days, even in the clearest conditions. Maybe it was a dream, like his earlier vision of being pursued by a man whirling an axe. But Geoffrey knew the difference between being awake and asleep. He knew what he'd seen. He feared the worst, yet was unable to say exactly what he feared.

Despite this, he fell into a deep sleep and woke refreshed. It was two or three hours later. The sun was bright outside and the sky a buoyant blue. For a moment, he forgot where he was and imagined himself back in London. Then he looked about him. Ned Caton was still slumbering, fully dressed but on his back now. Alan's bed was empty. There were sounds from around the house. Now the birds were singing and the dogs barking. What should he say if Alan asked him what he was doing hanging out the window in the misty hour of dawn? But Audley had been half asleep. Geoffrey decided to say nothing. He would not ask Sara Storey why she was taking an early morning stroll and he certainly would not mention it to her husband either.

Then he became aware once more of the sounds from downstairs. This was only the second morning he'd awoken in Semper House, yet there seemed something out of place about the noises. Birds sang and dogs barked, yes, but otherwise there were lengthy periods of silence followed by bursts of running feet. The easy mood in which he'd risen from sleep at once evaporated. He swung out of bed at the same instant that the door to the chamber burst open. It was Alan Audley. His face was pale, his black curls more disordered than usual.

'It is terrible, Geoffrey, terrible!'

He was almost shouting. Ned Caton stirred.

'Quiet yourself, Alan. What is terrible?'

'Sara Storey is dead.'

'What? Who's dead?' said Ned, struggling to wakefulness.

'She has been murdered down there,' said Alan, gesturing towards the window. Geoffrey said nothing but Alan's news, shocking as it was, did not somehow come as a surprise. What else except a terrible thing could have occurred? It was what the visions of the night, the sleeping and waking visions, had told him.

Geoffrey returned to the spot where he'd gazed out at the cloudy dawn. This time the view was clear down the terraces and across the sparkling river. But his attention was fixed on the herb garden. In the central point, marked by the bust of Aesculapius, was a cluster of people, among whom he recognized some of the household. They were looking or pointing at something on the ground, hidden from Chaucer's view by the box hedge. The gate, which had been shut when he'd glimpsed the figure in the mist, was open. Even as he gazed, a couple of the servants ran along the path, slipped through the gate and disappeared behind the hedge. Ned Caton came up behind him to look out. He grasped at Geoffrey's shoulder.

'Sara? You are sure it is Sara?'

The question was directed at Alan Audley. He said, 'I have seen her, seen her where she lies. And next to her – '

Alan never finished what he was about to say for Ned uttered some incoherent exclamation. Then, at a run, he left the chamber. Chaucer turned back to Audley, standing uncertain in the middle of the room.

'There is nothing we can do down there at the moment. Enough people are chasing to and fro. Compose yourself, Alan, and tell me what you have found out.'

'You are very composed yourself, Geoffrey. You are still in your night-gear. How can you be so calm? Wait a minute. I remember now. I woke up as it was getting light. You were standing by the window just as you are standing now. Except that it was open and the cold air was coming in and you were looking out. What did you see? You saw something, didn't you?'

'I saw something.'

'What?'

'I'm not quite sure what I saw. Tell me all you know first.'

Geoffrey pulled on his leggings and replaced his nightgown with a shirt. He considered putting on a doublet but then thought that the day would be warm whatever horrors awaited them. He fussed about his clothes, giving Alan time to gather his wits, giving himself a distraction from the dreadful news. Which Alan now proceeded to deliver. Audley had pieced together the story from the garbled account of several servants. Perhaps it was Chaucer's influence which caused him to tell it in a relatively ordered fashion.

Alfred Portman had discovered the body of Sara Storey. He was accustomed to rise early, since this was the best time to gather herbs for his remedies and concoctions. (It is well known that plants are at their most vigorous and efficacious in the hours following sunrise.) In fact, on this morning he had not gone to the herb garden as early as usual since he had been working late on the previous evening. When he did, he was surprised to discover that the wicket gate was open. He entered and found the mistress of the house lying face down near the centre of the garden. She had been savagely beaten about the head. At this point, Alan paused. The whiteness of his countenance had been replaced with a flushed look.

'This is the worst part, Geoffrey. One of the worst parts.'

'Worst? Worse than a corpse?'

'No, I do not mean that. But it is bad enough. I recognized the weapon which was used to kill poor Sara . . . it was lying next to her body . . . '

He faltered, yet Chaucer knew what he was going to say before he continued.

' . . . it was the club which I took from the ground the day before yesterday, the one wielded by that woman on the upland.'

194

'You're sure?'

'Yes. Not that I picked it up for a careful look. It was stained with blood.'

He shuddered. Chaucer repeated, 'You are sure, Alan?'

'Yes, the haft had been whittled and shaped in a certain way, to fit snugly into a woman's hand. I remember noticing that when I picked it up.'

A chill came over Chaucer. He thought of the nut-brown woman lovingly chipping away at the handle of the weapon so she could use it to better effect.

'God's bones, man. I wondered why you'd taken it in the first place.'

'I don't know, Geoffrey. I didn't know what I was doing after the attack either. Perhaps I took it to stop her getting her hands on it again. She was worse than the men, that woman. There was a look in her eye that I've never seen in a man's. They shouted and they whirled their axes about but she would have battered us to death without a word.'

'Very well. But what did you do with the club afterwards?'

'I forgot about it, to be honest. I fastened it to my saddle-pack, then when we arrived here our horses were taken off for stabling, and it slipped my mind.'

'Griffin brought our bags in later while we were standing in the hall.'

'He didn't bring the club though. He must have left it in the stables. As I said, I forgot about it.'

'No doubt he thought you'd hardly need to defend yourself from attacks inside Semper House,' said Geoffrey.

'Semper is a dangerous place,' said Alan. 'People are dying on every hand. Animals too. They are dying. That little dog of Sara's.'

After a quiet beginning, there was a hectic quality to Alan's words. Chaucer tried to calm him.

'You cannot be blamed for the death of Sara Storey, Alan. I know you were sleeping tight in your bed when all this happened.

Someone found the weapon, either by chance or because they knew it was there in the stables. If we wanted to protect ourselves from violence, we'd have to lock up all knives and sticks and stones. And then we'd still have our fists.'

'Even so . . .'

'It might have been one of our ambushers, come back to try their luck again.'

There was a curious comfort in considering that Sara Storey might have been attacked by an outsider, one of the wild folk who haunted the woods. Yet, even as he spoke, Chaucer did not really believe his own words. Their assailants on the upland above the house were brutal and murderous but they weren't foolish. For one thing, the attackers had run away when they were outnumbered. They would hardly take the risk of entering a well-secured estate, would they?

'I do not blame myself, Geoffrey, though my guts did a dance to see that I had supplied the instrument which killed the poor woman. No, it is something else which troubles me. The finger of blame has already been pointed. When Alfred Portman went into the herb garden, the first thing he noticed wasn't the body on the ground but a man who was on the far side of the garden. When this man saw him he slipped off.'

'Through the gate?'

'No, Portman was standing near the gate, blocking the way. There are gaps at the base of the hedge. The man ducked down and wriggled through one of them. He got away.'

'Portman saw who it was?'

'His sight is not so good. He wears spectacles. At first he thought it was his master, Richard Storey, and was waiting to be greeted.'

That seemed characteristic of the soft-spoken and deferential cousin. Alfred Portman would not speak first but would indeed wait to be greeted. There was some odd reluctance in Alan Audley to say more and a reluctance in Geoffrey to press the point. Alan stood awkwardly in the centre of the chamber. Chaucer glanced out of the window again. Figures were still scurrying about the garden. Soon, he and Alan would have to go down there themselves. But it seemed important to get the story straight first and, in any case, Chaucer was in no hurry to visit the site of a murder.

'So it was not the doctor of physic in the garden?' he prompted.

'It was not Richard but *Edgar* Storey,' said Alan. 'Father and son are the same height so I suppose Portman mistook the one for the other. What was conclusive was that Portman saw Edgar's black dog, Hector, with him. The dog keeps company with no one else. It squeezed through the hedge after Edgar. Portman wondered why the son was in the herb garden and then he saw this terrible sight on the ground.'

Geoffrey sat on the edge of his bed. He felt a weight on his shoulders, as if someone was pressing him down.

'So it seems . . . it looks as though . . . Edgar Storey might have attacked his stepmother.'

'Why else would he run away?' said Alan.

'He had already run away, remember. He left the house yesterday after Sara accused him of poisoning her little dog. The question is why he came back. Yet his father predicted he wouldn't stay away. He said he wasn't suited for life in the wild.'

'He ran off when she called him a murderer. And now he may have become one. Do you think it is possible, Geoffrey? That a son should attack his mother – his stepmother?'

Anything's possible, Chaucer thought. Aloud he said, 'There was no love lost between Storey's children and their new mother. But it is still a distance from there to murder.'

'What did you see? You saw something when you were at the window this morning.'

Swiftly Chaucer outlined the scene which he'd witnessed when he'd got up to piss. The early mist, the view into the herb garden, the figure in white (which must have been Sara Storey). He hesitated before mentioning the black-clad shape but Alan had been frank with him and he owed his friend no less than a complete account. Nevertheless he stressed his indifferent eyesight, the cloudiness of the weather, the fleeting glimpse only. He added that he had seen Edgar Storey on the previous evening, skulking among the trees as the storm was rising. A man and a black dog taking shelter. Perhaps the son was so consumed with rage and bitterness that he'd never left the grounds of Semper but brooded all night and then, when light began to dawn, crept back to the herb garden where he'd encountered the woman who'd accused him of murdering her little dog . . . another argument had ensued . . . Edgar had equipped himself with the club, had . . .

'So it was him?' said Alan Audley.

'Who?'

'It was Edgar Storey you saw down there this morning as well.'

'I do not know even whether it was a man or a woman. It was someone in a black mantle, is all I can say. Do not repeat my story to anyone else, Alan. We must be careful how we proceed. As you say, this is a dangerous place.'

'If it *was* Edgar you saw in the garden, then he must have hung about there for some time – an hour or more. Why would he be doing that?'

Chaucer was pleased to see Alan using his powers of reason again. The more calm heads in such a situation, the better.

'A murderer may haunt the scene of his crime, I suppose,' he said. 'Perhaps he was turned to stone by what he'd done. When Alfred Portman entered the garden, he came back to life. Or it might be that Edgar was the one who'd first discovered the body and he fled by instinct, fearing to be accused.'

'Then his fears are justified, since he is accused by the household whisperers.'

There seemed no more to say so the two of them left the chamber and made their way through the house where everything was silent. Out of doors a glorious summer morning lay all about them, as if in mockery of the human drama. On the other side of Semper, where the terraces stretched down to the river, were clusters of people, conferring with their heads together or standing in silence. Among them Chaucer saw Pietro Cavallo and William Bailey, together with Juliana Barton. In addition was the Italian sailor who had crossed the river yesterday evening with his master, and John and Francis, Bailey's men. On these latter faces there seemed to be no more than curiosity. This was not their business, although it would make an interesting tale to tell later in the taverns of Dartmouth or Genoa. Ned Caton and Alice Storey stood by themselves, Ned with his arm around the doctor's daughter. The girl's expression was impassive. Chaucer wondered what must be going through her head, with a stepmother dead and a brother fled in panic from the scene.

Among the people were scattered some of the household dogs. They sat or lay in the morning sun, undisturbed but not inclined to play. Then all attention was turned towards the entrance to the herb garden. Through the narrow wicket gate shuffled a little procession. First came Richard Storey, accompanied by Bridget Salt. She had been weeping and her colour was high. The doctor of physic walked stiffly and his face was a pale, unseeing mask. After a moment came a makeshift stretcher borne by Griffin in the lead and the bespectacled Alfred Portman at the rear. On the stretcher was a sheet covering a body. The shape beneath was slight, hardly seeming to disturb the concealing sheet. Both men had their heads down and moved as if they were bearing a heavy burden, although in truth Sara had been a light, almost frail thing.

As the party drew level to where Geoffrey Chaucer and Alan Audley were standing, the sheet slipped and the head and shoulders of the corpse were revealed. Someone gasped and a woman's sigh carried through the still air. Sara's head was angled away from Chaucer. She was bare-headed and her fair hair was blotched with gouts of blood which had crusted and grown dark. There were plentiful marks of blood too on her white gown. Alfred Portman, with an instinctive quickness and delicacy which was surprising, leaned forward and draped the sheet over the face of the corpse once again. Chaucer was reminded of the way he'd attended to the corpse of Giovanni the previous evening. Griffin looked up and caught Chaucer's eye, then his squinty gaze flicked sideways to Alan Audley. Richard Storey and Bridget Salt, who were several yards ahead, did not look round but continued their slow progress towards the house.

Geoffrey thought this was the same garb which Sara had been wearing when they arrived at Semper House less than forty-eight hours ago (although it felt as if weeks had passed since then). More important, this glimpse of white seemed to confirm that the figure he'd seen from his window in the early hours had indeed been the doctor's wife. He'd taken it for nightclothes but he had been wrong. And, more important still, the fact that she was dressed for the day rather than for bed at the time she'd been murdered was significant – even if Chaucer couldn't see why yet. There was something else about the body, the head and shoulders, which nagged at him but he could not run it to earth.

He thought these thoughts about the bloodstained dress and other matters in an attempt to master the sharp pang of sorrow which ran through him at the sight of the woman. He'd hardly known Sara Storey, but the vision of her battered head and bloody shoulders as she lay on the stretcher shook him. He'd seen enough violent death on the battlefield and elsewhere, but here in a domestic setting it felt wrong, it felt out of place. The skull was so thin and the life was so easily taken. The woman was so young, so recently married and with her life extending before her. He recalled that she was without parents, perhaps the last of her line. He crossed himself and uttered a silent prayer for her soul. Geoffrey Chaucer resolved that, if he could assist in tracking down her murderer, then he would do his utmost. Beside him, Alan Audley muttered some words under his breath, something between a prayer and an exclamation, and Geoffrey knew by instinct that his companion had the same feelings.

The party with the body disappeared round the corner of the house. There was an extended pause, as if no one was certain what to do next, whether to return indoors or to resume the broken business of the day. Then came a cry from one of the groups on the grassy terrace. The cry came from William Bailey's man, Francis. He was pointing down towards the river. Everybody crowded to the edge. About halfway down the slopes and under the shadow of some trees was a man with a dog, a black dog. It was Edgar Storey. He was standing stock still, looking up at them. He had his hands on his hips. Chaucer saw he was wearing a dark mantle.

What followed might have been comic, in other circumstances. The individuals on the bank, the mayor and his men together with Juliana Barton, Cavallo the ship's master and *his* man, and many of the Semper House servants, scrambled down the slope in pursuit of Edgar Storey. Several of them were so eager that they slithered or tumbled on the grass. The dogs joined in the chase, their yapping the only sound. Chaucer had seen a similar reaction in men who are at last committed to battle after a period of suspense, a mad scampering towards action. He might have feared for the bodily safety of Edgar Storey if the young man had put up a fight or tried to run once more. It mattered little that those dashing towards their prey had hardly known Sara Storey (or liked her very much). Their blood was up. There was a murderer – a supposed murderer – to be hunted down.

Fortunately, young Storey stood quite unmoving. Chaucer put a restraining hand on Alan Audley's arm, as if to say that this was not their immediate business, best leave it to the others, and watched as the pursuers reached the shade of the trees. They fanned out around Edgar Storey and his hound, which barked at his yapping fellows but, like his master, made no move to get away. Instead Edgar gestured upwards and started to climb the slope, accompanied by Hector, with the escort forming a loose ring about them as they went.

'He's giving himself up,' said Alan softly. 'That is not the behaviour of a guilty man.'

Chaucer wasn't so sure but he said nothing. The only people remaining on the upper bank were Ned Caton and Alice Storey, together with some of the older women of the household. Everyone's attention was fixed on the spectacle of Edgar Storey climbing up the terraces with a loose-limbed stride. Geoffrey was aware of a movement in the corner of his eye. He turned. The doctor of physic was standing a few paces off. His face remained masklike but he was clenching and unclenching the hands which hung rigidly at his side. He must have been alerted by the cries of the dogs, or perhaps someone had run into the house to tell him that his son had been found.

It only took a couple of minutes for Edgar to reach their level, although it seemed much longer. The young man had outpaced his pursuers who were climbing the slopes in varying states of breathlessness. Richard Storey stared at his son but said not a word. Edgar tried to meet his eye but he was not equal to the intensity of his father's gaze. He hung his head. His clothing was creased and stained, not surprising since he had spent a stormy night out in the open. There might have been blood on his black mantle but it was impossible to tell without a closer examination. There could be no doubt, however, about the streaks of blood on his face or (Chaucer noticed, looking down) on his hands which, in an odd imitation of his father, were curling into fists and then uncurling again. The two men might have been separated by a generation but there was a mirror effect in their postures, their shared height, and the queer, rhythmic movement of their hands. Hector looked uneasily from father to son, his tail lowered. Chaucer glanced at the dog then gazed more carefully. With horror he observed too that the dog had blood on his muzzle. It reminded him of the dog by the hut on the upland, and he recalled Sara's accusation that Hector had killed her pet Millicent.

Now Griffin and Portman appeared, having stowed Sara's body inside the house. The squint-eyed Griffin came to stand near his master while Alfred Portman took up a position a little behind Storey. Geoffrey wondered whether they were there to protect the doctor from an attack by his own son, a reasonable fear given what had occurred, maybe. No one spoke. By this time most of the pursuing party had returned to the terrace. William Bailey, red-faced and short of breath, approached Storey and drew him to one side. Eventually he recovered himself sufficiently to deliver a few soft sentences. As mayor of the town over the water, he possessed some authority in this situation. Storey had to bend his head to listen. He nodded and in turn said something quiet to Griffin and Portman. The doctor's cousin and assistant crossed over to where Edgar was standing. Portman was shorter than the son and had to look up into the other's face. His spectacles reflected the morning light.

'Will you come this way, master? For your own safety, will you come this way?' he said, his voice like the rustle of dry leaves but somehow carrying through the still air. With the same gentleness which he'd shown when replacing the make-shift shroud over Sara's face, he touched Edgar's arm and inclined his head in the direction of the house. Edgar, who had not said a word this whole time, walked off beside Portman. Hector, the dog with the bloody muzzle, trotted obediently at their heels. The son did not look at his father as he passed though Storey continued to fix him with an unrelenting stare.

When the group had gone out of sight round the corner of the house, William Bailey sought out Chaucer.

'I have told the doctor that he should keep his son secure while this matter is investigated. He must be kept under lock and key in case he tries to escape again. This is a difficult matter.'

'Of course it is,' said Chaucer.

'I mean that the doctor is accustomed to running things on this side of the water. He does not welcome the intervention of Justice Mortimer over here.'

'He'll have no choice,' said Chaucer. 'There is a fugitive from the law, a possible murderer.'

'Edgar is no fugitive,' said Alan Audley. 'He did not try to escape this time. He turned himself in.'

'This is a difficult matter,' repeated Bailey, paying no attention to Audley.

'You have done the right thing, William,' said Geoffrey.

'I am hoping to get your advice. Do you consider that this young man attacked and killed his stepmother?'

'It would appear so,' said Geoffrey.

'I have heard that there was an argument between him and the lady yesterday.'

'A family quarrel, no more,' said Alan Audley. 'Surely you're familiar with those, Master Bailey?'

'Nevertheless it must be taken into account,' said Geoffrey quickly. 'Everything must be taken into account.'

He saw that Alan's attempts to defend Edgar were having the wrong effect on the Dartmouth mayor, who had bridled at Audley's words. He observed also that Bailey's casual, robust manner had been replaced by a shrewd watchfulness. He recalled the man's brother, Harry Bailey, the innkeeper of the Tabard. Under the guise of good cheer which was so necessary to a tavern host, Harry too had a sharp mind.

William Bailey nodded at Geoffrey but pointedly ignored Alan. He went back to the group which consisted of Pietro Cavallo and Juliana Barton, and their attendants.

'Come on, Alan.'

'Where are we going?'

'To the herb garden.'

Geoffrey drew Alan off towards the open wicket gate, as much to distract him as anything else. Also, he was curious to examine the scene of the murder. Often quite minor details which could be revealing were overlooked. He'd had experience of this.

13

There was no one else in the garden. The air here was enclosed and scented with herbs. The smell was delicate but heady and, somehow, far removed from any human taint. Their feet crunching on the gravel walk, they made their way to the centre where stood the bust of Aesculapius. In the area immediately around the figure were patches of blood and the confused imprint of many feet. The morning sun had long since dried the blood and darkened it. Chaucer squatted down and poked at the gravel surface. He swivelled round and looked at the beds nearby as if they might yield up evidence. But he could see nothing beyond the luxuriant vegetation. He looked up at Alan.

'The club which was used to kill Sara, do you know what happened to it?'

'It was here earlier. Someone must have taken it.'

'It's not the kind of thing you'd want to leave lying around.'

'If only I had left it where I found it!'

Geoffrey straightened up and spoke firmly. 'I say again, Alan, do not blame yourself. The person set on murder will find the means. You've said nothing about the club to anyone?'

'No, not yet. But Griffin might remember that it was fastened to my saddle-bag when we arrived.'

Geoffrey thought of the way Griffin's sly gaze had slid on to Alan as he was bearing the stretcher. For sure, the doctor's servant was aware of who had brought the murder weapon into

207

the Semper estate. It would be better if Alan came clean about it now, before he was implicated in this death. He knew Alan had nothing to do with the murder, but rumours quickly took hold. He was about to say as much when they were interrupted by the arrival in the garden of Ned Caton and Alice Storey.

The couple halted opposite Geoffrey and Alan. Alice's face was determined. She glanced for a moment at the stains on the ground and a shudder passed through her frame.

'My brother Edgar did not do this deed,' she said.

'I do not think so either,' said Alan.

'It looks bad for your brother,' said Geoffrey, growing impatient with these assertions which ran against all the evidence.

'Listen to what Alice has to say, Geoffrey,' said Ned. His normally equable features showed the strain of what was happening. 'She has proof that Edgar is innocent. Listen to her.'

'Proof?'

'As good as proof.'

Geoffrey did not point out that proof was either proof or no such thing. Instead he waited for Alice's story.

She had, she said, seen her brother the previous night or rather in the early hours of the morning. Had seen and spoken with him. She and Edward had spent some time in conversation together in her apartment in Semper, well after midnight. (It was a measure of how serious the situation was, that none of them grinned or made a knowing remark at the reference to a 'conversation'.) Eventually Edward had left to return to the chamber which he shared with Alan and Geoffrey.

Alice had extinguished her candles and lain down to sleep. But, restless with thoughts of all that was happening in the household and the disappearance of Edgar, she had risen from her bed. Something had drawn her to the window. She looked out. The very first glimmers of dawn were showing, though all was cloudy and mist-shrouded. Her window was above the terrace, near the visitors' chamber. She had seen a figure standing there, gazing up. He saw her in turn. It was her brother. She'd hardly recognized him but he was accompanied by his dog Hector. Quickly she wrapped herself in a mantle, made her way through the dark and empty house, unbolted a side door and slipped round to the terrace.

There Edgar was waiting for her. He was in a terrible state, alternately angry and despondent, and shivering all the time. Alice urged him to return to the house. It was not for his health or hers that they should stay outside. He could not return, he said. He had been accused by that woman — he refused to utter the name of Sara — of killing her wretched dog. His father had taken his new wife's side, as usual. Everybody was against him. The whole world hated him. It took Alice a deal of time and effort to soothe him. For as long as she could remember, she'd had influence with her brother. Maybe it was to do with the absence of a mother. She, Alice, was older (and, thought Chaucer as he heard the measured way in which she told her story now, she was also calmer and wiser). He'd always listened to her in the past. Alice said that it was inevitable that their father should take Sara's part in any argument, and that in any case he'd had nothing to do with the accusations of poisoning a dog. She insisted that Sara had not been in her right mind when she charged Edgar with the deliberate death of little Millicent. She said that, by running away, Edgar had made it appear that he did indeed have something to hide. He must come back. The whole business would be forgotten by morning. (This was before the murder, of course.) Her brother was a good, kind man. He wouldn't hurt a fly.

'It is true, Master Chaucer, he would not. Why, I have seen him in tears before now over the death of a dog. He is not so different in that regard from poor Sara.'

'What did he say to all this?'

209

'He promised me he would return. He gave his word.'

'But Edgar didn't come back into the house straightaway – or did he?'

'No. I know that he did not come back.'

'So he preferred to stand shivering in the cold dawn?'

'He was on the point of coming indoors when that wretched hound of his was startled by something which it saw or heard. Hector dashed away into the dark, down the terraces. Edgar said that he must fetch Hector. He ran off in pursuit. I waited for several minutes more, growing colder and not liking being outside on my own at that time either. In the end, I gave up and went inside. I thought that since Edgar had given his word to me he'd be back sooner or later. I knew he wouldn't abandon Hector to the night. And he did keep his word. You saw just now how he walked calmly up here.'

'Yet you know that he was seen much earlier this morning by Alfred Portman, here, in the herb garden.'

Geoffrey indicated the patch of stained ground near where they stood. He did not have to spell out his meaning.

'That doesn't prove that he killed our stepmother,' said Alice.

'No, but the fact that he ran off does not help. Nor the fact that there are marks of blood on his face and hands.'

'Whose side are you on, Geoffrey?' said Ned Caton. 'Naturally he ran off – he was startled and frightened.'

'And the blood?'

'Perhaps that came from another source altogether, or perhaps he was examining the body and unwittingly marked himself.'

'I am eager to get at the truth, as you are,' said Geoffrey. 'Like you, I do not believe that Edgar killed Sara Storey. I am merely saying what has already been said and witnessed by others. If we are to defend your brother, Alice, then we must understand the strength of the accusations against him.'

'You will help us, Master Chaucer? You will help my brother?'

'I will do all I can.'

Alice smiled for the first time that morning. She grasped Ned's hand and, reassured, said, 'I believe my brother will give a complete and satisfactory account of what happened, and it will be as Edward says. He was foolish enough to touch the body, maybe because he was seeing whether Sara was beyond recovery, and then, when cousin Portman entered this garden, he panicked and ran off.'

'Let's hope so.'

But Geoffrey was by no means convinced that this would be enough to exonerate Edgar. The young man might swear innocence all summer and come up with a cartload of plausible reasons for his behaviour, but it still looked bad. Men had gone to the gallows on evidence which was much less compelling. Chaucer kept quiet about this, though. Nor did he mention the black-clad figure which he'd glimpsed in this very place, together with Sara Storey, since this strengthened the likelihood of Edgar's guilt. Alan wasn't likely to refer to it either, for the same reason. No use to add to the distress of Alice, or of Ned Caton who'd taken up Edgar's cause with a lover's zeal. Besides, Chaucer was inclined to believe in Edgar's innocence for all that the facts seemed to be against him. He was a moody, introspective person but he did not bear the murderer's stamp.

Through Chaucer's mind flashed the sequence of events of a few hours earlier. Alice Storey rising from her bed and going to her brother in the attempt to stop him sulking and persuading him to return home. The young man promising to do so but instead racing off in pursuit of his dog. Then, a little time later, he, Geoffrey, had got up to piss, and glimpsed from the window the two individuals in the mist-shrouded garden. One of them was Sara, beyond a doubt. And the other . . . was it Edgar Storey? A second – or third – sighting of the hapless son of the household had occurred later, after the sun had risen and driven off the mist. Alfred Portman, out gathering herbs, had witnessed Edgar take fright and squeeze through the box hedge.

Chaucer looked about the garden. He caught the eyes of the bust staring at him. Aesculapius, that wise and aged physician, had seen everything. Unfortunately he had taken a vow of silence. Meanwhile Alice and Ned and Alan were talking quietly. Chaucer's impression of the previous day, that these youngsters had formed a kind of alliance against the rest of the world, was reinforced. There was a determination in them, and a faith in Edgar's innocence. Alice in particular was a resolute individual, not one to be easily deterred or frightened. A question occurred to Geoffrey.

'When you were talking to your brother last night, you said that something disturbed Hector so he ran off. Think back, Alice. Do you remember hearing or seeing anything yourself?'

'I don't believe so. But then I haven't got Hector's senses. He was probably chasing a will-o'-the-wisp.'

'And after your brother went off in pursuit of his dog, you were alone out on the terrace. Did you sense anything then?'

This time Alice sounded less sure. 'If you are by yourself in the dark, you can never be certain what is happening inside your head and what is happening outside it.'

'Even so, if there's anything you can remember it might help your brother in his plight.'

'I thought there was someone else in the half-light, I had the feeling that I was being watched.'

'Watched? From where?'

'I don't know exactly. From somewhere between the house and the outbuildings perhaps. Everything was obscured by mist. But the feeling was strong enough to drive me indoors, that and the cold.'

'Someone from the household?'

'It was too early for anyone to be about their duties. And this was no fine morning in spring . . .'

'. . . no morning such as a lover might roam abroad in,' said Geoffrey. 'No, it was dank and miserable, as you say. But, Alice, you did not actually see anyone?'

'No.'

'You ought to have woken me,' said Ned. 'You ought to have come to our room and woken me. You should never have gone outside alone and unprotected.'

Alice shot him a look which suggested she was well capable of looking after herself. Alan Audley said, 'Ned – sorry, Edward – was right out of it, dead to the world on his back. Too tired even to shift out of his day-gear. What had you been doing to our Edward, Alice, to fatigue him so?'

There were some embarrassed glances and smiles, and Alan's remarks lightened their mood for a moment. Only a moment though, for Griffin now came into the herb garden. Whether it was to do with his sidling motion or his squinty gaze, there was something unsettling about his presence. He said to Alice, 'Your father wants to see you.'

Ned made to move off with Alice but Griffin held up his hand, open-palmed, as if to indicate he should stay where he was. Ned might have brushed Griffin aside but Alice said, 'It is all right, Edward. Enjoy the sunshine and the scents of this spot.'

She seemed to have momentarily forgotten that 'this spot' was the scene of a murder and, in truth, it was quite easy to do if you didn't cast your eyes over the scuffed and stained ground by the head of Aesculpius. Griffin turned his back on them and was about to follow Alice Storey when Audley said, slightly louder than necessary, 'Stay yourself, Griffin.'

The little man looked round and pulled his cap lower over his brows.

'Master?'

'I think you know, Griffin, that the instrument which was used to do this dreadful deed was brought to Semper House by me. It was strapped to my saddle. I picked it up after we were ambushed beyond the hill.'

Chaucer noticed that Griffin did his best to appear surprised, as if this was all news to him. But perhaps he was merely taken aback that Alan was confessing to bringing the murder weapon to the house. He said nothing.

'Come, man, you must have observed a great club when you were fetching our bags from the horses.'

'Now you mention it, master, I did. I asked myself what a gentleman was doing with such an implement when he ought to have been wielding a sword. And you say it was this very thing which was used to attack my lady? Well now . . .'

Griffin had known all the time, of course. Chaucer wondered whether he'd been hoping to use the information to apply pressure to Audley or to extract money from him. Now that Alan had 'confessed', the opportunity had gone.

'You did not bring it into the house, Griffin,' said Geoffrey.

'Why no, sir. My lady would have fainted to see such a great instrument. And besides why should you want such a thing indoors?'

'So what did you do with it, Griffin? You could not have left it strapped to Master Audley's horse.'

Griffin went through the pretence of thinking. He scraped his hand across his stubbly chin. 'Threw it in a corner of the stall, I suppose. What use was a club in Semper House?'

'Useful enough to kill your mistress,' said Geoffrey. 'Show us now where you left it.'

He was pleased to have put the objectionable servant on the defensive. Griffin shrugged in a show of indifference and led them from the herb garden. They walked along the edge of the upper terrace, deserted by now, and approached the scatter of outbuildings and penthouses which lay on the far side of Semper. Among these were the stables, a long timber building. They entered a warm, dungy world. There was a wide walkway with horse-stalls leading off it. From the stalls emanated soft scuffling and champing sounds. As in the herb garden, there was something reassuring about the stable, possibly to do with the absence of human beings.

But no, there were already human beings in here, at least three of them. Talking quietly at the end of the walkway. The interior was dim but a shutter was open at the far end and the morning sunlight threw a halo round their heads. Yet at first Chaucer couldn't make out who the people were. Then he was surprised to see the thrice-widowed Bridget Salt. She was deep in conversation with . . . who was that? Ah, one of the Genoese sailors who had accompanied Pietro Cavallo across the Dart on the previous evening, the only surviving one after the death of Giovanni. Chaucer recalled that Bridget Salt's first husband had been a Pisan by the name of Antonio. What more natural than that she should like to converse in that tongue which, she had assured him, she had a smattering of? 'The Italian language is fitted for romance,' she'd said. Maybe the sailor, who was a fairly good-looking fellow, brought back memories of that first husband. There was still something odd about the encounter, though. Standing near the two adults was a young lad.

Mistress Salt looked up to see Griffin, Chaucer and the others approaching. She broke off her conversation, quickly it seemed, and joined them. The Genoese sailor and the lad stayed at the other end of the walkway. The horses which Geoffrey and his companions had hired in Exeter for the final stage of their journey were stalled next each other. Alan Audley stepped to one side, rubbed his bay mount on the nose and spoke softly to it.

'So you say, Griffin, that you discarded the club in this place because you didn't wish to bring it into the house?' said Chaucer.

'As far as I can remember, master.'

'Remember a little harder if you please.'

'Now it comes back to me that I unstrapped the club from this gentleman's saddle and put it . . .' Griffin paused and cast his eyes about the walkway. '. . . put it there, in the corner near the door.'

There were brooms and rakes for sweeping and cleaning the stables piled in the angle of two walls. Chaucer walked over to the spot. Together with the brooms were leather buckets and a mound of cloths and blankets. Everything was arranged haphazardly, and a few rakes had fallen over where someone might have tripped on them. A length of rope which should have secured the bigger items in the corner trailed on the ground.

'Who is responsible for the stables?'

'That is easily answered,' said Griffin, beckoning. 'Tom, come here.'

The lad who'd been standing at the far end of the stable shuffled forward. He had fair hair, a hank of which hung over one eye giving him the look of a pony. He hunched his shoulders and stood with hands clasped.

'Is that how you keep this place?' said Geoffrey, indicating the jumble in the corner.

'No, sir, they like things tidy. I's beaten if things ain't tidy.'

'Then why are they in a mess now?'

'Dunno, sir.'

'Did you leave them in that state last night?'

'No, I swept and cleaned up here last night. I put them things away and made all fast with the rope.'

'Did you notice a club when you were clearing up yesterday, a club among all the gear?'

The boy shook his head, as if to clear the hank of hair from his vision.

'Dunno, sir,' he repeated.

'You haven't touched the brooms this morning? You haven't been cleaning out the stables?'

'No, sir. I ain't done nothing this morning, no sweeping, no cleaning – on account of – on account of . . . '

'On account of what?' said Griffin sharply.

'Of – of the dead lady,' said Tom. 'Nobody done nothing this morning on account of the dead lady.'

His voice sounded as if it was about to crack. Bridget Salt put an arm on Tom's shoulder.

'That's all right, Tom. No one would expect you to do anything. Go and tidy up now.'

'A minute, Mistress Salt,' said Chaucer. 'Do you sleep here in the stables, Tom?'

'I sleep outside, sir.'

'Outside? Show me.'

The boy led Geoffrey out of the building into the sunshine. He pointed to a low wooden construction to one side of the stables. It reminded him of a dog-kennel. The entrance was covered with canvas sacking.

'That's my house, sir,' said Tom with a touch of pride.

Geoffrey stooped and lifted the canvas over the kennel entrance. He peered inside. There was a pile of straw on the ground which still bore the impress of a body. It was just big enough to accommodate a lad of Tom's size, although when he grew a few more inches he'd have to sleep with his feet sticking out of the entrance. He noticed something glinting among the straw. He picked it up. It was a brooch in the shape of a heart with an inscription surrounding it. The inscription read *Amor vincit omnia*. Chaucer stood up, letting the sacking fall back into place. He held up the brooch.

'Where did you get this?'

'Picked it from the ground this morning, sir. Didn't mean to keep it, sir. I was going to give it back to – to . . . '

'To who?'

'Whosoever it is's. Honest, I weren't going to keep it, sir. Don't tell.'

'All right, Tom, I believe you,' said Chaucer, though he was inclined to think that the boy had intended to keep the brooch from the way it had been thrust into the straw of his kennel, not quite deeply enough. He slipped the brooch into a pocket. 'Show me exactly where you picked it up.'

The boy pointed to a spot close by the entrance of the stable.

'You were in here last night?' said Geoffrey, indicating the kennel-like structure.

'Well, I ain't got nowhere else.'

'Did you hear or see anything after you'd gone to bed?'

'How could I hear or see, sir, if I was sleeping?'

'You locked the stables when you'd finished for the night?'

'Locked 'em? No, sir. I don't do no locking up. It is Griffin who does the locking up. Anyway, I couldn't've locked up 'cause there was someone going to sleep in the stables.'

'Who? Who was in the stables?'

'The man Mistress Salt was speaking to. He was sleeping in the stables last night.'

'That's what he said to Mistress Salt?'

'I dunno what he said to her. They were talking in a foreign tongue. But I know the man was in the stables 'cause I seen him, singing and staggering about. And weeping he was too.'

'Very well, Tom. We'll go back inside now.'

They returned to the stable, where Alan and Ned and Griffin and Bridget Salt looked curiously at them. Chaucer nodded towards the corner and Tom went over and began tidying up the fallen brooms and rakes. He stacked them against the wall and replaced the rope, looping it round a nail. Chaucer didn't bother to examine the area further. There would be nothing to see now.

'What were you searching for?' said Bridget Salt. 'I don't understand.'

'The implement which was used to kill Sara was taken from here, we believe,' said Alan Audley.

Bridget gave a little gasp. Yet, as with Griffin, it seemed to Geoffrey that there was something considered about her reaction. He glanced towards the end of the stable. The Genoese sailor was no longer standing but rather had slumped down against one of the stall posts. Geoffrey was wondering how best to question Bridget but she spoke first.

'His name is Marco. He's still the worse for wear from last night. He was drinking deep with the others in the household after the death of his ship-mate. Drowning his grief. You wonder what I was doing talking with him just now, Master Chaucer. For one thing, it is a pleasure to me to converse in the Italian. It was my first husband's tongue, you know. For another, I was condoling with Marco over the death of poor Giovanni.'

Of course, there had been more than one death in Semper House over the previous twelve hours or so. It appeared that Mistress Salt was ready with a kind word or a gentle touch for all and sundry. That spoke well for for her, didn't it?

'I understand that this Marco was sleeping in the stable,' he said.

'I told him he should sleep here,' said Griffin. 'It's more comfortable than rocking on the waves, I dare say. He prefers a straw-bed to the ocean bed, I dare say. There was such a press of people in the house that we couldn't find space for everyone indoors.'

That was true enough. While visitors such as the mayor of Dartmouth or the ship's master would expect to be accommodated inside the house, an unimportant (and unexpected) guest such as the Genoese sailor could count himself lucky to be somewhere dry and sheltered. Chaucer was about to ask Bridget if the sailor had reported hearing or seeing anything during the night but then reflected that he could speak to the man himself. Later, perhaps, when the man was upright. The chances were that he would be no good as a witness if, as Tom had described him, he'd been under the influence. It seemed,

219

however, that Bridget Salt had more to say to Chaucer. She drew him to one side.

'Do you believe in dreams?'

'It depends what they say,' Geoffrey said. He suddenly remembered the interrupted tale which he'd been telling his children, the one about the cock and the hen and the fox.

'I do not usually set much store by dreams and visions, Master Geoffrey, but Sara came to see me last night. She could not sleep easily, she said, even though Portman had provided a draught for her.'

'A draught of valerian and marjoram,' said Geoffrey.

'Probably,' said Bridget Salt. 'That is Portman's province. Anyway, Sara woke in fright and her husband was not there to console her. She had been dreaming that someone was trying to kill her.'

'A warning?'

'It seems so.'

Geoffrey felt his scalp prickling. 'Did she give any details, Mistress Salt?'

'She said that she was in a room and that there was someone outside the door who was waiting to kill her. She knew she would be safe as long as she remained in the room but at the same time something was drawing her towards the door and she knew she would be compelled to open it, sooner or later, and then she would die. She could hear the person breathing on the other side of the door.'

'She had no glimpse of this person?'

'No, but she sensed that he was wearing a mask. She feared seeing his face more than anything else.'

'He? She believed it was a man?'

'I questioned her upon this very point and she said she couldn't be sure. It might have been a woman. All she knew was that they were masked, and waiting, and breathing beyond the door.'

'What happened next?'

'She woke in a sweat and shaking. She came to me. I tried to comfort her, told her it was probably something she'd eaten at supper and also that she was oppressed by the death of that shipman like the rest of the household. I said that it might have been the effect of the sleeping draught itself. Eventually she calmed down and returned to her chamber. I would not have mentioned this if nothing had happened for Sara is . . . she was . . . a woman inclined to fears and false alarms. But this was a dream that came true.'

It was, thought Geoffrey, as revealing as most dreams – that is, hardly at all. And even if Sara had glimpsed the identity of the individual behind the mask, that would hardly count as evidence.

'You've told her husband of the dream?'

Bridget hesitated before replying. 'No. Now is not the moment. He has other things on his mind. To tell the truth, Master Geoffrey, this is a burden that I want to get off *my* mind. If I had paid more attention to Sara's fears, if I'd taken her more seriously, I would have allowed her to couch in my chamber and then perhaps she would have been saved.'

'You are not to blame, mistress,' said Geoffrey. 'You soothed Sara Storey and did what you could to explain her dream away. If we obeyed our nightmares we'd never get out of bed in the morning.'

Bridget Salt looked grateful. Geoffrey observed Alan and Ned eyeing him curiously, wondering what they were talking about. Something occurred to him.

'Was Sara in her nightclothes when she came to your room?'

'Why no. She said she was so wrung through with sweat when she woke from her dream that she had put on her day things again.'

So the one question which had occurred to Chaucer as he gazed at her body, the significance of Sara's being dressed for day rather than night, was answered. Yet this raised another one, something that had been nagging at the corner of his mind.

'Was she wearing her pectoral when you saw her last night?'

He pointed to his own chest, at the equivalent place to where Sara's pearl-crusted cross had hung.

'She never took it off,' said Bridget Salt. 'She wore the cross by day and night. Richard had given it to her as a wedding gift, and she believed it kept her safe from harm.'

'But she was not wearing it just now, I mean when her body was being brought out of the garden.'

'I did not notice whether she was or not.'

'She was not, I am sure.'

'Then it must have been taken from her by force. She would never have relinquished it.'

'Or it was taken from her after she'd been murdered,' said Geoffrey.

He thanked Mistress Salt for her help and rejoined his companions.

'What now, Geoffrey?' said Alan Audley.

'Now we take stock,' said Chaucer.

Geoffrey and his companions were not the only ones taking stock. At a point on the higher ground overlooking Semper House were two men and a woman. They were dressed in drab greens and browns which blended with the grassy earth. From their vantage point in the trees and bushes they could watch not merely the comings and goings on the terrace but also the activity within the herb garden. They had observed the discovery of Sara's body, the flight and return of Edgar Storey. They were able to see the trio of individuals for whom they had lain in ambush not so many days before, the plump gentleman and the two younger ones.

They were used to waiting. But, as if to pass the time, the man called Bull took an item from within his jerkin. He closed his fist round it and held out the fist to the others. Then, like a conjuror, he opened his hand. In his wide palm there nestled a finely wrought cross decorated with pearls. There was a fragment of silken thread still attached to it. The man pinched the thread between meaty thumb and forefinger and dangled the cross in the air. The woman with the nut-brown complexion made to grab at it but he closed his hand tight about the ornament again. The woman's large breasts jiggled under her smock and the man, enjoying the sight, once again dangled the cross by a thread. As if by instinct, the woman made a second lunge while the man jerked the cross once more out of reach, and laughed. The other man, the one whose face was marked by a scar in the shape of a Z, looked affronted as if to say, How did a rogue and a villain like you lay your thieving hands on a token of our saviour? The man with the cross rose to his feet and placed the object tantalizingly on the ground. Then he mimed a clubbing action, before bending down to snatch up the pectoral, as if he was indeed tearing it from the neck of a body.

So the question of how the man had come by the cross was answered. But Zed still looked affronted, as though he should have been given the opportunity to wield a club and thieve the item too.

Then they settled down to wait again. They were used to waiting. They were used to overseeing death.

14

Chaucer and his companions assembled in their chamber on the upper floor of Semper House. Geoffrey was not sure how to proceed, and had suggested they come here partly because he wanted to be away from prying eyes and ears, especially Griffin's. What to do next? The original reason for visiting this western port had been to investigate the disappearance or theft of a cargo of alum. He had failed to uncover the truth behind the event, and it hardly seemed to matter at this stage. The murder of Sara Storey overshadowed all else. And now, through some ill-considered words, Chaucer had committed himself to aiding Edgar Storey and proving the young man's innocence.

This was a task made considerably harder by some news which Ned Caton brought. He'd exchanged a few hurried and hushed words with Alice Storey when they re-entered the house. She was too distressed to say much more. Her father had summoned her because Edgar had indicated that he'd talk to no one but his sister. Edgar was under guard in one of the many rooms in Semper, a prisoner in his own dwelling. Yet, when Alice confronted him, he would give no account of why he'd been discovered in the herb garden by Portman, of how he'd come to have blood on his hands and face. He refused even to say outright that he had *not* killed their stepmother, but merely shook his head vigorously when Alice pressed him.

'So what do we do now, Geoffrey?' said Ned, echoing Chaucer's own thoughts. 'It looks bad when a man will not defend himself.'

'Sometimes it looks worse when a man defends himself too clamorously,' said Alan, who was so assured of Edgar's innocence that he was grasping at straws. 'The man who shouts that he is not guilty has something to hide.'

'There is talk of taking Edgar back across the Dart and handing him over to Justice Mortimer,' said Ned. 'In fact, this would have happened already if it weren't for his father's authority here.'

'Perhaps the son did this deed after all,' said Geoffrey. 'There is nothing to say that he did not and there is no one else to blame.'

'Is there not?' said Alan Audley. 'I do not think that Sara Storey was greatly loved in this house or beyond it either. What about Juliana Barton, for example? Did you observe how the two women greeted each other yesterday evening? Sara was fearful of the madam. Perhaps they had an argument which led to something worse later.'

He paused and in the interval Ned jumped in with his penn'orth. 'There is always another possibility . . .'

'Which is?' said Geoffrey.

'That someone killed Sara in order to injure her husband. For sure he has enemies. Pietro Cavallo, for example. You saw the way the Genoese captain took the death of his nephew last night. Perhaps he holds Storey responsible. Or William Bailey. He certainly doesn't like the doctor.'

'No, no, such a murder must have been the act of a desperate individual,' said Chaucer. 'And whatever else Pietro Cavallo and William Bailey may be, I don't believe they're desperate.'

Yet even as he said the words he wondered. Who was to say that Cavallo or Bailey hadn't been driven to the act by some unknown crisis? He went on, more sure of what he saying, 'We do know that this act was carried out at a rush. The murderer seized the first weapon he or she could lay hold of in the stable.'

'If the club was still lying in the stable,' said Alan. 'Maybe it was removed beforehand.'

'Anyone taking it earlier would have done it without drawing attention to themselves. They wouldn't have left brooms and rakes scattered all over the place. But what was the murderer doing in the stable?'

The answer to something which had been baffling Geoffrey suddenly came to him as he was talking. You go to a stable to get your horse. You get your horse to ride away from a place. Suppose that Sara Storey's murderer was about to quit Semper, for whatever reason, when he (or she) was interrupted by the physician's wife. And the physician, what was his part in all of this? Did he know that his wife was absent from their chamber?

He had the answer to this question too, and sooner than he might have expected. Word came that the doctor of physic wished to speak to Geoffrey. But he was not the only one. Before Chaucer could talk with Storey, he was intercepted by Juliana Barton, friend to the mayor of Dartmouth.

'This is a terrible thing, Master Chaucer,' she said.

'It is, madam.'

'You may have heard me speaking heartlessly of Mistress Storey yesterday on the quayside. I regret those words now.'

'You couldn't know what was to follow,' he said.

'Indeed I tried to make it up to her by presenting her with a brooch at supper last night – you saw me, I believe.'

'I did,' said Chaucer. He felt his skin prickle. His hand went to his pocket and closed round the brooch which still nestled there.

'I regret that she took the gift in the wrong way. I don't know why, it was only a simple brooch with a simple saying on it.'

'What was the saying?' said Geoffrey.

'*Amor vincit omnia.* You know it perhaps. Love conquers all.'

'It is old as the hills. But would it not have been a more appropriate present from her husband rather than . . .'

'A woman who keeps an establishment in Sheep Street, you were going to say. Perhaps so, Master Chaucer, but the good doctor is not the kind of man to give his wife little gifts and tokens. There is not much romance in his soul.'

'Then it was good of you to make up his deficiencies, mistress.'

'I meant no harm by it,' said Juliana.

'I expect not. But here is the brooch again.'

He drew it from his pocket. Juliana Barton's face grew more flushed. 'It seems Sara Storey did not want it,' he said.

'True, she did give it back to me,' said Juliana, then clapped her hand to her mouth as if she'd spoken more than she intended.

'It was found outside the house this morning. It must have been dropped earlier.'

'Not by me, Master Chaucer, not by me. Sara *tried* to give it back to me, I should say, but a gift is a gift. I left it outside the door of her chamber last night where she might pick it up today.'

'You left it?'

'To tell you the truth, I was angry with Mistress Storey. She had spurned my gift and I certainly did not want it back.'

'You returned it in anger?'

Mistress Barton looked thoroughly uncomfortable. Chaucer pushed the brooch in her direction and the woman took it as though she were handling a knife by the blade.

'Forgive me, madam, I am summoned to speak with Richard Storey.'

And Chaucer went on his way, wondering why Juliana Barton had gone out of *her* way to assure him of her regret. A touch of guilt maybe that she'd talked slightingly of a woman who was now dead and given her an inappropriate token which had been returned and then returned again . . . or was there more to it than that? Had she been telling a lie when she claimed to have left the love-brooch outside Sara's chamber? Had she dropped it herself in the early hours outside Semper?

Chaucer and Storey met in the latter's office where Giovanni's body had been stowed. That body was now wrapped up and lying in an outhouse ready to be ferried over the water in the company of Pietro Cavallo and Marco. As for Sara Storey, she was lying in an upstairs chamber, watched over by Bridget Salt and other women of the house.

Outside it was bright and fair but the office was fusty with death, and the underlying scent of all the preparations which were concocted here. Storey showed marks of strain – hardly surprising, considering that he had a wife dead and a son likely to be accused of her murder – but he explained that he had asked to see Geoffrey because he wished to tell him what he knew of the events of the previous evening, or rather night.

Geoffrey saw that he was being appealed to. The doctor of physic was master of Semper, but a man tends to lose control of things when a murder takes place on his own premises. William Bailey, who remained on this side of the water, had some authority by virtue of his position but the doctor and the mayor did not see eye to eye. If Storey was going to account for himself to anyone, it would be to an outsider whom he considered of equivalent rank. Perhaps it was more a question of Storey unburdening himself, since he wasn't a man in the habit of accounting to anyone. This might have waited until the Justice arrived from Dartmouth. But Chaucer had gathered that Justice Mortimer's remit did not run easily on this side of the river. So, as an emissary of the London court, Geoffrey perhaps better fitted the bill. Or at least this was Chaucer's reading of the situation.

'I do not know what my wife was doing outside the house,' the doctor of physic began even though Chaucer had asked him no question. 'She sometimes rose early at this time of year but the weather was not clement this morning. It is not healthful to be outside at such times.'

'You didn't hear or see her leave your chamber? Forgive me, but you do – you did – share a chamber?'

'We do. We did. But I was not there last night. I was here, in this very office.'

'Working late?'

'I often work late, Master Chaucer. Sara had taken a draught which Alfred Portman had prepared for her and fallen asleep. I left her and came down here to continue my . . . studies.'

He gestured in the direction of a little side table. The stubs of a couple of candles sat there. Several books were scattered across it, and one volume lay open, as if in demonstration of those very studies.

'I did not expect to sleep soundly,' continued the doctor, 'after everything which had occurred . . . '

Now he nodded at the empty trestle table. Chaucer wondered whether anyone had slept soundly in Semper last night apart from the dead man who'd lain there and was now elsewhere. He did not mention the dream-story which he'd heard from Bridget Salt but it chimed with what Storey was telling him, at least as far as confirming the husband's absence from the marital chamber. The reference to the sleeping draught (which had not worked) also echoed Bridget's words. This much was confirmed as true.

'In any case,' said the doctor of physic, pursuing his last words, 'do you not find that your sharpest ideas, your highest thoughts, come to you when the world is hushed? Don't you find that, Geoffrey, as an educated man, as a man of letters?'

It was the same appeal which Richard Storey had made in the herb garden when they were standing by the bust of Aesculapius. We are alike, he was saying, we are both reflective individuals who read and study and ponder. And it was true, thought Chaucer, he did like sitting up in Aldgate when the rest of the house had gone to bed and all was quiet. Sitting among his books and papers, pen in hand, rereading his favourite lines of verse and mulling over his own writing. Though he wasn't so certain about the 'sharpest ideas' and 'highest thoughts' which Storey had mentioned. (Often, when he looked next day at what he'd written in the fastness of the night, his first inclination was to throw it away.)

'Was anyone else up and about?'

'No one. Or only Alfred.'

'Your cousin?'

'He was working in here when I came down.'

'What was he doing?'

Storey hesitated then said, 'I did not ask. He often works in here. He has the run of the place.'

'Did he stay?'

'No, I told him to go. I cannot think in company. He said he'd finished anyway. I read for some time. I had to light more candles. I read until I felt drowsy.'

'You fell asleep in here?'

'I must have done, I suppose, but eventually I hauled myself up to my – our – chamber for comfort's sake. It was already light by then. Sara had gone. I assumed she was about household business or, like me, that she had not slept well. I never thought that she . . . she was . . . '

Richard Storey swallowed hard and regained control of himself.

'Was your wife wearing the pectoral last night?'

'I – I expect so,' said Storey. 'Yes, she always wore the cross. I gave it to her on the day we married. She said that it kept her safe from harm. Why do you ask?'

'I don't think it was about her neck just now when she was being . . . '

Geoffrey did not need to finish the sentence. Storey shot him a fierce glance.

'My God, she would not have parted with it in this life,' he said. 'Who would have done this deed?'

Chaucer was not sure whether he was talking about the murder of Sara or the theft of the pectoral. He reflected on the different ornaments Sara had recceived at the beginning and

231

end of her married life: a cross from her husband, a brooch with *Amor vincit omnia* inscribed on it from the madam of the local brothel. He was on the verge of asking whether Storey had noticed that discarded ornament by the door of the chamber, where it had supposedly been left by Juliana Barton, but something held him back. Instead he said, 'The murder weapon was a club, I believe.'

'Yes,' said Storey. 'Brought here by one of your companions, I am told.'

So Griffin had known all the time, and had passed the information to his master. There was a tinge of blame in Storey's comment, as though it had been Audley who was somehow responsible for the deed by picking the club up in the first place.

'Where is the club?' said Chaucer. 'It may be needed again.'

A shudder crossed Storey's frame before he understood that what Chaucer meant was 'needed in a court of law'. 'I think that Alfred Portman has taken it. He asked for it and I did not want to look at it again.'

'Do you believe that your son Edgar did the deed? I mean the murder,' Chaucer said now. The question had to be asked, but neither man looked at the other.

'No,' said the doctor of physic.

'He refuses to speak, I am told.'

'Silence is not guilt. Besides, there is another thing which may be linked to the taking of Sara's pectoral cross . . . Some of the servants have reported seeing individuals in the grounds last night. It is possible that the rogues who attacked you on the upland came back to make another attempt. Did the club not belong to the woman who was with the men?'

'It did. But why would they come back? To rob the house?'

'Perhaps. There are wild people out there. It may be that Sara saw something suspicious in the early hours and went to investigate and . . . was set upon.'

Chaucer thought this was unlikely, given the timorous nature of the physician's wife. Anybody with any sense who 'saw something suspicious' would surely rouse the household, rather than venturing out alone.

'Who saw these intruders?'

'Griffin. It is his task to secure the house for the night.'

'He didn't mention seeing anyone to me,' said Geoffrey.

'He does not answer to you, Master Chaucer.'

At that moment there was a great commotion outside the door and, as if on cue, Griffin entered the office without knocking. Behind him in the doorway Chaucer was surprised to see the portly figure of William Bailey and his men, Francis and John. A tumble of words poured out of Griffin, who was usually so dry and spare of speech. It seemed that the very individuals whom Storey had been referring to had just been sighted on the upper fringes above Semper House. Two men and a woman, darkly garbed. But they'd seen that they'd been seen, and had made themselves scarce. It was necessary to take off in pursuit now, right now.

15

Richard Storey was out of the door before Griffin had finished his tale. They ran and stumbled through the house and towards the stables, Storey shouting orders that the horses be saddled. The rumour of the sighting had spread fast. There was other news too. The body of a dog – another dog – had been discovered in the grounds. It appeared to have come off worse in a fight. It was a mangy, mongrel thing, not one of the house breeds. Possibly it was the dog that had accompanied the trespassers. The report tended to confirm that they'd been in the grounds of Semper for some time.

Everything was confusion and excitement. Now Ned Caton and Alan Audley appeared, together with Pietro Cavallo and Marco, seemingly recovered from his sozzled state. Other male members of the house were arming themselves with clubs and swords and, in the case of Cavallo, with a crossbow. There was a store of weapons kept in a locked cupboard by the kitchen quarters.

Chaucer might have been inclined to be sceptical at this sighting except for the presence of William Bailey. The mayor was as eager as the others to make one of the posse and speedily secured himself a horse, although he had to be helped to mount it. Even Alfred Portman was taking part in the hunt. Geoffrey and his friends climbed on their hired horses. It occurred to him that he was no better armed than on the previous occasion.

235

Within a few minutes a group of some dozen men or more, on horseback and on foot, were cantering or running towards the gate accompanied by a motley collection of dogs. There was no sound apart from the thudding of the hoofs or the yapping of the hounds. As they crowded through the gate, the aged keeper of the lodge stood holding his arm out as if to direct them. He was pointing uphill. Above the house snaked the path, down which Chaucer and his companions had first descended on their arrival at Semper.

Geoffrey reached the crest of the hill a little behind the others, although ahead of the men on foot. The party had to rein in for an instant to let the horses recover. The open grassland stretched out on three sides, fringed by distant trees. Off to the left was the dilapidated thatched hut and the sycamore clump, site of that earlier ambush. And straight ahead could be discerned three shapes moving jerkily towards the wood, the presumed ambushers. Richard Storey, who'd taken the lead, looked round at the others with a mixture of gratification and anger in his expression before digging his spurs into his horse. There could be no question of allowing these malefactors to lose themselves in the woods this time.

Geoffrey urged his horse forward as the foot-followers reached the brow of the hill. He had hunted before, although it wasn't a pursuit he had much of a taste for. But he had never been part of a band or posse going after runaways and he was surprised to find how easily he was caught up in the human chase. His vision narrowed to the three figures nearing the shelter of the trees, as if they and the horsemen were all that the world contained. A scent of horseflesh and sweat and sunny grassland – and of something sharper and harsher – filled his nostrils. At that instant he regretted that he did not have a great sword or axe with which he might fell the fugitives, but the weapons cupboard had been bare by the time he got to it. Glancing beside him he saw the set, hungry expression on the faces of the other riders, the very look which must be on his own.

They reached the edge of the trees at the point where the fugitives had been seen entering. A descending track ran into the shadows but soon forked and then forked again. One of these must be the same path which Geoffrey and his companions had followed on their way to Semper House. If the fugitives had any sense they would have split up and made themselves scarce among the trees. The dogs ran in circles and up and down blind alleys but they had no scent to pursue. Then Alfred Portman slipped from his horse and, dropping down on all fours like a hound himself, examined the ground. He stood up and indicated one of the paths. Some signs of passage, invisible to the others, must have been apparent to him. Not merely an apothecary but a tracker.

They set off along Portman's path, which was fringed by ferns. Chaucer recognized it and, in particular, the dead oak that stood like baleful hands and a single thumb. The boisterous spirit of the group had given way to a more watchful mood. They were riding strung out, singly or two abreast. Some distance to the rear straggled the foot-followers. Every now and then a dog would dart into the ferns and the ripple of its progress would spread among the greenery. The pursuers strained their ears for any sound, they scanned the shadows for any movement. Although the posse numbered over a dozen, there were two desperate men and a ferocious woman in the woods whose eyes might be on them at this very instant. Geoffrey and Alan and Ned had particular reason to be wary, for they had actually been attacked by the trio. Geoffrey noted that Ned at least had armed himself with a sword this time.

Eventually they arrived at the turning where Chaucer and the others had taken the wrong direction two days before. Once again Alfred Portman descended from his horse and snuffed about the ground. Without speaking he pointed down the track, the 'wrong' one which led only to the dead end of a clearing. They penetrated deeper into the forest, where it was yet more quiet and gloomy. Chaucer remembered thinking that this would be a fine place for an ambush. There was comfort and safety in numbers but that didn't mean that an axeman might not do damage, severe damage, before he was brought down. They would have no qualms, these ambushers and murderers.

No birds sang and the dogs had fallen silent. The only sound was the clinking of bridles and the thud of hoofs. The path they were following petered out in the large clearing and then the tangle of bushes and brambles which fronted the cliff-like rock face. Chaucer glanced at Caton and Audley, sharing their bafflement. If this was where the trail led, then they had reached a dead end. The others, including Storey and Bailey and Cavallo, evidently thought the same. But Portman once again slipped from his mount and began to examine the ground.

At this point they were distracted by Griffin. He was staring intently back down the track. He pointed.

'There they are!'

The company wheeled their horses about. Chaucer looked but could see nothing along the length of the path. Nevertheless, by some herd instinct, the riders began to canter back the way they had come. Richard Storey was near the front and, after a few hundred yards, he shouted to Griffin to rein in. When the pursuers had halted once again, Storey gave vent to his anger.

'Where are they, man? You said you'd seen them.'

Three or four figures were indeed coming along the path at somewhere between a walk and a run but it was only some stray members of Storey's household who'd taken all this time to catch up with the main party. Griffin did his best to look sheepish and made some remark about being entitled to his mistakes, but Storey ignored him and said to Portman, 'You are sure this is the right track, Alfred?'

'I may be wrong, cousin.'

'I doubt it,' said the doctor of physic and without another word he indicated that they should go back to the point where the track petered out in front of the cliff. By this time the posse was in a state of chaos, literally uncertain whether it was coming or going. Yet to Geoffrey Chaucer this was a wild-goose chase, a distraction somehow from the whole business of Sara's murder. He gazed at the rock face. What now?

A couple of dozen feet above the point where the pursuers were milling about in front of the cliff, the two men and the woman looked down at the posse. The trio were concealed on a ledge that was screened by bushes. They lay stock still, the only movement the heaving of their chests as they recovered breath after the relentless dash across country. Their faces and limbs were scratched and torn from the breakneck ascent they'd made of the rock face. Fortunately, the pursuers were making so much noise, what with the jingling of harness and the shouting of suggestions and counter-suggestions, that any sounds the hiders made were covered. Behind the ledge where they lay prone was a narrow entrance into the rock face which, like the cliffs fronting the sea, was fissured with cracks and shallow caves. It was the intention of the leader, Zed, that they should slip into the entrance as soon as the band below had given up its pursuit. They could not move now without alerting the riders. But he had reckoned without the hot-headedness of his brother.

'It's that bastard Griffin,' hissed Bull, hardly able to get the words out in his anger and exhaustion. He gripped the haft of his axe. 'He has betrayed us. He has led them to this place.'

Zed grasped his arm to prevent him moving.

'No, he led them *away* from us.'

'And now he has brought them back, the bastard.'

'Stay still, you fool.'

Molly tried to clap her hand over her man's mouth but before she or Zed could prevent him, Bull had risen unsteadily to his feet. He gave a great yell and brandished his axe. Down below, the hunters looked about in confusion before some of them grasped where the cries were coming from. Among them was Storey's servant, Griffin. He glanced up towards the perch on the rock face, from behind which emerged the wild, shrieking shape. The horses shied away and jostled to clear the space at the end of the track. Griffin must have seen something which the others hadn't for he seemed to flinch and hunch lower in his saddle. But it was too late. There was a whirring sound and a blur as an object travelled through the air.

The thrower's aim was not perfect – if he had intended that the axe-blade should strike Griffin four-square in the face – but it was sufficient to deliver a mighty blow to the top of the servant's head. Griffin tumbled from his horse and the axe dropped with a clatter beside him. The thrower stood whooping on his perch and shaking his fist. But his triumph was short-lived. At least one of the party of pursuers had the presence of mind to respond. It was Pietro Cavallo. Swift as thought, the ship-master raised the crossbow and loosed a bolt. The shaft struck the axeman full in the throat and threw him back against the wall of rock at the rear of the ledge. Then – whether in some involuntary response or because he knew his life was all but over – the man burst through the concealing bushes and launched himself into the air for a final assault. He flew down, with arms flailing and blood streaming from his throat like a banner. He crashed into the bare ground. The blow drove the crossbow bolt right through the back of his neck.

'It is the man who attacked us,' said Alan Audley.

Chaucer also recognized the corpse, if only because of his bushy beard and the sheer bulk of him. Nor was this the end of things. At once another figure reared up on the ledge in the manner of a bear. He gazed at one of the bodies – the second body, not that of Griffin – sprawled in the clearing below and let out a wail that was less a war cry than a scream of grief. Now he too began to come down the rock face, not by launching himself through the air as his brother had done but by a scramble that was half descent, half fall. He was encumbered by his own axe and he landed among the scrub and brambles that fringed the base of the cliff. Yet he was strong and driven by a mindless fury and, within seconds, he had struggled to his feet out of the tangle of thorns, wielding the long-handled axe. He stood over the body of his companion, as if it should be protected even in death. This other individual Chaucer also recognized, for it was the man who had played dead by the stone hut.

By this time the pursuers had gathered their wits. There were a dozen of them or more, and most were armed with swords or knives or bows. They would not permit the living man to escape. Geoffrey was reminded of a cornered animal, a boar or a bear. Such a beast is at its most dangerous when brought to bay. It has nothing more to lose and will inflict what injuries it can before being brought down. Yet it will be brought down.

So it was with this beast. With more presence of mind than his companion, the man did not throw his axe for that would have deprived him of the one weapon he possessed. Rather he stood his ground, swinging the axe from side to side and glaring at the circle of horsemen. Chaucer, towards the rear of the pack, did not turn away but nor did he shove his way to the front. He had no desire to come within striking distance of the axe, but he was even more reluctant to be any nearer to the kill. If such a scene had occurred in a city, then reason and order might have prevailed. The axeman might have been persuaded to lay down his implement and surrender himself to the authorities. He might have been taken and tried, judged and executed by due process. And they did have authorities with them on this expedition, the mayor of an important town and a distinguished physician. Yet they were in no city but a wild wood. Justice and reason were suspended. On the faces of William Bailey and Richard Storey was the set expression he'd seen men wearing into battle – teeth bared, eyes somehow withdrawn into the head. There was no sound but the panting of horses and men.

Cavallo had reloaded. He once again directed his crossbow towards the fellow although his horse suddenly shied under him so that the shot went wide. But this acted as the cue for the circle to close about the man. A couple of the horsemen made to outflank him and then Alfred Portman – of all people! – achieved a hit with a stone he'd picked from the ground. It must have been luck for the doctor's assistant could see little that was beyond his nose. The man shrugged off the blow from the stone but it caused the blood to gush down from his cut brows and he was distracted for an instant, long enough for Ned Caton, one of the flanking horseman, to get in close enough for a swipe with a sword. Then, moving as one, the innermost riders tightened around the axeman and overwhelmed him by weight of numbers. Clubs and swords and fists quivered in the air. There was the sound of wood on bone. There were gasps and curses. Then, after what seemed many minutes but was probably only as many seconds, the hunters reeled from the scene, blood-spattered and exhausted but with curiously sated expressions like men coming away from a feast. Among them were Richard Storey and William Bailey, as well as Pietro Cavallo and Ned Caton. Despite the blood, none appeared to have sustained any severe injuries.

Now there were three corpses on the ground, that of Griffin with a fatal gash in his head, a second with a bolt through his neck and a third body much more hacked about than the others. The pursuers stood around in a loose circle, examining their weapons and the damage to their limbs or garments, but unwilling to look each other in the face. It was like the aftermath of a battle and, as in the aftermath, no one seemed certain of what to do next.

It occurred to Geoffrey that they had originally been in pursuit of *three* individuals, the two men presently sprawled on the earth and the woman with the nut-brown face. Had she escaped – or was she about to make a desperate attack of her own? He glanced up at the perch from which the two males had hurled themselves. He thought he saw the foliage stir, but it might have been no more than the breeze. After a time Chaucer dismounted, together with Alan Audley, and went to look at the bodies. Nearest was Griffin, still wearing his hat which had been part driven into the furrow of the wound by the force of the falling axe.

'He was unlucky,' said Alan. 'It might have been any one of us.'

Geoffrey had not trusted Storey's servant from the moment he'd seen him sitting by the forest track before they ever arrived at Semper House. Now he gestured towards the first of the axemen and said, 'More deserved than unlucky. Did you see the look that one gave him when he threw the weapon? For sure, they knew each other.'

'A look is not much evidence.'

'Then why choose a mere servant to kill when you have a mayor and a physician to hand? I'd wager a good deal that Griffin was accomplice to the dead men.'

'What would be the purpose in throwing an axe at your accomplice?' said Alan. Like Chaucer he spoke in an undertone.

'Perhaps they thought they'd been betrayed.'

'It was Griffin led us here.'

'No, it was Alfred Portman led us here. Griffin tried to distract everyone by claiming to have seen something in the opposite direction, remember. It was Richard Storey who pulled him up and stopped him going any further.'

They were interrupted by a groan from Storey himself. By now those who'd participated in the killing of the leader of the robbers were coming back to life and inspecting their handiwork. The doctor of physic was looking down at the body of the first of the men, the one who'd done for Griffin. He had been rolled over on to his back.

'Look, Geoffrey, look.'

Storey was pointing not at the man's bloody throat, from which the end of the crossbow bolt protruded, but at his chest. This was only partially covered by a leather jerkin and nestling among a mat of hair was a cross. Chaucer at once recognized it as the pectoral which Sara Storey had been wearing before her death, her husband's gift on their wedding day. There were tears in Storey's eyes. He reached down and, almost tenderly, raised the dead man's head so that he might slip the cross and cord from about his neck. It was tricky because of the impediment of the crossbow bolt, and when he stood up again his hands were shaking and covered with fresh blood. He slipped the pectoral into a pocket of his cloak.

Storey did not have to say anything. The finding of the cross about the neck of the man on the ground was proof enough of who had killed his wife, if further proof were needed apart from the innate murderousness of this band of outlaws and their proximity to the place of the crime.

Geoffrey said, 'You know your fellow Griffin is dead too. I believe that he was in league with these men.'

Storey looked surprised. Chaucer gave his reasons, and then asked the doctor about something which had been nagging at the back of mind.

'Before we arrived at Semper House, you had sent Griffin to watch out for our coming?'

'Yes, and he informed us that an ambush had been laid for you. I sent him out because I knew the dangers of the woods. He'd seen the fellows waiting – these very ones, no doubt.'

'How long did it take you to saddle up and ride to the ground above the house?'

'A few minutes, I suppose. There was no time to be lost.'

'The time had already been lost,' said Geoffrey. 'We took the wrong path in the woods, as a matter of fact we ended up at this very spot. In the process we must have forfeited at least two hours . . .'

'I think I understand you, Geoffrey, but perhaps you could spell it out for me.'

'Your man Griffin deliberately delayed alerting the household that ambushers were lying in wait. He intended that the rescuers should arrive on the scene *after* we had been disposed of. In truth, you only just got there in time.'

Storey stroked his trim beard. 'You may be right, I suppose. Now I recall he did his best to spread alarm through the house, telling Sara for example and frightening her thoroughly, before he came to see me. And he was not breathless when he did so but curiously composed. Even so I am unwilling to think ill of Griffin, especially now that he is dead.'

Chaucer wondered what more evidence was required to implicate the late servant. He observed that the mayor's man, Francis, seemed to agree with him, for he was standing over the body of Griffin with a kind of sneer on his face. But Geoffrey was saved from replying to Storey by an excited shout from higher up. Since it was apparent that the dead men had been concealing themselves on the ledge, a few of the more agile pursuers had scrambled up the cliff – finding foot- and handholds in the rock face or clinging on to tufty outcrops of vegetation – to see what was what. Leading off the ledge was an entrance to a cavelike chamber in the rock. And within the chamber, which was dry and spacious, were various items. Items such as barrels of wine and bales of cloth and chests full of valuables . . . and sacks of alum.

Geoffrey was relieved that he was not expected to clamber a

couple of dozen feet above the ground to inspect the finds. It was evident that they'd stumbled across, or been drawn to, a nest of violent thieves. Furthermore it was soon confirmed by Pietro Cavallo – who for all his size demonstrated a surprising nimbleness in scaling the rock – that the alum was indeed the remnants of the cargo from the *San Giovanni*, not all of it but sufficient to be worth retrieving. Worse than thieves the dead men were, for the loot in the cave could only have been salvaged from ships wrecked upon the coast, wrecked by accident or deliberately. The explanation for the scuffed and muddied state of the track leading down here was obvious: it was a regular route for the villains who carted their loot to the hidden cave. There was a general air of satisfaction and congratulation in the party, all except for Richard Storey, who looked thunderous at the news.

'By God,' he said, 'there has long been talk of a band of wreckers and land-pirates in the area but I did not expect them to be operating under my nose.'

'Calm yourself, doctor,' said William Bailey. 'They are dead now and what is lost has been found – some of it found at any rate.'

'They are the ones who robbed your warehouse?'

'It would seem so,' said Bailey. As he spoke, he was looking not at them but at Francis who appeared reluctant to move far from his position by Griffin's body. Chaucer had the impression that, had Francis been by himself, he might have started searching the corpse, possibly all three bodies. He gave voice to another thought that had been troubling him.

'There was a woman as well.'

'She cannot be of much account without the men,' said Storey.

'You have not experienced her at close quarters. She may be the deadliest of all.'

A shadow passed over the doctor's features but he recovered and said, 'At least some justice has been procured for Sara's death. But there is much to be done here.'

The three bodies had to be taken care of, together with the stolen items from the cave. All of this would require wagons and labour to shift, a day's work or more. Storey detailed his cousin Alfred Portman to take charge of the business. There was more to Portman than his appearance and manner suggested. For all his soft-spoken deference it had been Portman who'd literally sniffed out the way to this spot and who had even distinguished himself in the action by flinging a stone at the head of one of the axemen.

Most of the party returned to Semper House where the women – or at least Alice Storey and Juliana Barton – were anxiously waiting for them. There were gasps and cries at the blood which stained the hands and garments of the hunters followed by swift relief at the realization that the blood was none of theirs. Bridget Salt seemed less concerned at the dangers to which they had been exposed, but she expressed her gratification at the death of the wreckers. 'For you know,' she said to Geoffrey, 'my last husband, Edward Salt, was master of a vessel and he came to grief at sea. He was not deliberately lured on to the rocks, but I have long thought that in the annals of human wickedness such a crime is among the worst – perhaps the very worst. To lure sailors with the false promise of safety, and all for the sake of a few barrels of wine! Their bodies should be displayed on gibbets by the shore as a warning to others!'

Geoffrey agreed with her, at least as to the wickedness of the crime. He suspected, however, that the corpses of the axemen perhaps together with Griffin's would be buried in the woods since it was unlikely that a priest would agree to inter them in sanctified ground.

So it seemed, after all, as though a double offence had been solved: the identity of Sara Storey's killers and of those who had robbed William Bailey's warehouse was one and the same. The general belief was that the robbers had been hanging about the grounds of Semper in the hope of pilfering from the house or outbuildings, probably with the connivance of Griffin. There had been some hints of their presence. Edgar's dog Hector had run off into the darkness and no doubt it had been Hector who had seen to the wreckers' mangy mongrel. Chaucer recalled the blood on Hector's muzzle and the sound of barking in the night. Alice too had the sense that she was not alone outside. 'I had the feeling that I was being watched,' she'd said to Chaucer. And further proof was provided by the fact that the weapon which had done Sara to death was the very club which the woman had been wielding on the upland. By chance, or aided by Griffin, the wild woman had retrieved it from the stable where it was stowed. Chaucer wondered whether she had administered the killing stroke herself. He had not been jesting when he said to Storey and Bailey that she was the most deadly of the three.

Sara Storey must indeed have been alerted by some disturbance out of doors – by her own admission she had been unable to sleep. Showing a courage or recklessness that was not in her character, she had ventured outside in the early light, had been set upon by the band in the herb garden and relieved of the single item of value on her person, the pectoral cross.

The first thing to do on the return to Semper was to free Edgar Storey from the unofficial custody in which he was being held. The young man accepted his liberation with the same queer passivity with which he'd accepted his imprisonment. He made no comment on hearing of the death of the land-pirates, but took himself off to some corner of the estate in company with his faithful Hector.

Geoffrey's mission to Semper seemed to be concluded. In a day or so he would begin the journey back to London with Alan Audley. (Ned Caton was to stay with Alice for the time being.)

It was all over. Or almost over.

16

Later that same day, William Bailey together with Juliana
Barton were being ferried back across the waters of the
Dart. Pulling on the oars of the mayor's boat were his men,
Francis and John. The sun glittered on the water, and the
mayor and his mistress were sitting in the shade of the awning
which hung over the stern of the little boat. It was a warm
afternoon, full of the promise of summer to come. The bloody
start to the day – the pursuit of a band of land-pirates and the
death of three men – had been left behind them on the other
shore.

Like the others, William Bailey had cleaned off the worst
of the marks of that morning's carnage. But his normally
ebullient manner was replaced by a subdued thoughtfulness. As
they were drawing near the harbour crowded with cogs and
merchant ships and smaller vessels, Bailey spoke for the first
time since they'd set out.

'Do not go to our usual mooring, Francis. I wish to visit
Master Mortimer. He has his own mooring place and we shall
go there instead.'

'Mortimer?' said Francis. The mayor's man looked up at his
master. 'The Justice?'

'Aye, the justice of the peace. There is only one Mortimer
with a house large enough to have its own landing stage.'

And, indeed, Bailey could see James Mortimer's house from
where he and Juliana were sitting in the stern. Situated on the

inner reaches of the port, it was not as grand as Richard Storey's but was similar to his in having its own access to the river. Like most justices, Mortimer was not a professional lawyer (and for that reason he stood more highly in Bailey's estimation) but a landowner. If Edgar Storey had been brought to face the law in Dartmouth, he would have been examined by Mortimer in the first instance.

'You want to tell him what has happened, master?' said Francis. Beside him, John appeared to be paying no attention to the conversation but continued to ply his oar. William Bailey did in fact intend to report to James Mortimer on the deaths of Sara Storey and the two villains. The justice of the peace would require a full accounting. There were statements to be taken, there were questions to be asked and answers filed. But he had made the remark more because he wanted to see Francis's reaction. And, sure enough, the little oarsman looked uneasy.

'You will not require us after that?' he said.

'You have other plans on this fine afternoon?'

'I need to go to the warehouse and see that all is safe and secure,' said Francis, 'since the stolen cargo of alum will be returned there in due course, I expect.'

'You do, do you?'

'Yes,' said Francis uncertainly. He was used to being given a free rein by his employer. He was not used to being questioned. He became distracted from his task and his blade hovered above the water while John continued to pull hard. The vessel started to turn in a circle.

'I would like you to be present when I see Master Mortimer,' said Bailey.

'Me, master? But I have nothing to say.'

'Oh, I think you do, Francis. You will explain to him your association with Storey's man, Griffin.'

'The dead man?' said Francis, as if there was more than one person called Griffin in this tale. 'I scarce knew him.'

'Mistress Barton here says otherwise. She heard from a kitchen-girl in Semper House that you were talking all quiet and private to Griffin last night.'

'A man may talk,' said Francis grudgingly. By this time he'd given up any attempt to row. Bailey indicated that John should stop, and the little boat slopped up and down on the edge of the harbour.

'Bessy says that Griffin said something to you about friends out in the dark. He threatened you as if he knew you well.'

This was Juliana Barton speaking out. She'd been listening intently to the exchanges between William and Francis.

'Bessy?' said Francis. Who was . . .? Oh yes, that girl with the tits in the kitchen. 'You cannot trust the word of a slattern.'

'*I* trust her,' said Juliana. 'I know Bessy of old.'

'One of your needlewomen, was she? One of your whores?' said Francis, and at once saw he'd made a bad mistake. The colour came into Juliana's face and Bailey gripped the side of the boat.

'There is something going on, Francis. I've always trusted you but I see now that I have been mistaken.'

The mayor hadn't intended to say so much, had intended merely to take Francis with him to the Justice and assess the servant's response. But he was provoked by the little man's insolence and what had been suspicion hardened into certainty. John did not know where to look. His glance flickered between the mayor and his female companion in the stern, and the view across the river. He shifted slightly as if to distance himself from his place on the thwart next to Francis.

Bailey persisted. It did not occur to him that they were bobbing about in a boat several hundred yards from dry land, and that none of them was able to swim. William Bailey had no fear. Besides he was bigger than Francis, and believed he could knock sense into any man.

'You will tell Justice Mortimer how you have been assisting with the thefts from my warehouse.'

'That's bollocks – by your leave, master.'

'It is not bollocks, Francis, but God's honest truth,' said Bailey. Every denial from the other confirmed what he was saying. He gripped more tightly to the side of the boat. 'When Master Chaucer and his friend were on the quay yesterday morning I saw they were spattered with mud. I saw that at once. They'd been snooping round the back in Hobbs Lane where there is another entrance to my property as you well know. I asked myself whether they'd been prompted to do that by something they'd discovered *inside* the warehouse. So I did a little investigating myself on the upper floor.'

'You couldn't get your fat arse up there,' said Francis. 'By your leave, sir.'

'But John could get his thin one up there – and he did. Tell him what you found, John.'

Francis looked at John as though his fellow had stabbed him in the back. John hung his head and shifted further away from his rowing companion. He began to speak but could not get much out, what between his fear and his stuttering, so William Bailey took over once more.

'The pegs to the shutter-bars had been tampered with so that a thief could get in from Hobbs Lane,' he said.

'Get in from the *outside*, mark you,' said Francis.

'Your response comes too quick, Francis. An innocent man would scratch his head and wonder what I was talking about. And someone had to replace the pegs afterwards – from the inside,' said William Bailey, unknowingly echoing Chaucer's words. 'Someone had to know the layout of the warehouse and show how it might be done in the first place. Remember, Francis, I asked you why the *Gee-vanny* cargo had been stored on the first storey when there was nothing wrong with the ground floor, plenty of space there.'

'And remember, *sir*, that I said it was the ship-master Peter the Horse who commanded the alum should be stored up top.'

'You said he waved his arms about and talked a deal of foreign words. I ask again why the cargo of alum was stored on the upper floor when there was room down below. And my answer is, so that you and those land-pirates could get at it from the backside because there was too much coming-and-going along the river-front.'

'Suit yourself, master,' said Francis, 'but it's your backside you're talking out of – with respect.'

'We'll let Justice Mortimer be the judge of that. Take up your oar again and row towards his landing place.'

There was a moment when Francis might have disobeyed the command. A moment when he might have hoisted his oar out of its rest and swung it wildly at the mayor or his woman. William Bailey saw the blaze of fury and revolt in the servant's eyes, and saw it as rapidly die away. Bailey was almost disappointed. His blood was still up, from the bloody encounter of the morning. But then Francis seemed to slump in his seat. Perhaps he was yet affected by the tone of command in Bailey's voice. Perhaps he realized that there was nothing to be gained by braining the mayor and slipping overboard – even if that could have been achieved – since they were still hundreds of yards from shore. Perhaps he remembered that he, like the other occupants of the boat, was unable to swim. Anyway, he grasped his oar in both hands once more, and John did likewise, and the boat began to carve a new passage across the harbour waters towards the house of James Mortimer, justice of the peace for Dartmouth.

William Bailey may have been lulled by Francis's air of compliance for he too slumped back in his padded seat in the stern, and Juliana Barton patted his arm as if in reassurance. Within a couple of minutes they had reached the stone flight of stairs cut into the bank that fronted Justice Mortimer's property. Bailey indicated that John should secure the boat to one of the mooring rings set at intervals on a wooden pile next to the stairs. As John was straddling the gap between vessel and shore, rope in hand, Francis suddenly leapt up and pushed at his fellow so that John tumbled into the river. Then he was up the steps, fast as a ferret from his hole. The others were distracted by John's floundering in the water and the violent rocking of the boat which had already begun to move away from the bank. By the time Bailey had seized the oarsman's hand and dragged him inboard, Francis had vanished over the top of the bank.

Bailey made no move to go in pursuit and John was too soaked and confused to be any use. Instead the mayor contented himself with calling Francis a series of names. Then he seized an oar himself and eased them back towards the mooring. He fastened the rope to a ring while Juliana Barton and Francis clambered ashore and up the stairs. A path ran along the bank, leading in one direction towards the harbour where there was the usual bustle of activity. Of Francis there was no sign.

The mayor said to his mistress, 'Well, at least that proves one thing.'

'What's that, my dear?'

'The innocent do not flee. That man is guilty as sin.'

17

'Where are we going?' said Geoffrey Chaucer for at least the second time since they'd started.

'I would prefer not to say before we arrive,' said Bridget Salt.

The poet and the widow were riding across country beyond the bounds of the Semper estate. It was the day after the night-murder of Sara Storey and the hunting down of the land-pirates. Geoffrey and Alan Audley were due to leave on the next day since there seemed to be nothing more to detain them in Dartmouth. But Bridget had requested his company for a visit she wished to make. She'd kept their destination a secret, assuring him that it was only a couple of miles away on the coast. When Geoffrey had hesitated, she'd said, 'Come now, Master Chaucer, you are surely gallant enough to accede to an old woman's desire for your company. Do not look so worried. I will protect you from the wild men of the woods. Anyway, my son-in-law's writ runs on this side of the water.'

Geoffrey refrained from saying that Storey's writ didn't seem to run particularly successfully. He stared at Bridget Salt. Indeed she looked determined enough to see off a whole pack of marauders. She was attempting to be playful but Geoffrey could see that it was an effort. He supposed that, like the rest of the household, she had not shaken off the terrible events of the last few days. Perhaps in keeping with her sombre mood, she had substituted her usual bright gear for a dark riding mantle.

'It is not the wild men I'm thinking of,' said Geoffrey. 'They are safe underground since Alfred Portman buried them in the woods where they belong. But there is a woman still on the loose.'

Chaucer wasn't speaking entirely in jest. The image of the woman with the nut-brown complexion, and (more to the point) probably armed once more with the kind of implement which had been used to batter Sara Storey to death, had haunted his dreams of the previous night. Still, this she-outlaw would doubtless be apprehended in due course. There were some other loose ends to this business besides. He'd heard a report that Francis, the mayor's man, had been in league with Griffin and was implicated in the theft of the alum from his own master. Francis had escaped before he could be brought before the local justice but the ratlike servant would likely be more concerned with saving his own skin than getting vengeance on those who'd unmasked him. He could no longer be a danger. So, his curiosity sparked by Mistress Salt's request, Geoffrey had taken the hired horse on which he had originally arrived at Semper and set off with her on this mysterious outing.

They cantered through sun and shade with the river to their right hand. In the distance he could see the gleam of the sea. Geoffrey had the leisure to appreciate again the beauty of the setting. Yet he would not have exchanged it for his dwelling in the Aldgate gatehouse or even for his wife's lodgings in the Savoy Palace. It seemed to him that there was more wickedness and crime at the heart of this green country than was to be found in the dingiest and most impoverished district of London.

When they reached an open area of grassland at the top of the cliffs, Bridget Salt reined in. Over their shoulder, though hidden by the lie of the land, lay the entrance to the Dart and the harbour within. The breeze brought with it the tang of salt.

Gulls were borne aloft at the edge of the cliff. A scatter of sails was almost lost in the immensity of the prospect which unfolded before them. The sea was calm, with waves that were no more than wrinkles. Chaucer pulled his hat down. His companion was shading her eyes with her hand and gazing out over the water.

'I think I told you, Master Geoffrey, that my third and last husband was a ship-master.'

'You may have mentioned it once or twice, madam.'

'His ship went down not far from here. Every spring and autumn I ride to this point and pay my respects to his grave. His bones are lying there below us.'

She spoke with a curious detachment. Something told Geoffrey that they were making this trip for another reason than for Mistress Salt to pay her twice-yearly 'respects'.

'He was not lured ashore by false lights, I know. He was not ruined by human wickedness like the unfortunate victims of those men in the woods. Instead, Edward perished in the worst storm on this coast for many a year. But although he is lost, others may be saved.'

So saying, she wheeled her horse away from the cliff-edge and set off at a canter in an easterly direction. Geoffrey followed. After a few hundred yards the land dipped into a small valley, through the middle of which ran a churned-up path leading down towards the sea. Bridget Salt once more reined in and this time she dismounted.

'The track is steep,' she said, 'and besides I do not wish to alarm Mags by galloping up to her door. We shall leave the horses here.'

There was an old dwarf-oak at the head of the path, hunched against the prevailing wind. Hoof-marks in the mud indicated that this was a place where horses were regularly tethered.

One they'd secured their mounts, Geoffrey paced downhill beside her. The banks on either side of the path enfolded them.

The way was steep and slippery and the gurgling of an underground stream was audible above the distant sounds of the sea. Bridget Salt was sure-footed and waved away the offer of a steadying hand. Chaucer thought it best to ask no more questions, and only now did his silence prompt the widow to speak.

'Mags has lived down here for many a year. Her house once belonged to a samphire-gatherer. He died of the pestilence when I was no more than a girl. Mags pays no rent since no one else wishes to live in this spot. People think it is cursed. She does not care. She has the gift.'

'The gift?'

'Of seeing the future, sometimes. She can tell a man who his enemies are. Or his true friends. I pay her to keep a light burning whenever the weather turns foul. The light marks the entrance to the mouth of the river. Any vessel which is storm-tossed or benighted may steer to safety when they see her candle. I do this in memory of my late husband and so as to reduce the world's supply of widows.'

'Then you are doing the world a service,' said Geoffrey.

'There are enough widows as it is. I am also preserving the stock of men,' said Bridget with a twinkle of her customary mischief. 'Tell me that I am doing good, Master Geoffrey.'

'We men are in your debt,' said Geoffrey. He answered lightly, yet he meant what he said. Even so, he wondered what they were doing, visiting a witch – for a witch was surely what this Mags person was. Chaucer visualized a withered crone, as the woman must be if she'd been living here since the three-times widow was a girl. As though she could read his thoughts about the purpose of their journey, Bridget Salt said, 'I have been talking to Marco.'

'Marco? Oh, the sailor from the *San Giovanni*.'

'The one who was sleeping in the stables on the night of Sara's murder.'

'Marco was drunk-asleep,' said Geoffrey, recalling that the man had scarcely been able to stand upright the next day.

'Even so, he saw things, he heard things,' said Bridget Salt. 'Unless it was all a dream. I hope it was all a dream. The lady Mags will tell us if it was a dream.'

Geoffrey Chaucer glanced at her. Her mouth was set firm. At once he felt cold, even though the day was mild and no more than a gentle breeze was blowing in their faces as they scrambled down the track. Bridget suddenly halted. She fumbled under her dark cloak and brought out an object which she kept concealed in her clenched hand.

'This will assist the lady,' she said, unfolding her hand and letting fall a cross. It swayed on a cord. Chaucer recognized Sara Storey's pectoral cross with its pearls. He had last seen it being loosened, almost delicately, from the neck of a dead man. He felt colder than before.

'You took it from Richard Storey?'

'Took it? I asked my son-in-law that I might handle it for a time, in memory of Sara. He made no objection.'

Chaucer thought of the odd collection of objects that had clustered around Sara's murder. The pectoral cross which Bridget Salt now replaced under her cloak. The inscribed brooch which had passed backwards and forwards between Sara Storey and Juliana Barton. The club which had been employed to murder Sara, and which had originally been the property of the wild woman in the woods before being gathered up by Audley and which was now, according to Storey, in Portman's safe-keeping. What did the doctor's assistant want with the club? He was a man who looked as though he had never handled a weapon in his life. But Geoffrey remembered his prowess in the hunt yesterday, the way he'd thrown the stone at one of the axemen. The club . . . something about the implement snagged at his brain but he couldn't pin it down.

Geoffrey Chaucer and Bridget Salt moved on and rounded a corner and came to a kind of shallow basin where the path widened before dropping down again. In the middle of this space was a dilapidated house, more of a hut than a house. It was boggy underfoot and the place was gloomy and sunless, surrounded with scruffy trees. Beyond lay a wide expanse of sea.

A woman was standing in the doorway of the hut. Chaucer's first thought was that this could not be Mags the witch. The woman was tall and imperious with a hawklike nose and flowing grey hair. She nodded slightly on seeing Bridget Salt.

'I've been waiting for you,' she said.

Then, as Chaucer thought that this was indeed Mags and that the remark about 'waiting' was probably intended to impress, the woman in the door added, 'I hear your steps. I hear your horses' hoofs. You will not take Mags by surprise. I lit a candle the night afore last. Weather was bad.'

That had been the night of the storm, the time of Sara's murder.

'We wish to have your counsel, Mags,' said Bridget. 'We wish to consult you.' She spoke more quietly than Chaucer had heard her speak before. He understood that Mistress Salt was nervous of the woman, who had not shifted from her stance in the doorway.

'Him too?' said Mags, inclining her head at Geoffrey.

'Geoffrey has an interest in this.'

'Geoffrey has come far to visit Mags,' said the hawk-nosed woman. Chaucer nodded. Almost despite himself he felt apprehensive, even though identifying him as a stranger to the region did not take great powers of divination.

Bridget Salt once again reached under her mantle and extracted the cross which had been the property of Sara Storey. She walked forward and handed it to Mags. The woman took it without comment and held it in her open palm. She had long, quite elegant hands, clean ones, the hands of a lady. If she felt uneasy at holding the image of the Saviour she did not show it.

'The person who wore this is dead,' said Mags.

'Yes, she is dead,' said Bridget with a glance at Geoffrey.

'She did not die alone.'

'That is what I wish to discover,' said Bridget. 'Who was with her when she died?'

'Mags does not know anybody's name.'

'I am seeking not a name but a picture.'

'We'll see,' said Mags.

She turned and disappeared inside the hut. Bridget moved closer to the door, which hung off a single rusted hinge. The breeze whistled eerily in this spot. Through the doorway Chaucer glimpsed a deep-set aperture in the opposite wall which gave a view of the open sea. A lantern was set in the centre of the gap. He was reluctant to peer further inside the dwelling-place. He heard noises from within, mumbled words, the pouring of liquid, the sound of tearing cloth, an animal squeak. A black cat suddenly shot out of the door between Chaucer's legs. He jumped.

'That is Gib,' said Bridget, almost with pleasure at recognizing the animal.

They waited. Chaucer strained to hear more but heard nothing. After a few minutes, Mags called out for Bridget Salt to enter. The widow was gone some time. There was the sound of conversation but not much of it. When Bridget came back out of doors she wore a grim expression.

'You must look too,' was all she said. Her voice was strained.

More uneasy than ever, Geoffrey Chaucer entered the witch's house. There were gaps in the roof and walls as well as the window space so it was well lit, after a fashion. Yet for all the patches of sun there was a dank, unwelcome air to the place. Mags was sitting on a makeshift stool behind a ramshackle table. She was holding the cross in her hand. There was nothing on the table apart from a small bowl, a disc-shaped piece of metal and a loop of ragged, dirty material tied with a loose knot. Geoffrey recalled the sound of tearing cloth. He was reminded of a woman who sets up her tent at a fair and professes to clear up the mystery of the future in exchange for a coin or two. But there was something simple and austere about this setting as there was about Mags herself. Nor did he think any money had changed hands.

'Put this on,' said Mags to Geoffrey, gesturing first at the strip of cloth and then towards her eyes.

'Why?'

'To clear your vision.'

How can I see anything if I'm wearing a blindfold, thought Geoffrey. But such was the commanding power of the woman's voice that he obeyed, reluctantly slipping the fabric band over his eyes. He was slightly fearful but did not think he would come to any real harm. He waited in the dark, listening for signs that Mags had moved her position. His mind wandered in the dark and time seemed to be suspended. He suddenly grasped what it was that had been tantalizing him about the club, the implement with which Sara Storey had been beaten to death.

After a few moments Mags instructed him to remove the blindfold. Her voice came from a distance. He blinked at the light. Had his vision been 'cleared'? Perhaps it had, but the interior of the hut looked exactly the same. Mags held out the small bowl. He took it. A colourless liquid lay at the bottom. He was obviously meant to drink it. Now he baulked. Suppose that it was some drug or poison? But Mags, as if divining his fears, said, 'It is a preparation to clear your mind, Geoffrey. Mistress Salt will tell you as much.'

Chaucer raised the bowl to his nose. The contents were odourless as well as colourless. He was reluctant to drink yet more reluctant to appear timorous in the eyes of this weird woman. And if Bridget had already drunk from the bowl . . .

He tilted it and swallowed a little of the liquid. It was fiery like aqua vitae, and burned his gullet before settling with a warm glow down in his guts. Not unpleasant but he was not tempted to take another draught. Did his mind feel clearer now? He did not believe so. Not a whit clearer.

Now Mags handed him the piece of metal from the table. It was made of tin and slightly convex like a mirror. But the surface was badly smeared and scratched and Chaucer thought that it would never have done for a fine lady.

Nevertheless it was as a mirror that Mags intended Geoffrey to use it, for she told him to take the object near the window where the light was stronger. 'Look into it,' she said. He made to wipe the circle of tin clean on his sleeve but Mags told him firmly to leave it be, and repeated, 'Look into it.'

Chaucer angled the tin so that it caught the light. He attempted to catch his reflection. But it was no use. The curved surface was so cloudy that it was like breathing on a square of glass and then trying to peer through. He glanced in puzzlement at the hawk-nosed woman who sat without moving on her stool by the the table, clutching at the pectoral cross. She nodded as an indication that he ought to persist.

Chaucer did so, and the cloudy surface began to clear, again like a sheet of glass. And, as it cleared, Chaucer almost dropped the piece of tin in surprise – and fear. He was not a vain man and rarely glanced at his mirror-image, but he was familiar with his own appearance: the fullness in the cheeks, the neatly trimmed beard, the slightly hooded eyes (which his wife Philippa always claimed were his most interesting feature, even an attractive one). Yet, as the image of a face started to emerge through the smears and spots on the surface of the tin, Chaucer found he was looking not at himself but at another individual . . . and one that he knew.

Instinct almost caused him to jerk his head round, but some fragment of reason told him that if the person was that close,

close enough to produce a reflection in the mirror, then he would be feeling the other's breath on his bare neck. And he felt no one's breath. His skin crawled, and he was split between wanting to hurl the object away from him out of the window and wanting to examine the image more closely. Instead he turned the disc over but the back had been covered with a dull black paint which revealed nothing. He glanced at Mags.

'Well,' she said, 'have you seen what you desired to see? Have you seen, Geoffrey?'

'I don't know.'

He tilted the mirror for a second time and once again almost let it fall to the ground, for now the features which he could clearly distinguish were his own, the full cheeks, the hooded eyes. Geoffrey Chaucer, to the life. It was as if one image had been wiped away to be replaced by a second, truer one. Yet the first picture had contained a kind of truth also.

He returned the mirror to Mags and, in exchange, she handed over the cross. Dimly, he understood that the consultation was over. He stumbled through the open door, his mind in a whirl even as some small, clear corner of it wondered whether this was the effect of the potion which he'd drunk. Outside Bridget Salt was waiting for him. Chaucer leaned against the doorpost. He felt exhausted.

After a while the poet and the widow began to retrace their steps up the rutted track. Neither of them seemed willing to say anything, or rather it was as if each was waiting for the other to speak first. Instead they concentrated on the ascent. Geoffrey was wondering how the trick had been played – how Mags had conjured that image on to the circle of tin. Yet a whisper told him that it was no trick.

It was only when they reached the tethered horses and regained their breath that Bridget Salt said, 'Marco told me of this. I didn't believe him but now I see it must be true.'

'He saw . . .?'

Geoffrey was curiously reluctant to name names.

'Yes, he saw, drunk as he was,' said Bridget. 'And you recall that Sara Storey had a dream in which she feared that someone was waiting outside her door to kill her? The person was wearing a mask. She feared seeing the person's face more than anything else.'

'Yes,' said Geoffrey.

Dreams . . . mysterious images in mirrors . . . masked faces . . . it was all one to him.

'I fear that we have just lifted the mask,' said Bridget Salt.

18

Pietro Cavallo, the master of the *San Giovanni*, sat inside his crib on board his own vessel. The ship remained in her Dartmouth dock but it was almost ready to put to sea again. Indeed, it only required the reloading of the cargo of alum sacks which had been discovered in the cave in the woods and which were now awaiting shipment over to this side of the water. The matter was in the hands of Alfred Portman. The doctor's assistant had assured Cavallo – speaking in his own tongue, for Portman had a good grasp of Italian – that the goods would be safe in temporary storage in Semper House. He would make sure they were well guarded.

Nevertheless, Cavallo didn't altogether trust Alfred Portman. It had been the quiet-spoken man who had made the first approach to him after the *San Giovanni* had been wrecked and brought into Dartmouth harbour. Somehow word had got out that Cavallo was carrying a double cargo to Fowey. There was the alum which was intended for the merchant by the name of Latchett, and there was the other item, tiny by comparison but perhaps its equivalent in value. For another customer dwelt in the town of Fowey, a doctor called Raymond Lamord who was expecting delivery of the precious vial which Cavallo had purchased from Barak in the port of Genoa and which he kept under lock and key in his chest during the voyage. It had been this vial which Cavallo had retrieved just before the *Giovanni* was cast so violently on to the shore.

Within a couple of days of their arrival in Dartmouth, Alfred Portman had sought out Pietro Cavallo in his temporary lodgings in Fore Street and explained that he knew there was a secret substance in the ship-master's keeping. Instinctively Cavallo's hand went to his breast. He felt the outline of the leather pouch which was snugged beneath his jerkin. If Portman was aware of the movement he didn't show it. He said he was prepared to offer a sum, a good sum, a fair sum, in exchange for the vial. How much? said Cavallo. How much, supposing him to be holding such an item? Portman named a price, with reluctance it seemed. In fact, there was an air of constraint to everything the man said. But he did name a price. Cavallo considered it. The sum was good. Actually it was more than he expected to receive from Raymond Lamord. But he thought that by holding out he might extract an even higher price. He hummed and hawed. He claimed that he was under an obligation to deliver the vial to Master Lamord. Portman merely looked unhappy and repeated that his offer remained open. Then the doctor's assistant slipped out of the house in Fore Street as unobtrusively as he had arrived.

Cavallo sat and thought. It might be to his advantage to sell the vial here and now, without the delay and risk that would be involved in carrying it on to Fowey. To tell the truth, its possession made him uneasy. From the moment it had been handed to him in the dark back room of the Genoa tavern the vial and its contents had made him uneasy. The death by water of Barak the merchant – an accident, yes, but who could be absolutely sure? – had followed hard at heels on the sale. Then the voyage across the seas to England, a voyage which had been suspiciously free of trouble until its closing hours when the *Giovanni* was lured on to the rocks. Had the survival of his vessel and her occupants been on account of the vial? Or had the precious object somehow brought misfortune on their heads in the first place? Cavallo couldn't tell. It might be one, it might be the other. Yet his instinct was to rid himself of this dangerous vial. And now an offer had come from an unexpected quarter . . .

True, he was under an obligation to Master Raymond Lamord, whom he had met and negotiated with on previous voyages and who had first commisssioned him to obtain the vial. Yet what did he owe to an Englishman who was conducting surreptitious business? Then Cavallo considered that he could pretend that the vial had been lost in the wreck of the boat. Who was to gainsay him? The article did not appear on any manifest of freight but was being shipped privately, in a negotiation whose precise details were known only to Barak (who was dead), Lamord (who had not yet received it) and Cavallo (who still had it in his possession). Even so, the shipmaster hesitated. This wasn't so much on account of any scruple as because he thought he might get more money by holding out a bit longer. Cavallo resolved to wait a day or two for Alfred Portman to come up with a higher offer. Then, and only then, would he surrender the vial and its precious contents.

But in the intervening period his cargo had been thieved from Master Bailey's warehouse. Cavallo's first instinct was to blame the mayor, who after all had the keys to the place. No, not his first instinct, but his second. His first instinct had been to turn with fury on his hapless nephew and throw him into the cold waters of the Dart. But poor old Giovanni had nothing to do with the theft. That had become plain when Cavallo was approached once again by an Englishman, not by Alfred Portman this time but by Griffin, sly servant to Richard Storey. Griffin had brought a note with him – a note penned in Italian and undoubtedly written by Portman – saying that he would recover his cargo when, and only when, he had given up the precious vial. For which of course he would still be paid, a fair price, a good price. The cargo was merely being held as a kind of surety for the vial, in exchange for which he'd receive the money. As proof of that, Griffin had brought with him a purse full of coin. Cavallo looked up from the note. Griffin was dangling a chinking purse in his sly hand.

So the mayor William Bailey had nothing to do with the theft, after all. It was villains like Griffin and Portman who were responsible. They were in league! Cavallo's first response now was to became angry, again. Then he reflected more calmly, helped by the sight of that dangling purse. He did not have to come out of this situation the loser. He would hand over the vial, he would get the money, and later he would have his cargo back. The Genoese unbuttoned his jerkin and handed over the pouch, vial and all, to Griffin. In exchange he took hold of the purse. He was not so proud as not to inspect the contents. He told Griffin that, if the missing cargo was not returned within two days, then he would go to his master Richard Storey and to the mayor of the town. He had some difficulty communicating this information but Griffin seemed to get the gist. In fact, Griffin looked uncomfortable, insofar as such a sly fellow could look uncomfortable. Then he left.

And afterwards things went from bad to worse. The cargo was not restored to him. Some interfering visitors arrived from London, bent on investigating the theft. A theft of which Cavallo was innocent but in which he had now become complicit by his dealings over the vial. The arrival of the Londoners raised the stakes. Actually, Cavallo had taken to Geoffrey Chaucer. For a moment he even saw how this new twist in the affair might be turned to his advantage. He might get compensation from the English court – for he was well aware how far the English wanted to keep in the good books of the Genoese – and, eventually, he might recover the alum. Of which there was still no sign. Meantime poor Giovanni had fallen ill. At first Cavallo hadn't thought there was much wrong with his nephew. But the physician Storey thought differently.

He had offered – no, he had demanded – that Giovanni should be brought across to Semper House on that ill-fated evening. And look what had happened! Not merely did Giovanni perish but the pretty young wife to Storey had been cut down during the night.

It was some small compensation that those responsible had been tracked down and dealt with so speedily. Cavallo remembered with pleasure how he had fired the crossbow bolt at the axeman. It was especially gratifying that this was the band which was to blame for luring his boat on to the rocks. Cavallo was also pleased at the demise of Griffin. That sly fellow had been well rewarded with an axe to the head. They had even recovered most of the missing cargo. Most of it, not all.

Now, as Cavallo sat in his crib on board the *Giovanni*, he reflected that he was still entitled to some compensation. The Fowey merchant Latchett would not pay him in full if he was a few bags short, and he would have to explain to the physician Lamord how he had lost the precious vial, spinning some tale. Unless of course he could get the vial back again, as some sort of recompense for his losses and inconvenience. Once again, anger and impatience flared in the ship-master. Griffin was dead, he would get no more from him. But Alfred Portman was still alive. He would go to Portman and get his due.

The mayor's man, Francis, was walking through the woods on the far side of the water. He was no longer in the mayor's employment of course and, strictly speaking, he was slinking rather than walking through the woods. But, however he moved, he had nowhere else to go. Dartmouth was no longer safe for him. By taking to his heels as his master's boat touched the shore by the house of Justice Mortimer he had confirmed his guilt. He wished he'd had a cooler head, he might have brazened it out. But Bailey's questions had provoked him so! And with his mistress Juliana sitting beside the fat bugger and reporting on what that Semper House slattern had overheard, so that Francis's association with Griffin was revealed, things had taken a desperate turn.

Francis had hidden out in Dartmouth overnight and the next morning he had been ferried across the river – he still had friends in the town, and friends with small boats. Now he thought he might head out of the region altogether and try his luck in another place. But first he was determined to recover something from the wreckage of *his* plans. Well, they weren't *his* plans exactly . . . but much of the labour and the risk had been his.

It had been Francis, as Bailey correctly surmised, who had arranged for the robbery of the alum from the warehouse. He had personally rigged the pegs to the shutter-bar on the gable so that access could be made from the outside. Until the theft of the alum, he and the others had contented themselves with minor pilfering. Small losses – the odd sack, the occasional cask – were not noticed, and anyway Francis had charge of the records and accounts where much might be concealed by a judicious smudge of ink or slip of the pen. During any robbery, he made certain he was at a distance so he was well shielded from blame. He left the actual commission of the thefts to Griffin and the band of men, and Molly of course. Francis's job was simply to ensure that the pegs were replaced afterwards. The taking of the alum cargo was a bigger operation altogether and, for this, Griffin had insisted on his presence. They needed as many hands as they could muster. The sacks had been removed and ferried in sessions across the water and then carted to the cave in the woods through which he was presently slinking. Francis had wondered aloud whether it was worth the labour of stealing the alum in the first place, but Griffin told him that it was all part of a bigger scheme with which he needn't trouble himself. He would get his due reward. Except that he had not been rewarded, hence his conversation with Griffin outside the kitchen in Semper House.

And now Griffin was dead, and Francis was inclined to shed no more tears over his corpse than Pietro Cavallo had done – that is, none at all. Also dead were the two men, Zed and Bull, whose presence had always (to be frank) intimidated little Francis. He was dimly aware that the trio had not restricted themselves to warehouse robbery but were involved in the much more dangerous business of bringing ships to grief on the rocks. Francis chose to remain as ignorant as possible. He was frightened of the law, yes, but he was more frightened of the bearded brothers. But not as much as he was intimidated by Molly. There was a flinty glint in that woman's eye. She was handy with her club and her knife, and woe betide anyone who came within her reach if she was minded to use them.

It was desperation, and a burning sense of injustice, that now caused Francis to be walking in the woods. He had no money, his remaining few coins having been expended in paying for last night's lodging and getting across the river (his friends were not so devoted that they would harbour a fugitive for nothing). So his thoughts had turned to Molly as a last resort. He was well aware that she had escaped from the slaughter of the day before. Like Geoffrey Chaucer, he had caught that movement in the foliage concealing the cave entrance. He knew too that the cave was not the only place where the spoils from wrecks and robberies were stored. He was entitled to a share, a small share, of anything that was left. Molly could not refuse him, surely? All he needed was a few portable items, a few little leavings – a clasp, a brooch – which he might trade for cash in a neighbouring town or village. Then, when he had a bit of cash in his purse, he'd quit this region for good.

He was frightened of Molly but, when you came down to it, she was only a woman, and scarcely an inch taller than Francis. Now that her man was dead she might be looking for comfort. Francis thought that, if push came to shove, he might be able to provide her with comfort – at least once. Yes, he could bring himself to do it with her once. Francis believed himself to possess a certain charm for women. That slattern in the Semper House kitchen, for example, Bessy, the one with the big tits, she had definitely been warmed by his conversation. Her cheeks were flushed by more than the dying flames of the kitchen fire. In fact, if Griffin hadn't appeared, there was no saying what might have happened between him and Bessy.

Francis allowed himself several moments of hot day-dreaming while he slunk through the trees. He was following the path which led past the queer-shaped oak tree, the one that stood up like a pair of splayed hands, and which then descended deeper into the woods. All around him was gloom and silence. But he was so carried away in his thoughts that he was almost oblivious to his surroundings.

He made slow progress but eventually reached the clearing that fronted the cliff face. There were signs of the skirmish of the previous morning, many foot- and hoof-prints, flattened areas of grass and shrubbery, darker churned-up patches of mud and blood. Francis cast his eyes up towards the ledge on the cliff but he could detect no stir of movement in the concealing bushes. He was about call out 'Molly!' but the silence of the place sudddenly filled his ears and he became reluctant to break it. He knew that she was as watchful as a bird. If she was hiding up there then, sooner or later, she would peer out and see Francis, her friend Francis who had come to comfort her. And if she was somewhere else, out foraging, then she would surely return to this spot, like a bird coming back to its nest. It was the nearest thing which Molly had to a home. In that, she was more fortunate than Francis, who had no home, no home at all.

Overcome with self-pity, he wandered round the edge of the clearing. He was tired. He had not eaten that day nor had he taken more than a crust of bread on the previous one. A fugitive from justice cannot sit and drink and dine. He wondered whether Molly was out foraging for food, whether she'd be cooking later. Francis dreamed again, this time of coneys sizzling on a spit over a fire. Or he dreamed of a drink, something a little more spirited than the brackish water in pools in the wood. The cave had been used as a store for stolen barrels of wine, he knew. No doubt they'd all been removed by now. But perhaps one had been overlooked. A cask of Bordeaux that might be broached by him and Molly. And, when they'd drunk the Bordeaux and eaten the roasted coney, he'd comfort Molly, oh yes he would.

Francis found that he was wandering in a kind of circle in the clearing. If Molly was hiding up in the cave, then she would certainly have heard him by now, since her ears were as sharp as her other senses. It followed that she must be abroad in the woods, getting their supper. He sat down on a bank of earth near the edge of the clearing. Christ's bones, but he was tired.

The earth on the bank was soft and he seemed to sink into it like a cushion. He put out a hand to steady himself. Then he leapt to his feet. The earth was freshly turned. He was sitting on a grave. Straightaway he understood that this must be the burial place of one of the axemen – and then he saw another mound a few feet behind the first. And, Jesus!, a third one beyond that. Griffin too must have been interred where he'd fallen. Common sense might have told Francis that no one was going to bother transporting these ne'er-do-wells to a spot where they could enjoy an honest Christian burial. But, to Francis, it was as if these graves had been deliberately sited so as to scare the life out of him.

With his scalp prickling and his skin covered in goosebumps, he gazed round at the clearing as though more graves might spring into view. He looked up at the pale band of sky which was visible above the rock face. He turned his head to snatch a glance at the dark mounds behind. If the occupant of one might suddenly shoulder his way to the surface, his head all gory and his hands bent on vengeance . . . Were the bodies buried deep enough to keep off the wolves and the other creatures of the forest? But, he asked himself, who cared about a pair of felons and a servant called Griffin? Who cared if their rotting flesh was torn from their carcasses and their bones left to bleach in the sun? Who cared for poor old Francis?

Francis was not sure how much longer he could wait for the return of Molly. Suppose that she was not coming back to her lair in the woods, suppose that she'd abandoned it for good? Hardened as she was, could even she bear to look at the freshly dug grave of her man? Would she not have taken to her heels and fled the county?

Francis was on the point of doing likewise, of taking to *his* heels. If only he did not feel so light-headed and sick down in the guts. If only he knew in which direction to go for safety. Every path seemed to be strewn with danger and dead men.

But the three dead men were shortly to become four, as a small figure darted from behind a tree at the edge of the clearing. Molly had indeed been on the forage but she had not troubled herself to bring back the rabbit or coney from the net where the quivering thing had been trapped. Nor had she bothered to kindle a fire and cook the little creature, but had torn at it with her sharp teeth. Torn at it while it was yet warm and fresh, so that her mouth and her teeth were all bloody and slimed.

Molly was by now closer to a forest animal than she was to a town-dweller. She had never been far from the wild state, but the death of her man Bull had pushed her over the edge. Yet Molly did not use her teeth on Francis as she had on the trapped coney, or at least not at first. She still possessed the knife. She crept up on his rear. Francis was a town-dweller, unused to the sounds and the silences of the wood. When no more than a pace from the man, she jumped up and clung fast to his neck with one hand even as her legs entwined his waist.

With her free hand she brought down the knife on the exposed flesh of his neck and face, and then she employed her teeth. Anyone observing the scene might have thought that a grim and one-sided game of pig-a-back was in progress. Francis staggered forward under her weight but he did not fall to the ground until the blood started to gush into his eyes from the gashes on his brow.

When it was over, Molly stood straddling the body and wiping at her mouth. The death of Francis was some small vengeance for the killing of her man. Francis, who had been part of the group which had pursued them to their lair. But it was not enough. There was at least one more individual who had to pay the price. And there would be justice in it too. Some part of Molly's mind could still consider questions of justice. Images of the herb garden passed through her head. The early, mist-shrouded morning. The white-clad figure of the young woman, the attack on her by the dark-mantled figure who had, until now, been the protector of Bull and Zed and herself. After the woman had been left, unmoving and bleeding on the ground, Bull had approached the body and snatched the cross from around her neck. Why not? They were used to robbing the dead, these three.

On the Dartmouth side of the water, William Bailey and Juliana Barton were once again clambering into the mayor's personal ferry, to be transported across to Richard Storey's house. John manned one of the oars while an unimportant newcomer to these pages – another of the mayor's servants called Michael – took the second blade, in the place of Francis the fugitive. Bailey had explained to his mistress that he'd received a report from an informant in town that Francis had been observed crossing the river. From the moment the fellow had slipped through his fingers at the foot of Justice Mortimer's garden, Bailey's anger at his one-time servant had grown only stronger. Now that he'd had the opportunity to look back over the records and accounts connected with the warehouse, he saw that this man had been involved in pilfering from him for years.

Bailey, a generally shrewd judge of character, was angry with himself that he should have been regularly deceived. But he was more angry, much more angry, with Francis. He took a private oath to bring that 'faithful' servant face to face with the full rigour of the law. Then came the tip-off that Francis had been spotted crossing the river. But Bailey had failed to persuade Justice Mortimer to authorize a posse to pursue the villain on the other side, Mortimer's view being apparently that they'd never track the felon down in the woods and, besides, he was only a minor player, wasn't he? Hardly worth bothering with, when the rest of the band had been dealt with, so *summarily* dealt with. There was disapproval in Mortimer's tone, as though he was unhappy with the rough justice meted out in the woods. And indeed Bailey knew that Mortimer disapproved of Richard Storey, thinking that the doctor of physic had grown too big for his Dartmouth boots.

So William Bailey at once thought that he'd cross the river on his own account and go to see the doctor on the far side and get the man to assemble his household for another chase, the second in as many days. For sure, Richard Storey would be eager to take part. Storey had surprised Bailey by his eagerness in hunting down the land-pirates. The mayor recalled the look of satisfaction on the physician's face at the death of the axemen. But then, Bailey considered, those men had been responsible for the death of that fragile creature, his wife Sara.

Would he feel the same if anything happened to his wife Constance?

At this instant, no, he wouldn't.

Constance was the reason why Juliana Barton was accompanying William Bailey on this expedition across the water in pursuit of a fugitive. Not that Juliana had any particular interest in whether Frances was apprehended or not. Rather, it was that Bailey welcomed her company. For Constance – normally Constance the meek and mild – had suddenly turned on her husband over his friendship with 'that woman' in Sheep Street. Of no use for Bailey to protest that his friendship with Juliana Barton was innocent, since it was not innocent. His wife had proof. What proof did she have? She showed him. And said, did he take her for a fool? Anyway such a 'friendship' could hardly be innocent since it was well known just what sort of needlewomen occupied the house called the Shorn Lamb under the tender eye of Mistress Barton.

Bailey had more or less been driven out of his own house by a hail of curses. Pots and skillets might have followed if he hadn't made himself scarce down the street. Given her present state, absenting himself from Constance for a while seemed the most prudent course. What better way than to burn off his guilt and anger by pursuing a real villain over the water. Just at this point he ran into Mistress Barton. She was agog when he told her he'd fallen out with his wife. She would go with him, she said, and he could tell her about it, all about it. They talked low in the stern of the boat.

'What proof? You said she had proof.'

'This,' said William Bailey, holding up a brooch with a long pin. It was inscribed *Amor vincit omnia*. 'It fell from my pocket and Constance picked it up. How in God's name did it come to be there?'

'I put it there, Will,' said Juliana. 'It was given back to me by Master Chaucer.'

'How did *he* get it?'

'It's a long story,' said Juliana. 'No one seemed to want my gift. I thought it was perhaps ill-omened. I slipped it in your pocket.'

'Juliana, you are a fool. It is ill-omened.'

'But how did Constance know that it came from me? Not that it did come from me, not directly.'

'Constance has known all the time, I fear. She is no fool. This . . . this wretched pin was the last straw.'

'Did she really throw things at you, Will?'

'She would have done if I'd stayed to receive them.'

'Poor William. I have always said that she's a shrew.'

'She is not,' said Bailey. 'She is no shrew, but a quiet and docile woman.'

These – and the remark about her not being a fool – were perhaps the most approving words that he'd spoken of his wife in five years. Juliana Barton saw that she'd said the wrong thing. She recalled, with a pang of unease, how Sara Storey had seemed to threaten her or, at least, to reprove her during the brief conversation in the passage. Sara saying, 'Husbands should not deceive their wives.'

'What?' said Bailey.

'Nothing, my dear.'

'No, you said something just now. What was it?'

Juliana hadn't noticed she'd spoken aloud. She was compelled to repeat the words, hastily adding that they weren't hers but Sara Storey's.

'What on earth did she mean by that?' said William Bailey. 'Richard Storey is no deceiver.'

19

Alfred Portman closed the door of the doctor's study. He was tired from the various tasks which he had discharged over the previous days and tired from the thought of all that was still to come. He had been instructed by his cousin Richard Storey to oversee the burial of the three men in the wood and the recovery of the alum cargo and other items from the land-pirates' cave. He had done his duty, making certain that the bodies were given as decent a burial as their wickedness deserved, and then ensuring that Master Bailey received back his stolen cargo.

But there were heavier matters weighing on Portman's mind than the return of a few sacks of alum or the interment of a handful of villains. He recalled the procession of death which had trailed through Semper House lately. First the demise of Sara Storey's little dog Millicent, then the death of Giovanni, the Genoese sailor, and hot on the heels of that, the murder of Sara herself. Then three more deaths in the woods. He thought of the conversation he had had earlier that day with Edgar Storey, the young man no longer sullen but distressed and tearful, holding on to Hector's fur as though the hound was the only living being he could trust.

Portman picked up the club from its place in the corner. His employer and cousin had told him that he no longer wished to gaze on it. Not surprising, considering that it was stained with blood and wisps of hair and fragments of other stuff. Yet

Portman did not fear to look on the murder weapon. Rather he brought to it the same curiosity which he brought to all things. He hefted the club in his hands and swung it experimentally. The handle of the club had been whittled to fit a small hand, a woman's hand. As it happened Portman's hand was not large either, and the handle fitted snugly.

He replaced the bloody club in the corner and walked over to the shelf which contained pots and specimen jars. He took down from it a small earthenware pot. He removed from it a small bag. It was the same bag which he had unfastened and whose contents he had employed when Giovanni's body lay on the trestle table. He hefted the bag in his stained palm but did not open it. The grains inside were ground from the horn of the unicorn. Such an exotic (and expensive) product had been brought from the East, like much of the doctor's armoury of potions and tools of discovery. Unicorn horn was an infallible pointer to . . .

Well, it would all come out in a moment.

Alfred Portman replaced the bag in the pot and the pot on the shelf. He gathered up paper and pen, and settled himself at the table. He adjusted his glasses and bent low over the sheet. Then the door opened.

'What are you doing?' said the doctor of physic.

'I am about to write a story, cousin.'

'Story?'

'Call it a confession then,' said Portman, his gaze flickering towards the club in the corner.

'What have you got to confess to, Alfred?'

'Oh, it is not mine.'

'The day is fine,' said Storey. 'You should not stay and fust in here. Why don't we go for a walk and you will tell me all.'

So the two men walked in the herb garden with the head of Aesculapius at the centre, and Alfred Portman told his story. A story about a wealthy doctor of physic who had, by chance, discovered that a very valuable item – a priceless item – had been purchased by a rival in the town of Fowey. The rival was a man of learning by the name of Raymond Lamord. The item, small enough to tuck into a pocket or store inside a purse, was being ferried from the East via the city-port of Genoa. It was in the safekeeping of the ship's master, a gentleman called Pietro Cavallo.

The ship was wrecked before it could reach Fowey. Wrecked not by chance but by design. The land-pirates who had committed this terrible act had long dwelt in the woods not far from this very spot. They and the doctor of physic had an 'understanding'. He permitted them to go about their business unmolested while they – through the agency of villains such as the doctor's servant, a man by the name of Griffin – ensured that the doctor received a share of their takings.

When the doctor heard of the priceless item which Cavallo had with him, he despatched his assistant, a lowly relation, a cousin, to go and buy it. The cousin was not happy with this errand. He suspected the doctor of wrongdoing, all sorts of wrongdoing, including his association with the land-pirates. For a long time he had been gathering evidence against the doctor. Nevertheless he did as he was told on this occasion and went to see Cavallo. But the ship-master hesitated and seemed to think himself under an obligation to Lamord in Fowey and the cousin went away without a firm answer. So, as a lever to encourage Cavallo to part with the item, it had been planned that the ship's cargo of alum (also bound for Fowey) should be . . . confiscated. This was arranged by Griffin, and the plan carried out by him and others including the land-pirates. And it worked. Cavallo subsequently sold, or surrendered, the item in exchange for a bag of money and the promise that his goods would be returned.

The two cousins circled the herb garden. Storey was silent. He glanced at the head of Aesculapius. He sensed rather than saw the bloodstains that still spattered the ground round the stone head. Eventually he said, 'What happened next?'

This was merely the prologue to a tale of woe, said Alfred Portman. At last the doctor of physic had got his hands on what he craved, his appetite the stronger perhaps because he had been denied it at first. But, in the delay, things had begun to go wrong. The theft of the alum had caused trouble, the ripples of it spreading out as far as London. There had been accusation and counter-accusation. The King's second son, John of Gaunt, had sent down a deputation to investigate the matter. Even so, the doctor was not too concerned. His reputation – and his arrogance – were like armour to him.

He decided to put the substance, the potion, which he'd purchased to the trial. Perhaps he had delayed because he was afraid that the potion would not work. Perhaps he was afraid it *would* work. Anyway the doctor tested it out first on a little defenceless creature, the dog belonging to his wife. The dog had been poorly. He reasoned that the substance could do no harm. He was wrong. Perhaps he miscalculated the dose. Perhaps the dog was beyond recovery before it was 'treated'. Anyway, the dog it was that died. The lowly assistant thought this, that the dog had been poisoned, and he was unwise enough to say so in public. This was fiercely denied by the doctor.

Angry and dissatisfied, the doctor saw an opportunity to try the potion again, this time on a human subject. It happened that a member of the Genoese crew had fallen sick with a fever. The doctor suggested that the man, by the name of Giovanni, should be examined and treated by him. Once again, the potion failed. In fact, it was sufficient to kill the man outright when he might otherwise have recovered. The assistant suspected some foul play in the matter. He himself had inspected the dead man, and taken scrapings and samples from the discharge round his mouth and nose. These he submitted to the test, employing a preparation of powdered unicorn horn. As Master Storey was aware, the powdered horn was an infallible indicator of poison. The test verified the assistant's suspicions. But he did not confront the doctor. He required a further proof.

Further proof came, but not in a way that anyone could have desired. It seems that the doctor's wife had also begun to grow suspicious of her husband. She was an anxious woman, prone to fears and bad dreams. But not all bad dreams are unfounded.

Here Alfred Portman paused. He glanced sideways at the stony face of Richard Storey. The assistant's voice was drier and softer than ever. The doctor felt pity for his cousin.

'Let me continue the story,' he said. 'Let me stop you speaking any more. Let me save your throat.'

The gate to the herb garden opened at that moment, and Storey and Portman paused in their walk to witness the entry of Geoffrey Chaucer and Bridget Salt. They were not alone. Behind them came Edward Caton and Alice Storey, together with Alan Audley and Edgar Storey who was holding fast to Hector's leash. Pietro Cavallo strode through the little gate, and in his wake came the mayor William Bailey and his mistress Juliana Barton. These figures stood at a little distance. If the mood had not been so grim, one might have thought that they were waiting for applause at the conclusion to some drama.

'Only one last word, cousin,' said Alfred Portman, 'and then I shall be silent for good. Edgar saw you early that morning. He saw you with Sara. He saw . . . what happened. He has told me everything.'

Richard Storey glanced at his son, but he could not hold the young man's gaze. He looked round at the ring of faces, most of them accusing, and a couple uncomprehending.

'How did you know it was the club that belonged to the woman, Richard?' said Geoffrey Chaucer. 'You said to me that it was the woman's club yet no one saw her wield it but we three on the upland. You knew it belonged to the woman because you were familiar with the land-pirates. They were your agents. You offered them your protection in exchange for a cut from their activities. When they were no longer any use to you, when they became an active danger, you took the lead in hunting them down. Your writ runs on this side of the water.'

'I did not mean it to happen,' said the doctor of physic. He held himself upright. He spoke to the group which stood about him in a half-circle. As if he too was taking part in a drama, he spoke to no one in particular. He addressed them all.

'Sara was beside herself. She said she knew what I was doing. She accused me of killing her little dog. She was holding a brooch in her hand. She was jabbing at me with the pin of it. She said nothing of the sailor. She accused me of trying to kill her, which was assuredly untrue. She was wandering about the house. I made to comfort her and to quieten her down but she took flight outside. She went towards the stables, as if she was going to mount a horse and flee into the night. I don't know what happened next. I was . . . unwilling that she should leave in such a disturbed state of mind. I did not wish her spreading her wild stories about the place. I took the first thing which came to hand. It was a club. I ran after her to this very garden. I swear that I intended her no harm, but rather I meant to frighten her into submission. The next I knew she was lying here, all covered with blood, and I had done the deed.'

'I saw you, father,' said Edgar. 'You did not know that I saw you but I did, from a corner of the garden. Later I looked at the body of Sara. Her blood was on me.'

'Master Chaucer and I saw you too,' said Bridget Salt. 'We have been to visit the witch on the cliffs. We saw your face in her mirror.'

Alice Storey sobbed, and she buried herself in Ned Caton's arms. Edgar stared at his father, as if seeing him for the first time. William Bailey and Juliana Barton looked at each other.

Pietro Cavallo adjusted his cap. He did not understand these English.

'In God's name, what was it?' said Alfred Portman. 'What was the substance you wanted me to purchase at so great a price? You never told me.'

For answer, Richard Storey reached inside his doublet and drew out a silken pouch. He unfastened it and took from it a glass vial. He held it at arm's-length up to the sunlight. The vial was half full and the liquid inside was the colour of dull gold.

'It is the elixir,' he said. 'The elixir of life. It was made in the East by a wise man and brought thousands of miles across the sea. Lamord of Fowey wanted it but I got it first. It has been the quest of the wise and the curious since the creation of the world. A substance that will turn back disease and hold off death. A potion to preserve youth in perpetuity. An item which will cure all.'

He lowered his arm. A look of desolation crept over his features.

'It does none of these things though. Instead it shortens life and brings ill fortune.'

He unstoppered the vial and tilted back his head. The golden thread spooled from the tube and trickled into his upturned mouth. When it was finished, Storey wiped at his beard and looked at the company. They stared in turn, waiting.

But nothing happened. If the doctor of physic had been expecting the contents of the vial to take an instant effect he was to be disappointed.

Geoffrey Chaucer made to step forward. Storey must be apprehended. The doctor of physic must be brought before justice, he must be taken over the water to face the law. Before Geoffrey could take a pace, there was a crashing on the far side of the garden. A figure burst through the hedge, a small figure like a malevolent imp or demon. It was dressed in filthy rags and howling. Crouching for a second, it surveyed the group gathered near the bust of Aesculapius. Then the figure seemed to fix on Richard Storey. Alfred Portman backed away. Shrieking, it leapt frontwards on the doctor of physic, wrapping its legs about the man's waist and clinging about his neck. An arm flew up and a knife was outlined against the sun. The arm descended, the knife was buried in Storey's neck. He tried to shake off the nightmare-shape but Molly clung tight to him. She did not release her hold until she'd plunged the knife in half a dozen times. Then she jumped off him like a cat from a tree and darted back in the direction she'd come. She vanished through the hole in the hedge.

Richard Storey stood for an instant longer, one hand clasped to his neck. Blood fountained from his wounds. He began to rock on his feet and then crashed to the ground at the foot of the bust of Aesculapius and in the very place where he had lately struck down his wife Sara.

20

J a'far had not prospered. His careful plan, whereby Ali would steal the elixir from his uncle Ragab while he would profit, had failed in every respect. First, Ali had burst into the house while Ragab was still up and about. Taken by surprise, his uncle had stumbled and fallen, cracking his head against the filigreed chest. Ja'far had kept his own head as best he could. He instructed Ali to take the precious vial and run with it to the house with red shutters by the harbour where the merchant Barak would be waiting.

Ja'far was disappointed in Ali. His friend had let him down. He saw no reason why Ali should not pay for the death of Ragab, but of course only once he had returned with the ring from Barak, which was being given as a token of more money to come the next day. Once that had happened, once Ja'far had been paid, he would consider reporting Ali to the authorities. But, even as he was gazing at his uncle's body (with a mixture of fear and anger and self-pity), there was a thunderous rap at the door. It was the kadi or magistrate, accompanied by two of his servants, toting their whiplike rods of office. The kadi said that the neighbours had reported trouble, the sound of breaking wood, shouts and cries. A man had been witnessed lurking in the alley by the cemetery.

Ja'far's heart quailed but he thought fast. Yes, it was true, there had been trouble, terrible trouble. A wicked intruder had broken into his uncle's house and surprised the poor, defenceless old man as he was working in his chamber. The first Ja'far had known of this was the crash of breaking shutters and the shouts, which had also been heard by the neighbours. He had raced downstairs and flung open the door of Ragab's room, to see the old man lying in a pool of blood and the intruder making off through the open window. And Ja'far led the way to the chamber where his uncle lay.

Did he recognize him? said the kadi.

Who? said Ja'far.

The man who fled, said the kadi.

Ja'far was about to say yes, that it was a young fool by the name of Ali. But something made him pause. He pretended to think. No, he had only had a glimpse of a back scurrying away. He could not think who would do such a wicked thing, especially as it was well known that his uncle was not a wealthy man, but one wholly dedicated to his studies and research.

Meanwhile the kadi's servants were strolling about the room, flexing their whips and examining the curious apparatus of flasks and tubes rather than paying attention to the dead man. They picked up vials from their resting places and peered at them with suspicion. It was almost a relief when the attention of one of them was caught by a movement in the courtyard beyond the window. But relief turned to alarm when Ja'far saw that it was Ali, already returned. Fortunately he could count on the young fool for a display of panic. Once again Ali took to his heels, and stumbled off into the night with crashes and curses. The magistrate's men gave chase but came back without their quarry.

In one way, Ja'far was relieved to have had his story so promptly confirmed. For there was little doubt that this was the original intruder, the man responsible for Ragab's death. But the kadi did not seem entirely satisfied and he wondered aloud why the still unknown man should have taken the risk of returning to the house. Ja'far could not answer him. Instead he finally gave way to grief at his uncle's death. There was that good old man, still lying on the floor in his own blood. He wept and wailed. And, after a time, the kadi left him alone even though he still seemed dissatisfied.

The next day, once he had attended to the funeral arrangements for Ragab, Ja'far made his discreet way to the port to see Barak. The merchant was due to sail on the boat to Genoa by the evening tide. He found Barak but the merchant refused to keep his side of the bargain. Yes, he had the elixir in his grasp. But where was the ring which he'd given to Ja'far's accomplice? Ja'far of course had no ring since Ali had disappeared into the night before he could hand it over. That would have to be taken into account, said Barak. The ring was valuable. And he, Barak, had heard stories of trouble last night in the old quarter of the city. One man dead, another one almost apprehended. Would the trouble have anything to do with Ja'far? That too would have to be taken into account, as would the down payment he'd already received.

In the end, Ja'far received only a fraction of the worth of the vial. He had to be content with this. Just as he had to be content when he heard that a corpse had been discovered in the wasteland beyond the cemetery. A corpse ravaged by the dogs that dwelt there. There was a valuable ring in the corpse's possession, perhaps stolen in the course of the robbery of Ragab's house. And even this Ja'far did not acquire, since the kadi said that he would retain it pending further investigations.

So Ja'far was left in the dilapidated house by the cemetery. From time to time he looked at his uncle's scientific apparatus, asking himself whether he too could create the elixir. But he had none of Ragab's skill or patience or learning. He pondered the rack of vials. He even wondered whether he had given the right one to Ali. Was it possible that the elixir of life was still in his possession?

21

'Finish the story, father,' said Thomas.

'Story?'

'The one about the cock and the hen and the fox,' said Elizabeth.

'Where was I before I was interrupted?' said Geoffrey.

'The fox had just seized the cock, Chauntecleer,' said Philippa. 'The cock who would not pay any attention to his wife. What was her name now? It began with P, didn't it?'

'Pertelote. That advice was only in the matter of his diet,' said Geoffrey. 'Chauntecleer was also right, in that he should have paid attention to his own dreams. The dreams were warning him of his enemy.'

He paused. They were sitting in the Savoy Palace apartment. It was the end of the day. A fine day in summer, no need for a fire now. The children were about to go to bed. Philippa was sitting with Lewis on her lap. Elizabeth and Thomas were sitting on the rush-strewn floor.

'Why have you stopped, father?' said Thomas.

'Nothing,' said Geoffrey. 'Just thinking . . .'

Thinking of Sara Storey's dreams, of the enemy who waited beyond the door, the enemy who was her husband. He came back to the present.

'Anyway, Chauntecleer was well and truly caught. Russell the fox had trapped him by flattery . . . or fattery, Thomas. He had seized him in his mouth and set off towards the wood. The other occupants of the farm cried out in their pursuit. The old woman who lived there, together with her daughters – '

'You didn't mention her daughters before,' said Elizabeth.

'Ssh,' said Thomas.

'Well, that was probably because they don't play much of a part in the tale. The rest of the farmyard, I say, gave chase, the geese honking and the ducks quacking and the cows mooing and the human beings crying. But the distance between them and Chauntecleer and Russell was simply too great, and besides they were no match for the speed of a fox. If Chauntecleer was to be saved he would have to do it himself. When they got to the edge of the wood where the fox lived, Russell paused for a moment as though to appreciate how easily he'd outrun his pursuers. This was Chauntecleer's chance, his only chance, his last chance.

'He said, "Now that you've got this far, why don't you tell them where to go? You've won, victory is yours. That pack of fools will never catch a clever fellow like you." Russell didn't hesitate. "You're right," he said. "I'm cleverer and quicker than the whole bunch of them, including you, Chauntecleer."'

'Or rather this is what he would have said if he'd had the opportunity to get to the end of his speech. For no sooner had he opened his mouth to utter the first word than the cock broke free and flew up into the nearest tree, well out of Russell's reach. When the fox saw that it was his turn to be fooled, he put on his most honeyed tones and pleaded with Chauntecleer to come down again. He meant no harm, he said. He apologized if he'd frightened him by snatching him so roughly from the farmyard. All he wanted was for Chauntecleer to accompany him to his house in the woods and sing for him, for he loved music and a fine voice above all things. But Chauntecleer was not to be tricked a second time and by now the old woman and her daughters were drawing near, and so Russell slunk back to his lair in the wood and the bird flew down from his perch in the tree and was restored to his proper position in the farmyard. Where you can be sure he listened to his wife Pertelote's advice in future, at least in the matter of his diet.'

Geoffrey sighed and sat back in his chair. It was good to be home again, even if it was in the luxury of the Savoy Palace.

'What is the moral of the story, father?' said Elizabeth, who in her seriousness did not believe in stories which had no lesson to teach. When she was older Chaucer would tell her that most stories contained no lessons, none whatsoever.

'The moral, Elizabeth? Beware of flatterers. Think before you speak. Pay attention to your dreams. Is that enough of morals? We have reached the end, I think.'

Not quite the end though. The end, for the time being, comes with Geoffrey Chaucer sitting in the Tabard Inn in Southwark. It was the same summer's evening. He sipped at his ale. He was tired, not merely after the several days' journey back from Devon, but from walking across from the Savoy to his house in Aldgate (all was well, his books were safe) and then over the bridge to the south bank of the river. He had passed on the greetings of the mayor of Dartmouth to his brother, Harry Bailey, the tavernkeeper. Harry had his brother's bluffness and merely said, 'How is the old bugger? And his wife?'

'They were well when I left,' said Geoffrey.

And indeed William Bailey had patched things up with his wife Constance, it seemed. No more harsh words, let alone the pots and skillets that might have flown. Nevertheless, Geoffrey wondered how long it would be before Bailey trundled back to the arms of Juliana Barton, or Juliana flamed once more into the mayor's life. Similarly, he had left Edward Caton with Alice Storey. It seemed as though Semper House would be run by her, and by Bridget Salt, now that its owner was dead at the hands of Molly (who was still at large).

The mood of the inhabitants was fragile. Ned and Alice in particular were appalled not merely that Storey had – in a fit of anger or panic – slain his own wife but that he had also plotted to destroy Chaucer and the others before they arrived at his house. For there could be little doubt that the ambush had been staged with the connivance of the doctor, eager to ensure that no one from London should arrive to investigate the theft or any of the murky business with the land-pirates. The slowness in reaching them, which Geoffrey believed was Griffin's trick, had been Storey's own delay. Geoffrey wasn't so sure, however, that the doctor had ordered the killing of his own prospective son-in-law. It seemed to him that, during that confused skirmish on the upland, the wild woman had at first tried to protect Ned Caton by flinging her arms about him. It would have been enough perhaps if Chaucer and Audley had been killed or injured. For certain, they would have been compelled to abandon their mission.

Anyway the doctor of physic was no longer here to be questioned and brought to justice. He had attempted to finish his own existence with the so-called elixir of life, although it had not given him death straightaway. Not before the wild woman intervened. Perhaps Storey had swallowed the potion in the knowledge of the legal punishment that awaited him. Any lord of the manor who conspired with wreckers was to be tied to a stake in the centre of his own property and the house burnt down around his ears. This was the law of statute, as Sir Thomas Elyot had reminded Geoffrey when he gave a full account of all that had happened down in Dartmouth.

Elyot was disturbed to hear of Storey's guilt, which was especially shocking in a man of learning who had been in favour at the royal court. Sir Thomas showed his anxiety and displeasure by frequently shifting the items on his table-top, the pens and piles of paper, and putting them back not quite aligned. Sir Thomas's eyebrows drooped rather than bushing out. But at least the affair had been resolved, he said. Said it several times. The cargo of alum, most of it, had been found. Pietro Cavallo had set sail again in the *San Giovanni*, bound for Fowey. The alum would be duly delivered to the merchant by the name of Latchett. The treaty between England and Genoa would be preserved. What Cavallo would say about the elixir to Raymond Lamord, Storey's rival, Chaucer did not know. Presumably the Genoese ship-master – who had escaped very lightly, considering his complicity in the business – would come up with some story. It wasn't so hard to come up with some story.

The Tabard Inn was filling up. There was a bunch of people who were assembling here before starting off on a Canterbury pilgrimage. You could identify them by a certain look, at once pleased and pious. Chaucer recognized some of them, as if they were old friends. They were familiar types, a knight and his squire, a prioress, even a doctor, as well as some less reputable-looking individuals. They looked as though they would have their stories to tell as well.

Geoffrey's thoughts returned to the elixir. The elixir of life. The substance which would preserve youth and cure disease, guard against age and slow the march of death. Something that would last for ever, or as good as ever. He wondered if that was one of the reasons why the doctor of physic had called his house Semper. All nonsense, of course. Nothing on earth was for ever. He wondered also that a clever man like Richard Storey should have given credence to such things. Let alone have killed in pursuit of them. But then perhaps it took a clever man to be such a profound fool.

And the idea of a story occurred to him. A story which was to do with the elixir, the fabled water of life. *Ab-e-hyat*, it was called. It would be created in the East of course. The East of the fables, the East which is the home of marvels and prodigies. Words and sentences started to shape themslves in Chaucer's head as he sat in the comfort of the Tabard Inn. A man, an old man, would be working in his secret chamber. He would live in a broken-down house near a . . . let me see . . . near a cemetery. Yes, a cemetery.

And it would start something like this: 'After the heat of the day, the cool of evening was refreshing. People were strolling in the streets or chatting on corners . . .'